Praise for the Crime of Fashion mysteries

"Lacey Smithsonian skewers Washington with style."
—Elaine Viets, national bestselling author of *Murder with Reservations*

"Devilishly funny . . . Lacey is intelligent, insightful and spunky . . . Thoroughly likable.   —*The Sun* (Bremerton, WA)

"Byerrum spins a mystery out of (very luxurious) whole cloth with the best of them. . ."   —Chick Lit Books

"Fun and witty . . . with a great female sleuth."
—Fresh Fiction

"[A] very entertaining series."
—The Romance Reader's Connection

Raiders of the Lost Corset

"A hilarious crime caper . . . readers will find themselves laughing out loud. . . . Ellen Byerrum has a hit series on her hands with her latest tale."   —The Best Reviews

"I love this series. Lacey is such a wonderful character. . . . The plot has many twists and turns to keep you turning the pages to discover the truth. I highly recommend this book and series."
—Spinetingler Magazine

"Wow. A simplistic word, but one that describes this book perfectly. I loved it! I could not put it down! . . . Lacey is a scream, and she's not nearly as wild and funny as some of her friends. The story line twists and turns, sending the reader from Washington, DC, to France, and finally to New Orleans. . . . I loved everything about the book from the characters to the plot to the fast-paced and witty writing."
—Roundtable Reviews

"Lacey is back, and in fine form. . . . This is probably the most complex, most serious case that Lacey has taken on, but with her upbeat attitude and fine-tuned fashion sense, there's no one better suited to the task. Traveling with Lacey is both entertaining and dicey, but you'll be glad you made the trip."
—The Romance Reader's Connection

Hostile Makeover

"Byerrum pulls another superlative Crime of Fashion out of her vintage cloche. . . . All these wonderful characters combine with Byerrum's . . . clever plotting and snappy dialogue to fashion a . . . keep-'em-guessing-'til-the-end whodunit."
—Chick Lit Books

"So much fun." —The Romance Reader's Connection

"The read is as smooth as fine-grade cashmere."
—Publishers Weekly

"Totally delightful . . . a fun and witty read." —Fresh Fiction

Designer Knockoff

"Byerrum intersperses the book with witty excerpts from Lacey's 'Fashion Bites' columns, such as 'When Bad Clothes Happen to Good People' and 'Thank Heavens It's Not Code Taupe.' . . . Quirky . . . interesting plot twists."
—The Sun (Bremerton, WA)

"Clever wordplay, snappy patter, and intriguing clues make this politics-meets-high-fashion whodunit a cut above the ordinary."
—Romantic Times

"Compelling. . . . Lacey is a spunky heroine and is very self-assured as she carries off her vintage looks with much aplomb."
—The Mystery Reader

"A very talented writer with an offbeat sense of humor and talent for creating quirky and eccentric characters that will have readers laughing at their antics."
—The Best Reviews

Killer Hair

"[A] rippling debut. Peppered with girlfriends you'd love to have, smoldering romance you can't resist, and Beltway insider insights you've got to read, *Killer Hair* adds a crazy twist to the concept of 'capital murder.'"
—Sarah Strohmeyer, Agatha Award–winning author of *The Cinderella Pact*

"Ellen Byerrum tailors her debut mystery with a sharp murder plot, entertaining fashion commentary, and gutsy characters."
—Nancy J. Cohen, author of the Bad Hair Day Mysteries

"Chock full of colorful, often hilarious characters. . . . Lacey herself has a delightfully catty wit. . . . A load of stylish fun."
—Scripps Howard News Service

"Lacey slays and sashays thru Washington politics, scandal, and Fourth Estate slime, while uncovering whodunit, and dunit, and dunit again."
—Chloe Green, author of the Dallas O'Connor Fashion Mysteries

"*Killer Hair* is a shear delight."
—Elaine Viets

Other Crime of Fashion Mysteries
by Ellen Byerrum

Killer Hair
Designer Knockoff
Hostile Makeover
Raiders of the Lost Corset

Grave Apparel

A CRIME OF FASHION MYSTERY

Ellen Byerrum

A SIGNET BOOK

SIGNET
Published by New American Library, a division of
Penguin Group (USA) Inc., 375 Hudson Street,
New York, New York 10014, USA
Penguin Group (Canada), 90 Eglinton Avenue East, Suite 700, Toronto,
Ontario M4P 2Y3, Canada (a division of Pearson Penguin Canada Inc.)
Penguin Books Ltd., 80 Strand, London WC2R ORL, England
Penguin Ireland, 25 St. Stephen's Green, Dublin 2,
Ireland (a division of Penguin Books Ltd.)
Penguin Group (Australia), 250 Camberwell Road, Camberwell, Victoria 3124,
Australia (a division of Pearson Australia Group Pty. Ltd.)
Penguin Books India Pvt. Ltd., 11 Community Centre, Panchsheel Park,
New Delhi - 110 017, India
Penguin Group (NZ), 67 Apollo Drive, Rosedale, North Shore 0745,
Auckland, New Zealand (a division of Pearson New Zealand Ltd.)
Penguin Books (South Africa) (Pty.) Ltd., 24 Sturdee Avenue,
Rosebank, Johannesburg 2196, South Africa

Penguin Books Ltd., Registered Offices:
80 Strand, London WC2R ORL, England

First published by Signet, an imprint of New American Library,
a division of Penguin Group (USA) Inc.

First Printing, July 2007
10 9 8 7 6 5 4 3 2 1

ACKNOWLEDGMENTS

Thanking everyone who has helped keep my spirits up, answer my questions, and inspire me in the process of writing this book would be impossible. Please know that I am grateful to you all. First I must thank my patient husband, Bob Williams, who is my number one helpmate, friend, and supporter.

My sincere thanks go to Mary Ann Grena Manley of Project Northstar, and to "Breezy," for giving me insights into the plight of the homeless and children at risk. Any factual errors are mine alone, of course. I am also grateful to my editor, Anne Bohner, and my agent, Don Maass, for their guidance.

I want to make a special acknowledgment, which I neglected to make in an earlier book, to the teacher who first interested me in Russian history. Reg Holmes made the Russia of Peter the Great and Ivan the Terrible come to life with a great deal of detail and humor. He is not responsible for any factual errors in *Raiders of the Lost Corset*, Lacey's previous adventure, but the book benefited greatly from his inspiration.

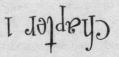

Chapter 1

It was bad enough that everyone in Washington, D.C., was blaming Lacey Smithsonian for that notorious editorial in *The Eye Street Observer*.

For the record, Lacey did *not* write the tirade that started the tempest in a Christmas teapot that came to be known around *The Eye* as "Sweatergate."

Sweatergate. The editorial that viciously bashed all lovers of "festive yet fatuous" seasonal Christmas wear, the "egregious" necklaces of twinkling Christmas lights, the red-and-green mufflers with "tinkling bells that jingled," the garish holiday cardigans overrun with Santas and elves and snowmen and tiny electrified reindeer that made the viewer's eyes "throb like a visual toothache from one too many sugar cookies."

Yes, it was bad enough being blamed for attacking that innocent seasonal fashion icon, the Christmas sweater. But it was the whispers in the newsroom that Lacey Smithsonian was "ruining Christmas" that really singed her curls.

If I'm ruining Christmas, Lacey thought, *heaven knows I've got help.*

During the holiday season, the showy sections of the District of Columbia were at their glittery best. From Union Station, with its enormous wreaths beribboned in red, to Georgetown, with every lamppost decked with greenery and gold bows, the Nation's Capital looked festive, happy, and welcoming. It was the season of peace on earth, goodwill toward men. That, however, was not the case at *The Eye Street Observer*, the city's third-tier newspaper, where Lacey Smithsonian pounded a keyboard.

The newspaper had donned its holiday finery in the lobby

for all the Washington world to see, with wreaths of green and a lavish tree in white and gold. However, upstairs in the offices overlooking Farragut Square, the paltry poinsettia plants scattered around the newsroom added mere spots of color, registering nary a blip on the peace and joy scale. It was the newspaper business as usual, but a little worse than usual. Reporters torn between pressing deadlines and the need to take care of holiday errands and attend family events were snappish and unseasonably tense.

Even without the specter of Sweatergate.

Editorial writer Cassandra Wentworth was the real author of those rancid anti-Christmas sentiments. But she was doing nothing to dispel the widespread suspicion that it was Lacey who had rained curmudgeonly curses on every wearer of a festive Christmas sweater and every bearer of seasonal cheer. After all, if anyone made snarky comments in print about what anyone else in the Nation's Capital was wearing, it had to be *The Eye Street Observer's* resident fashion reporter. Didn't it?

The editorial landed Lacey smack in the middle of a grudge match between her two least-favorite people in *The Eye's* newsroom: food editor Felicity Pickles, the brawny queen of the bakery-and-bistro beat, and Cassandra Wentworth, the scrawny voice of the politically ultracorrect who wielded the unbylined poison pen on *The Eye's* editorial page.

Lacey wondered idly who would try to kill whom first. If this were a boxing match, she thought, bantamweight contender Wentworth would be glowering and spitting in one corner and heavyweight champion Pickles fuming and pawing the canvas in the other. Lacey would be the unhappy referee caught in the middle.

Cassandra was a first-rate ruiner, a one-woman holiday destroyer who wouldn't be happy until every sugarplum was pickled and every candy cane was crushed. Figuratively speaking, of course. For Cassandra, no one should be happy until everyone in the world was happy. As that was unlikely, no one deserved to be happy at all. Ever. Not even a little. Nope. No way. *Just look at the facts, people, the situation is too dire to indulge ourselves in frivolity and twinkling lights and mere holly jolly happiness. Put down those candy canes, people, these are desperate, miserable times! Act like it!*

Ms. Wentworth lived her life as an eternal penitent, apologizing for crimes she did not commit. She wept for whales and thought globally and walked for the cure, and she was always on the lookout to stamp out the politically incorrect thought, in herself and in others.

But why did Wentworth have to make everybody else so miserable? Lacey found herself thinking. Couldn't she at least keep her miserable opinions to herself?

Of course that was why *the Eye* employed both Lacey Smithsonian and Cassandra Wentworth. For their opinions.

As far as Cassandra, avenger of all wrongs, was concerned, "Jingle Bells," colored lights, and all other holiday gaiety paved the road to hell. The gaudy and conspicuous consumption of the season depressed her. She tried to bear up, but Christmas got under her skin, like a tag digging into the back of her neck until she had to rip it out.

Cassandra hated Christmas—the green and red of it, the constant caroling on the radio, the shopping, buying, and giving of it, the candy making and relentless baking of it, the card sending and "happy holidays" of it. In short, she hated everything that most other people loved about the annual holiday season. They added up to a litany of insults.

Ultimately, however, it was Christmas sweaters that made Cassandra crack: Food editor Felicity Pickles and her collection of Christmas and other novelty sweaters.

For most of the year, Felicity wore shapeless smocks in a depressing palette of earth tones and faded floral prints. But when fall kissed the air and the days grew shorter, she suddenly embraced her wardrobe of eye-popping, seasonally themed sweaters with a love that only a mother could bestow on a balky child. She adored them all, pullovers, cardigans, the occasional puffy sweatshirt.

In September, Felicity's sweaters bore a harvest of red apples, ABCs, miniature schoolhouses, and the leaves of autumn. On the first of October, orange pumpkins and golden haystacks appeared and ushered in scarecrows, witches, and ghosts with electrified eyes.

November called forth a veritable Thanksgiving turkey of a sweater, complete with the real tail feathers of some unfortunate Butterball. Then there was her famous acrylic Pilgrim sweater, sporting the entire Plymouth colony sharing their feast with tiny Indians.

By the day after that harvest festival, Felicity's sweater mania was in overdrive. Christmas washed over her wardrobe like Santa's tsunami. Wool, cotton, or one hundred percent acrylic, her sweaters blazed with Christmas bulbs, sang with choirboys, shivered with snowmen muffled in crimson and green and plaid with icicles in gold and silver, ho-ho-hoed with Father Christmas in velvet-trimmed burgundy Victorian tableaus, and on-Dasher-on-Danced with Santa Claus, the jolly old elf himself with his sleigh and tiny reindeer. She was a woman possessed.

Heads turned as Felicity waltzed by in the newsroom, and not just because she daily offered the fruits of her food column's labor—whatever she'd cooked that day for research, usually something sweet and fattening. There may have been a few giggles behind her back, but Felicity didn't mind. She knew that every Christmas she became the center of newsroom attention and she wasn't about to give that up. Her ostentatious good cheer clashed conspicuously with Cassandra's philosophy of ascetic suffering. Slights were noted and snarls were snarled. There was bound to be a collision soon.

Would they really come to blows over something as silly as a Christmas sweater? Lacey wondered. It was beginning to look a lot like . . . disaster. A fashion disaster. Even though she was the paper's official fashion pundit and style scribe, her essential fashion philosophy was: *You can wear what you want, but you can't stop people from laughing.* She wasn't laughing anymore. Lacey and the rest of the reporters in the newsroom awaited the coming showdown with a mixture of trepidation and anticipation.

It came during the first week of December, just days before the annual company Christmas party. Cassandra trudged like a tiny troll down the hall from her corner and headed to Felicity's desk, where a tray full of star-shaped sugar cookies awaited the overfed masses. Bright blue sugar crystals trailed down the aisle that separated Felicity's desk from Lacey's, proof that the cookies were popular, as well as colorful and messy.

Cassandra didn't like to be seen eating, but even she couldn't resist the call of the carbs. She always took what Felicity offered, often wrapping it in a napkin and scurrying back to her desk to nibble on her treat like a lonely mouse with a forbidden treasure. Cassandra now stealthily picked up a cookie covered with azure sugar.

Lacey wondered whether Cassandra could appreciate the way Felicity's sweater color-coordinated with the cookies. The sweater was ice blue, accented with white rhinestone-studded stars that danced around the collar, bordered the bottom of the garment, and circled the cuffs. In Felicity's Christmas collection, this particular sweater was restraint itself.

The shade brought out her aqua eyes and pink cheeks, bright against her clear pale skin and long dark auburn hair, making Felicity appear soft and approachable. To Lacey, there was still the hint of a chubby malevolent doll about Felicity, a doll who might whip out a sharp knife and slice more than your cake. But Lacey's opinion of her had begun to soften. The food editor had recently fallen hard for Harlan Wiedemeyer, the newspaper's so-called "death-and-dismemberment" reporter, and love, however it had come calling, had improved Felicity's disposition. So perhaps it was love, and the Christmas season, and not the sweater that had softened her, Lacey thought.

Restocking the cookie plate, Felicity waited expectantly for some word of acknowledgment from Cassandra. It was part of the deal. The unspoken agreement: Felicity offered fattening goodies, reporters repaid her with fawning flattery. Lacey rarely indulged in either and tried to keep her mind on writing her "Crimes of Fashion" column.

"What do you think, Cassandra?" Felicity prompted her.

"What do I think?" After working at *The Eye* for more than a year, Cassandra still didn't know how to play Felicity's game. "Works and plays well with others" wasn't on her resume. "I think you could feed a village in India with what you paid for that *thing* you're wearing," Cassandra said. "That and the hundred other tacky travesties you've been wearing since September. It's vile, it's unnatural, it's—"

The words seemed to spill out of her uncontrollably, as if from the mouth of the smart-alecky thirteen-year-old Mean Girl that Cassandra might once have been. Felicity, who in fighting trim had fifty pounds on Cassandra and could probably break her into bite-size pieces with one hand, took a moment for this to register.

"What did you say?" She took a step into Cassandra's space.

Cassandra was a lightweight, but toned and athletic. She could no doubt turn cartwheels around Felicity, if necessary.

"You heard me," she taunted. "You and that lowbrow petroleum by-product you call a sweater, that monument to wretched commercial excess."

Blue sugar flew as Felicity snatched back the tray of treats. Then she plucked the remains of Cassandra's cookie right out of her hands and told her where she could go, and it wasn't back to her desk, but to a region far warmer than Washington in August. Lacey could no longer pretend to be working on a "Crimes of Fashion" column when a crime of passion was about to take place right in front of her.

"People are starving in the world—" Cassandra began. It was possibly her favorite way to begin a sentence, but she didn't get far this time.

"I'm sure you can show them how to do it the right way, you miserable, skinny, bony, anorexic, bulimic, self-righteous little runt." Felicity's eyes were slits of blue fire.

"I am not anorexic!" Cassandra had quite a shriek for being so bony. "You glutton! Obesity kills and causes high blood pressure and diabetes, overconsumes your fair share of the world's resources, and leads to global warming! And you're not just a victim of it, you're a carrier too!"

Lacey tried to lighten things up to defuse the tension. She should have known better. "Cassandra, you've got your next editorial right there. 'Christmas sweaters mean global disaster: Why does our government suppress the awful truth?'"

"You think I'm joking! Everything is just a joke to you, isn't it?" Cassandra had a weird look on her face.

Lacey laughed. Of course she was joking. Cassandra Wentworth writing about something as trivial as fashion? Even to stop the worldwide menace of the Christmas sweater?

Felicity moved in ominously. Reporters crowded around for the smackdown, eager for a ringside seat. Unfortunately, at that moment, Douglas MacArthur "Mac" Jones, their editor, was hard on the trail of blue sugar crystals leading to the promised land of Christmas cookies waiting on Felicity's desk. He approached, his large eyebrows knit together, bringing a glower to his café au lait complexion. The eyebrows and mustache seemed to compensate for his gleaming bald head. Mac was a mix of races, and he favored no one race over another. He was an equal opportunity spoilsport.

"Break it up, ladies," Mac ordered. "People would think you don't have enough work to do. You got time on your hands? You got time to debate instead of writing stories? Well, you don't. Back to work!" He picked up a cookie and stared them into submission. The crowd broke up. Reporters retreated grumbling to their stories and deadlines. Order was restored. Mac picked up another cookie.

Cassandra withdrew, sans her blue sugared treat. She retaliated for her humiliation later that day by writing a scathing editorial. Not about food or fat people or global warming, but about those selfish people who offended the very Earth itself by the wearing of seasonal accessories, the comic ties, the cheery little elf ears and Santa hats, and of course, the Christmas sweaters. She even used specific examples from Felicity's wardrobe. The piece appeared in the next day's Eye, unbylined as per the newpaper's usual practice with the house editorial, and swifter than Santa's reindeer it became known around the office as Sweatergate.

The day after the diatribe appeared, Felicity did not cook. Nor did she bake. Nor did she supply the hungry news troops with sweet sustenance. She did, however, wear a loud purple sweater covered with saucy-eyed elves and a pair of purple Christmas bells in her ears that announced her presence every time she turned her head.

Reporters suffered sugar withdrawal. Mac amped up his grumpiness. The lack of seasonal treats resulted in a rush to empty the snack machines. Bereft reporters were seen standing in the middle of the newsroom and pleading, "Anybody got a cookie? Anything at all?" It didn't make for a happy working environment.

When her fans asked Felicity about her latest culinary adventures, she said darkly that she simply wasn't in the mood. "I don't know if I'll ever be in the mood again," she sighed. "After what I've suffered . . ."

Whether they covered sports or cops, every time Cassandra or Felicity passed by it fed the newsroom's daily desire for gossip and sensation. Reporters took sides, bets were placed, and bookmakers agreed the odds (and popular opinion) were stacked against Cassandra. After all, she never fed them anything but her opinions, and those often required an antacid chaser.

Tensions were running high, with no rapprochement on the horizon. Finally Tony Trujillo, *The Eye*'s dessert-addicted police reporter, grabbed Lacey's sleeve and begged her to intervene. Just as he did, Felicity's tinkling purple bells sailed out of the office, along with Felicity and all hope of the return of Christmas Goodies Past.

"Lacey, you gotta do something! We're dying here! Besides, Smithsonian, you know this is all your fault."

Chapter 2

"Me? What can I do?" She arched one eyebrow and glared at him. "And what do you mean this is all my fault?!"

"*Madre de Dios!* It will kill our Felicidad not to bake. She'll dry up like a prune. The balance of power will shift. The North Pole will melt, civilization as we know it will end. And three words: No. Christmas. Cookies." His brown eyes pleaded with her. He smiled, his even teeth bright against his olive skin. Tony was handsome and he knew it, setting female newsroom hearts to pitter-patter, but Lacey was immune to his charms.

"You're breaking my heart."

"You sit next to her. You're friends."

"Ha!" Her desk was across the aisle from Felicity's, and Lacey considered this proximity a thankless burden. "It's common knowledge that she hates me. You try, she can't resist your charm."

"I already tried. Nada. Besides, she owes you," Tony smirked. "She'll listen to you. You set her up with the jinx, and she loves him." He shrugged toward the desk of Harlan Wiedemeyer. Most people at *The Eye* considered Felicity's boyfriend to be a bringer of bad luck. But Felicity, who had already suffered the indignity of having her minivan blown up outside the newspaper offices after developing a crush on Wiedemeyer, was now considered impervious to his peculiar hexing abilities.

"Harlan Wiedemeyer is not a jinx, and Felicity is a big girl," Lacey said. "A very big girl. I try not to get in her way."

"Do something," Tony pleaded. "If you let this go on you're gonna ruin Christmas."

"I'm caught in the crossfire, Tony. And I am not ruining Christmas!"

"You are too. It's all your fault Cassandra wrote that Sweatergate thing. You goaded her into it. The Wentworth *bruja* is jealous of you, so she writes a column just like yours! Her version, anyway. Felicity wound her up, but you pointed her in the direction of disaster."

"That's not my fault!"

"Cassandra created Sweatergate and pissed off Felicity, who now is not doing what she does best. Cooking, baking, bringing us food, feeding the troops. What about our Christmas cookies?" He looked as mournful as a little boy who'd been sent to bed without his dessert. He flicked a speck of dust from the toe of one black lizard skin boot.

"You're not going to turn that into Cookiegate, are you?" Lacey said.

"You know what I'm talking about, Lacey. You started all this. Not your intention, I know, but you gotta do something."

Everyone knew what Trujillo was referring to: Felicity Pickles's legendary once-a-year Christmas cookie extravaganza, her crowning culinary achievement. Lacey could just imagine the orgy of dough mixing, rolling, cutting, shaping, throwing, baking, sprinkling, and sugar decorating that took place in Felicity's kitchen to produce her annual pièce de résistance. Lacey liked to think that Felicity lived in the forest in a gingerbread house with cream cheese icing on the roof. In her mind's eye Felicity's cookie-baking scene included Hansel and Gretel fattening up in the pantry.

Felicity annually produced a Christmas cookie display that would make Betty Crocker blush. On one magical day in mid-December, she would bring dozens of different kinds of cookies to the office. It happened every year, it was a Christmas *Eye* tradition, and the denizens of the newsroom were trained like a pack of Pavlovian dogs to watch (and whine and whimper) for it.

"Everyone expects it, Lacey. Christmas at *The Eye* won't be the same without it."

"Don't whine, Tony," She was thinking.

"The cookies," he moaned, "think about the cookies."

"Now you're whimpering."

Felicity's many trays of artistically arranged treats would include cookies in the shapes of poinsettias, wreaths, Santa Claus, reindeer, and angels. There were Moravian spice cookies and there were brown sugar drops and coffee and spice drops, applesauce cookies, butterscotch cookies with burned butter icing, oatmeal cookies, ginger creams, coconut jumbles, and macaroons. The food editor piled on the date bars and lemon bars. There were cookies with raspberry and cherry fillings. Cookies iced and sprinkled with colored sugars and dotted with red and green gumdrops. Cookies with exotic names and familiar names and cookies with no names at all. Felicity demanded nothing in exchange for her efforts—except lavish thanks and eternal love.

"Don't forget about the gingerbread cookies," Tony said.

"How could I forget?" Lacey snapped. "I could never forget the gingerbread cookies. Why, they practically do the tango, Tony. They could stage a newsroom revolt and publish their own paper."

Felicity made gingerbread boys and girls for every reporter and editor, personalized with their names in red or green icing. Her yearly cookie ritual was a not-to-be-missed event. Even publisher Claudia Darnell made an appearance for her own gingerbread girl. Lacey had a problem with the cookie feast because she had a problem with Felicity. And the fact that the entire newsroom had been seduced into loving Felicity by her compulsive feeding of them. Lacey considered the whole thing naked emotional blackmail, and it was just another excuse to pack on five pounds during the holidays.

Lacey turned her back on Tony and stared into her computer screen, the silent code in the newsroom for *This conversation is over.*

"All I ask is for you to try, Lacey."

"Go away, Tony. I am not responsible for Sweatergate, and I'm not responsible for Felicity's baking or not baking. I'm not ruining Christmas." *Everyone else is ruining my Christmas,* she added silently.

"You are, you know!" Tony left with a dark look. "You're ruining Christmas!"

Cassandra's editorial brought more nasty repercussions for Lacey. She opened her e-mail: Another reader convinced that fashion reporter Lacey Smithsonian had written the snotty editorial cursing Christmas clothing: "You're not a crime of fashion, Smithsonian. You're a crime of nature. Do you think you're witty? You're not!"

Lacey was one of the better known names at the paper, thanks to some sensational stories she had broken in the past few weeks. She allowed herself one sigh of self-pity. She had just come off the scoop of her career, finding a legendary corset full of Romanov jewels. It was good while it lasted. At work, the heady glow continued for about a week. A couple of weeks and it was old news. And in the newsroom, old news is no news at all.

Obviously, Lacey thought, her less stable readers believed Sweatergate was some psychotic personal vendetta, and Smithsonian must simply be too craven to put her name on it. Unhappy e-mails followed, along with several personally delivered letters from the more seriously outraged members of the reading public.

"My grandmother wears Christmas sweaters," one of them said. "And she has more taste in one little finger than you have in your whole body! I'm through reading you!" *If only that were true,* Lacey thought. People who swore they were through with her column inevitably read it again and were outraged again. And wrote a letter again. Another wrote, "What kind of twisted, hateful worm would attack something as innocent as a harmless Christmas tie that lights up and plays 'God Rest Ye Merry, Gentlemen'? I'll have you know my granddaughter gave me that tie!" Still another member of the reading public said, "Watch your back, Miss High-and-Mighty Smithsonian, you might find yourself bloody in the snow with no one to rescue you."

Lacey was willing to take her lumps for the columns that she actually wrote. She was not willing to take the heat, however, for Cassandra Wentworth's incendiary opinions. Mac said it was no big deal. Mac said it would blow over. But every time she checked her e-mail there was another vile message or three. She forwarded them to Cassandra, but that didn't help.

Lacey's reputation was at stake. She had no choice but to fight for her honor, such as it was.

She decided to set the record straight and pen a small fashion apology, not on behalf of Felicity or Cassandra, but for the common woman, the average Jill, the woman who gets no respect, the woman who loves the flashier aspects of the holidays. Christmas is a holiday that seeks to embrace all mankind,

Lacey reasoned, including those with taste and those who can't resist the tacky.

In light of the threats, she needed to cover her back, her front, and everything in between. Lacey was reduced to defending Christmas sweaters in order to defend herself. She hoped she wouldn't regret it.

The truth, when she dared to acknowledge it, was that Lacey didn't hate Christmas sweaters at all. They amused her, they comforted her, they lifted her spirits, and most of the time they made her smile. She applauded those brave few who dared to wear one to the office. At least they broke up the dreary sartorial color palette of Washington, D.C., which in winter tended to turn as drab and depressing as the Potomac River mud. The city took itself far too seriously all year long. If a Christmas sweater was a cheap laugh, at least it was a laugh.

Lacey remembered fondly all the outlandish and joyous and just plain preposterous Christmas sweaters she had known, scrupulously avoiding using any of Felicity's as examples. At a department store cosmetics counter, Lacey had recently seen a cotton candy blonde of a certain age, looking like a bonbon plucked from a platter of pretty pastel petit fours. The blonde was wearing a powder blue skirt and a powder blue Christmas sweater. Or perhaps the sweater was wearing her. The sweater was framed with white ostrich feathers and featured a white Christmas tree decorated with silver rhinestones. On her wrist she wore a charm bracelet from which dangled a silver jingle bell. In her heart, Lacey imagined, giving the blonde the benefit of the doubt, was the joy of Christmas. Lacey recalled this image and took a deep breath.

But how to begin? She concentrated. At the beginning, of course.

FASHION BITES

It's Not a Matter of National Security, It's Just a Christmas Sweater.

That's right, it's just a sweater. Go ahead and wear it. Wearing that uniquely resplendent garment of seasonal delight, replete with Rudolph and Santa and their friends, the Little Toy Soldier, the Nutcracker, or the Snow Queen, will not cause the terrorists to win or the polar ice cap to melt. It will not cause wars, except possibly at this very newspaper, nor will it cause (or cure) cancer. It's just a sweater.

Your craziest Christmas sweater may make people smile, or laugh, or question your taste or your sanity, but the bottom line is that it is your choice, your decision, and you are free to make it. It's time to lighten up, people! After all, it is the Season of Light.

Christmas sweaters are as welcome on my holiday landscape as Björk wearing a stuffed swan to the Academy Awards. Comedy on the hoof is always welcome, and that Icelandic songstress in a swan can lighten up my Oscars any time she wants. After all, do we want our stars to always be tastefully attired? No. We want them to spurn common sense, to wear what strikes their fancy, to be brave, to be festive, even foolish. So let's think about those Christmas sweaters.

Are they festive? Of course. Are they foolish? I plead eye-of-the-beholder here.

Are they stylish? Almost certainly not. But who cares? Most Christmas apparel in Washington, D.C., is merely more of the same old same old: gray, beige, black, navy blue, and more gray. A little taupe, for the daring. *Don we now our grave apparel!*

You're almost ready to give up hope that there's even one person out there willing to celebrate the season. And then, suddenly, *there she is.* She walks into the restaurant on Connecticut Avenue. A woman who makes you stop and stare. She is wearing a white turtleneck, a red corduroy jumper, knee-high red leather boots, and a sweater that simply makes the outfit. It might make it outrageous, but it also might make it sublime.

The sweater is a black cardigan trimmed in white faux fur, and circling the garment are puffy grinning Santa Claus faces, made from felt and cotton balls. This woman is in her element. She may not even be wearing this sweater as an ironic statement. But that's okay, because Christmas is not about irony. At least she's making a statement.

And then you notice other diners sneaking a look, smiling, chuckling, because, well, someone had the nerve to wear it. It's not even an expression of neo-retro-pseudo-faux-satirical-ironic-postmodern anything. It's Christmas! If someone wants to wear a holiday sweater or a stuffed swan, why not? Or a stuffed turkey, just to keep it seasonal.

So celebrate your season, whatever the season. Do it in style, whatever style that may be. And maybe, just maybe, we in Washington should learn not to take ourselves so seriously. If you feel compelled to wear an outward expression of your inner feelings, now is the time. Don't let the fashion curmudgeons tell you not to listen to your heart, even if your heart yearns for a sweater encircled with a chorus line of high-kicking Rockettes who light up and sing. Get your kicks this Christmas! Don't be afraid to march to the beat of that distant drummer. Or maybe just the beat of the Little Drummer Boy.

Pa rum pa pum pum!

chapter 3

The following afternoon everything seemed to be going so well. Lacey was rushing, like her fellow reporters and editors at *The Eye*, to make an early deadline. Publisher Claudia Darnell's annual Christmas-slash-holiday party would fill the National Press Club that night, the first Friday evening in December.

There was no apparent fallout from Lacey's Christmas sweater "Fashion Bite," either positive or negative. It was accompanied by an Editor's Note that it was in fact editorial page writer Cassandra Wentworth who had written *The Eye*'s previous editorial on this subject, and not fashion writer Lacey Smithsonian, as many readers had assumed. "*The Eye Street Observer* regrets any confusion in the minds of our readers," etc.

Christmas has been saved, Lacey thought. *And my hide along with it. Just in time for the party.*

Then she glanced up from her midafternoon decaf.

Like a small dark specter of doom, Cassandra appeared on the horizon. She looked like a bony knobby-kneed insect in her black tights and yellow windbreaker. She was striding purposefully toward Lacey, her streamlined yellow helmet tucked under her left arm, a grim look on her face.

No matter how cold it was, unless there was a foot of ice and snow on the ground, Cassandra rode her bike to the office. She saved fuel. She saved the planet. She was "carbon neutral." She was a shining example for the rest of the slobs who worked at *The Eye*. No rest for the ecologically correct. But first there was a fashion reporter to torment. Cassandra had a mad gleam in her eye. She gestured at Lacey with a wadded-up page of their newspaper.

"Just what do you call this?" She threw the thing at Lacey. She missed.

"Bad aim? It works better if you make it into an airplane. Like this." Cassandra stood and fumed as Lacey deftly folded the page into a paper airplane with part of the headline visible: IT'S JUST A CHRISTMAS SWEATER! She launched it back at Cassandra. "My Fashion Bites column. Via airmail."

The spirit was willing, but the newsprint was flimsy, and the plane fell to the ground. Cassandra stomped her yellow running shoe on Lacey's column.

"Everything's a joke to you! You contradicted everything I said!"

"Really? Everything?" Lacey said. "I wasn't keeping a tally of everything you ever said. I mean, who has the time?" She stretched. "Lighten up, Cassandra, it's just an opinion, a little fun. It's Christmas."

"You're defending Felicity Pickles!"

"I'm not defending Felicity." That would be the last thing she would do. Lacey looked around to see who might be listening. Luckily Felicity wasn't around. "I just don't advocate ripping Christmas sweaters off little old ladies and shipping them off to third-world countries. Um, the sweaters, not the little old ladies."

"That's not exactly what I said." Cassandra puffed out her chest in indignation.

"I paraphrased."

"You made fun of me!"

"I have not yet begun to make fun," Lacey retorted. "And don't you think there's room for more than one opinion on any given issue? And a little fun too?"

"Opinion? Is that what you call it? This drivel?"

Lacey felt her cheeks blush red, but she decided it was more interesting to watch Cassandra quiver in indignation than to get indignant herself.

"Opinion. Yes, that's what I call it." She decided to change the subject. "But speaking of Christmas and not its sweaters, aren't you going to change into something festive for the office Christmas party tonight?" She surveyed the woman's bike togs. "Okay, maybe festive is the wrong word. Something more suitable. Gravely and somberly celebratory. You know: 'Don we now our grave apparel'? Fa la la la la?"

"It's a *holiday* party, not a Christmas party!" Cassandra corrected her. "And I don't think I could be happy eating like a pig and swilling booze like a camel when there are oppressed people in the world who will never be able to enjoy a nice holiday party."

"Camels swill booze?" Lacey leaned back in her chair. "I had no idea. But you'll miss Felicity's outfit." Lacey had no idea what Felicity would wear, but she had faith in Felicity's Christmas spirit. "I'm sure it will be festive. Ferociously festive."

"Everything's just hilarious to you, isn't it?" Cassandra picked up Lacey's column off the floor. She crumpled it up into a ball and with a surprising show of fury pitched it at Lacey once again. Lacey caught it. "You and Felicity Pickles can wear nothing but holly and ivy and choke on your mistletoe, for all I care!"

"You forgot the part about the starving oppressed masses." Lacey looked at the ball of paper and tossed it neatly over her shoulder into the wastebasket without looking. "And mistletoe is poisonous."

"You're disgusting." Cassandra swung her yellow-and-black backpack over her shoulder and stomped off. "You people! All of you!"

All of *who*? Lacey wondered. "That's hardly the Christmas spirit, Cassandra!" she called after the hunched form receding down the hall. Lacey fished her crumpled column from the wastebasket and flattened it out. But she had no time to brood over Cassandra's hostility; she had to change her clothes. It was nearly time for the party and Lacey was determined to have a good time, even if it killed her.

The entire newspaper was humming with anticipation over tonight's Christmas party. It was "black-tie optional," an instruction that never failed to send reporters into spasms of panicky indecision. How black-tie is "black-tie"? How optional is "optional"? Wouldn't that rumpled blue blazer do just as well? Navy blue is just *like* black, isn't it? But who wants to be the only guy at the party *not* wearing a tux?

The male managers were all expected to wear tuxedos, even the grouchy and generally ill-dressed Mac Jones. But there was also a festive final touch intended to jump-start the holiday spirit: A jolly red-and-white Santa cap was mandatory wear for the male managers. The female managers were merely ex-

pected to be attired "formally," sufficient challenge in itself for
the Washington women of the Fourth Estate. For them, the
Santa caps were "optional." Lacey did not know for certain, but
she suspected that Claudia was having a little joke with her
Santa motif. There was a certain amount of grumbling over this
"black-tie optional/Santa hat mandatory" dress code, but Lacey
knew newshounds everywhere loved free food and liquor.
They'd wear much worse than a tux and a Santa cap for free
food and liquor. For free food and liquor they'd wear nothing
at all.

The Eye Street Observer wasn't known for its well-dressed
staff. Reporters, especially in Washington, D.C., tend to believe
what they write is far more important than what they wear.
Lacey tended to agree, but she regretted that her colleagues at
The Eye set the style bar so low.

For day, blue jeans or khakis with polo shirts were a typical
male reporter's choice, along with that rumpled blue blazer if
he had to cover something on the Hill. Getting tuxedoed up for
the Christmas party wasn't a reporter's favorite official duty of
the year. A few of the female reporters appreciated fashion and
dressing up, but many considered it grossly unfair that dressing
up was so easy for the men: Tuxedo? Check. Santa cap? Check.
Ready to party, dude! Lacey recalled some odd and entertaining female fashion choices from last year's party. She hoped her
coworkers would hit similar heights this year.

Who knew it was possible to find a floor-length black velour
turtleneck dress? Lacey visualized this as a cocktail party dress
for a bohemian ex-nun. At least it contrasted nicely with the
"retreads," the ancient bridesmaid's dresses pulled out of the
closet once a year. It's long, it's satin, it's a weird color, it's in
my closet: Hello Christmas party! Or as one young reporter in
a fluorescent neon green departure from good taste that positively screamed BRIDESMAID DRESS had confided to Lacey,
"I wore this in a wedding! Wouldja believe it? It *totally* doesn't
look like it, does it?"

Another told her, "My sister made me buy this stupid dress
for her stupid wedding. Why buy something new every year
when I've got this? Merry Christmas!"

There would, no doubt, be several varieties of the velvet
peasant sack dress, a dressed-up hippie look: Laura Ashley goes

to the Renaissance Fair. But at least it was usually colorful. Burgundy and purple seemed to be the popular choices.

Another current female reporter favorite was the amorphous and practically colorless New Age offspring of this peasant sack dress, in ecologically correct hemp and cotton. The tax reporter at *The Eye* had several. Her black and gray and beige office attire came entirely from earth-friendly online catalog sites. Clad last Christmas in yet another shapeless, structureless, earth-toned, natural-fiber sack that might have held organic potatoes in an earlier life, she had boasted to Lacey how these fit her *every* time, even though she *always* ordered through the Web. "It's so amazing! Smithsonian, you should write about this in your column!"

Lacey hoped there would be some delicious fashion disasters at this year's party, but she could never write about them. Too dangerous. She grabbed her garment bag and tote bag full of essentials and dashed into the ladies' room to transform herself for the evening before heading for the National Press Club a dozen or so blocks away. It wouldn't do to have the fashion reporter show up looking less than fabulous, or at least what passed for fabulous at *The Eye*. But before she could make progress on her fabulous look, her cell phone rang. The number looked familiar, but she couldn't quite place it. "Hello?"

"Smithsonian. This is Wentworth."

Lacey groaned. Cassandra had been gone for all of three minutes. "Cassandra. What a pleasure. Now what?"

"We're not through with this. I'm taking your egregious piece of junk journalism contradicting my editorial and everything I stand for to the managers' meeting on Monday." Cassandra was technically some sort of minor manager, although she didn't appear to Lacey to manage much of anything, least of all her emotions. "We need to speak with one voice at *The Eye*."

"And that would be your voice?"

"Are you mocking me?" Cassandra's voice lifted an octave. "The managers' meeting will deal with this! This isn't over!"

"Knock yourself out, Cassandra. This call is over." Lacey hung up with a silent oath, vowing that Cassandra would not ruin her evening. Or her Christmas spirit. She swung open the ladies' room door.

LaToya Crawford, the pretty African-American Metro section reporter, was rummaging in her purse for lipstick. She wore her trademark long jet-black pageboy, with never a hair out of place. It looked beautiful and bulletproof. She glanced up at Lacey.

"Girl, you look frazzled. You do need a Christmas party. What's up?"

Lacey gazed at her reflection in the mirror under the ghastly fluorescent lighting and smoothed her hair. "Just a little run-in with the one and only shepherdess of the downtrodden of the Earth."

"Ewww, Cassandra? What's she jumping on you for? No, wait. I know." LaToya laughed. "That Fashion Bite you wrote? Musta pushed all her buttons. Cassandra thinks Christmas sweaters are destroying the ozone layer or something."

"You're psychic." Lacey grinned.

"Doesn't take a genius, what with Sweatergate casting its pall over the entire office." LaToya smoothed lipstick over her lips. "And that Wentworth witch has got no sense of humor."

"Some people never get one. And they can actually take others' away." Lacey wondered what Cassandra could actually do to harm her. Bore the other managers senseless? Write another wretched editorial, attacking motherhood and apple pie, and blame it on Lacey? She pushed the thought from her mind.

She hung her garment bag and opened it, revealing her dress for the evening, one of her Aunt Mimi's vintage evening gowns. It was a perfectly simple cocktail-length dress from the 1940s, featuring a sweetheart neckline and sheer organdy sleeves decorated in subtle velvet polka dots. The dress was a sapphire blue velvet that made Lacey's blue-green eyes look dark and mysterious—at least that's what she told herself. She slipped out of her suit and into the dress. She admired her reflection in the mirror and felt better already. Her silky light brown tresses skimmed her shoulders in a soft wave, parted on the side with subtle blond highlights, courtesy of Stella, her stylist. As Stella would say, it was "very Rita bleeping Hayworth."

"Take that, Cassandra," LaToya cackled. "That ain't no pair of yellow bike shorts you got on."

Lacey smiled. Once again she silently thanked her late great-aunt for leaving her a trunk full of wonderful vintage clothes from the late great twentieth century, chiefly the 1940s and a few gems from the 1930s. Not only was this vintage wardrobe fun and fabulous, Aunt Mimi's clothes were one of a kind.

"And I thought I was the only one who was going to look good here tonight!" LaToya exclaimed. "Where did you get that dress?"

"The usual place." Lacey grinned at her. "Just a little something from Aunt Mimi's trunk."

"Honey, I wish she was my Aunt Mimi."

"Your dress is beautiful, LaToya, and it suits you perfectly. You look terrific." Lacey admired the clean lines of the simple sleeveless A-line dress that LaToya wore. The bright red showed off her beautiful caramel-colored skin and flattered her curves. Lacey hoped she looked just as dramatic, in her own way.

"It'll do," LaToya said, skimming her hands over her perfect hips. "So where is that other crazy woman, Felicity Pickles?" LaToya asked with a smirk. "Your little buddy."

"Please. It's not my day to watch her."

"Whatever she's wearing, I bet it's gonna be good. You know, good meaning bad. As opposed to bad meaning good."

"You have a premonition? A feeling?" Lacey asked.

"Moi? I'm hoping she comes as a human aluminum Christmas tree, with a battery-operated color wheel in one hand and a big shiny star perched on her head."

"I hope you're right. She disappeared early this afternoon." Lacey stroked some blush on her cheeks. "Maybe she had to get her star polished."

"What about the eco-bitch, Cassandra? She coming to the Christmas party?"

"Doubtful. She seems to have a phobia of drunken camels."

"That's a shame. Only kind of camel I like. Course, she's got that no-sense-of-humor thing going on." LaToya vigorously rubbed lotion into her hands, then sprayed perfume with a circular flourish. "I was hoping for a knock-down, drag-out fight between the two of them. Maybe a food fight. A girl can dream, right?"

"And get us kicked out of the National Press Club? Please! I was rather hoping for a quiet evening." Lacey closed her eyes for a moment and thought about her date, Vic Donovan. She was hoping to get him in a quiet corner somewhere in the course of the evening. *Mmmmm.*

"I'm talking live entertainment. And who better? Felicity Pickles and Cassandra Wentworth? Two humorless white girls tearing it up in front of the Christmas tree? Front page news."

"Make sure Hansen's there to get it all on film."

"Film is so last-century, Lacey," LaToya said, slipping a tiny camera from her shiny gold purse. "I got my digital. Smile, honey, you look gorgeous." She took a picture of the two of them grinning into the mirror.

Meg Chong, a general news reporter, swept through the ladies' room door and cheerfully plopped down at the counter between them. She peered into the mirror and applied her mascara. Meg was tiny and stylish and wore her long black hair in a high ponytail decorated with sparkling jewelry. Her silver spaghetti strap dress left nothing to the imagination and the back dipped well below her waist. Lacey felt chilly just looking at her.

"Quite a dress, Meg! Won't you get cold in that?"

"How can I get cold when I look so hot?" Meg smiled. "Besides, I'll be warm enough with one of our hot sportswriters draped over my shoulders all night."

"Which one?" LaToya asked, her eyes wide in the mirror.

"Does it matter? They are *all* hot!" Meg laughed and the others joined her.

Lacey's cell phone rang. She retrieved it from the pocket of her suit jacket hanging in the garment bag. The number on the screen made Lacey groan again. Cassandra Wentworth's cell phone. "Yikes! It's her again!"

"Who her?" LaToya leaned over her shoulder and glanced at the number. "Oh, that her! The eco-witch. Don't answer it. Let her grinch someone else tonight. Later, baby."

LaToya gathered up her things and she and petite Meg Chong, freshly mascaraed, swept out of the ladies' room chattering, leaving Lacey alone to face the wrath of Wentworth.

Lacey stuck her tongue out at her phone. She pressed the button to reject the call. No doubt Cassandra had recovered her wits and thought of something new and wicked to say to her. Most people, Lacey thought, when they came up with a snappy comeback a minute too late, would simply call it old business and forget about it. Not Cassandra. She was the mistress of the drive-by insult, and no insult was too stale to deliver. And she would back up over you on her fat-tired mountain bike just to make sure you got it.

The phone rang again. Lacey sighed. What insult could possibly be so perfect that Cassandra simply couldn't wait to say it? Lacey was curious; her fatal flaw. She narrowed her eyes at the phone. Bracing herself, she clicked the answer button. Lacey gazed at her reflection in the mirror and thought she struck just the right note of cool disdain, her right eyebrow raised imperiously.

"Merry Christmas, Cassandra, it's been simply ages."

"You have to come!" A high voice pleaded urgently. "The lady is hurt." The voice sounded young and upset. *This is definitely not Cassandra,* Lacey thought. *Is this a child? Did I read the number wrong?* Lacey glanced again at the screen to make sure it really was Cassandra's cell phone calling her. It was.

"Who is this?"

"You have to come now! She's hurt bad. Please."

"Who's hurt?"

"The lady!"

"I don't understand. Who are you? What's your name? Why are you calling me?"

"She's bleeding." The voice rose higher. "Outside! The lady is bleeding! You have to help!"

"A lady is bleeding? Who is she?"

"The lady! The lady with the phone. I don't know her name. You have to come now! Now!" The little voice edged toward hysteria.

Lacey's stomach did a flip. "Calm down." She said it for herself as well as for the voice on the phone. "Who are you? Why do you have her phone?"

"You have to come now! She could die!"

"All right. I'm coming, but where? You have to tell me where."

"Outside! You have to hurry!"

Lacey grabbed her evening bag, her garment bag, and her tote with one hand, the phone glued to her ear. She opened the ladies' room door with one elbow.

"It'll be all right. Just tell me where you are."

"Outside! The alley. Are you inside?"

She dashed down the hall to her desk in the newsroom and dropped her baggage. The newsroom was nearly empty, though there was some last-gasp activity in some of the offices ringing the large room. She saw Mac on the phone in his office. She grabbed the soft chocolate brown mouton coat that had been Aunt Mimi's and headed for the newsroom door.

"Are you still there? Stay where you are. Maybe I should call the police."

"No! You can't. You can't call the police!" the voice screamed. "You have to come."

Lacey raced past the notoriously unreliable elevators to the stairway exit. She slipped off her blue velvet high heels, scooping them up with one hand, and sped down several flights of stairs and into the lobby of the newspaper. She paused for a moment in front of the elaborate Christmas tree, decorated in gold balls and bows and white lights, to put her shoes back on.

"Are you with Cassandra?" she asked the voice on the phone. "Is that who's hurt? Where are you now?"

"I'm with the lady. She came out of the building and got hurt. In the alley. Hurry!"

Lacey stepped outside the front door of *The Eye* and took a moment to get her bearings before heading toward the alley. She caught her breath and tugged her jacket on while juggling her phone from hand to hand. Words from angry e-mails came back to her. "Watch your back, Miss High-and-Mighty. . . ." She looked around.

Indian summer had lingered far into the fall. In December, the golden days still were comfortable with the kiss of sunshine. Washington had yet to see a single snowflake, but the nights were chilly and crisp in anticipation of winter. Lacey heard a Salvation Army bell somewhere in the distance. Behind it, sirens near and far were ever-present on the city's soundtrack, and the air was thick with diesel exhaust from the city buses, reminding her she was in the busy District of Columbia.

There were two main exits from *The Eye*'s building, one in the parking garage, which opened to the alley, and the front doors that faced Farragut Square across Eye Street to the north. The Square was a block of neat green park with diagonal walkways converging on the statue of Admiral David Farragut at its center. Lacey noticed the white Christmas lights twinkling at the entrance of the Army and Navy Club, which faced the park on its east side. Lacey assumed from the stream of formally dressed couples passing through the Square that the very elegant club was the scene of a Christmas party that night.

There was another population in the Square, in striking contrast to the fancy-dress partygoers. Homeless people began to claim the park benches at dusk to store their meager belongings for a few hours, or for the night. Several of them seemed to live in makeshift lean-tos attached to the benches. Lacey noticed a middle-aged black man with a stocking cap pulled down to his eyebrows, standing by a bench right across the street from *The Eye*, wrapped in a quilted sleeping bag. His name was Quentin and he was a regular. He seemed to be gathering his belongings, perhaps heading for a meal at a shelter.

Crowds were heading for the escalator down to the Metro station on one corner opposite the Square. The sidewalk was a bustle of commuters on their way home or to shop, or to meet friends at a happy hour at a neighborhood pub. Laccy pushed her way through the throng. She realized the voice on the phone had been silent for a moment.

"Are you still there?" she asked. "Are you still in the alley?"

"Yes, but hurry! I think she's gonna die!"

"Keep talking to me. What's your name? Why were you in the alley?"

"Just hurry! Please!"

Lacey turned left into the alley, conscious of the strong garlic aroma from a nearby Italian restaurant. In contrast to the busy street, the alley was calm and empty of traffic. Lacey slowed down to take in her surroundings. She was breathing hard. The alley behind *The Eye* was shaped like an L and it made a sharp turn behind the building. The street entrance was well lit, but there were deep pockets of shadows at the turn.

The voice on the phone sounded genuine to her. Lacey couldn't believe this was some elaborate joke of Cassandra's. The woman seemed to lack the most basic rudiments of imagination or humor. Lacey told herself she was foolish to be chasing off down a dark alley at the sound of a frantic voice, but it was a child's voice. Even so, she looked around carefully to make sure she wasn't being followed.

"Am I in the right alley? Where are you?" The voice on the phone was silent.

Just past the turn in the alley, a woman lay on the ground next to a featureless brick wall. No one else was visible. At first glance, the woman might be taken for one of the homeless people who clung to whatever bit of urban turf they could find, a nook where they might spend the night and not be hassled. But on second glance, Lacey saw it wasn't a homeless person. This woman wore black tights and yellow running shoes. There was no sign of a yellow bike helmet, but there was a bike thrown up against the wall. The frame looked bent. Lacey caught her breath.

It was Cassandra Wentworth. Dark liquid was seeping through her mud brown hair, strands of which had come loose from her ponytail. But that wasn't what caught Lacey's attention. It was what else Cassandra was wearing: a Christmas sweater.

It was a masterpiece of its kind. Knitted Santas and sleighs and reindeer frolicked festively among red and green Christmas trees and fat knitted snowflakes. It was decorated with embroidered-in strings of multicolored Christmas lights, tiny but real. A music chip concealed somewhere inside the sweater was playing merrily and the bulbs were flashing, synchronized to the tinny mechanical sound of a tune Lacey knew well.

The sweater was playing "Jingle Bells."

chapter 4

"She got hit on the head."

Lacey heard the same small urgent voice she'd heard on the phone. It came from behind her. She turned around to see a child stepping out from behind a large greasy blue Dumpster. She clicked off her cell phone.

"Did you see what happened?" Lacey peered at the small figure.

The child stood still and wary, poised to run. "Maybe."

"Will you tell me your name now?"

The child said nothing. All Lacey could see was a blue-and-white striped shepherd's robe with the hood pulled down to the child's eyebrows. The shadows and glare from the yellow streetlights high above the alley didn't help. A reckless little boy, Lacey thought, judging from the voice and the shepherd's robe. *A little wayward shepherd boy, strayed from the Nativity pageant. But there are no sheep here. What's he doing in our alley?*

As curious as she was about the boy, Lacey turned to examine the woman lying on the ground. Carefully gathering up the folds of her velvet skirt, she bent down next to the still figure in the grimy alley. Cassandra was breathing, but she didn't respond to Lacey's voice or touch. Lacey felt for a pulse and found one, but it seemed weak.

She became aware of another presence, uncomfortably close. The little shepherd had crept silently up to Cassandra on the opposite side and squatted over her, leaning so close to Lacey that their foreheads nearly touched. Lacey looked up to see a pair of dark brown almond-shaped eyes staring at her intently, framed by the blue-and-white striped woolen fabric.

Lacey caught a whiff of that earthy smell that comes from play-ing outside in the dirt. And perhaps a little motor oil.

"Is she dead?" the shepherd asked.

"No."

"Because if she's dead I didn't do it." It was the kind of statement someone who always got blamed might make.

"I believe you," Lacey said. "Did you see who did it?"

"A man." Her companion appeared to be about ten or eleven years old, but Lacey decided she was perhaps not the best judge of children's ages. He appeared to be part black, part Asian, and maybe some white, Lacey guessed. It was hard to tell, the light was so bad and the face so dirty. An exotic mix of ethnici-ties, but not uncommon in the Nation's Capital. Lacey stood up and rubbed her hands to warm them.

"She's alive. It's a good thing you called someone. I have to call for help."

Feeling sick to her stomach, Lacey fought the guilt of hav-ing argued with Cassandra moments before someone came along and knocked her in the head. She took another close look at her. There were small red and white slivers of something on the ground and some were speckled in the woman's hair near the wound.

Lacey dialed 911. She reported a woman assaulted in the alley off Eye Street Northwest across from Farragut Square. She told the dispatcher she would wait for the ambulance and clicked off. She heard a siren, but there were always sirens in the background in the District. It faded in the distance.

"You saw what happened?" she asked the child.

He sized her up silently and pressed his lips together.

"Really, you can tell me," Lacey said. "After all, you didn't hit her. Right?"

"I didn't." The little shepherd remained squatting over the limp form of Cassandra, peering at her as if she were a giant science experiment, a very interesting one, one that might roar to life without warning. Cassandra, whose skin was normally pink and weather-roughened, looked deathly white, her lips a chalky gray color. The alley suddenly seemed very quiet.

"It stopped," the shepherd said, and Lacey realized he was talking about the Christmas sweater. The lights had stopped flashing and the tinny sound of "Jingle Bells" was suddenly blessedly still. Grimy little hands started searching the garment.

"What are you doing?"

"Something makes it turn on. The music." Dirty fingers pressed a button at the bottom of one sleeve. The lights started flashing again and "Jingle Bells" tinkled a reprise.

"You probably shouldn't play with that," Lacey cautioned.

"I'm not hurting it!" he protested, displaying a logical side. "I like to know how things work."

"Yes, but—" But what? He wasn't hurting Cassandra. Could the sweater be evidence? And what would it tell anyone? "Never mind. Did the man put this sweater on her?"

The child stood up. "He laughed when he was doing it, like it was the funniest thing in the world."

"Did he say anything?"

"He just laughed. He was dressed like this Santa Dude."

" 'Santa Dude'?"

"Yeah, a dude wearing a Santa hat? You know, those hats like Santa wears?"

Lacey nodded. Like the Santa caps the managers would be wearing to *The Eye*'s party this evening. The shepherd lifted his face to hers, his eyes clear.

"The Santa Dude. Did you see his face?"

"He's a white guy. Like Santa. No beard, though."

"Was this guy wearing a full Santa suit? Red and white? Reindeer?"

The shepherd gave her an exasperated look. "No reindeer! Just a Santa hat. The Santa Dude. This Santa Dude is rude, with a bad attitude. He had squintchy eyes." The shepherd boy made an angry face and squinted. He opened his mouth in a fierce grimace. "Like that."

"What happened?"

"I just saw the lady and the Santa Dude yelling. She was on that bike." He gestured to Cassandra's bent mountain bike. "So he grabs her off the bike and she hits him with her bike helmet."

"She was going home. Was he waiting in the alley for her?"

The child shrugged. "The Santa Dude hit her with this thing, this giant candy cane."

"A what?" Lacey had the feeling she was being had. "Like a red-and-white striped candy cane?" *Oh, please, a candy cane!*

"Like I told you!" The shepherd glared at her, offended. "The biggest one I ever saw. I swear. This big!" The shepherd gestured with both hands spread wide, indicating the size of the alleged giant candy cane weapon. Then he acted out the drama in the alley. "And the Santa Dude holds it up way high over her head. This candy cane? She gets really quiet, and she's kind of little. He's bigger. And I think maybe she tells the Santa Dude to stop or go away or something? Whack! The dude cracks her in the head with it." The boy gestured the blows. "She just stands there for a second and there's lots of blood. And he does it again and again and again, and she falls down. And he puts the sweater on her."

"That sounds pretty scary." *And pretty strange.* Lacey had seen the shards of red and white and wondered what they were, but she wasn't about to touch them. *Fragments of the weapon?* Lacey bent down again to check Cassandra's pulse. She was still breathing, but her skin was cold. "Hold on, Wentworth. You're tough. You'll make it."

"She looks bad," the shepherd said. He squatted again to get a better look. "You think she's gonna die?"

"Where did he have the sweater?"

"I don't know. I was hiding. They were screaming."

"What did they say? And where were you?"

He looked up at Lacey. "I didn't hear all the words. I was hiding behind the Dumpster." He showed her the narrow gap behind the large trash container. It would just hold a child. "And then I peeked out. Like this." Lacey saw just a flash of blue-and-white stripes and a pair of dark eyes peering out. "Because you got to know your circumstances in this town, you know," he counseled wisely. "I could have been whacked too, you know. Like the lady."

"That's true. You're pretty smart." Lacey checked to make sure Cassandra's chest was still moving. "She'll be okay." Lacey hoped her words weren't just bravado.

"That's good," the shepherd agreed. "We're really saving her, huh?"

"Yes, we're saving her. What else did the man do?"

The shepherd thought about it for a moment. "He looked up and saw me. He points his finger like a gun. He starts coming after me. But I squeeze behind that old Dumpster again. He's like way too big to get me in there." The shepherd's eyes were very large.

"And he didn't catch you," Lacey said. "What made him leave?"

"A car came down the alley. The other end. So the Santa Dude, he ran away. But the car turned off, like to park in the garage or something."

"You're all right, then?"

"Sure." The shepherd looked around as if to make sure there was no Santa Dude in the alley. "Sure I am. I'm always all right."

"That's a nice costume." It looked homemade to Lacey, perhaps sewn out of a wool blanket. "Are you late for a school pageant tonight or something? Should I call your parents?"

He ignored the question. "Do you think the lady's going to die?"

"I don't know." Lacey wondered if she should say something more hopeful for the shepherd's sake.

"Yeah, me neither. But she could die, right? People die every day in D.C." The child was silent for a moment. "What's her name?"

"Cassandra. Cassandra Wentworth." Lacey looked at her watch, then at the child. *Where the hell is that ambulance?!* "What's your name? And where are your parents anyway? Are you meeting them somewhere?"

"You ask a lot of questions," the boy said.

"So do you," Lacey said. "Why were you in the alley?"

"Why do you ask so many questions?"

She could ask him the same thing. "It's my job. I'm a reporter."

The shepherd cracked a small smile. "That's a funny job. All you do is ask questions?"

"I do. And after I ask questions I write stories about the answers." A siren suddenly howled in the distance and grew louder. "I work for the newspaper in this building, *The Eye Street Observer.* That's where Cassandra works too. She's a writer too. My name is Lacey Smithsonian." She extended her hand. "And you are?"

He shook her hand very formally, but he didn't offer his name. "Lacey Smithsonian? And you're a reporter. And your phone number is " He rattled off her cell number. A quick learner. "Are you going to put this in the paper?"

"I don't know. Someone will."

"You gonna mention me?"

"You're a hero. You saved her. So maybe we will. What's your name?"

He seemed to finally consider this, rolling it over in his mind, but the name was not forthcoming. He touched Lacey's mouton coat with its thick fur. "I like your coat. It's soft."

"Thank you. It's warm. It was my aunt's."

"Hand-me-down, huh?" He nodded sagely. "I know all about that."

"Yes. A hand-me-down. Tell me something," Lacey said. "You picked up her cell phone?"

"It fell on the ground. You can make it call the last number it called, you know? I figured you must be her friend, so you would come and help her."

Cassandra's friend? He didn't know that Lacey almost didn't answer the call. A twinge of guilt hit her. "Where is her phone now?"

"I don't know." The child made a dramatic show of looking up and down the alley. He shrugged. "Musta lost it."

Lacey smiled and lifted her eyebrow. "You got a hidden pocket in that robe?" No answer. "How old are you anyway?"

"Fifteen."

"Uh-huh. I think you're more like ten. Or eleven."

Offended, the shepherd set her straight. "I am totally almost thirteen!"

"So you're twelve." Lacey could believe twelve. A small twelve.

"Almost thirteen! Twelve and three quarters." The little shepherd boy smiled, showing pretty white teeth. But he froze at the sound of police sirens suddenly almost on top of them.

"The police are going to want a statement," Lacey said. "I'll help you."

"Nuh uh. I don't talk to the police. It's my policy." The boy started walking, then running, as the blue-and-red flashing lights of a Metropolitan Police car entered the Eye Street end of the alley. An ambulance was right behind it.

"Wait! You won't get in trouble. I promise!" She started to follow him, but she didn't want to leave the injured Cassandra. "There could be a reward," Lacey shouted. "A reward from the newspaper. Wait! Come back!"

But the child was running fast now. Lacey caught a final glimpse of blue-and-white stripes flashing under a streetlight at the far end of the alley. Then the little shepherd boy was gone.

chapter 5

In moments the alley was full of people, the ambulance, three police cars and the newest member of *The Eye* staff. With her freckled face, Kelly Kavanaugh looked like a kid on her way to study hall. Her straight brown hair hung to her shoulders and her straight bangs reached to her eyebrows. Kavanaugh wore khaki slacks, a lightweight green windbreaker zipped up to her neck, and a pair of cross trainers. The junior member of the police beat was not dressed for the office Christmas party.

Okay, you're a cops reporter, Kavanaugh, let's see you report, Lacey thought. *Let me know if there's a fashion clue I can decode for you.*

The EMTs were checking Cassandra and preparing to lift her into the ambulance.

"Whoa," Kavanaugh exclaimed. "Cassandra Wentworth from *The Eye*? What's she doing in that awful sweater, Smithsonian? I thought she wouldn't be caught dead in those!"

"You're right about that. But she's not dead."

"So far. So it's someone hacked off about that Sweatergate thing?"

Lacey shrugged. Kavanaugh didn't need any help with the obvious. They had no more time to talk before a youngish policeman approached and wanted Lacey's statement. He took her out of earshot of the young and hungry reporter and Lacey filled him in on the details of how she found Cassandra. But he didn't believe her.

"A boy? In a shepherd's robe? And he's gone now? Right. You been drinking, miss?"

"No, officer, and all I can say is: This is the District."

The cop appraised her and took in the alley. "Yes, ma'am."

Lacey repeated the story the child had told her. She retraced the path from Cassandra to the Dumpster for the officer's benefit, and there hanging on the Dumpster she noticed a tiny piece of torn fabric. Its blue-and-white threads matched the little shepherd's robe. She pointed this out. The cop sighed. His partner came over to look.

"So now you believe me?"

The second cop gave her a slight inclination of his head. "It's the District, ma'am." He reached for the scrap of fabric.

"Hey, don't touch that," the first cop said. "We'll let the forensics boys pick that up."

The second cop looked at him and laughed. "Forensics. For the lab."

"Yeah, forensics." They both laughed. "Right. They'll be all over that. At the lab."

A detective finally showed up, a tired middle-aged black man named Sam Charleston from the Second District. The uniformed officers stood aside and Lacey repeated her story to him.

"So, you'd describe this suspect as black or white or what?"

"Suspect? He's a witness, detective," Lacey said. "And he's a mix of Asian, black, and maybe some white. Just my guess."

Detective Charleston rolled his eyes. "No one on the beat's going to stop and figure that one out. Not even a place on the report for all that. What's his skin look like? Dark, light, medium?"

"Medium lightish, maybe, but—"

"Okay, we got an Hispanic teenager," he called to the young cop. "In a blue-and-white jacket. Put it out."

"Hispanic? Wait, I don't know that," Lacey cut in, "and actually it was a shepherd's robe, not a jacket, and he did say fifteen, but then he said twelve and—"

The detective threw her a look that stopped her cold. "Yeah, that's our suspect."

"No! I didn't say that," Lacey protested. "He's not a suspect! He's a witness. He called for help."

Charleston stroked his jaw. "Right. Maybe he was just waiting to hit you over the head too. Take your Christmas shopping money, credit cards, phone. Maybe he had an accomplice that ran away before you made it to the alley. You show up, he invents a cover story."

"You think he's lying about the candy cane? Who would make that up?"

"People will say anything. Let's say I'm open-minded."

"But I really don't think this kid hurt Cassandra!" She wondered if the little shepherd really could have had something to do with the attack. The kid wouldn't know about Sweatergate. How could he? "The attack on Cassandra was personal. Sort of a grudge. What would some little boy have against her? What's the kid's motive?"

"Motive?" The detective snorted. "Who cares about his motive? All I care about is who did what. Assault in an alley, victim hit in the head? Pretty common. We'll see if we got us a serial."

"Cassandra wrote an editorial about Christmas sweaters. It was negative. Lots of people were angry, writing e-mails—" Lacey froze. That could have been her on the ground, attacked by one of the angry e-mailers.

"I hate the holidays." Detective Charleston closed his eyes for a moment and sighed deeply. "Look, lady, you've got a bleeding victim here and this Hispanic teenager's the last one seen running out of the alley? He's the suspect."

"If you think he's the suspect, why don't you think I'm the suspect?"

He gave her his best cop stare. "Lady, you're making me tired."

The EMTs were settling Cassandra into the ambulance when Lacey felt a warm hand on her shoulder. She was still shaking her head over how a mixed-race child who was a witness to a crime and had tried to help had somehow become a teenage Hispanic suspect. It was easier for her to concentrate on the boy than to think about how close she might have come to Cassandra's fate.

"Lacey, are you all right?" The words came with a lovely wave of testosterone, a voice full of concern.

"I am now." She touched the hand and turned and smiled up at Vic Donovan. Even though his eyes seemed troubled, she noticed how handsome he looked in his tuxedo. She hugged him tightly. Lacey didn't know how long she had been standing in the amber light of the alley, but it felt like forever. It might have been only half an hour. "How did you know I was here?"

"Lucky guess. You're not at the Christmas party with me, where you're supposed to be. So I just looked for the cops. I always figure that if there are flashing lights and sirens anywhere nearby, Lacey Smithsonian is bound to be involved. And look, I was right."

"Very funny. You're just drawn to excitement." She broke the hug and he reached for her hand. "It's the ex-cop in you. Like a moth to a flame."

He smiled, his green eyes crinkling. An unruly lock of his curly hair fell over his forehead. "Just like you. But are you the moth or the flame?" Vic kissed her. "So what's going on here?"

"Short or long version?"

"Short now. Long one over drinks later."

She briefed him and he shook his head. He wrapped his arm around her. "So you probably saved your buddy Wentworth's life, you and your mysterious little shepherd. Pretty exciting." Vic looked at her hopefully. "Any chance you're too traumatized and upset now to go to that ridiculous office party?"

"Not a chance, Donovan." She stared him down. "I may be upset, but this dress is immune to trauma, and I am showing you off in that beautiful tuxedo and you're not weaseling out of it."

"So this is the Smithsonian-shows-off-her-man event?"

"I warned you." Lacey tickled his ribs. "You're the trophy."

"Just think, sweetheart, if you had just said yes way back when, we could have been happily bickering like this for years. You really want to go to that silly thing at the Press Club? Just to see Mac in a Santa cap?"

"You bet. You're already dressed to the teeth, Vic. So am I. We deserve it. And I have to let people know——"

"Because it's news?"

"Yes, but it affects the paper too. Besides, if I don't go to the party, I'll just brood about this awful attack, the spooky alley, the weird sweater, the strange little shepherd boy——"

"And before you know it, Lacey Smithsonian's taking a personal interest in the case." Vic folded her hand in his. "And that would be too much excitement for me. So, my dear, let's party. We'll drink to forget. We'll dance the night away."

"You have no faith," she started to say.

"Au contraire, my sweet reporter. I have all the faith in the world in your ability to get involved where you don't need to. Smithsonian rushes in where angels fear to tread."

"Hey, buddy, you're lucky you have me."

"I never said I wasn't lucky." Vic suddenly swept her into a hug and kissed her till her knees felt weak. "I'm very lucky."

He escorted her back upstairs to her office so she could pick up her bags. Most of the desk lamps were out in the newsroom. Lacey noticed cub reporter Kavanaugh in a pool of light at a desk in the far corner, referring to notes, presumably typing up her story about the incident in the alley. It looked like a lot of effort for what would be a two-paragraph brief, and it wouldn't even make tomorrow's paper. It was after deadline, the edition had already gone to bed. The attack on Cassandra wouldn't see print until Sunday. Kavanaugh was engrossed in her story. She didn't look up and Lacey didn't bother her.

Vic grabbed Lacey's bags from her desk. "Ready? Carry your books, little girl?" Having a boyfriend to carry your packages was a good thing, she decided all over again. Vic squired her back to his Jeep and then drove them to the National Press Club. Where she had been looking forward to seeing all the newspaper's managers clad comically in Santa caps. But it wasn't so funny now.

Lacey stepped out of the Jeep and wrapped Aunt Mimi's coat around her against the sudden chill. It was unthinkable that anyone at *The Eye* could be the mysterious Santa Dude.

Wasn't it?

chapter 6

The lights of the National Press Club gleamed over Fourteenth Street Northwest, across the street from the historic Willard Hotel. Just a short walk from the White House and the museums on the National Mall, or a short drive from Congress, the Press Club was surrounded by theatres and shops and restaurants. Lacey knew they ranged from moderately priced (where reporters paid for their own meals) to excessively overpriced (where reporters might dine with sources on the company's tab, if they were lucky). Tonight's entertainment was on the newspaper's tab.

The annual Christmas-slash-holiday party was as glittering an event as many of the paper's employees ever saw. The Press Club wore an air of understated elegance, its dark wood-paneled entrance and deep blue carpets studded with designs of gold medallions. Flanked by the flags of the fifty states, an impressive Christmas tree stood near the brass-railed stairway up to the upper-level lounge. Glittering lights, evergreen bows, and poinsettias in red and pink and white were everywhere.

It was a chance for the regular reporters to mingle in a place where they felt they belonged, by right of their profession, but they didn't, by right of the hefty membership dues. At *The Eye* it seemed that only editors and managers were members of the Press Club. Lacey wasn't a member, but she had been there a few times for the occasional media briefing. She always loved to visit the place. It made her feel like a legitimate reporter, not merely a fashion reporter.

The walls were covered with photos of famous journalists, from the ubiquitous Helen Thomas, the reportorial bane of presidents, to Margaret Bourke-White, the glamorous photo-

journalist who made her name in the 1930s and '40s and '50s.
All the usual famous male journalists were present and ac-
counted for too, but Lacey's attention focused on her role models, the women of the Fourth Estate. Missing, of course, were
her fictitious role models, the ones closest to her heart, great
dames like Hildy Johnson, played by the fabulous Rosalind
Russell in *His Girl Friday,* and the irresistible and intrepid
flame-tressed Brenda Starr from the comics.

Lacey checked her mouton jacket. She and Vic took a quick
turn through the party before moving through the receiving
line. With its warren of cozy interconnected rooms, the National Press Club was the perfect place for a large party to
spread out and still feel like an intimate gathering. The buffet
line was set in one room, with a prime rib station in the corner
and open bars strategically placed. Many of the partygoers
would round off the evening with a sherry or liqueur upstairs in
the club's Reliable Source Bar, a Washington journalists' hang-
out overlooking Fourteenth Street and the Willard Hotel.

A middle-of-the-road rhythm and blues band was playing in
another room and the more musical members of the staff were
already dancing. The corner room was the most popular: the
pastry room, featuring a dazzling array of pastries, chocolate
cakes, pies, ice cream, and a cappuccino bar. Atop one long
table, a marzipan yellow brick road flanked by rows of candy
canes led dessert-lovers to a large decorated gingerbread house.
Lacey half expected to see a tiny gingerbread replica of Felicity Pickles, the newsroom's Gingerbread Witch, luring little
gingerbread Hansels and Gretels to their sugary doom. She
would no doubt soon be along in the flesh, and in an amazing
Christmas outfit, as foretold by LaToya. But Lacey's attention
was captured by the candy canes, giant novelty candy canes
nearly as big around as her fist and almost two feet long. Giant
candy canes! She thought of Cassandra in the alley and what a
preposterous attempted-murder weapon a candy cane would
make. But she was amazed at how big these were.

Lacey and Vic looped back through the maze of party rooms
to find the formal receiving line. She looked down an impressive row of red-and-white Santa caps, a dozen or more of them,
their white puffball tails bobbing merrily atop the heads of *The
Eye*'s managers, both male and female. *Was the assailant someone here,* she wondered, *or was this just a weird Christmas*

party coincidence? Was black-tie-and-Santa-cap the party fad this year?

Their publisher, Claudia Darnell, had recruited a mostly good-natured crew of Santas, but Lacey's editor Mac, his Santa cap pulled down over his bushy eyebrows like a thug's stocking cap, looked like the Christmas elf voted Least Jolly.

Lacey took another look to make sure all the newspaper's managers were wearing their festive headgear, shaking her head at the charmingly ridiculous sight of grown men and women, serious journalists all, in tuxedos and formals—and Santa caps.

Claudia looked elegant in a red silk sheath dress that displayed her toned arms. Her blue eyes were set off nicely by her deep buttery tan and her sleek ice blond hair was styled in a French twist. The Santa cap edict didn't seem to apply to Claudia; after all, it was her newspaper, and her party. Claudia was a woman of a certain age, fifty-something, but she had a killer figure and a proven magnetism for male attention. Even Vic had appreciative eyes for her. Lacey elbowed him gently in the ribs.

Men flocked around Claudia now, worker bees adoring their queen, and not just *The Eye*'s staff, but also her invitees, K Street lawyers, lobbyists, politicians, liberal and conservative. They all had a healthy respect for the power of the press, even *The Eye*, particularly in Claudia's attractive hands. They wouldn't dream of snubbing her annual Christmas party.

As soon as Lacey approached, Claudia pulled her aside. The jungle drums of the newsroom gossip machine had already reached her.

"It's true then? Cassandra Wentworth was attacked in our own alley?" Claudia asked. Lacey nodded. "Oh my God. How is she?"

"Alive but unconscious. They took her to George Washington University Hospital."

Lacey could see Mac edging near them with a troubled look. Even with his brows knitted crossly, the Santa cap cocked crookedly on his head gave him a comical look.

"Now what, Smithsonian?" He growled in that editorial voice she knew so well.

Surprised he hadn't heard, Lacey quickly explained what she saw in the alley.

"Someone's attacked *The Eye*?" Mac's eyebrows rose in his familiar scowling arch.

"Whoever it was left her wearing a Christmas sweater," Lacey said. "A little Sweatergate message?"

"Not one word here tonight about Sweatergate," Mac warned. "I don't ever want to hear that word again."

"I'm sure Cassandra is in good hands." Claudia inserted herself back into the conversation and put her hand on Lacey's arm. "But there's nothing we can do right now. And as awful as this is, she's lucky you were there to call for help."

Lacey was about to correct the misimpression that it was she and not the little shepherd boy who had really saved Cassandra, but Claudia turned back to the receiving line with a final instruction. "Let's not cast a pall on this party for everyone else, shall we?"

Lacey was effectively dismissed. She broke from the receiving line to retrieve Vic, who'd been watching on the sidelines.

"Everything okay?" He put his arm around her waist.

"I'm not supposed to ruin the party with my bad news."

"Sounds like good advice," Vic said. "You did what you could, sweetheart. You did good. You might have saved her life." Lacey nodded and rested her head on his shoulder for a minute. "It's out of your hands now, anyway, isn't it?" She pulled away and gazed at him. Concern lit his jade green eyes.

"Yes, and it's not a murder case, so you can't blame it on me and my alleged magnet-for-murder thing. Can you?" Vic just smiled. She grabbed his hand and led him in the direction of the open bar. "Come with me, you handsome thing. Who can I show you off to?"

The party rooms were beginning to fill up, but she immediately saw one of her least favorite people, Peter Johnson, who pointedly turned away. Johnson was a Capitol Hill reporter whose exalted political beat covering Congress barely contained his inflated sense of self-importance. He somehow thought being a Hill mole made him sexy, to Lacey's mind a psychotic delusion. They had butted heads before.

A glance told her that Peter Johnson was being true to his dweeby Washingtonian fashion sense and dyed in-the-wool conformist nonconformism. To this formal black-tie event he had worn a brown corduroy jacket, rumpled and stained khaki slacks, a blue denim work shirt, and a violently purple-and-red-and-blue Jerry Garcia tie. *Not wearing a tux really sticks it to the Man, dude! And my tie totally rocks the power structure.* He had begun wearing his thinning hair in a ponytail. Lacey thought it was a sure sign of an impending midlife crisis.

Johnson skipped the receiving line and strode to the bar right past Lacey and Vic, as if he were expecting someone. Lacey assumed it was Cassandra Wentworth. She had seen the two of them exchange furtive longing glances, even though they both seemed to have grudges against the world and no idea what to do with any feeling warmer than contempt.

Johnson had always shunned the holiday party as a trivial frivolity, but this year Lacey guessed he was a man with a mission: Consume enough free liquor to actually talk to Cassandra. He apparently hoped against all reason she would deign to be there. He shot Lacey a dirty look. She briefly considered telling Johnson about Cassandra, but what was the use? Besides, Claudia had said to keep it quiet.

"Who is that jerk?" Vic asked. "I don't like the way he looks at you."

"That's sweet of you, darling." Lacey smiled. "That jerk is Peter Johnson, our Hill reporter. He's under the mistaken impression that I'm forever trying to steal his beat. As if."

"Shall I set him straight?"

She laughed at the thought of Johnson landing flat on his pride in the middle of the floor. "Tempting, but people might stare. And worse, write."

"Hey, Lacey, Vic!" A loud voice hollered from behind them.

She twirled around to see Harlan Wiedemeyer, *The Eye*'s "death and dismemberment" reporter, looking like a jolly little elf in a tuxedo that strained across his chest and a bright red cummerbund around his substantial belly. He was carrying a huge candy cane. And on his head, not a Santa cap, but a pair of brown felt reindeer antlers. He pressed the tip of one antler and the ears lit up in a happy blinking antler dance to the tune of "Santa Claus Is Coming to Town." This was just the type of sartorial statement of seasonal cheer that Cassandra Wentworth had been trying to stamp out. *If Cassandra weren't already in the hospital,* Lacey mused, *Wiedemeyer's musical antlers would send her there.* She felt a stab of guilt. *But she didn't deserve what happened to her. And where did Wiedemeyer get that big candy cane?*

"Nice antlers, Wiedemeyer," Vic said. Lacey thought he was just being polite, but Vic had a big smile on his face. He was getting a charge out of this chubby little elf in a tux and antlers. "I'd like to see the reindeer those came from."

"Amazing what you can pick up at the drugstore, isn't it? These babies will positively pickle that pompous Wentworth witch." Wiedemeyer stroked his antlers fondly. "She wouldn't dare show her face here, would she? Nah, she's probably out making some other poor bastards miserable tonight." Everybody was a "poor bastard" of one kind or another in Harlan's world. He waved the candy cane, as delighted as a little boy waving a brand-new baseball bat. "And have you seen the size of these babies? They're all over the place."

"She's not coming," Lacey said, but Wiedemeyer wasn't listening. Santa caps and giant candy canes were everywhere. The little shepherd boy was telling the truth. *This is a nightmare,* Lacey thought.

"I'll just have to wear my antlers to work then." He snatched hors d'oeuvres from a nearby tray. "I can't imagine what's keeping Felicity. She's been telling me how great this shindig always is. I even got all dressed up for her." He hit the button on his antlers and they started twinkling again.

"I'm sure she'll appreciate it," Vic said, nudging Lacey's arm. "I got all dressed up too, but I forgot my antlers. Lacey says she's going to show me later how much a woman appreciates a man in a tux."

"Victor Donovan!" Lacey grabbed his arm meaningfully and gave him The Look.

"You think so?" Wiedemeyer's antlers seemed to perk up. "You think she'll show me too? I mean Felicity, you know, not, um—"

"How could Felicity resist a man of your impressive antlerage, Harlan?" Vic said. "But maybe you should save your batteries for her, don't you think?"

"Well, gosh, yes." Harlan blushed. "Absolutely! Oh, boy!" Wiedemeyer was in such a dither he didn't even have some bizarre tale plucked from the day's news for them. Wiedemeyer loved the D & D beat and was always willing to share, and the more bizarre and/or disgusting his tale, the better. Reporters who saw him coming down the hall with a juicy tidbit often developed an urgent need to go interview a source, any source, anywhere but in the newsroom. But tonight there was no talk of exploding toads, or fish with human teeth, or male bass in the

Potomac laying eggs, or some idiot bank robber handing over a threatening note with his personalized deposit slip.

"I guess I better go find my little sugar cookie!" He marched off, antlers flashing, candy cane waving like a baton in search of his lady love. Who would, no doubt, Lacey thought, be wearing that aluminum Christmas tree LaToya had hoped for.

Veteran police reporter Tony Trujillo found Lacey and Vic through the increasingly thick throng of merrymakers. Tony was escorting a pale cool blonde in an ice-blue dress whose thin straps were struggling to hold up her cantilevered bosom. The blonde wore her hair in an improbable flip and sported a chunky necklace of marble-sized faux pearls. Another blonde, Lacey thought, in a long line of Trujillo's blondes. Tony introduced her as Linda Sue Donahue.

"I'm just dying to get to know you, Lacey." Linda Sue spoke with a soft Southern accent. "Why, Tony talks about you all the time! Is it true y'all're always getting into trouble? And so creatively?"

"I don't get into trouble nearly as often as Tony does," Lacey said. "For instance, he's in trouble right now without even knowing it."

"Oh my! You're going to have to tell me everything! But first I have to run off to the little girls' room to fix my face." Linda Sue tottered off toward the restroom on her spike heels and Tony looked sheepish. Lacey lifted her eyebrow at him. Her Look was getting lots of practice tonight.

"Hey, Lacey." Tony loosened his collar with his index finger. "I don't know where she got that stuff."

"Really?" Lacey gave in to a grin. "I do. By the way, she looks a little chilly. Is that the whole dress, or is there more to it?" It was even skimpier than Meg Chong's little silver number.

"Don't worry, I'll keep her warm." Tony winked at Vic and watched his date walk away with an appreciative leer. Lacey rolled her eyes.

"How soon can I whisk you away from here?" Vic whispered to Lacey.

Tony stuck his face in between them. "You guys can't go yet, everyone's got to stick around for the festivities."

"What is he talking about?" Vic asked Lacey.

She had forgotten to mention the "entertainment" portion of the evening to Vic. On purpose. "Claudia Darnell always makes some announcement, usually patting us on the back for our hard work, blah blah blah. It's considered rude to leave before then."

"And the skits, Lois Lane," Tony prompted. "Tell him about the skits."

"We can skip the skits and head for the bar." Vic looked from her to Tony and back again, expecting an explanation. "Some jokers on the staff think they're the equal of the Capitol Steps comedy troupe," Lacey said. "They are not."

"The skits are killer, man," Tony picked up. "Inside newspaper humor. Satire about politics, journalists, scandals, current events, whatever. Like the year Lacey got the fashion beat, you know, when the former writer died in her chair? Classic skit. Hilarious. Haunting. Dead editors on stage. The Death Chair. Practically Shakespeare."

"More like the Three Stooges, with an extra stooge or two," Lacey said. "Tasteless. Rude, crude, and socially unacceptable. Songs, dances. It's a stretch to call it satire, Vic, or even funny. But the good news is we can slip out as soon as the lights go down."

"Aw, come on, Lacey, it's hilarious, man. Unless you're one of the victims."

"Got it," Vic said. "Any victims we know tonight?"

"No telling, but Lois Lane here is a pretty good candidate. In fact, with her track record this year, it's for certain. There have been more bodies, you know."

Lacey rolled her eyes. She took Vic's arm and was about to steer him to the buffet, but Kim Jones, Mac's petite Japanese-American wife, appeared in a break through the crowds and took Lacey's elbow. Always tasteful, Kim wore a dark plum silk dress, her hair gathered in a low bun wrapped with a silk ribbon. She was afire with curiosity. Mac was trailing behind her with a buffet plate full of chicken wings, his Santa cap slipping.

"Lacey! What did I hear about a child witnessing the attack tonight?" Kim asked. "And how on earth did the boy get ahold of you?"

Lacey gave her an abbreviated version. "I couldn't get many details out of the kid," she said. "But if it weren't for him being in the alley—"

"But that's terrible! Where were his parents?"

"Like I said, my little shepherd was stingy with personal information."

Mac listened and munched another wing, standing attentively by his wife. Kim looked especially petite next to Mac's bulk. She seemed to have a calming effect on him.

"And in an alley?" Kim shook her head.

"Boys like to explore all kinds of dirty places," Vic said. Lacey felt her eyebrow rise. She tried to control it.

"Maybe," Kim said, "but behind *The Eye Street Observer* is no kind of neighborhood for kids." Kim accepted a glass of wine from her husband. "Mac and I love kids."

"Kim thinks every kid should have organized activities," Mac teased. "She'd give them all little Day-Timers."

"Ha, they already have Palm Pilots and cell phones," Kim said, placing a gentle hand on Mac's arm and gazing fondly at him. Love is a funny thing, Lacey thought. "Mac is terrific with children," his wife continued. "He coaches Little League."

"Little League?" Lacey tried to envision Mac's smooth dome in a baseball cap.

Her editor set his glass down on the tray of a passing waiter. "Maybe we could get a softball team organized at *The Eye*," Mac suggested. "How's your pitching arm, Smithsonian?" Lacey just stared in horror while Vic and Tony laughed. "Nah, you're probably better at catching those fly balls."

"I found her!" Harlan Wiedemeyer yelled from one of the bars in the foyer. His voice carried over the crowd, which he parted with his candy cane. "I found Felicity!"

Oh, lucky us. Lacey tried to become invisible, but that never worked for her. Harlan had Felicity's hand in a death grip and he was dragging her through the crowd toward Lacey's little group.

"Here comes trouble," Mac growled. He took Kim's arm and began to steer her away.

"He's not a jinx, you know, Mac," Lacey said. "You told me yourself there's no such thing as a jinx."

"I know," Mac said. "Don't believe in jinxes. Silly superstition. But bad things happen when Wiedemeyer's around. And my wife wants to dance. Bad things happen when I don't dance with my wife."

Kim beamed at Mac and took her husband's hand. "Happy holidays!" They disappeared in the direction of the music.

Vic leaned into Lacey. "I wish I had a camera when you two

heard about Mac coaching Little League. The looks on your faces? Priceless."

"Dude," Trujillo said. "Mac as a coach? Hard to wrap your head around."

"Even scarier: A team at the paper," Lacey said.

"Your boss is not exactly Ivan the Terrible," Vic said.

"No, Vic, but I do think Mac could frighten small children. He scares me."

"Darling, you scare him," Vic replied. "The tough-guy act is to cover his fear."

"I'm with Vic, here, Lois Lane," Trujillo said. "But I bet his Little Leaguers play their little butts off for him."

Lacey heard a faint noise coming from her purse: Her cell phone was ringing. She could barely hear it over the party noise. Cassandra's number was on the screen. She flipped it open and dragged Vic away to a quieter corner at the end of a hallway.

"Hello?"

"So is she okay?" The voice of the little shepherd came through. "The lady. Is she dead?"

"No, she's alive," Lacey said. "The ambulance took her to the hospital."

"Cassandra, right? That's her name, right? Is she gonna live?"

"I think so. All because of you. But where are you? Hey, and what's your name? Are you all right? Are you at home now?"

"I'm good. I gotta go."

"Wait a minute, you haven't told me anything. I need some more information." She felt Vic's hand on her shoulder.

"You worry too much," the boy said.

Lacey knew the kid wouldn't have called if he hadn't been worried too. Quite the little Boy Scout. "We need to talk. I need to know—"

"She's alive. That's okay then. Bye." He hung up, leaving Lacey to stare at the phone. She hit the button to redial and listened to it ring. But the little shepherd was cagier than that. He didn't pick up.

Vic looked at her, his dark brows knit over inquisitive green eyes. "Something you want to tell me, darling?"

Where to start? "I guess in all the excitement, I forgot about the cell phone."

"The kid has Wentworth's cell phone? Aha. You know of course the cops can trace it, if they get a judge to sign a warrant. And I recognized at least two or three judges at this party. Course, they'd have to know about the cell phone." She gazed up at him, her eyes large and troubled. "Now don't look at me like that, Lacey. I'm on your side."

"But Vic, the cops think the kid is a suspect. I can't believe it. He's just a little boy. Who tried to do a good deed. And he did! I can't just sic the cops on him!"

Vic leaned against the wall and drew her to him in an embrace. "Maybe. But did you think that maybe even a kid could be an accomplice in a crime that went wrong? Maybe develop an attack of conscience after it soured?"

"Yes, but not this kid. It doesn't feel right. He was just in the wrong place at the wrong time. Maybe he was screwing around in the alley, skipping out on the Christmas play, then saw something he shouldn't. But involved in the attack? No."

Vic hugged her. She closed her eyes and breathed in the warm spicy scent of him. "This is your call, Lacey. Much to my chagrin, your instincts are usually right on target, when it comes to bad guys anyway. If you think the kid is really just a good Samaritan, maybe he is."

"So you didn't hear the part about Cassandra's missing cell phone?"

"What cell phone?"

Lacey Smithsonian's

FASHION BITES

The Office Holiday Party:
Land Mine—or Booby Trap?

Christmas. It's the most wonderful time of the year. And the most stressful. Add the challenge of shining at the annual office holiday party, standing out with style and assurance. Dressing for this high-tension event can blur the fine line between Dress to Impress and Dress to Transgress. This high-stakes high-wire balancing act is not as easy as it sounds. Remember, you've got to go back to work with these people Monday morning.

After all, this is Washington, D.C., the stuffy bastion of sartorial conservatism that just happens to house the government. Wacky, creative, and revealing outfits won't win you brownie points or gold stars here. Unless you're an intern looking to trade your resume for a torrid tabloid liaison, in which case you don't need fashion advice from me. *Just a thong in your heart.*

The Washington office party isn't merely about free food and drink and conviviality. It's about offering the unwary opportunities for fashion fiascos. Your office gossips will dine on these delicacies for months, even years. Some typical pitfalls:

- You show up at the black-tie office fete in your blue jeans and corduroy jacket, and that one rumpled tie you always keep folded up in your jacket pocket just in case you have to "go formal." Your CEO's first question: "Uh-oh, who let the reporter in?!" His second question: "How do we get rid of him?"

- That low-cut micromini dress that shows off all your assets, right down to the bottom line? Hot for after hours at the club. Not so hot for prime time with your coworkers. Ice cold, if you want that coveted corner office on K Street. Spare the top of the office food chain the visual inventory of your tattoos and piercings. Nothing too short, too tight, too see-through, or too low cut. If you must share, do it among friends. Your boss may say he or she is your friend. She's not. She's your boss. *Quick test: Ask a friend for a paycheck.*

- The invitation said "black tie optional." You show up wearing "casual Friday." Your subconscious fashion statement: "I don't get paid enough to dress up! What I wear has no bearing on how well I do my job. Besides, black tie is stuffy and old-fashioned. I gotta be me, dude!" Your boss's subconscious hears: "You don't care enough to wear your very best, so maybe you don't care enough to do your very best, in this stuffy, old-fashioned town. Be yourself somewhere else, dude." And you haven't gotten a word in edgewise. Hint: In Washington, the word "optional" often means "mandatory." When in doubt, let your tux do the talking.

- Different rules for different folks. Your company's Vice President of Obscure Facts and Irrelevant Nonsense wears the same utterly bizarre office party outfit every year? *Smile!* It's probably considered a charmingly eccentric company tradition by now. You can dish about it the next day with your *real* friends. Remember, when *you* get to be the Vice President of Obscure Facts, you can wear your own charmingly eccentric office party outfit. As long as it's not too short, too tight, too see-through, or too low cut.

Ah, the office holiday party! Socializing with those wacky coworkers who drive you crazy all day! It sounds like such a good idea, so festive and carefree. Oh, it doesn't? *Why?* Because it's really just an extension of your workday, a little more relaxed, and a little more dangerous. Your office persona and performance are still on display, but you may be off your guard.

Your bottom line (which should be covered *completely* by your little black dress, by the way): Appropriate party wear shows respect for yourself and your host. At the office party, your host is your boss. *Yeah, no stress there.* What you wear can speed your way to the top. Or out the door.

Huppy Holidays!

chapter 7

"Here she is!" Harlan Wiedemeyer, a bundle of nerves over-wrought from love, came running down the hall with Felicity Pickles in tow and nearly ran Vic and Lacey down. He shook a branch of mistletoe over Felicity's head and kissed her awkwardly. They both blushed. "Have mistletoe will travel," Wiedemeyer declared.

Is this really Felicity? Lacey wondered. *The festive Felicity, shameless purveyor of seasonal excess?* The woman looked uncommonly subdued for the office Christmas party. Felicity's sleeveless red wool dress made her large arms look shockingly white. She wore a pair of shiny Christmas balls at her ears. That was it. No singing reindeer, no dancing elves, no tinsel. No aluminum Christmas tree. Felicity looked like the Grinch had stolen her Christmas.

"Gee. Nice dress, Felicity," Lacey said. "Very, um, tasteful."

Felicity looked daggers at Lacey. "This is not what I planned to wear. I mean I *was* going to wear it, but there was *more*." She looked distressed. "Something really special."

"But you look lovely, buttercup," Wiedemeyer protested.

"Someone stole my sweater!" Felicity roared. "My new Christmas sweater that goes with this dress. I had to special order it months ago, and it's gone." She turned to Wiedemeyer. "It was at my desk and someone stole it! I can't believe it. Who would do that to me?"

"But everyone loves you," her distraught boyfriend insisted.

It was all too clear where this was going. Lacey felt Vic's hand on her shoulder again. He knew what she was thinking.

"That sweater of yours, Felicity, it wouldn't be bright red,

with an embroidered string of Christmas bulbs that actually
light up, like Harlan's antlers, would it?"

Felicity's eyes went wide. "Yes! It does. It's beautiful!"

"And does it play 'Jingle Bells'?" Lacey's bad feeling was
getting worse.

"That's it! That's it! Have you seen it?"

"Oh yes. Unfortunately, I think I have."

Tony and his date rejoined the group. Linda Sue seductively
draped one arm around his shoulders. Tony took her hand and
kissed it absently.

"What did I miss?" Linda Sue said. "I'm all ears."

"And Wiedemeyer's all antlers," Tony added. "Now me, I'm
all—"

"I think I saw it earlier." Lacey knew she shouldn't talk
about it, but she was too curious now to obey Claudia's gag
order against spreading the bad tidings and ruining the Christmas party. Besides, Lacey was a reporter. *Gag order? What gag
order?*

"Tell me!" Felicity was in her face. "What did you see?"

Lacey looked around to see who might be lurking and eavesdropping. Even this far corner of the Press Club was filling up
with black tuxedos and a rainbow of recycled bridesmaid's
dresses.

"Cassandra Wentworth was attacked in the alley tonight behind *The Eye*. When I saw her she was wearing your sweater,
Felicity. Or one that looked remarkably like it."

Felicity's mouth dropped open. "My sweater? But Cassandra hates my sweaters. I don't get it."

Peter Johnson, on his way to the bar, overheard and elbowed
his way into the circle. "What's this about Cassandra? What
happened to her?" He grabbed Lacey's shoulders with both
hands and was about to shake her. "Tell me!"

Vic intervened with one practiced arm. Without even
spilling his beer he moved Johnson about three feet straight
back. "If you want to speak to Ms. Smithsonian you'll do it respectfully," Vic said, his former chief of police persona emerg-
ing. "By that I mean in a tone of respect. And without using
your hands. Am I clear?"

Johnson gulped. He was no match for the muscular Donovan in any dimension, and he wasn't used to being treated so
physically. He was used to getting away with bullying people

verbally under the protection of the Fourth Estate. Lacey reflected that this boyfriend business had some major pluses. She
introduced the two of them. Johnson offered his hand to Vic
hesitantly, as if he were a little uncertain whether he'd get it
back. Vic shook hands, then indicated Johnson could now address Lacey. Respectfully.

"Ms. Smithsonian," Johnson said carefully, tucking his
hands behind his back, "*please* inform me! What's all this about
Cassandra?"

She related the basics. He absorbed the story with a grim
face and announced his intention to rush to Cassandra's side
and do something, anything.

"She was unconscious," Lacey said, "and she's probably still
in the emergency room or intensive care. They probably won't
even let you see her yet."

"Nothing you can do for her right now, Johnson," Vic said.
"Time to let the cops do their thing."

"You didn't follow the ambulance?" Johnson demanded of
Lacey.

"No. There was nothing I could do, Peter. Or you."

"We'll see about that." Johnson stormed out to play Cassandra's knight in shining armor, or her belated knight in faded
corduroy.

Wiedemeyer watched all this with amazement. "Holy
tamale! That drip Johnson's got the hots for Cassandra Wentworth? Poor bastard!" He hit the replay button on his reindeer
antlers, and the lights started flashing again. The antlers played
"Deck the Halls." Felicity looked as if she were in shock.

A smile played over Trujillo's lips. "Ah, they say there's
someone for every poor bastard, Wiedemeyer. You think that's
true, amigo? Felicity, what do you think?"

"I don't know," Felicity said. "Why would she steal my
sweater?"

"Oh, I just love romance," Linda Sue said. "And all this excitement! My goodness, this is an interesting party y'all throw
here. And by the way, Lacey, that is a darlin' dress. Absolutely
darlin'! Where on earth did you get it? It looks positively
vintage."

Linda Sue's perkiness might eventually get on her nerves,
Lacey thought, but with Vic standing protectively by her side,

Lacey was feeling just fine. And it was always amusing to see Tony's personality change into Tony Terrific, the smooth seducer.

"And where is my poor sweater now?" Felicity asked, leaning against Wiedemeyer for support.

"It probably went into the ambulance with Cassandra," Lacey said. "That's the last time I saw it. She was still wearing it."

"Or it could be headed for the evidence locker by now," Vic suggested.

"She was actually *wearing* my sweater? When she was attacked? It was right *on* her?" Felicity wailed as if Cassandra had infected it with the plague or worse, cooties. *Sometimes,* Lacey thought, *we never grow up and leave the schoolyard.*

"Don't worry Felicity, we'll get you another sweater," Wiedemeyer consoled her.

"I don't want another sweater." Something occurred to her and the color drained from her face. "You don't understand, Harlan! If she's wearing my sweater, people are going to think—"

"They'll think you attacked Cassandra," Lacey said. "That's what you're thinking." The thought had crossed Lacey's mind, but she'd discounted it. As irritating as Felicity could be, she was a fellow reporter, and reporters fought the world, not each other. Maybe that theory would be tested tonight.

"That's just crazy talk." Wiedemeyer patted Felicity's hand.

"I wouldn't hurt anyone," she moaned. "Not even Cassandra."

"But you did fight with her," Trujillo said. "We were all there in the office."

"Those were just words," Felicity said. "Nothing happened."

"Felicity, where were you today?" Lacey asked. "I didn't see you much this afternoon. How did you lose the sweater?" Felicity looked confused. "Think. Where did you last see the sweater?"

"It was in the office." Felicity took her hand back from Wiedemeyer and rubbed it. "I hung it on the back of my chair, but I was running around. When I came back to get ready for the party, it was gone. I looked all over for it, then I went home."

"Home?" Wiedemeyer said. "No wonder I couldn't find you."

"Why did you go home?" Trujillo asked.

"To see if there was another sweater I could wear, but nothing worked with this dress, with this red!" Felicity rubbed her exposed arms. "Everyone has seen all my other sweaters. This one was brand-new. It was special."

"Where did you go after work, Harlan?" *You and your giant candy cane?* Lacey reached for Vic's hand.

"Krispy Kreme, of course." Harlan Wiedemeyer turned toward Lacey, his antlers bobbing. "I was a little nervous about the party. Being nervous always makes me hungry. So after I put my tuxedo on, I decided to get a bite and check out their special seasonal doughnuts. Red and green sprinkles." He inspected his tuxedo as if for stray sprinkles. "Say, I'm getting a little hungry now. How about that buffet line, Felicity? They have shrimp. You love shrimp. Shrimp will cheer you up."

"They have shrimp?" Felicity gazed into his eyes. "I don't know, I don't think I'm hungry."

"Of course you are, my little scallop. You don't need that old sweater, Felicity. I'll buy you the gaudiest damn Broadway musical of a Christmas sweater money can buy." He took her hand and led the way to the long food line.

Vic wrapped his arms around Lacey and pulled her away into a darker corner. "Alone at last." He tipped her face up. He was about to kiss her. *Oh yeah,* Lacey thought, *this is what I got all dressed up for tonight!*

"Yeah, man, alone at last," Tony said. "Now we can talk." Trujillo had followed them for a debriefing, with Linda Sue in tow. "You didn't think you could get away without spilling the whole story, did you?"

"We had hoped. Yes," Lacey said.

"Oh no, we want to hang with the cool kids," Linda Sue said with a self-mocking smile that made Lacey like her more. "And Tony says y'all're the coolest."

"It's weird, man, an attack on a journalist, right in our own back alley," Tony said. "You don't think Felicity did it, do you, Lacey?"

"I hope not." Lacey thought Tony was thinking about Felicity's cookies more than Felicity.

"Who's the cop on the case?"

"I talked to a Detective Sam Charleston. You know him?"

"Nope." Tony shook his head. "Heard the name. So who do you think got to her? You get a description? And what was the weapon?"

"I wasn't a witness," Lacey didn't want to sound like a fool. "Something big and hard, he said. Perhaps a giant candy cane."

"That's helpful," Tony grumbled. "Couldn't the kid do any better than that? Didn't he see the actual attack?"

The ambient party noise was growing deafening. The four found themselves huddling as if on a football field. "The sweater looks bad for Felicity," Lacey suggested. "From her description there's really no question it's her sweater." She reflected that if Felicity were to attack someone it would be with food, not with a blunt instrument. *But wait,* she thought, *candy canes are food.*

"Is Cassandra the one who wrote that mean little thing on Christmas sweaters?" Linda Sue asked. Lacey nodded.

"I thought you said a man attacked her," Tony said.

"The little shepherd said the 'Santa Dude' did it," Lacey said.

"I'm lost," Linda Sue said. "Who's the Santa Dude?"

"Felicity is big enough to be a Santa Dude," Tony said, and Linda Sue laughed. She told him she needed a drink. They headed toward the bar. "We'll be back," he warned.

"The sweater strikes me as pretty clumsy," Vic said to Lacey once they were alone. "A neon sign pointing to your pal Felicity. But it's a nice obvious clue for someone who's got too much work to do to look for the little things."

"You mean the cops?"

"Cops are pretty overworked in this town," he said.

"And the candy cane?"

"That's just showing off," Vic said. "Unless it was just the only thing at hand. If in fact the weapon was a candy cane. Who knows."

"Felicity's never been my favorite person," Lacey said, "but I find it hard to believe she did this."

"Oh, really?"

"If she tried to kill Cassandra, wouldn't Felicity be worried about her being unexpectedly alive and talking? She didn't even ask about Cassandra."

"Could be taken a couple of ways, and neither one looks good for Felicity." Vic took a swig of his beer and eyed the partygoers swirling around them. "Either she knows what condition Cassandra is in and thinks she'll die, or she's a completely unfeeling witch who couldn't care less. And that might make her a pretty good suspect too."

"That sizes it up pretty neatly," Lacey said, sipping her champagne.

"The thing really lights up and plays 'Jingle Bells'?"

"Like Harlan's antlers." She wiggled her fingers above her head. He laughed.

"What a pair they are. There really is someone for everyone, isn't there?" He put his arms around her.

"There is for me,' she said.

Tony and Linda Sue returned with drinks and the four of them grabbed an open table. Tony and his date took chairs across from each other and gazed into each other's eyes. Lacey tossed Vic a knowing glance. She gave Tony's new relationship a month, maybe two. Tony's dating history, in so far as Lacey knew it, consisted of his own personal Blonde of the Month Club, with an occasional extension for a second month. He had in fact told her once, ruefully, that his average relationship was about four and a half dates. The half date was the inevitable breakup date, where someone got dumped in the middle of dinner and decided not to hang around for dessert.

"Lacey baby!" LaToya broke through the crowd. "You didn't tell me about some creep in the alley putting the hurt on our poison pen writer."

"I never had a chance," Lacey said. "And Claudia said not to—"

"Well, it'll be all over the party soon enough. Peter Johnson just raced out of here like his pants were on fire, hollering something about Wentworth and Smithsonian. Just thought you should know." Lacey looked up. Faces in the crowd were peering at her. Fingers were pointing.

"Looks like Felicity's got a grudge against Cassandra," Tony said to LaToya.

"Lots of people have a grudge against Cassandra." LaToya was enjoying being in the thick of breaking news, like any reporter. And every reporter knows it's sometimes hard to tell news from gossip. "She's that kind. Pisses people off. Makes you want to pop her one."

"Someone did," Tony said.

"About time too. But what about you, Lacey?" LaToya sat down on the edge of their table, smoothing her satin skirt.

"What do you think? Of course, my prime suspect is Miss Pickles, who I am deeply disappointed to say is wearing nothing at all like an aluminum Christmas tree, or even those cheesy light-up antlers like her boyfriend, the jinx. I was hoping Felicity'd at least be wearing a tree skirt and a ton of tinsel. Nada. Pretty suspicious behavior, for her. So of course she tops my list of suspects. Then there is *you*."

"Me?" Lacey sat up straight. "Say what?"

LaToya smiled wickedly. "You had words, harsh words, with our Cassandra before she left tonight. You told me all about it yourself."

"Is this true?" Vic was now also on alert.

"Wentworth was psycho over our Miss Smithsonian's valiant defense of the Christmas sweater." LaToya had a tabloid style of talking and writing. "Cassandra threw the newspaper at our Lacey, inciting who knows what murderous passions."

"Oh, please." Lacey laughed. "She threw my wadded-up column at me, Vic, and I made a paper airplane out of it and threw it back. I found the whole thing mildly amusing. Cassandra didn't find it nearly as amusing as I did."

"When did this happen?" Vic asked. Everyone was leaning in so close, Lacey felt she needed air.

"Right before I changed clothes. When I asked her what she was going to wear to the party, she flew out of there like a bat on a bicycle," Lacey said to Vic's arched eyebrow. "She was wearing her bike clothes."

"Everyone's waiting for you to confess, Lacey," Tony smirked.

"Confess what? That I was more interested in getting gussied up for the party than letting Cassandra ruin my evening? I confess. And then she called me up to abuse me some more. I was in the ladies' room when her call came in on my cell phone. And then the second call came, telling me a lady was hurt in the alley. I was standing right next to you, LaToya. You told me not to answer the phone! And then you left."

LaToya made a rueful face. "Oh, that's right, I did say that. Damn, girl, I'm your alibi! There goes another suspect. Guess you're off the witness stand for now. You'll be chasing this phantom attacker then, won't you? No Pulitzer in this tawdry little tale, though."

"Give it a rest, LaToya," Tony said. "Don't you have men to chase?"

She gave him the evil eye. "I don't have to chase 'em, Trujillo. All I gotta do is crook my little finger." She stood up and straightened her dress with her hands, letting them linger on her hips. "Tootles for now, people. By the way, you're a fine-looking specimen, Miss Lacey's boyfriend." LaToya leaned into Vic. "If that girl ain't ultra-nice to you tonight, who you gonna call? Just call on me, wonderful, beautiful me. LaToya Crawford."

"Ah, I'll keep that in mind." Vic cleared his throat and looked to Lacey for help.

Suddenly, the lights flashed off and on again and spotlights swept the room, finding and then following Claudia Darnell to the stage. The PA system played Don Henley's "Dirty Laundry," the rock anthem of journalists everywhere, drowning out the sweet R & B from the dance band in the room next door. This was the signal for the announcements and entertainment. She waved at the crowd and then gestured for the applause to stop.

"It has become a tradition here at *The Eye* to lovingly, and not so lovingly, lampoon some of the year's most memorable moments, both in the news and in our newsroom. We are not the stuffed shirts of the Fourth Estate; we leave that up to *The Washington Post*," Claudia said. The crowd roared. "As you know, the First Amendment of the Constitution is precious to us, and the free speech in these skits is Constitutionally protected. They are unrestrained, unpredictable, uncensored, practically unrehearsed, and maybe even not yet written, but keep in mind, I did not write them, I have not seen them or approved them, nor am I responsible for any tasteless, juvenile, satirical atrocities that may take place on this stage tonight. I plead the Fifth Amendment. And now please join me in welcoming the Not Ready for K Street Players!"

The crowd applauded as props were placed for the first skit, the most notable a gated picket fence draped with several loud Christmas sweaters. Rumbling through the room the word "Sweatergate" became a chant. "Sweatergate! Sweatergate! Sweatergate!" Lacey assumed that the Not Ready for K Street Players had not been informed that Cassandra Wentworth was in the hospital and possibly near death. That might be too tasteless for even reporters to make fun of.

Three male sportswriters sashayed onto the stage in drag.
One wore a yellow bike helmet and bike shorts and a ballet tutu
and carried a giant Styrofoam pencil skewering a Christmas
wreath; apparently he was Cassandra Wentworth. The next man
wore a big gaudy Christmas sweater and a muumuu and carried
an overflowing cookie jar: Felicity Pickles. On his head he
wore a miniature aluminum Christmas tree. *LaToya must have
been channeling this image,* Lacey thought. *Or else she'd seen
a run-through.* The third burly sportswriter sported a big blond
wig in a pageboy style, tottering high heels, and a women's suit
stretched tight over his chunky frame. He gleefully issued oversized fashion citations to everyone onstage and in the first row
of the audience, tossing them from a giant parking ticket pad,
while blowing a shrill police whistle and hollering, "Fashion
Police! Crime of Fashion! Fashion Police!" Lacey rolled her
eyes and pasted her biggest phony smile on her face. *I am not a
blonde,* she repeated to herself. *I may have blond highlights, but
I am not a blonde, and this will all be over soon.*

She might have turned on her heel at this tacky spectacle,
but Vic was holding her tight and trying not to chuckle too hard.
Trujillo laughed until he had to sit down, Wiedemeyer thought
it was hilarious, and the skit hadn't even begun yet. Felicity was
frozen where she stood, like a deer in the headlights.

The trio of sportswriters indulged in a little Three Stooges-
style slapstick squabbling. "Cassandra" whacked the other two
over the head with her giant pencil. Then they joined hands and
danced and sang a medley of customized Christmas carols, including "Away in a Blazer," "Here We Come A-Needling,"
"Have Yourself a Fattening Little Cookie," and "Who Dressed
Ye, Merry Gentlemen?" It ended in a three-way slap-down,
until "Santa Claude," a grouchy Santa figure in a loud plaid
suit, obviously meant to be Mac Jones, showed up. Santa
kicked their butts off the stage and threw miniature candy canes
to the audience.

The crowd roared. All but Smithsonian and Pickles.

chapter 8

"It could have been worse," Vic consoled her.

"Yes, it could have been worse." *They could have beaten each other bloody with giant candy canes.* Lacey's face was burning with embarrassment.

"You looked the best, Lacey, even in drag," Trujillo said. Linda Sue agreed.

A roomful of eyes were on Lacey. The Not Ready for K Street Players, still in costume, bustled over to much applause on their ill-fitting high heels with a staff photographer, to have their pictures taken with Lacey and Felicity. Lacey tried to smile graciously, but her face hurt from the effort. The stage was being set for the next skit. Lacey looked to Vic for help.

In the next room they could hear the band playing a slow blues number. Lacey glanced longingly toward the music. The laughing crowd couldn't reach her there.

"Want to dance?" Vic said.

"What took you so long, cowboy?"

He took her hand and led her to the dance floor. This would be their first real dance, she realized, at least the first one in public, since a brief but memorable turn on a dance floor in Sagebrush, Colorado, one New Year's Eve. That dance ended in a kiss that had haunted her for years, and it was the last time she had seen Vic until he unexpectedly reappeared in her life this spring. It had taken a long time for them to become a couple, and then a long time to overcome their "issues." Now Lacey wasn't about to let a single invitation to dance get away.

He held her tight, one hand on her waist and the other holding her hand. He brushed her fingers with a kiss. She swayed to the music, following him effortlessly. Vic made it all so easy.

"You've done this before," she said.

"I'm a man of many talents. Didn't you know?"

"I'm still finding out."

The band played some lovely slow songs from the early Frank Sinatra playbook. Lacey and Vic danced without speaking. Other couples made more of a show on the dance floor, but Lacey was content just to hold him and inhale his familiar aroma of spice and cloves. She willed herself to forget the awful skit and the rest of the evening, everything except being held by Vic Donovan. But the picture of the little shepherd boy in the alley kept popping into her head. She sighed.

"You thinking about the skit?" He held her closer.

"Trying not to. I'm thinking about the kid. What was he doing in the alley?"

"Lacey, a boy doesn't need an excuse to be in an alley. Goes with being a boy. You said he was wearing a costume?"

"A shepherd's robe. An escapee from a school Christmas pageant? Maybe a church Nativity scene?" She gazed up at him. "Would a boy run away from that? Would you?"

"As fast as I could, if I had to wear a costume. So tell me where there's a Christmas pageant in that neighborhood?"

"Beats me. There's a couple of churches, but it's not a homey neighborhood," she said. Eye Street at Farragut Square in the District wasn't a neighborhood full of children. It was all business, only a block from K Street, the heart of D.C.'s financial and legal district. Lacey rarely saw children on the street there.

"And yuppie parents here don't let their kids out of their sight, let alone roam the city after dark," Vic said. "Of course, boys generally will find a way to get off the leash. Back in Sagebrush, that boy'd be shooting up street signs."

"He called for help. Seemed like a nice kid. Pretty mature, except . . ."

"Except what?"

"He wouldn't tell me his name."

"So the kid didn't want to get into trouble. He wasn't supposed to be there."

"He accused me of asking a lot of questions."

"Imagine that. You, asking a lot of questions."

"Are you making fun of me, Vic?"

"Not me, honey." He swung her around, then brought her

back smoothly to his arms. "In my professional opinion, this boy's behavior is consistent with being a boy."

Lacey saw Tony and Linda Sue take to the dance floor. Apparently the skits next door hadn't kept their attention either. Wiedemeyer was trying valiantly to cheer up a tearful Felicity. His musical antlers were bobbing back and forth like a fool's cap.

"So, boys will be boys, Vic? What about the cops calling the kid a suspect?"

"I trust you. If he was part of the attack, why hang around? Calling the kid a suspect sounds like an overworked detective going a little too much by the book. But don't worry, they'll probably never find the boy anyway. Kids are hard to find."

Lacey leaned against his shoulder. The adrenaline that had kept her wired all night had dissipated and she suddenly felt exhausted.

"I'm not going to get involved with this one, Vic."

"Sure you're not, Lacey."

"Really. I'm not kidding. I don't even like Cassandra Wentworth."

"Right." He held her close and dipped her gently to the music.

"And I can hardly stand Felicity Pickles, and she can't stand me. We simply detest each other quietly now. So why should I get involved?" Lacey wasn't sure she was convincing herself, much less Vic. She spun under his arm. "So really, Vic, I'm not going to have anything to do with this—" She caught her breath. "This incident in the alley. I don't care if one of them attacked the other one, I don't even care who hit whom and why and who saw what and why the boy was in the alley and where he is now. I don't care."

He brought her back to his arms. "Just who are you trying to convince, Lacey?"

"You don't believe me?"

"You don't believe yourself. Why don't I try to keep you busy, and we'll see how much energy you have left to investigate with."

"You'll keep me busy?" She arched one eyebrow at him. "You must have a lot more time on your hands these days."

"We hired more investigators to help handle the load. Besides, I've got better things to do at night than pull surveillance."

"Such as?"

"Keeping you warm. I'm hoping for a really chilly winter."

Lacey was glad the lights were low. She suspected she was blushing. Even though she'd been dying to show Donovan off tonight, she felt the glare of attention from every side. Lacey had been enjoying the winks and nudges from her friends at the paper, and when they caught sight of the handsome Vic Donovan, they were gratifyingly impressed. He looked particularly alluring when that dark curl fell over his forehead and his green eyes were focused only on her.

"So what do you think of my plan for the holidays?"

"I approve. And Vic, I'm really not getting involved this time, only . . ."

"Only what?"

"I'm worried about my little shepherd boy. Do you think he could be a target of this nutcase who cracked Cassandra over the head?"

"Not if he takes off the shepherd's robe." Vic stroked her neck. "He's only a target as long as he's identifiable. Without the robe he's just another kid. He didn't know the assailant, right? And from what you told me, the assailant probably didn't get a good look at him. Too busy."

"So you think the kid is not in any danger?"

"Probably not. The kid goes to his Christmas pageant or whatever it is, he comes home, he takes off the costume. It goes back in the church basement till next year. End of story, end of trouble. For him. Maybe not for Cassandra, though."

"You're right. Of course," Lacey said. "Unless this shepherd's robe thing is a new fashion trend. Crèche couture?"

"Look on the bright side, honey. At least it's not another Christmas sweater." Vic's eyes were caught by something behind Lacey's back. "And don't look now, but I see cops at this party."

"Where?" She spun around.

"There. Plainclothes. You can always tell."

She saw Felicity being braced by two men, one black, one white. They were wearing sport coats, not tuxedos, not Santa caps. And Vic was right, the trained eye of a cop, or a reporter, could tell at a glance they were plainclothes detectives. A distressed Harlan Wiedemeyer sprinted toward Lacey and Vic. He was sweating and his hair stuck out from his head where his antlers had fallen off in the rush.

"They've got Felicity," he spluttered. "The cops! They want to ask her some questions. They've got my sugar cookie! Heartless bastards!"

"That's what they do," Vic said, steadying Wiedemeyer with a hand on his shoulder. "Just like reporters. Your sugar cookie has nothing to worry about. Does she?"

chapter 9

"It's too obvious," Lacey said, dropping her keys on Aunt Mimi's trunk in front of her blue velvet sofa. "The Christmas sweater thing is just too obvious." *And why are we still talking about this?* Lacey wondered. *I am not getting involved!*

"Cops like obvious," Vic said. "They like things that fit. And people do stupid obvious things. They'll like the sweater connection to Pickles."

Vic removed his jacket and took off his tie.

"You look cute," Lacey said.

"Cute, you say?"

She hung up his coat and stared at him. "Yeah, very cute."

"Not handsome, thoughtful, brave, clean? Heroic?"

"Yeah, that too," she admitted. "And cute."

"Well, I am cute. Just so we're clear," he said. The red light on her phone was blinking. "Uh-oh. Are you going to answer that?"

Lacey sighed and pushed the PLAY button. "It's probably just my mother."

"Lacey, honey, are you there?" It was her mother. "Are you sure you can't come home for Christmas? This is your mother calling."

She rolled her eyes at Vic. "Told you."

"I could call that boss of yours," her mother continued on tape. "That nice Mr. Jones. If that would help. Do you think that would help?"

"Oh yeah, that would really help," Lacey muttered under Vic's laughter.

Rose Smithsonian had been trying for weeks to entice her daughter to join the family at home for the holidays. She hadn't come right out and said that Lacey was ruining Christmas for them, but the subtext was crystal clear. "Well," her mother sighed, "maybe you could come for New Year's then. Call me." She hung up.

"That was fun." Lacey waited for the next message to play, expecting part two of Mom's message. "She probably forgot something. Another scenic detour on the guilt trip."

They were both surprised when the caller turned out not to be her mother.

"Lacey, it's Jeffrey. Remember, Jeffrey Bentley Holmes? It's been a while, I know, but I'll be in Washington next week for a fund-raiser, and well, if you're free, I'd love you to be my date."

"Jeffrey Bentley Holmes?" Vic's face was quizzical.

"But we can talk about that later," the message continued. "Among other things."

"Other things?" Vic inquired.

"I have no idea." Lacey shrugged her shoulders.

"I know we have lots of things to talk about," Jeffrey went on, "and you're probably surprised to hear from me. So let's go to lunch. I'm on the road, I'll be hard to reach, so I'll call you at work Monday. Looking forward to seeing you. Bye."

Vic was wearing his dark sardonic look. "Something I should know, Lacey?"

"Vic, you know the last time I heard from Jeffrey he was in a monastery. Getting his head together."

"Not becoming a priest? That's too bad."

"He was on retreat."

"Doesn't sound like he's on retreat now. More like he's on the advance." Vic put his arms around Lacey. "And he's advancing on the state of Virginia, moving in on you."

"Jeffrey was a friend to me, that's all."

"The way I heard it, he wants a date."

"He doesn't know that we're a couple. I'll just have to let him know I'm taken."

"On your date?"

"No silly, at lunch." She kissed him. "I think it's so cute that you're so jealous."

He kissed her back. "I'm not jealous, but they say he is rich and handsome." It was true. Jeffrey Bentley Holmes was rich and handsome.

"But you're rich, Vic. And I didn't even know it. I thought

you were just a good-looking ex-cop on a salary. You're rich and cute."

"I'm 'comfortable,' Lacey. Bentley is rich."

She laughed. "And I didn't even know how comfortable. We could talk about how jealous you are, or you could make yourself useful."

"Useful, huh? So just being rich isn't enough for you anymore?"

Vic moved into the small pass-through kitchen. He took out a pan, grabbed the milk from the refrigerator, chocolate and sugar from the cupboard. "And by the way, I'm not jealous. Just curious. And cute, remember?" He made hot chocolate for them while Lacey slipped out of her shoes.

"I'll find out when he calls." She joined Vic in the kitchen. "What a night."

"You worried about Felicity? She's a big girl," Vic said, stirring the hot chocolate. "That's not what I meant. She is a pretty big girl, but you know what I mean. She can take care of herself."

"Yeah, all she has to do is start cooking again. She'll have the entire newsroom wrapped around her hot cinnamon buns in no time. They'll start a legal defense fund just to save her buns from prison." Lacey laughed.

"Lacey, I can't believe we're talking about anyone's buns but yours." He drew her toward him for a kiss, and then poured hot chocolate into two mugs and topped them off with a squirt of whipped cream. He made her sit down on her velvet sofa to sip some chocolate and unwind. Lacey was finding it hard to concentrate on anything but Vic. Not even his delicious hot chocolate was distracting her.

"Okay, Vic. No more buns. For the moment. Let's solve the crime right now, so I can stop thinking about it, okay? Felicity could have done it, right? She was missing in action this afternoon. She doesn't have much of an alibi. She was angry. She could have waited for Cassandra and attacked her." Lacey sipped and Vic licked the cream off her lips. "Wrapping her up in the Christmas sweater would have been stupid and obvious, but like you say, people do stupid obvious things all the time. She even had a motive, although I know how you cops hate that nebulous concept."

"It all fits. Nice, neat, obvious, and possible," he said. "And

Felicity had a big obvious motive. Cops like obvious." Lacey slurped her hot chocolate again and murmured with pleasure. "You're making those little 'ummm' noises," Vic said. He smiled his wolfish smile. A gentlemanly wolf, she thought.

"Ummm." She smiled back. "You've made hot chocolate before, haven't you?"

"Once or twice. Good for what ails you, my mamma always says."

"I know what else is good for what ails me." She set the cup down and slid onto his lap. She put her arms around his neck. "I could do that 'ummm' thing again. Lots of ummms. Big ummms."

"Ummm yourself," Vic said, and that was the last time anyone mentioned Felicity or Cassandra until morning.

chapter 10

"Scotland the Brave" filled the air with the sound of bagpipes and drums, announcing the start of the Scottish Walk, the annual parade that opened the Christmas season in Old Town Alexandria, Virginia.

This event was always on Lacey's calendar and she was delighted to find it was now on Vic's as well, though she suspected he would be there partly to ride herd on his security agents, watching over some of the valuable vintage cars featured in the Walk. He and Lacey arrived well before it started, and they strolled up and down several blocks before finding the right spot.

"You're just casing the place, aren't you?" she asked. "You're on the clock today?"

"You're a very suspicious woman, you know that?" Vic took her hand and kissed her fingers. "Just making sure we can see everything. You don't want to miss the cute little Scottie terriers in their cute little kilts, do you?"

Alexandria was founded by Scots in the middle of the eighteenth century, long before that upstart village known as Washington, D.C., was ever carved out of the swamp across the Potomac. That Scottish heritage was honored by the city with a gathering of the clans from up and down the East Coast every year on the first Saturday of December for the Scottish Walk. Dozens of tartan-clad clans took over the streets of Old Town in full regalia and colorful kilts with pipes and drums. Step dancers and pipe bands in kilts (and sometimes Santa caps) marched in formation up and down streets named King, Queen, and Duke, St. Asaph and Pitt and Fairfax, all lined with colonial townhouses.

The Scottish connection also mustered a host of St. Andrews societies and the Lord Provost of the City of Dundee, Scotland, Alexandria's sister city. This wasn't the parade for Shriners in tiny cars and clowns (that was the George Washington's Birthday parade in February), although in a similar vein it did feature local politicians from the city of Alexandria and the Commonwealth of Virginia. A sitting U.S. Senator from Virginia was occasionally called upon to serve as Grand Marshal. These visiting dignitaries waved to the crowd grandly from vintage automobiles. Some even walked in the parade, gamely taking to the street among the bagpipers and high school marching bands. And dogs.

The parade was full of dogs of every breed with any imaginable kind of Scottish connection: Scottish terriers, cairn terriers, Dandie Dinmont terriers, Scottish deerhounds, shelties, Westies, Airedales, border collies, and seemingly every sheepdog on the East Coast, not to mention a gaggle of greyhounds. Some of the canines were even putting on the dog in their kilts and tam-o'-shanters and the occasional Santa cap.

The sky was a brilliant blue and the day promised perfect parade weather, just cool enough to require a jacket. Lacey wore a plaid shawl over her forest green jacket and congratulated herself for looking so festively Scottish. Vic wore his usual jeans, black sweater, and black leather jacket, looking handsome as ever. She loved looking at him, and he hugged her close to him.

Lacey and Vic and their fellow commoners on St. Asaph Street had their choice of watching the Scottish Walk or gazing into the windows of the grand townhomes, where parties of expensively groomed people turned out in plaids and Brooks Brothers jackets to gaze down on the clans and the hoi polloi, champagne flutes in their manicured hands. The Donovans had a fair share of Scottish blood and Vic's parents usually attended one such party in one of the elegant colonial homes on St. Asaph.

"Will we be seeing your folks?"

"Nah, I'm sparing you that pleasure, for the moment. We'll be with them tonight at the concert."

Lacey was a little disappointed that she wouldn't get to see the inside of one of those gorgeous homes. She'd have to wait for the annual house and garden tour.

"You'll thank me, really," Vic broke into her thoughts.

"Why is that?"

"Nadine heard about the incident behind your building last night. She would have devoured you with questions today. She will tonight. Brace yourself, babe."

"You seem to manage to deflect your mother's interrogations pretty easily. And I still can't believe you really call your mom 'Nadine.' "

"That's her name," Vic shrugged. "I call her Mom too. And I've had years of practice evading her questions." He smiled at her, his eyes barely visible behind his aviator-framed sunglasses. Lacey knew his eyes would be crinkling up at the corners.

"How'd she find out about it, anyway?"

"I don't know, she heard it on the news or something."

"The news?" Perhaps, Lacey thought, Vic hadn't quite evaded Nadine's latest interrogation. "I didn't think it was on the news."

"Nadine is very plugged in. Get you some hot cider?"

She nodded and Vic sauntered off. A stand on the corner was doing a brisk business in cider, coffee, and cookies.

Lacey found herself watching the children watching the parade. There was no little shepherd boy, no flash of a blue-and-white robe. She had to trust that Vic was right: No robe, no danger. Even so, she still found herself wanting proof that the child was okay. A child of twelve wandering the streets of the District alone at night was in danger by definition, even without witnessing a crime.

"Hey, Lacey!"

Brooke Barton, Esquire, waving from down the street, was striding toward her, sporting her favorite accessory, her boyfriend Damon Newhouse. They both wore trench coats over jeans and black boots and matching Burberry scarves. They were the same height. They strode together in perfect unison. And even though Brooke's long blond hair pulled back in her predictable ponytail contrasted nicely with Damon's short cropped black hair and Van Dyke beard, they had achieved the very same look, right down to their identical square black sunglasses. *A sort of human twin set,* Lacey thought. She hoped this phase of their relationship would soon pass. Brooke at thirty-something still had the air of a very proper young

Washington lawyer; Damon at the same age was still cultivating a baby beatnik vibe, as if he were the Last Hipster, still forever *On the Road.* And yet somehow they seemed to fit each other perfectly.

Lacey tried not to grumble over Damon's presence, because Brooke was so fond of him. His was a world crammed with crackpot political conspiracy theories, alien abductions, subliminal messages broadcast via cell towers, top-secret pheromone jammers, sinister pollutants in the Potomac. He drove Lacey slightly crazy. But Brooke could be just as bad. In her world, everything was a conspiracy. No doubt they thought the Scottish Walk was a front for some kind of Celtic unification group bent on world domination, not just a demonstration of pride in a common ancestry. Lacey found herself smiling at the thought. Then she told herself, for heaven's sake, do not share that theory with Brooke and Damon! She'd be reading it on the Web Monday morning. With her own name attached to it as a reliable source. Brooke was forever telling Lacey to check Damon's notorious Web site, Conspiracy Clearinghouse, aka DeadFed dot com, to keep up with the "reality behind current events," but Lacey figured all she had to do was wait for these two to open their mouths.

"More excitement at *The Eye*?" Brooke inquired with a knowing smile.

"The drums say Smithsonian is once again mixed up in a police incident." Damon smirked at Lacey. He almost licked his chops. "In the alley with a candy cane? My my."

"Really?" Lacey said. "Could those drums have come from a police radio?"

"And no story in today's *Eye*? A cover-up?" he said. "Exactly what is your newspaper hiding?"

"Let Lacey explain," Brooke said. "There's always an explanation."

"Deadline, Newhouse!" Lacey said. "It happened past deadline, so it didn't go in the paper. Mac certainly wasn't going to print a special edition just for a mugging, not in the District. You'll just have to wait for tomorrow's edition to get the prizewinning paragraph from the police log."

"You did write a story then?" Newhouse persisted. "About that suspicious attack in the alley? So you know what it really means?"

Lacey sighed. She looked around to see if Vic was coming back with their cider. A brace of vintage Bentleys and Rolls-Royces rumbled slowly past in the parade, filled with interchangeable local politicians waving at the crowd.

"Strangely enough, I didn't write the story, and I have no idea what anything means. I just called the police," she said. "I swear I don't know what came over me! There's a woman lying on the ground bleeding and I do something wacky like that. What was I thinking?"

"Okay, okay," he grumbled, "you did your good citizen thing, and then what?"

"And then Kelly Kavanaugh, our new police reporter, wrote the story. What little story there is." *Curse Damon and his one-track conspiracy theory mind,* Lacey thought. He was, she knew, cooking up some bizarre theory, even as they stood there. *Gangs of renegade elves from the North Pole are taking revenge on skeptics like Cassandra who don't believe in Santa!* "It might not even make it into print. The only news hook is that Cassandra works at the newspaper."

"And you found her. That's a news hook right there. Whenever you're involved, Lacey," Damon replied, "I'm sure it'll make headline news sooner or later."

"Just watch the parade, Damon."

Brooke took his arm. "We'll grill her later, darling. I'll help you."

"Medium rare, please, with a little marinade," Lacey said.

"That would be wonderful." Brooke linked both their arms in hers. "The two of you working together. My two favorite people. What a team we make! Just like in Paris last month, hunting that fabulous corset, right, Lacey?" *Where's Vic when I need him?* Lacey scanned the crowd for him, but it was too big and too dense. "I know you'd really get along and respect each other," Brooke the peacemaker said, "if only you could work together on more big stories like that one."

"You know you're my role model, Smithsonian," Damon said with a grin.

"Oh please. Cut the bull, Damon. What do you want, really?"

"Not much. If you could just put a word in for me at *The Eye*?"

"What? You want a job? At *The Eye*? You're serious?"

We don't have a science fiction beat, Damon, she wanted to say.

"It would mean so much to me," Damon said. "I could be a stringer for special investigative reporting? Stories that could tap my unusual expertise and contacts?"

"DeadFed dot com is not exactly the kind of resume they're looking for."

"Great! Thanks, Lacey. I'll e-mail my curriculum vitae to you first thing. You're the best."

Lacey turned to Brooke. "What word do you people use for *no* in your parallel universe?"

Brooke leaned in close, ignoring her in the same blithe way Damon had mastered. "You need to be careful, Lacey. From this attack on Wentworth, it looks like someone is going after reporters. I can get you a Taser cheap. I'd tell you to just get a Glock nine millimeter, but you'd be a little dangerous with a gun."

"One editorial writer getting assaulted in an alley does not make a vendetta against reporters! And I don't need a gun to be dangerous, Brooke. Tell Damon that."

"You've been lucky so far, Lacey, but one of these days—"

"I always have you to bail me out, Brooke."

"That's true." Brooke changed direction. "So what's your theory then? About this madman in the alley?"

"I don't have a theory," Lacey said. "The fact is, Cassandra Wentworth is a pill, she aggravates everybody, and somebody attacked her. And that is not a quote, Damon."

"It's personal then?" he asked.

"Could be. Or not." Lacey craned her neck to see over the crowd. Another tartan-clad pipe and drum band marched by in formation. "Have you seen Vic anywhere?"

"Cassandra Wentworth is an editorial writer?" Brooke said. "Oh, she couldn't be the same one who wrote that nasty Christmas sweater editorial? The one everyone thought you wrote? Even my mother was upset with you. I told her of course you didn't write it, it didn't have your flair and it was utterly humorless so it couldn't be you, but she was hard to convince. She is the soul of taste you know. Well, Washington taste anyway, and she hates those tacky acrylic things, but she does have this one white wool Christmas cardigan with just the tiniest edging of holly, she's had it for years, and she was stricken! Positively stricken! *The Eye* denigrating Christmas sweaters! Mother only wears this old thing when they go to buy the tree and the occasional caroling party," she continued, "but it's a tradition with her. Taking away her Christmas sweater would just ruin her Christmas."

"Brooke, my love," Damon cut in before Lacey could say a word, "that editorial wasn't really about Christmas sweaters. That was obviously just a cover. This Wentworth woman is some kind of agent provocateur behind her eco-radical facade."

"You think?" Brooke trained her baby blues on him. "Mother will be so relieved."

Damon was obviously deranged, but Lacey bit her tongue. She liked Brooke's mom. She wanted Mrs. Barton, with her real pearls and perfectly bobbed blond hair, to wear her holly-edged white Christmas cardigan without fear of ridicule from *The Eye*.

Vic reappeared and saved the day with two cups of hot cider. He handed Lacey one and Brooke the other and smacked Damon on the back. "How's the parade going?" Lacey blew on her cider and sipped.

"Thanks, Vic. So, Lacey, what's the suspect really like?" Brooke asked. "The kid in the shepherd's costume. Hispanic kid, right? About twenty?"

"First of all," Lacey started to say, then stopped. "No comment! Where did you get that?" It troubled her that they knew about the child. It must have been in the police report, the so-called Hispanic teenager in the blue-and-white jacket, but how did Damon get police reports?

"A source." Damon looked smug.

"No fair going all no-comment, Lacey," Brooke complained. "I'm your lawyer."

"Not while Damon is your fly on the wall."

"We are soul mates, we share everything," Brooke said. Damon stood by her in silent agreement.

"I rest my case, Counselor." Lacey turned back to the parade and listened to her friends grumble behind her back. "Are you here to pump me for information I don't have, or watch the parade?"

The leader of the next marching clan wore a huge black fur helmet and carried a staff. He stopped, commanding a moment of silence with his upraised staff, and then lowered it. The bagpipes and drums tore into "Brian Boru's March." Vic put his arm around Lacey's shoulders and she felt chills go up her spine. She wasn't sure whether it was Vic or the bagpipes, but she liked the combination.

"Are you sure it was a kid who attacked your copy editor?" Damon broke into the bagpipes. "And not a midget or a dwarf? Maybe a gang of renegade dwarves who—"

"Gang of dwarves?!" Lacey growled. "Are you off your meds, Damon? Where do you get this stuff? Good Lord! Listen, Newhouse, and listen good! The perpetrator of this particular crime was not a midget, the assailant was not the child, the child was a witness, and the child was a child. Not a dwarf. Not a pygmy. Not an alien in child's clothing, or some sort of half-human Creature From the Potomac Lagoon. And Cassandra is not a copy editor, she's an editorial writer! Are we clear on all this?"

"Just asking, Smithsonian. One journalist to another." Damon sniffed, wounded. A truck full of laughing children crept by in the parade, the kids pelting the crowd merrily with candy.

"I don't mean to intrude on this fascinating conversation," Vic broke in. "However, Wentworth suffered a head injury, right? Might be difficult for a child, a midget, or a dwarf to inflict a head injury on a standing adult."

"Good point," Brooke said.

"Aha! Unless of course, the child, midget, dwarf, whatever it was, used a ledge or a ladder to commit the assault," Damon persisted. "Any ladders in the alley, Lacey?"

"No, Damon, no ladders." Lacey sighed wearily. "Maybe the tiny assailant dropped an invisible anvil on her head from a passing balloon, or the alien mother ship! But maybe it wasn't an evil alien dwarf or a tiny Spider-Man with an attitude. Maybe it was an ordinary human adult with some ordinary human motive, who was seen by a good human kid who had the smarts to elude the attacker and call someone for help. Just a theory."

"Hmmm. What if a very small suspect attacked your copy editor after she was already lying on the ground?" Brooke asked.

"Two separate attacks?" Damon said. "Fascinating theory, Brooke."

"You people are crazy!" Lacey said. "One attacker! One witness! One child!"

Brooke's face lit up. "The dwarf attacked Cassandra *after* she'd already been struck down! The second attacker theory makes so much more sense, doesn't it, Damon?"

"I'll cover all this in tomorrow's story on DeadFed," Damon said.

"Another story?" Lacey said. "What was the first story?"

"*The Eye* didn't bother to write it"—Damon sneered—"so I scooped you on the Web. Last night."

"You haven't seen Damon's Web site today?" Brooke looked shocked. "Honestly, Lacey, you don't check DeadFed daily for what's going on behind official Washington?"

"Believe it or not, it's not the first thing on my reading list. No offense." Lacey sighed. "I never even check my e-mail on the weekends. Much less DeadFed." Damon Newhouse's imagination was stirred by aliens, Bigfoot, the Jersey Devil, imagined conspiracies that lurked in the halls of Congress. His vision of journalism took its cues from the Web pages of Matt Drudge and The Smoking Gun and the airwaves of Art Bell. Now his curiosity was tickled by events in the alley behind Lacey's own newsroom. Not a good thing, Lacey thought.

"We had better things to do." Vic winked. Brooke and Damon laughed.

"Someone had to dig for the real story," Damon said. "So I guess it's my scoop."

"Oh, please," Lacey said. "Scoop? I'll tell you what it's a scoop of."

"It's okay, Lacey," Vic put a calming hand on her arm. "Damon writes in a completely different, um, style than you do."

"Yeah, it's positively extraterrestrial," she shot back.

"That's why I love him." Brooke put her arms around her cyber beatnik. "He's definitely not K Street." They kissed. Vic smiled at Lacey, and she felt momentarily guilty for dismissing Damon as a nutcase. He and Brooke were both crazy, but they were good together.

"So Damon," Vic said, interrupting their kiss, "in your, um, alternative theory of the crime, why do you suppose they're after the Wentworth woman?"

"They?" Lacey asked Vic. "Who are 'they'? The little people of Damon's imagination? Maybe the kid was a leprechaun!

Cassandra Wentworth hasn't written anything about the Little People pro or con, that I know of, but maybe she wrote it in a secret code. You'll have to look into that, Damon."

"Boy, I must have stepped on someone's toes today," Damon complained.

Brooke stepped in between them. "Damon, you have to remember Lacey found the woman bleeding after the attack. It must have been traumatic for her."

Not as traumatic as it was for Cassandra, Lacey thought. She realized she should have felt guilty for not being more traumatized by the attack, but she wasn't. Cassandra Wentworth was so unpleasant to be around, it was hard to feel even the normal level of human sympathy for her. But why would someone attack Cassandra? What could have tipped someone over the edge into rage? Was the sweater a real clue or a red herring?

"You have that look on your face," Vic whispered in her ear. She flashed her eyes at him. "That look you have when you get involved in one of these messes. This time keep me in the loop, sweetheart. Okay?"

"Watch the parade." Lacey sipped her cider. A tartan-clad regiment of foot soldiers circa 1776 marched to a halt in the middle of St. Asaph Street. At a shouted command from their commander, they shouldered their antique rifles and fired in ragged unison. Only blanks, but lots of noise and great clouds of sweet-smelling smoke from their black powder charges. The crowd cheered. Little kids all around them laughed and clapped their hands.

Next came a Scottie terrier club in an array of colorful plaids, led by their Scottie terriers, some black, some white, some wearing tartans and tams. Delighted children on the sidewalks ran into the street to pet the dogs. One sprite about eight years old declared to her mother, standing next to Lacey, that she "only petted the softest ones."

"I forgot they had dogs in this thing!" Brooke said. "Did I tell you I'm thinking of buying a dog?"

"You don't have time for a dog, Brooke," Lacey said. "It would starve to death."

"I'll hire a service to walk it and feed it and groom it and all that. I'd love to have a happy puppy to come home to every night."

Lacey looked at Damon with his puppylike eyes, but Vic

nudged her gently and she refrained from stating the obvious. "Yeah, that would be nice," she said.

The marching tartan-kilted clans kept coming, Campbells and Gordons and Wallaces and MacDonalds and MacDuffs and MacSomething-or-Others who strutted down the street, the pride of the Highlands. Lacey enjoyed them all: the colors, the variety, the sheer number of people of every kind, all proud to claim their clan and their tartan.

Her favorites from years past were there too, the Clan Hay, marching in their distinctive clan tartan, the younger members of the clan pulling a little red wagon with a bale of hay. As they marched they shouted the stirring yet simple battle cry of their clan: "Hay! Hay! Hay!" Happy onlookers shouted back, "Hay!"

But when Clan Lamont strode proudly by in their blue-and-green Scottish tartans, she was riveted by the unexpected sight of someone she knew. His name was definitely Lamont. The large and muscular Detective Broadway Lamont stood out among a platoon of pale blond and redheaded Lamonts. But she had never pegged him for a Scot.

Detective Lamont of the Washington, D.C., Violent Crimes Branch was large, forceful, African-American—and apparently Scottish as well, at least a wee bit of him. Lacey had whimsically imagined that he was named Lamont because he was a mountain of a man. She felt a nudge in her side.

"Is that really who I think it is?" Brooke's voice carried over the crowd.

Lacey lifted one eyebrow. Lamont caught sight of her in the crowd and gave her the smallest possible nod of his head.

"Only if you think it's the one and only Broadway Lamont."

chapter 11

"Is Broadway Lamont on the Wentworth case?" Damon asked, his mouth agape.

"No, some other detective caught the case," Vic said, "and Lamont's probably thrilled about it. Seeing as how he's such a personal friend of Lacey here."

"Introduce me," Damon said to Lacey. "Please? He's a local law enforcement legend. And he's a friend of yours, right? From our last case, the legendary lost corset hunt?"

"Oh please. The man is busy marching with his clan," Lacey said. "Or didn't you notice? And you don't want to interrupt Broadway Lamont when he's busy marching. Or talking. Or eating. Or working. Or anything. Besides, we're not exactly friends, although I don't think he'd arrest me on sight now, like he wanted to do once upon a time."

Lacey had developed a grudging fondness for the big detective, but she preferred him when he wasn't breathing down her neck demanding information. And now she knew a little something about him that she never would have suspected: his Scottish family connection. He looked very proud to be marching with Clan Lamont in that mighty kilt. She wondered how friendly he might be with a certain Detective Charleston. And whether Lamont might be able to see beyond the obvious that Vic kept telling her cops were so in love with.

Santa Claus, wearing a red-and-green kilt and riding atop a giant fire truck, signaled the end of the parade. His appearance animated the crowd into a slow-moving but hungry throng. It was time for lunch, and soon every seat at every Old Town restaurant would be filled with parade-goers.

Brooke and Damon departed for brunch with her folks. Vic

and Lacey headed straight to Union Street, a popular restaurant and pub on the street of the same name, near the Potomac River, a friendly place with warm wood accents.

Before they could even order drinks, a large man in a kilt, kneesocks, and brogues joined them. He wasn't carrying a gun, but he was armed with an impressive fancy dress dirk swinging in its scabbard, a large matching kilt pin, and a smaller dagger—a Highlander's *skean dhu*—tucked into one of his black kneesocks. Vic shook his hand and moved from his side of the glass-partitioned booth to join Lacey on her side, allowing Detective Broadway Lamont to take the seat opposite them.

"So glad you could join us for lunch, Broadway." Lacey smiled. "I was afraid you hadn't gotten our invitation."

The detective turned to Vic. "You like a smart-mouth woman, Donovan?"

"Yeah, I like 'em feisty." Vic jabbed Lacey playfully in the ribs and she jabbed back. "I like 'em smart-mouth and smart."

"Then I'd say you're in luck," Lamont said. "Big time. I'm meeting my clan here, but here you are too, so we can have us a little visit."

"It's funny you never mentioned you were Scottish," she said.

"You never asked," he said with a chuckle. "Part Scottish. My great-great-grandfather was one Fergus Lamont. In fact, Lamont means lawman, so they tell me."

"So we're all a little Celtic here," Vic said, as their waiter arrived. They ordered two Guinnesses for the lawmen, and an iced tea for Lacey.

"Speaking of lawmen, Smithsonian, I hear you're up to your neck in my business again," Broadway Lamont said, his deep dulcet tones cut with a trace of sarcasm.

"And that business would be marching in parades?" Lacey asked. "Nope. I'm a watcher, not a marcher."

"Playing games with me, Smithsonian." He favored her with his special intimidate-the-suspect grimace. "I'm talking about the woman attacked behind your office last night. Name of Wentworth. Off critical this morning but still unconscious."

"You working that case?" Vic asked.

"No, thank the Almighty for small favors."

"You're taking an interest, though," Lacey said, trying not to sound like a reporter.

"Negative. I don't know if this heart could take another Smithsonian predicament. Takes years off a man's life, Donovan. Take a warning from me." Their drinks arrived and Lamont took a deep swallow of Guinness. *Marching in a parade can work up a powerful thirst,* Lacey noticed.

"I understand there's a certain sweater of interest," Lamont deadpanned. "A certain Christmas sweater. That one of your fashion clues? 'Cause my colleague Detective Charleston wasn't much interested in it, until I explained that a fashion reporter was involved in this thing and she had this theory about fashion clues."

He was enjoying himself. Lacey could just imagine the two cops yucking it up at her expense. She was glad she wasn't there to enjoy the moment.

"But your buddy Charleston doesn't work violent crimes, Broadway. Or as someone once explained to me: In the District, if they're still alive, it's not a violent crime. How'd you happen to be discussing it?"

"You think cops don't talk, Smithsonian? They talk. Hell, that's half of what we do. Other half is listen."

"I'm not getting involved in this thing."

"That true?" Lamont looked at Vic.

"That's what she tells me," Vic said.

"Yeah, I thought so," Lamont said, shaking his head. "Up to your neck again."

She favored him with the famous Smithsonian Look. It didn't seem to be working.

"Listen, I don't care if you get all tangled up in this, as long as I'm not involved. But I gotta tell you, Smithsonian—" He interrupted himself for a long drink of stout. He licked the foam off his lips. "You got some kind of trouble mojo."

"So I've heard."

"That's true, Lamont," Vic said. "She has heard that. From multiple sources."

"So if I'm all tangled up in this thing, then what can you tell me?" Lacey picked up her menu.

"Not a damn thing."

"Cops talk, right? And listen? You must have heard something."

Lamont's brows knitted in suspicion. "Such as?"

Lacey decided on the steak sandwich. "Your favorite *Eye Street* reporter, and no, it isn't me, is of interest in the case."

"I don't have any favorite reporters. That's an oxymoron. Like jumbo shrimp. Military intelligence. Who is it?"

"What about Felicity Pickles?"

The detective coughed and shot her a glare beneath his brows. "Little Miss Cookie Baker? You're kidding. You're saying she's involved?"

"She's been questioned," Vic said. "You didn't know?"

"Lotsa people get questioned," Lamont said. "All the time. Didn't hear any names."

"The sweater seems to belong to the Pickles woman," Vic said. "The one that was found on Cassandra Wentworth? The fashion clue?"

The big detective nodded. "So that's the smoking gun of Sweatergate, I guess."

"How did you hear about Sweatergate? I thought that was in-house information."

The waiter took Vic's and Lacey's orders, steak sandwiches, medium rare. Lamont waved at the first arrivals of his clan. "You got a new cops reporter, don't you?"

"Kelly Kavanaugh?"

"Oh yeah. That's her. Regular Chatty Cathy, Charleston said."

Doesn't he look like the cat who swallowed the canary, Lacey thought. "So she talked about Sweatergate and made Felicity look bad?"

"It just shows you never know," Lamont said.

"Know what?"

"That a woman can cook like an angel and still be capable of turning to the dark side." He drained his Guinness.

"Wait a minute!" Lacey put down her iced tea. "You don't really think Felicity attacked Cassandra?"

"Lacey Smithsonian." The detective chuckled. "I think anyone is capable of doing anything, given the right circumstances, the right mixture of passion and anger and something lethal in your hand. Up to and including murder. That goes for you and me and Miss Felicity Pickles and my Aunt Abigail. But it would be a damn shame if your Felicity did it."

"And why is that?"

"Because that woman has baking in her bones. She takes

pure pleasure in it. There ain't nothing like quality baked goods in prison. You can get damn near anything you want in prison, so they tell me on the street. But Felicity Pickles's double-frosted maple cinnamon sticky buns? Not one of them. No way." Broadway leaned back in the booth. "And she has brightened my day on the rare occasion I've had to visit your offices. Usually on Lacey Smithsonian–related business, I might add."

Lacey refrained from saying that his business was just as often Felicity's-baked-goods related. She had an indelible image of Broadway Lamont sitting on her desk like a giant, with a cinnamon roll in each hand. "You're all charm, Broadway."

He smiled broadly, a charming predator's grin, and stood up to leave.

"That's what they tell me. Gotta go, rest of my clan is here."

chapter 12

The crowd at the Folger Shakespeare Library Saturday evening was of the tweed-jacket-and-patched-elbow type, rather than the Elizabethan doublet-hose-and-bodkin type. They were distinguished and rather professorial, but not very Elizabethan. *It's so hard to find a nice doublet these days.*

Ensconced in an imposing marble neoclassical building on Capitol Hill, just a block from the Library of Congress, the Folger Shakespeare Library was one of the world's leading research centers on the works of Shakespeare. It was also dedicated to the study of early modern Western literature, according to the pamphlet Lacey picked up inside the front door. And the Folger boasted one of the most unusual small theatres in the District.

This handsome Elizabethan theater, a near-replica of Shakespeare's Globe, presented a distinguished season of plays (mostly Shakespeare, of course) and early music concerts. Vic was taking Lacey to a Christmas concert there featuring the Folger Consort, specialists in medieval music. They were joining Vic's parents, Nadine and Daniel Donovan. According to Vic, the Christmas season officially began for his mother with a trip to the Folger to see the Folger Consort.

Vic and Lacey picked up their tickets and wandered through the exhibition hall outside the theatre. Their fellow post-Elizabethans were gathered there for a glass of wine before the event. The hall was long and formal, with high ceilings and dark wood paneled walls, tapestry-covered armchairs, and exhibits of texts from the Shakespearean research collection and historical vignettes of famous Elizabethans.

"Now this is what a library should look like," Lacey said.

"Like Shakespeare's own branch library. No bookmobiles for Our Will."

"Exactly! I love it." She feasted her eyes on the sumptuous decor of the hall. It was her first visit to the Folger and Lacey was looking forward to an evening where she could indulge in a little style surveillance out of her normal sphere. An evening where she wouldn't have to discuss Sweatergate or the incident in the alley or the relative merits of Cassandra vs. Felicity.

She surveyed the crowd for style notes. This crowd contrasted nicely with *The Eye*'s Christmas party crowd the night before. Men in distinguished-looking beards and sweater vests with tweed jackets, women in tasteful woolens and muted knits that could only have come from the Outer Hebrides. They wore an academic patina of intelligence, composure, and comfort, at least on the outside. *This is what my university faculty lounge should have looked like,* Lacey thought. *And never did.*

She saw a number of subdued holiday sweaters in tasteful green and red, but no gaudy seasonal prints or elf ears or Santa caps. No flashing Christmas lights or antlers playing "Jingle Bells." A young blonde in a fitted black satin suit with a burgundy velvet scarf at her throat wore the flashiest outfit on display, and Lacey assumed she was showing off for her date, a dull Hill staffer-type in a black suit and tie. Lacey noticed a family of three women all wearing pale pink sweaters. Nothing here for a column, at least not yet. No crimes of fashion at the Folger. *Hmmm,* she mused, *maybe that* is *the column?* SHAKE-SPEARE LIBRARY DECLARED FASHION-CRIME-FREE ZONE.

Lacey decided she fit right in with this very tweedily elegant crowd, in her long brown wool skirt and gold blouse with a wraparound collar. And to avoid getting a chill in this chilly marble building, she wore a shawl in shades of brown, cream, and burgundy. One of the drawbacks to being a fashion reporter, she discovered, was that people expected her to look perpetually sharp and pulled together. Lacey had always loved clothes and had a certain talent with them, but ever since she'd been shanghaied to the fashion beat, her wardrobe decisions played a much larger role in her daily life. There were days she thought her wardrobe *was* her life. Those were days she wished she could just stay in bed in her jammies and not have to make one more fashion decision. But tonight everything seemed to be coming together. Especially with Vic.

She took a moment to admire Vic in his gray slacks, dark blue turtleneck, and blue blazer. He ran his fingers back through his hair, but the dark curl that fell over his forehead was as rebellious as ever. She thought she might need to help him with that one little curl. She would run her fingers through it all night if she had to, and she was just reaching out to begin when Vic took her hand.

"Don't look now," he whispered in her ear. "Here comes trouble." Lacey frowned, but Vic was smiling. She turned around to witness his parents sail grandly through the doors of the Folger.

Nadine Donovan was a very well-preserved woman in her early sixties. She spied her son and his date and descended on them with open arms and a mile-wide smile. Looking elegant in a silk tunic with a subtle blue-and-green pattern over black velvet slacks, Nadine wasn't just a breath of fresh air, she was more like a gale force wind. Nadine originally hailed from Nevada and her voice still carried more than a trace of a broad Western accent. Lacey, coming from Colorado, thought she talked just like regular folks.

Growing up on a ranch in the West, Nadine learned to rope and ride practically before she could walk. However, Nadine Donovan could play the lady as easily as she could the cowgirl. She had acquired all the glossy patina of the well-bred, well-groomed Washington woman. Her soft brown hair was worn in a standard pageboy. Her makeup was flattering and natural. She was medium height with a slim build and her wardrobe, Lacey had already discovered, ran to Brooks Brothers, St. John knits, and the occasional pair of perfectly fitted blue jeans. She was a snob about her jeans. They had to be authentic Levi's, Lees, or Wrangler, not designer. "I have my standards," Nadine said.

Vic's dad, Danny Donovan, had a full head of white hair and the bearing of a general. He was a Southern gentleman with a military background, and he owned a thriving corporate security and private investigation company. The firm also had contracts with Homeland Security, contracts that often took Vic to undisclosed locations to do classified things he couldn't tell Lacey about. Danny was tall, as tall as Vic, Lacey noticed, and his eyes were the same green as Vic's. Despite his tough-guy credentials, Vic had told Lacey, he had long ago surrendered all domestic sovereignty to his wife. He couldn't control her and didn't try. Danny let Nadine take center stage. Vic told Lacey she would just take it anyway, whether you let her or not.

"Your dad and Nadine must have been quite a pair in their day," Lacey whispered.

"Don't kid yourself. They still are. That's why we try to take them in small doses. "

"Lacey! Vic!" Nadine gave them each a kiss on the cheek. "Isn't my son handsome?"

"Oh, is this your son, Nadine?" Lacey said. "This handsome guy I picked up on the street?"

"And she's smart too, Vic." She grinned and hugged Lacey.

"Don't fuss over them, Nadine," his dad said.

"Hello, Mother." Vic kissed her on the cheek, with a wink at Lacey.

"I saw that." Nadine said. "Now, Lacey, you're coming for Christmas dinner." That was already settled. "So I'm not going to beat around the bush or drop subtle hints, your dessert at Thanksgiving was out of this world. Would you mind bringing something for Christmas? It'll be easier than Thanksgiving, there'll only be twelve."

Lacey was dumbstruck, remembering the madness that overcame her at Thanksgiving. She had insisted on bringing a homemade dessert to dinner at Vic's parents' house. She and Vic had spent untold hours in her tiny kitchen making the most preposterously labor-intensive dessert, just as a trial run. And then they'd made it *again*. Only better. She was glad Damon Newhouse knew nothing about this episode. He would find in it proof that an alien force was in control of Lacey's brain.

"Vic helped me," she said. "A lot."

"And he can help you again," Nadine laughed. "I couldn't believe you tackled *Southern Living*'s famous pecan pie cake. It's a killer."

"I couldn't either. We got carried away. Didn't we, Vic?"

"Count me in," Vic added. "It was pretty ridiculous, though. There was batter on the ceiling. We used kitchen implements, no, wait, *scientific apparatus,* I had never seen before. It was like a science fiction movie. *Attack of the Pecan Pie Cake From Outer Space.*"

"But with a happy ending, and no blood spilled," Nadine said. "It was worth every second. People are still talking about you two. And your dessert was good too."

"Nadine," Danny said, "don't tease the young people. Sometimes they don't understand your sense of humor." He winked at Lacey. Nadine paid no attention to him.

"Seriously, Lacey, it was fabulous, and another spectacular dessert would just send your reputation over the moon. What do you say?"

Maybe it really was alien mind control, Lacey thought, that made her buy the expensive pie pans and the cooling rack and all the rest and spend hours making that infamous pecan pie cake. A cooling rack! No, the truth was she'd wanted to impress Vic's mom, and apparently it worked. All too well.

"I'd say you've got my number, Nadine. But I couldn't possibly do it without Vic's help. And he can clean cake batter off my ceiling."

Nadine laughed. "His ex-wife couldn't even bring anything to a boil. Except my blood."

"Mother, you are shameless." Vic wrapped his arm around Lacey's shoulders. "She's just teasing us. You don't have to make dessert. We'll just pick something up."

Lacey looked at Nadine, the cat who caught the canary. Vic's mother smiled and rolled her eyes. "Um, I'll have to take a peek at some cookbooks, Nadine."

"Yeah, maybe we can try something *really* complicated this time," Vic said.

"Christmas will be such fun with you there, Lacey," Nadine went on blithely. "We can talk girl talk. Recipes, clothes, men, those interesting little murders you're always getting involved with. You must tell me simply everything."

Vic groaned. "Dad, help me out here. How about some wine? All around?"

"Sean Victor Donovan, you know I can't be held responsible where your mother is concerned. This poor girl of yours is on her own, son," he said. "Heaven help her."

"I know," Sean Victor said. Lacey had learned at Thanksgiving that nearly every male in the Donovan family was named Sean something. His dad was Sean Daniel.

"Lacey can take care of herself," Nadine interrupted. "She's a resourceful girl. Just give her a steak knife or hairspray or something, she can turn anything into a weapon. For that matter, any woman can, can't she? Now Lacey, you simply must tell me more about all these adventures you've been having."

My brain just froze. "I'm really looking forward to the concert tonight," Lacey said. "I've never been to the Folger before."

"Let's take our seats, shall we?" Danny Donovan ushered them up the stairs to the front row of the balcony of the small theatre.

"We'll talk later," Nadine assured her as the lights dimmed. "You and I are going to have such fun. Pay no attention to our stuffy menfolk."

Inside the theatre, dark wooden galleries were aglow with greenery wrapped in white lights overlooking the stage. Carved wooden figures around the room appeared to guard the quiet space, and the ceiling featured a mural of a unicorn.

They sat on wooden chairs with red velvet seats. From their vantage point, Lacey could see the entire Elizabethan theatre. She whispered to Vic that they should see a play there. Vic nodded, smiling. Lacey was thinking, *Romeo and Juliet.* On second thought, *A Midsummer Night's Dream.*

The stage set for the musicians was simple. A Christmas tree with white lights stood well off to one side. The instruments, including flute and lutes, were in place waiting for the players. A guest soprano would be singing medieval carols, they would be transported to a Christmas long ago, and the incident in the alley would fade away, Lacey thought; perhaps for a few hours anyway. The lights dimmed, the stage lights and the Christmas lights brightened. The first notes from the lead violinist soared to the ceiling and the carols and the Corelli worked their magic.

At the intermission in the exhibition hall, Vic and his dad went to buy glasses of wine for the four of them. Nadine took the opportunity to drag Lacey over to a dark wood-paneled corner. "Lacey, you simply must tell me! When are you going to write your story on this attack in the alley last night?"

"How did you know about that?" Lacey began. "Did Vic tell you?"

"My own Sean Victor? No, my son is just like his father, as silent as the grave," Nadine said. "But it's all over Conspiracy Clearinghouse today. You know, DeadFed?"

That damned Web site! Again! Lacey thought. "Nadine! You don't really read that thing?"

"Don't I? Of course I do," Nadine laughed. "And I just wrote that darling Brooke Barton a little check to support them."

"Yes, that darling Brooke Barton . . ." Lacey sighed. Of

course it would be Brooke. "Wait a minute! How do you know Brooke?"

"Oh, her mother is an old friend of an old friend. I've been hearing about her for years, but we actually only met the other weekend at a Conspiracy Clearinghouse fund-raising event. Lovely family, the Bartons, and so well connected. I met Brooke and her father, and what's-his-name, her brother. Brooke tells me you two are thick as thieves."

Vic made his way through the crowd with a plastic glass of Cabernet Sauvignon for her. Danny followed with two more glasses and handed one to his wife.

"You didn't tell me about your mother's distressing secret habit," she whispered in his ear, while his mother was busy with his father.

Vic looked amused. "Which distressing habit would that be?"

"Now, Vic. I know there are so many of those," Nadine said.

"She reads DeadFed dot com!" Lacey said. "Why didn't you say something about it? Why didn't you warn me?"

"And ruin the surprise?" He brushed her face with his hand and kissed her forehead. "With Mother, it's usually more fun when she gets to pop the surprise herself."

"It's just a guilty pleasure, Lacey, like everything on the Web," Nadine said. "It's not gospel, I know, but really, there has to be something other than *The Post* to read in this town. And DeadFed always has such an interesting spin on things." Lacey must have looked dismayed, because Nadine went on. "Of course there's *The Eye Street Observer. The Eye* always has its own unique angle, don't you think?"

"That's true." Lacey sipped her wine and checked her watch, wondering how long before Act Two. "*The Eye* has its moments. And then it has all the moments in between those moments."

"I started reading your little newspaper last spring after Vic started complaining about it. It seemed some reporter he knew there was always getting herself involved in all kinds of trouble, flirting with danger, egging on killers, just asking for it." Nadine was enjoying her story. "Someone he knew from his past, amazingly enough."

"Really?" Lacey's eyebrow raised involuntarily and she

glared at Vic. "I wouldn't cross this woman if I were you, Sean Victor Donovan. She sounds like trouble to me."

"Mother, now isn't a good time," Vic said.

"Oh, she is trouble! This very striking fashion reporter, according to Vic, pretty and sassy and smart too," Nadine continued. "I liked her. And I thought, how on earth can a smart fashion reporter get in trouble writing about hairdos and hemlines? Well, good Lord! I found out! Didn't we all!"

"Concert should be starting again soon," Vic said, but nobody moved. Lacey raised her eyebrow. Danny tried his best not to laugh.

"Vic was so aggravated with this woman," Nadine continued, "I just knew he must have some sort of serious interest in her. This mysterious 'Lacey Smithsonian' person. Wants to protect people he cares about, you see. Takes after his father that way. Couple of overgrown Boy Scouts, the two of them. Aren't they adorable?"

Danny took his wife's arm and began to lead her away, back toward the theatre. "Nadine, it's time we got back to our seats." Nadine broke away from her husband's protective arm and stuck to Lacey's side.

"So, of course, I started reading your paper, Lacey, just to keep up on the players in this little drama, or else I'd never know what goes on with my own family. Then you started popping up on DeadFed. Good heavens, the stories they have about you, dear! But what I wanted to say is this. I know you don't have a car right now. That little misadventure with the car theft and the drive-by shooting and all? Such a shame. Your poor little Z. So I'd be more than happy to drive you on one of your little adventures. We'd have fun, Lacey. It would be a hoot." Lacey almost spit out her Cabernet on her blouse. She covered it with a cough. "And we can take the Caddy!" Nadine continued, reaching her point at last. "You can wear your vintage clothes, I will drive my vintage Cadillac, and we will solve crimes in high style. What do you say, Lacey?"

Nadine's everyday car, for trips to the grocery store or her bridge club, was a large, comparatively sedate, scarlet Mercedes-Benz. But for excursions to the country club or when she was out just "catting around," as she called it, Nadine drove her large unmistakable Cadillac, a 1957 Eldorado Biarritz convertible. A bright pink Eldorado Biarritz, a sleek monument to the stylish American excess of the mid-twentieth century, complete with fins out to here. Only 1800 were made, Nadine told Lacey later, and none as pretty as her "Miss Flamingo."

Father and son both looked pained. "No need to encourage her, Lacey. She'll find some excuse to take the Caddy out for a road trip anyway," Danny said.

Nadine looked so pleased with her idea, Lacey almost didn't have the heart to dash her hopes. "But Nadine, there is no mystery. There is no case. Not this time."

"That's what you say now, Lacey. From what I read, that's what you always say before you're up to your you-know-what in alligators. According to Vic, anyway. Oh look, showtime!"

The house lights were flashing, signaling the end of intermission. The concert was about to resume. Lacey reached for Vic's hand and led him back up the stairs in a rush behind his parents.

"If you ever want to get me alone tonight, darling," Lacey whispered in his ear, "get me out of going on a road trip with your adorable mother!"

chapter 13

"Where's the Sunday paper?" Lacey asked Vic sleepily. Brunch the next morning seemed to come all too soon, after a late night with Vic's parents, first at the Folger and then later over drinks at the bar at the Willard Hotel, all the while denying that she was champing at the bit to "slap on the old Wonder Woman bracelets," as Nadine called having an adventure, and tackle the investigation into Cassandra Wentworth's attack. Nadine seemed to have the oddest image of her, Lacey thought. *Wherever did she get the idea that I was a freelance righter of wrongs in heels and a vintage suit? Oh yeah. DeadFed. And she may have had a little help from Vic too.*

Lacey just wanted a nice unpretentious Sunday meal after Mass, where they arrived late, so they drove down Route One to El Puerto for their great Mexican food. Vic handed her a huge pile of newspapers and took a tortilla chip, dunking it in the salsa.

"Not this thing. I want *The Eye*, not *The Post*."

"You really want to see it?" Vic held the paper back, his face a practiced blank.

"What? Oh no. Let me see." She grabbed it. On the front page was the Cassandra Wentworth story. "Oh my God. Did it really deserve a box on the front page?"

EYE STREET OBSERVER WRITER ASSAULTED

Heroic "Little Shepherd" Witnesses Attack, Calls for Help

Observer Fashion Reporter First on the Scene

She gazed up at Vic and back down at the paper. The new cops reporter Kelly Kavanaugh had milked the story of Cassandra Wentworth's attack for all it was worth.

"I never told her any of this stuff. We barely said hello. Where did she get all this? And half of it's wrong!"

"I take it she got the information from an industrious and probably rather young cop," Vic said. "Feminine wiles and all that. Or maybe she's a real reporter after all."

"Feminine wiles! Kavanaugh's not that wily. Or feminine. And look, she's described the boy in the shepherd's robe, and even though I said he's a witness, she also quoted the cop saying he's a suspect. Either way, she could be putting the boy in jeopardy. Just in case the jerk who conked Cassandra in the head didn't remember the kid, she reminds him and gives him a description. This is irresponsible journalism!"

"Sounds like Kavanaugh wants a Pulitzer Prize."

"She wants a kick in the head, if you ask me." Lacey threw the paper down. "I can't believe Mac let her get away with this. You better be right about the robe, Vic. I hope he took it off and it's back in the costume closet in the church basement somewhere."

"Now you know how cops feel when they read the papers." He took another chip. "At least you're not named till the third paragraph."

"Let me see." Lacey sipped her tea and picked up the paper again. The story jumped to an inside page. She was still steaming when her attention was caught by a tiny news brief at the bottom of the page.

Holy Family Robbed

The Holy Family is a little more destitute than usual this year at the small stone church, Shiloh Mount Zion, in the Shaw neighborhood of D.C. The scene at the stable in the church's Nativity had been made cozier by generous parishioners, who had made new robes for the plaster figures. But not long after the traditional scene was put on display, persons unknown took several of the new robes, Metropolitan police report. Mary, Joseph, two of the

Wise Men, and a shepherd have all been left unprotected
from the onset of winter weather.

The theft might have been a prank by teenagers, according to police, or the work of homeless people who
gather in the vicinity. The church itself was not entered or
damaged, Church Pastor Wilbur Dean told *The Eye.* "I
don't know who would do such a thing! And at Christmas. It makes you wonder about people."

"Vic, read this." She handed the paper to him. "Robes stolen.
A shepherd's robe."

He read it and met her eyes. "A shepherd. No description of
the robes. Big shepherd or little shepherd? Coincidence?"

"Pretty coincidental."

"Coincidences happen." Vic reached for another chip. "A
known fact."

"I wouldn't be so sure that kid is safe." Lacey pulled out her
cell phone, got a number from information, and dialed the
church, even though she realized the pastor was probably busy.
After all, it was Sunday. A machine answered and she left a
message, identifying herself as a reporter with *The Eye* and asking Pastor Wilbur Dean to call her as soon as possible.

She wondered if the kid still had Cassandra's phone. Lacey
dialed the number. Maybe the little shepherd would pick up.
But it rang until Cassandra's voice message came on, saying
she couldn't come to the phone right now and please save the
planet and leave a message after the beep. Lacey didn't leave a
message. The kid wouldn't have Cassandra's password to access her voice mail.

"Lacey, please eat your enchiladas, they'll get cold. Or else
I'll eat them."

She took a bite. "If Kavanaugh could take the facts and
mush 'em together like she did, I can't imagine what Damon
Newhouse did with them."

"Don't even think about it," he said. "Ruin your appetite.
You gonna eat that taco?"

"Right. I won't. It will. And I am! Get your thieving hands
off my taco, cowboy. Taco rustler!" But of course she couldn't
get her mind off it until they returned to her apartment. And she
let the thieving taco rustler have half her taco.

* * *

Lacey raced past Vic and her front door to her office-slash-guest room, the second bedroom of her apartment, which had a lovely view of the Potomac River. Today, however, she barely noticed that wide ribbon of water that divided Virginia from Maryland, gleaming in the early December sunshine.

"I have a sick feeling about this." Lacey sat at her little antique writing desk and flipped open her laptop.

"I told you not to look at the paper," Vic said. "Do you really want to turn on the computer? It's Sunday."

"I have to do this." She powered up and dialed into her ISP to connect her woefully slow dial-up connection to the Internet. She preferred to surf the Web at work.

"Didn't you want to do some Christmas shopping?" Vic stretched out on the trundle bed, which was made up to look like a sensible sofa, his cowboy boots propped up casually. "Whatever DeadFed has to say will just bum you out. Guaranteed."

"You're probably right." She turned around while the Internet connected. "I know you mean well, Vic, but I have to know what insane flight of fancy has seized that little wretch Damon."

"Don't say I didn't warn you."

"Are you telling me you've already seen it?"

Vic closed his eyes. "I don't have to see it. Damon Newhouse is an open book. Written in an unknown language."

Lacey turned back to the screen. "Oh, no!"

SWEATERGATE, LACEY SMITHSONIAN, & MISSING SHEPHERD!

Cassandra Wentworth, op-ed page wordsmith at *The Eye Street Observer,* took a giant candy cane to the cranium Friday night at the hands of an unknown assailant, reportedly disguised in a Santa cap. Wentworth still lies unconscious in her hospital bed, Conspiracy Clearinghouse has learned. And the only witness to the savage attack is said to be someone wearing a shepherd's robe, described as a child. A child, or something much more sinister? This assault may be part of an orchestrated attack on the freedom of the press and the First Amendment. But by whom?

Or what? According to sources who requested not to be named, this purported "child" witness may in fact have been the assailant. This tiny suspect may in reality be a small man, a Little Person, midget or dwarf with criminal or paranormal, perhaps even extraterrestrial, connections. The perp may also be the perpetrator of a bizarre hoax calculated to delude *The Eye*'s ace fashion reporter, Lacey Smithsonian, whose ability to unravel a bizarre crime is unparalleled and well documented on these pages. What part in this attack was played by "Sweatergate," a strange scandal brewing deep inside *The Eye*'s newsroom and hidden from the public eye by newspaper management—until now? Is this attack part of a concerted effort to silence the press on some story *Eye* writer Wentworth had been keeping under wraps?

There was more. Much more. And all in Damon Newhouse's patented purple unparagraphed prose. "He's dead," Lacey said.

"Who's dead?"

"Damon Newhouse is so dead. I'm sorry, Brooke, but he is so dead this time."

"I was afraid you might not like it." Vic stood behind her and peered at the screen.

"The little bastard. He can't really believe this stuff, can he? Is it all just a big comedy act for him?"

"Who knows? Once he gets ahold of a story, all bets are off. Sweetheart, one thing I learned about the press as a cop: Once the barn door is open and the horse is running down the street, there isn't much you can do, except to say, 'No damn comment.'"

"He had the nerve to e-mail me his resume too." She was tempted to delete it from her e-mail. "He wants to be an investigative reporter for *The Eye*. Can you believe it?"

Vic chuckled. "You mean he's not gonna get the job now?"

"That's what the expression 'cold day in hell' was made for."

"On the other hand, if Mac hired him, he'd be Mac's problem, not yours. Damn shame he's Brooke's boyfriend," he said. "You can't actually kill him. She'd be upset."

"Yeah, a shame his crazy-ass theories aren't true. Then

maybe one of his space alien midgets would kidnap him and take him to another planet. It wouldn't be just the scoop of the century, it would be the scoop of the universe." Lacey turned and gazed at Vic. "I could deal with that. How many light years does it take to get to Pluto?"

"You can't send him to Pluto, it's not even a planet anymore. It's a dwarf planet, probably where his killer dwarf came from. No more direct flights to Pluto, you have to make that darn layover on Neptune." Vic rubbed Lacey's indignant shoulders as she steamed before her computer screen. "Try to stop thinking about it, Lacey, it'll ruin the rest of your day. And we have better things to do." Vic rubbed her shoulders just the way she liked. He lifted her hair with one hand and kissed the back of her neck, sending chills straight to her heart. "I could take your mind off your troubles," he offered. He kissed her some more. "Remember that layover on Neptune? It's nicer on Venus. Warmer climate."

"Keep talking, space cowboy. No, talking isn't enough. Keep kissing me," she said and turned the computer off. *Layover on Venus, here we come.*

chapter 14

It was late afternoon and the sky was turning toward twilight. Lacey and Vic had whiled away the afternoon in the only way that made them both forget the entire rest of the world. They never did get to go out Christmas shopping. Lacey turned over and whispered in Vic's ear.

"Would you like to go look at a crèche at a little church in Washington?"

He hugged her a little tighter. "But I'm so comfortable here. Your feet are so warm."

She didn't really like to think about going to church while lying in such a compromising position. She sat up. That was better. "We're going to have to move sometime. We'll get hungry."

"We'll phone for pizza and eat it in bed." She nudged him and he sat up. "Oh, let me guess. This wouldn't happen to be the Church of the Little Shepherd?"

"That's why you're such a good investigator. You pick up on all the subtleties." He raised one dark eyebrow and she giggled. "The pastor didn't call me back, so now I have to go pound on his door. I'm sorry we have to go there. It's this car thing. Or the not-having-a-car thing. I'd have to call a cab. Or your mother." She grimaced. "Scratch that."

"Good call. She drives that Cadillac like a maniac."

Lacey still missed her Nissan 280ZX, which had been stolen earlier in the fall and used in the commission of a vicious crime before being abandoned and stripped. She'd made a few half-hearted tries at replacing the Z, but she never had time to go car shopping. Most of the car dealers were so far away she needed a car to go car shopping. She'd had offers of cars from friends,

like Brooke and Miguel, but nothing seemed to click. No new
car could really replace the Z in her heart. It was fast, it was fun,
it was a semiclassic, and it held the road, at least when it was
running and some mechanic wasn't swimming to Japan for an
expensive part.

"And if I didn't drive you to the church, you'd find a way to
wander around up there in Shaw, wouldn't you?" Vic interrupted her reverie. "That's still a dangerous neighborhood, you
know."

"It's getting safer."

"Ha. I'm up." He leaped out of bed. "This way I get to keep
an eye on your exploits." She would have answered him, but he
kissed her instead.

"I've got to get a car," she said.

"No need, Your Ladyship. I live to drive Your Ladyship. The
Jeep awaits Your Ladyship's pleasure. As does your humble ser-
vant, Your Ladyship."

"Smart aleck. When you put it that way, how can Your Ladyship refuse?"

Half an hour later the Jeep pulled up in front of the little
church overseen by Pastor Wilbur Dean, the Shiloh Mount Zion
United Church and House of Prayer for All People.

"The name is bigger than the church," Vic commented. The
church was off Rhode Island Avenue near the U Street corridor,
an area that had experienced a major turnaround in the last
decade. The Shaw neighborhood was now part shabby, part
gentrified, sometimes a block of one next to a block of the
other. The contrast was striking.

But the block that harbored the tiny Shiloh Mount Zion
Church was still several years away from gentility. Vic drove by
slowly, looking for a place to park, a challenge in every neighborhood in the District, giving Lacey a chance to look at the
front of the church, a small but pretty stone and brick building
that had started out Episcopalian but was now a tiny nondenom-
inational church. Next to the church in a vacant lot stood a
weather-beaten wooden stable. A small knot of people stood
viewing it in the cold.

Vic drove past in search of an elusive parking space. He
spotted one a block away and Lacey spotted something out of
place in the neighborhood, as out of place as a diamond ring in

a box of rocks. A classic 1957 Cadillac Eldorado Biarritz in a shocking shade of flamingo pink was parked right across the street, taking up nearly two spaces. It was a bold thing of beauty. Lacey had seen a few other ancient Caddies in the neighborhood, some lovingly preserved, others held together with duct tape, rust, and Bondo. But this Caddy would be a showstopper anywhere. It was drawing its own crowd of admirers, six or seven men, hands in their pockets, grins on their faces.

"What on earth is your mother doing in this neighborhood? Detour from the McLean Country Club? That is her car, isn't it? There can't be two of those."

"I have no idea what she's doing here." Vic rolled his eyes. "This is all we need." Vic and Lacey joined the little crowd of Caddy fanciers and peered discreetly into the pink-and-white two-tone leather interior. It was Clubbed and the security system was blinking ON.

Lacey touched his arm, indicating the church down the street. "Shall we?"

"The Church of the Little Shepherd? I can hardly wait," he said.

The church was locked. No one answered when they rang the bell and pounded on the door. They walked around the building. It was too small to have a rectory or a residence inside. Lacey thought it looked almost too small to have pews. She and Vic proceeded to the empty lot next to the little church, where the wooden stable stood.

A dozen or so people stood gazing at the lighted Nativity tableau, the plaster figures, and the hay bales scattered around the ground and inside the wooden structure. Some were parents with their children. Perhaps Pastor Wilbur Dean liked the symbolism of placing the crèche in a vacant lot. It might highlight the plight of the Holy Family, who could find no room at the inn. Or maybe there simply wasn't enough room around the church. The stable once hosted a living Nativity with actors, but they had long since been replaced by statues. They were three-quarters human size, stripped bare of their raiment. Apparently the good pastor hadn't anticipated the unintended consequences of offering free clothes to thieves and the homeless.

Lacey tried to see what the little shepherd might have seen. Mary was beaming serenely. Next to her, Joseph bent protectively over the Infant in the manger. An angel stood on the roof. The three kings waited with their gifts, and there were two little shepherd boys. But Lacey didn't see what the child saw, the missing robes. Perhaps all her little shepherd saw was warm clothing, or a cool new coat.

The boy wouldn't have traveled far and most likely he lived close by, Lacey reasoned. On the other hand, they were about two miles from *The Eye*'s building down at Connecticut and Eye Street. Perhaps it was a small crime of opportunity. Maybe it was just too tempting to steal a funny-looking, old-fashioned robe and then go wander the streets in disguise, before wandering back home. Or maybe the shepherd was homeless, or not quite homeless, but on the edge of it, cold, desperate, and daring? Sleeping in an alley somewhere in a dirty shepherd's robe, unaware he might be in danger . . .

Too dramatic, Lacey, she told herself. *Knock it off, you're just torturing yourself.* The kid was probably having a good laugh about his big adventure. Playing with his PlayStation in front of a cozy fireplace.

Vic stepped into the semicircle of viewers next to his mother Nadine Donovan, who was standing next to another well-tended matron, a blonde in a bob and a camel-colored suede jacket. "Mother." His voice betrayed some exasperation. "What are you doing driving *that* car in *this* neighborhood?"

"I had to take the Pink Flamingo, Sean Victor. She has the only trunk that can handle our Christmas shopping. You know that." Nadine was unfazed by his tone. "No one would ever steal her, she's too noticeable to steal. It would be like stealing the *USS Enterprise*. Besides, your father had that cunning little LoJack system installed for me." She took his arm. "Just look at this! Isn't this such a sweet little church, and this Nativity scene? Oh my. So urban, so gritty, so touching."

"It's not exactly Bethlehem." Vic kissed her on the cheek and pulled away from her embrace.

"No," Nadine agreed. "It would be much warmer. But even Bethlehem isn't what it used to be, is it? And I'm so delighted to see the two of you here! We thought you might drop by. Let's get some hot cocoa after this, shall we?"

Lacey recognized the blonde as Brooke's mother, Trish Barton. Lacey hadn't realized they were friends. It didn't take a genius to figure out why they were here. *Shopping, indeed.* "Hi Trish," Lacey said. "It's Damon's lunatic Web site, isn't it?"

Trish Barton laughed. "I like how you get to the point, Lacey. Yes, DeadFed just mentioned that the Nativity scene here was plundered, including a shepherd's robe very much like the one described in your newspaper. Two plus two."

Nadine picked up the narrative. "And Damon is looking for a little man or a dwarf he believes wore the robe and witnessed or perpetrated the attack at *The Eye* the other night. How's your investigation going, Lacey? I see you're following the same trail of clues we are!"

Lacey could feel steam gathering in her head. "Of course, you read this on DeadFed."

"Something like a leprechaun, I imagine," Trish said. "But I think he also mentioned a hybrid race of gnomes? Something ghastly that happened in a petri dish in some secret government lab somewhere? Which just goes to show you shouldn't mess around with DNA. You probably know more about all that than we do, Lacey. We just decided to take a look, get in on the action. You and Brooke get to have so much fun."

"It was a child! The witness was a child!"

"Whatever you say, dear," Nadine said. She winked broadly. Clearly she and her fellow matron in crime believed Lacey knew more than she was telling. "DeadFed says you can be cagey like that."

Vic took Lacey's arm and pulled her out of earshot. "Sweetheart, let Damon do what he does best."

"Which is what? Confuse and obfuscate and trivialize the issue? He's not a journalist, he's a—"

"Yep, he is that, and you gotta admit he's really good at it." Vic kissed her forehead. "Maybe he's helping in his own way, just by sending other people off on wild goose chases, while you try and figure out what's up with that kid."

"Oh you're good. You know that, Donovan? So we let them assume some phantom dwarf or little person is on the prowl, no doubt kneecapping people so the aliens can abduct them, right?"

"It's getting nippy out here, isn't it?" Nadine drew her coat around her tightly to ward off a sudden breeze. "At any rate, we all know that Lacey Smithsonian will crack the case. That's what DeadFed says. After all, you found the poor woman, right dear?"

"DeadFed says a lot of things," Lacey protested.

"And I suppose that's not why you're here?" Trish Barton said. "You're not interested in writing a follow-up? I have it on very good authority that you never give up on a story."

"Good authority? You mean Brooke." Lacey smiled in spite of herself. It was good to have friends, even if they were a little too enthusiastic. Even if they were certifiably insane.

"And by the way, Lacey, thank you for your column on Christmas sweaters. I never for a minute thought you wrote that awful Sweatergate thing."

"You're welcome, Trish." At least the Washington fashion world was safe for women like Trish Barton, who could now wear their Christmas finery without fear of further abuse from *The Eye Street Observer*. Of course, there was always *The Washington Post* around to castigate people.

Now Lacey would also throttle Damon for telling the world about Sweatergate. She silently added it to her long list of motives for his demise. In the meantime, maybe she could have a little fun at his expense. Anything she said here would surely reach Damon.

"Actually, *Eye Street* reporter Peter Johnson is the lead on this story," Lacey said. "He thinks it has real potential. He's our ace Hill reporter, and he thinks this story may penetrate"—she paused dramatically and dropped her voice—"the highest levels of our government." Nadine and Trish Barton gasped at the audacity of those cunning little conspirators bonking reporters in alleys. "But don't tell Damon, whatever you do. With his sources, he'd be way ahead of Johnson in no time." They both murmured their assent and exchanged significant glances. *Take that, Newhouse.*

"Lacey was just telling me all that on the way over," Vic added decisively. "Now how about that hot chocolate? We'll walk you ladies to the Caddy, and then we'll meet you somewhere."

"How about that Love Café on U Street that sells those CakeLove cupcakes?" Nadine said. "I hear it's very popular and the cupcakes are simply to die for."

As they stepped away from the Nativity scene, Lacey reminded herself to keep her eyes peeled for the flash of blue-and-white stripes of a shepherd's robe on a streetwise boy who liked to take short cuts through D.C.'s alleys. This neighborhood was full of alleys. But she didn't see the robe, or any child who looked like her little shepherd.

Vic pulled Lacey close. "Don't worry about him. He's okay."

"He's just a little kid."

"Lacey, he lives in the District and he wanders the streets of Shaw and downtown to Eye Street? He's no stranger to trouble. He's obviously resourceful. Why don't we take care of the trouble at hand?"

"Your mother and Brooke's mother?"

"Enough trouble for one night, don't you think?"

As they started walking up the street toward the pink Caddy, Lacey could hear the words "DeadFed" and "little man" rustle through the small knot of conspiracy fans at the Nativity scene. *Oh good, the DeadFed Social Club is calling the meeting to order,* Lacey thought. *Why wasn't I informed I was on the agenda for the evening?*

Nadine took the wheel of the shocking pink Caddy. Lacey was giving her and Trish directions to the coffee shop on U Street when Vic's cell phone jingled. It was business interrupting pleasure, but Lacey thought he looked more than a little pleased. He wouldn't have to eat cute little cupcakes and hot cocoa with his mother and her pal.

"I'm sorry, honey, I gotta go handle something and it can't wait. Can you catch a cab back to Old Town?"

"She'll do no such thing," Nadine said.

"We wouldn't think of it," Trish added.

"We'll give you a lift back to Alexandria." Nadine waved at her pink Caddy.

"Okay, I guess," Lacey said dubiously. She wasn't certain she had ever ridden in anything quite so big. And pink. And proud of itself. "If you really don't mind."

Vic looked distressed by this turn of events, but his phone rang again. He gave Lacey a quick kiss, and his mother a stern look. "I'll call you later." And then he was walking briskly toward his Jeep.

Trish climbed into the backseat and Lacey took the front. Nadine eased Miss Flamingo away from the curb.

"Now tell us about the little boy," she said.

"You don't think it's one of Damon's space aliens?"

Nadine laughed. "If you say it's a boy, Lacey, it's a boy."

"Damon is sometimes swayed by his own enthusiasms," Trish said.

"Putting it lightly." Lacey tightened the aftermarket seat belt as Nadine stepped on the gas. As they rounded the corner and passed the alley, Lacey's peripheral vision caught a glimpse of blue-and-white stripes. "Wait, Nadine, I saw something!" The blue-and-white blur disappeared around the corner.

"Where?"

"There." Lacey pointed.

Nadine maneuvered the big car deftly down the street and around the next corner to the other end of the alley. She idled at the mouth of the alley. There was no sign of the robe, let alone the shepherd boy. "Which way? Was it this alley, Lacey?"

A shard of light reflected off a shiny surface in the alley, probably broken glass. Lacey peered through the darkness. The flapping tail of a blue-and-white robe could just be seen by the light of a back porch. Then it was gone. "Down the alley." This boy had a real affinity for alleys, Lacey thought.

The big pink car turned in and nearly filled the alley from side to side, but the boy was gone. Nadine stopped the car and Lacey got out. With Miss Flamingo following her at a slow crawl, Lacey peered down walkways and around trash cans, the sort of places a boy might find amusing, a place to elude nosy grown-ups. She called softly to him, so the boy would know it was her and not the Santa Dude driving a fancy new pink sleigh. There was no sign of him.

The crew of the Pink Flamingo repeated their hunt down six or seven more alleys in the Shaw neighborhood before they gave up on finding the little shepherd. They kept their rendezvous with the hot cocoa and the cute little cupcakes to lift their spirits. But Lacey's spirits refused to be lifted.

Shepherd boy, two, she thought. *Lacey, nothing.*

Chapter 15

"She wants to see you," Mac hollered as Lacey walked by his office with her Monday morning coffee. She ignored him. Mac's bellowing voice was part of the normal background noise of her morning ritual: Coffee, the daily news, and her e-mail, and at least a half hour of peace and quiet before beginning the never-ending struggle to find and polish a "Crimes of Fashion" column or a "Fashion Bite" before deadline.

Lacey barely noticed that style wise, everybody in the newsroom was back to normal after their Christmas party fling with "black tie optional, Santa cap mandatory." She wore a vintage blue heather tweed suit, the jacket trimmed with a light blue suede collar and cuffs, a copy of a Forties suit of Aunt Mimi's. Mac, no more in tuxedo and Santa cap, wore a dingy plaid shirt stolen from a depressed lumberjack and a striped vest from a singing waiter. His pants were a bilious shade of mustard from a desert commando. His tie was another clash of colors, not vintage, merely old. The outfit was topped off, of course, with blithe indifference. *Why does Kim let him dress himself this way?* Lacey wondered. *She must leave the house every morning before Mac gets dressed. That's the only explanation. But doesn't she see him come home looking like that?!*

"Smithsonian! You hear me?" Lacey stopped in her tracks, then stepped inside her boss's messy office. Mac's bushy eyebrows were jammed tight together. *Bad sign first thing on a Monday,* Lacey thought. She checked for signs of sugar inhalation, doughnut overdose, muffin mania, all conditions that might soften Mac's usual testy mood. Nothing. There was only one cup of java, black. Felicity must still be on her baking strike, she thought. *Uh-oh.*

"Who wants to see whom? And who cares?"

"Cassandra! She woke up. And you. That's whom."

"Me? She wants to see me?" Lacey sighed loudly. "Are you sure? She doesn't even like me." *Probably wants to finish yelling at me, right where she left off Friday night.*

Of course, Lacey was happy and relieved that she was still alive. But she had better things to do than listen to the woman rant. Cassandra had been unconscious for two days, so there must be a backlog of rants for her to catch up on. Lacey would get them all. It was a scary thought.

"It's a medical miracle. Go see her."

Lacey didn't have time for that. She needed more information about the theft of the Nativity robes at Shiloh Mount Zion Church. Pastor Wilbur still hadn't returned her calls. And if Lacey called Cassandra's number again, perhaps the kid would answer.

"You listening to me, Smithsonian?" Mac's voice jarred her from her mental to-do list.

"Of course, Mac." She could see him puffing up, ready to speechify. "I always listen to you." *Except sometimes when I don't.*

"*The Eye* will not rest until Cassandra Wentworth's attacker is caught, prosecuted, and jailed. Here." He handed her a flyer.

"What's this?" She looked at it. It offered twenty-five thousand dollars for information leading to the arrest and conviction of the assailant who cracked his candy cane over the skull of their editorial writer. "Only twenty-five thousand?"

"She's not dead," Mac said without apparent irony. "I'd also like to point out that the reward is for the public. Not for *Eye Street* employees, family members, et cetera. If you happen to solve this, Smithsonian, it's for the good of the paper. And the story."

"That figures." Lacey handed the paper back to him. "Why does she want to see me?" It was rhetorical. Of course Cassandra would want to see her, just to bark at her.

"Maybe she wants to give you a big hug and a thank-you. Or not. Get your butt over there. This is your story now." He returned to reading the newspaper.

My story? I already have a story! "What about Johnson? Last I heard, he was going to bust this story wide open, expose the mad attacker, scoop up a Pulitzer Prize."

Mac sat back in his chair and leveled his steely gaze at her. "Never joke about the Pulitzer, Smithsonian."

Everyone at *The Eye Street Observer* joked about the Pulitzer, that hallowed prize for excellence in journalism. *The Eye* was widely considered Pulitzer-proof.

"Can I joke about Johnson then?"

"Can I stop you?"

"No."

"You may not like Johnson, but you have to respect him."

"Okay, Mac, now you've stumped me. Why?"

"Johnson is a Capitol Hill reporter. He knows his beat. He's no genius, but he's not that bad. He's dogged, he keeps nipping at the heels of Congressmen and staffers." Lacey could feel her eyes rolling. "And he usually gets the job done. Eventually. Of course, he doesn't have your particular talent for attracting killers. You're our secret weapon, Smithsonian. I want you working this one."

"Uh, thanks. I think. But this Santa Dude guy is not technically a killer," she said. Mac's eyebrows knit tighter in response. "Okay, let's call it attempted murder. You like that better? Maybe I could psychically transfer my killer-magnet talent to Johnson?" *Happily, any time,* she thought. *Come and get it.* "Give me a break, Mac. I have real work to do, not this mystical peer-into-the-mind-of-the-killer mumbo jumbo."

"Nice try," Mac said. "This is a story, a big story. *The Eye* does not allow its employees to be attacked. An attack on one of us is an attack on journalism. You know that." He paused, stared at his coffee and took another sip. He seemed to be missing something, something sweet, something that Felicity had not baked today. And might never bake again.

"But there's no fashion angle."

"Ha. You got a singing and dancing sweater on a victim who had just attacked the very idea of singing and dancing sweaters! And you tell me there's no fashion angle? Not only do we have the most ridiculous sweater I have ever heard of, apparently it's Felicity Pickles's own special Christmas sweater. Smells like a setup to me."

"What about Tony? It's a police matter, that's his beat. That's what you keep telling me. Or Kavanaugh. She's the one who screwed up the story in the first place, why can't she unscrew it?"

"Forget Trujillo. He's on standby on this. And Kavanaugh is off this story. This calls for a fashion reporter of your very particular expertise."

"But Mac . . ." Lacey realized she was always trying to talk her way on to hard news stories. *Why am I trying to talk my way off this one? Oh yeah. It's Cassandra.*

"She's at George Washington University Hospital. Go see the victim. Get the story. Give me a break."

"I guess it's a nice day for a walk." Lacey sighed for effect. The hospital was not that far from the office for someone fond of walking. Lacey could stretch it out, look at Christmas decorations, do a little shopping. . . .

"Take a cab," Mac barked. End of discussion. She walked.

The smell of starch and medicine hit Lacey in the face. She didn't like the pungent aroma, and she didn't like hospitals as a general rule. They caused her a low-level anxiety that felt a little like death tickling her spine. But she took a deep breath and marched through the door, showed her identification to the guard at the entrance, bought a cup of mocha, and headed toward Cassandra Wentworth's room.

A middle-aged nurse with short curly brown hair and a nononsense manner met Lacey in the doorway and cautioned her not to fatigue the patient. The nurse wore scrubs that looked just like pajamas. The bottoms were green and the patterned top featured Disneyfied farm animals jumping over rainbows. A stethoscope dangled from her neck. White clogs completed her look.

Once upon a time, Lacey reflected, nurses wore white uniforms, white hose, sensible white shoes, and navy capes. A clever little cap topped their coiffure. Lacey loved that old-fashioned look, especially the navy capes. It was crisp and distinctive and professional. That was centuries ago. Today's Florence Nightingales apparently thought the traditional costume made them look antiquated. Nurses today wanted to look like nursery school attendants.

Gazing at the nurse's pseudo-jammies, Lacey warned herself never to wear elastic waistbands. *Give up on your waist and it's the beginning of the end for your figure, she thought. For* half a second, she pondered this topic as a "Crimes of Fashion" column. But no, this would be one of those inflammatory columns that would enrage her elastic-waisted Washington reading public, like pointing out the aesthetic horrors of wearing athletic shoes with suits and dresses. It might get a columnist hit in the head in the alley behind her office. Lacey sighed. *Is Sweatergate and its aftermath making me lose my edge, my eagerness to engage and enrage?*

"Head injury. Got that? Her blood pressure spikes, I'm holding you personally responsible," the nurse told Lacey. "Got that?"

Lacey nodded. "Another reason to leave soon."

"That poor woman's been through a lot. Don't make it any worse." The nurse marched silently away in her white clogs.

Lacey entered the room and unbuttoned her jacket, but she didn't take it off. She didn't plan on staying long. She set her purse down on a chair and checked her watch. Maybe Cassandra would order her off *The Eye*'s investigation. Maybe she'd refuse to talk to anyone but Peter Johnson. Maybe Lacey would be out of here in mere moments. She smiled for the first time since Mac's order to go see the woman.

The room was a double but Cassandra was alone, her bed positioned next to the window. Nobody looks their best in a hospital bed and Cassandra Wentworth was no exception. Of course, Lacey thought, she may never have seen Cassandra at her best.

As small as she was, Cassandra seemed even smaller in the large bed in a faded pink and white floral hospital gown. She never wore makeup, it was against some obscure subsection of her union rules, but she usually looked ruddy and healthy with her sunburned face and pink wind-chapped cheeks from all that eco-pedaling.

Today, however, Cassandra was ashen. Purple bruises colored the right side of her face. Straight mouse-brown hair streamed out from beneath a large white bandage on her head and lay lank against the pillow. Something liquid dripped through an IV into Cassandra's arm. She looked like she was asleep. Lacey was willing to wake her up, just to get this over with.

"Hello, Cassandra."

Cassandra opened her eyes slowly, as if they were weighted down with sandbags. "I'm cold."

"Nice to see you too." Lacey pulled the blanket up around Cassandra's shoulders.

"That's better," she croaked. "Water."

Not *please* get me the water. Lacey handed the invalid a blue plastic glass with a straw from a rolling tray near the bed. She checked her watch again. Cassandra slurped through the straw and coughed.

"They put some kind of tube down my throat. It hurts. And God knows what it's made of. Probably off-gassing carcinogens straight into my bloodstream."

"No doubt. Mac said you wanted to see me." Lacey stood by the bed. There was no place to sit and still maintain eye contact.

"What happened to me?"

"You don't remember?"

Cassandra handed the drink back to Lacey, who dutifully set it on the stand.

"I don't remember anything from Friday. It was Friday, right? Mac said . . ." Cassandra seemed reluctant to finish the thought. "He said you saved my life. Another coup for you, Smithsonian." She spat the words as if they burned her tongue.

"Gee, you're welcome. And that was an exaggeration. You would have pulled through without me."

"No. The doctor said I was lucky. I could have died." They shared an uncomfortable silence before Lacey spoke.

"Well, I'm glad you didn't die, even if you're not. What do you know about Friday?"

Cassandra looked away. "Someone attacked me and you found me shortly afterward. Your timing is impeccable, to say the least. That's all I know. Someone threw my newspaper away before I could read it. Probably didn't even recycle it. Can you imagine anything so stupid? I work for a newspaper, damn it! I want to read the paper." She sighed deeply at the injustice. "Tell me what happened." Again, no *please*.

"It wasn't me who saved you. I just called nine-one-one. It was really the kid, the little shepherd." Lacey described how she met the child in the alley who witnessed the attack. "He picked up your phone, hit the last number dialed. I won that particular lottery."

"You'll still get all the damn credit," Cassandra complained.

"No thanks." Despite Cassandra's situation, Lacey had an urge to pour the water jug over her. Only the thought of that tough nurse stopped her.

"The police asked me about a sweater. What sweater?"

"Apparently after the guy hit you on the head, he dressed you in a sweater."

Cassandra tried to digest this odd fact. "Why? Did he think I was cold and going into shock? I don't get it." She rustled the covers.

"Me neither. Pretty solicitous for an assailant," Lacey said. "And it was an unusual sweater."

"You're giving me a headache, Smithsonian. Don't talk in riddles. Why would this sweater be so important?"

"It was a Christmas sweater, Cassandra, and not just any Christmas sweater." Lacey sighed. "It was flashing little Christmas lights and playing 'Jingle Bells.'"

"Oh my God." Shock and puzzlement registered on Cassandra's face. She fell back against the pillow. "Because of what I wrote? Someone did this because of that? I've written really important things on vital world-shaking issues. But the sweater thing is what struck a nerve? What kind of crazy world is this?"

This was not the time, Lacey thought, to inform Cassandra that the sweater belonged to her archenemy, Felicity Pickles. Lacey told herself she was not going to get back into the middle of this feud. "Who knows why? I'm not supposed to tire you out. I'd better go. Your nurse threatened me with bodily harm. She looks pretty mean."

Cassandra smiled for the first time. "It's nice to have friends." Lacey assumed she meant the mean nurse, not Lacey. She didn't thank Lacey for coming. Lacey guessed that might be too much to hope for. Thanking someone might wear Cassandra out. The incident in the alley, as regrettable as it was, and Lacey's small role in saving her life, still didn't make them friends.

"If there isn't anything else," Lacey moved toward the door. "Get well." She picked up her purse and turned to go.

"Smithsonian. Wait." Lacey heard a big groan and Cassandra struggled rather dramatically to lift her head.

Lacey turned back. "Yes?"

"I want you to find out who did this to me."

"Me? Didn't Peter Johnson talk to you?"

"Peter?" Cassandra's face lit up momentarily. "No. What did he say?"

"He expressed an interest in doing just that. He's an experienced Capitol Hill reporter, you know." A reporter who couldn't find his own hind end with both hands and a map, Lacey thought, but she didn't say that. *Johnson wanted to throw himself in the middle of this? Let him knock himself out.*

Cassandra took her time, but she managed to sit up. "But you have a talent for—for—this kind of thing."

Do I have a "kick me" sign on my back? "Cassandra, the police are looking into it. And Johnson—"

"I want you to do—whatever it is you do."

Lacey groaned. "You don't really understand—"

"Mac said you would."

He did, did he? "I can only ask questions, Cassandra. You know that. If I come up with a question and someone to ask, I'll ask it. I promise."

"Very well." Cassandra closed her eyes and sank back against the pillows. "I'm glad that's settled. Where will you start?"

Settled? What made her think this was settled? "We could start with the supposed weapon, the giant candy cane? Do you remember that part?"

"I didn't write anything against giant candy canes." Her eyes opened wide again. "You're making some ridiculous point about Christmas, I suppose."

"I'm not. The guy in the alley might have been." Lacey briefly wondered what she might do right now if she had a large peppermint weapon at hand. *No,* Lacey thought, *I wouldn't use it. But I'd like to.* "Who do you think could have attacked you?"

"No one. People love me."

Did Cassandra want to talk about her popularity ratings? Lacey could count on several hands and feet the number of people whose noses wrinkled as Cassandra walked by. "Think a little harder." The patient's eyes filled with tears that did not fall. Lacey pressed on. "Do you have any enemies?"

"Of course I do! Big corporations, banks, developers, insurance companies, polluters, the government, the military, abusers of the Earth. The usual suspects. And if you mean someone closer to home, like the office, there's always Felicity Pickles with her unspeakably tasteless Christmas-in-the-trailer-park obsession." Cassandra shuddered and wiped her eyes.

"You're off her fresh-baked cookies list, that's for sure."

Cassandra's expression turned ugly. "Start with Felicity."

"I don't take orders from you. Can you expand that list

beyond Felicity? You've written a whole lot of editorials that offended people."

"My editorials are simply the unvarnished truth!"

And modest too. Lacey's head was starting to ache. "Whatever. You don't really believe Felicity did this, do you?" She sighed and leaned against the window. The glass was cool. People below were crossing the street, dodging cars and cabs, living their lives. Lacey wanted to join them. "You're the one who's responsible for Sweatergate, Cassandra, for which I'll remind you I was taking all the heat. Even I wouldn't infringe on someone's right to wear the ridiculous holiday garment of their choice. It would compromise my right to laugh at them. However, a lot of very unhappy people were writing to me, abusing me, threatening me, which could ruin a person's Christmas spirit. But now that everyone knows who really wrote it— *you*—maybe someone took it personally. Any candidates?"

"I'm proud of that editorial!" Cassandra's face was red with indignation, but not remorse. "My editorial was better than anything you could ever come up with. If you learned from me, Smithsonian, maybe you could write a good column some day."

"You're pathetic." The water jug was temptingly close and Lacey's fingers itched. She would have to leave soon or she would baptize this woman anew. "You simply hate everything, don't you?"

"I do not hate everything. Not everything. I have very high standards for—"

"You hate Christmas and you hate people who love it. Why?" No answer, just a glower on Cassandra's face. "You know why you were attacked? You're a Grinch. Let me clarify that for you. Grinch, grincher, grinchest. Shall I use it in a sentence, Your Grinchliness?"

"Take that back! I'm calling the nurse!"

Lacey headed for the door. "I'll call her for you. I'm out of here. Toodles, Grinchus Maximus."

She strode out the door and didn't look back. *That was a kindergarten moment,* she told herself ruefully. *But God it felt good!*

chapter 16

Lacey headed straight for the elevators, wondering what on earth she could use out of that preposterous interview to give Mac the story he wanted. Cassandra didn't seem to remember anything useful about the attack. According to her, either the entire world had a motive to try to kill her for exposing evildoers, or else no one did. Except Felicity Pickles. Lacey was also angry at herself for losing her temper with the victim of a vicious attack. An infuriating but presumably innocent victim.

As she approached the elevators, a man and a woman who had been sitting in a small alcove rose and followed her. A quick scan of their clothes told her they were well to the left of center. Lacey's well-honed Washington fashion sense enabled her to identify nearly every subspecies of Democrat and Republican at fifty feet. She pegged them as genus, *radical/liberal*; species, *shabby and proud of it*. With a nonprofit, Lacey guessed.

The man stopped her. "Excuse me, are you from *The Eye Street Observer*?"

"Maybe. Who are you?"

"Are you Smithsonian?" The woman spoke. "You're who Cassie wanted to see?"

"I'm Lacey Smithsonian. Who's Cassie?" Lacey couldn't imagine Cassandra with a nickname. She was Crazy Cassandra, the Portentous Prophetess of Doom, not a cozy little "Cassie."

"The nurse wouldn't let us in," the woman complained. "One at a time and only as requested by the patient, she said."

"She's a pretty tough nurse," Lacey said. "I wouldn't cross her."

"I'm Wendy. Wendy Townsend." She stuck out her hand.

Wendy was tall and plain and androgynous-looking, wearing a plain straight brown knit dress of eco-friendly material under a generic navy blue hoodie that had been washed till it faded. She carried a green canvas bag emblazoned with the slogan EARTH: LOVE IT OR LEAVE IT—BEFORE YOU POLLUTE ANOTHER MINUTE! Lacey noticed a red Earth-shaped logo for something called GARRISON OF GAIA. "We're friends of Cassie's. We've been waiting to see her."

Bouncing on her heels and shifting her weight from foot to foot, Wendy spoke with a breathy intensity. Her medium-brown, wild curly hair formed a perfect circle around her head. She wore no makeup, but she was wreathed in an overwhelming cloud of gardenia perfume. Lacey took an involuntary step back.

"And I'm Alex Markham." Wendy's companion shook Lacey's hand. "We're Cassie's housemates."

Markham looked like an aging grad student with his horn-rim glasses, shaggy brown hair, and neatly trimmed beard, speckled with gray. His jeans were frayed at the bottoms, his hiking boots were well worn, and he completed his look with a blue work shirt, a gray herringbone jacket, and, of course, the ever-present Jerry Garcia tie, a key fashion accessory for those tie-wearing Washington men who needed to project a certain middle-of-the-road, nonthreatening hipness. He seemed a mellow contrast to his companion's hyperkinetic energy.

Lacey realized she had never considered what Cassandra Wentworth's life might be like outside the office, but if she had, Markham and Townsend certainly fit the profile. But it was past lunchtime and Lacey was starving. She had no desire to hang around chatting in a hospital corridor.

"Nice to meet you. Gotta run."

"That gargoyle of a nurse told us she finally woke up, but she won't let us see her," Markham said. "I've been waiting around here for hours to see her."

"Actually," Wendy broke in, "we've both been here off and on for days, ever since it happened. Did she say anything? What did she tell you?"

"Not much. She was cold. She was thirsty," Lacey said, buttoning up her jacket. She left out Cassandra's royal command to get to the bottom of her assault.

"That's it?" Markham said. "Didn't she say anything about

what happened to her? Or who did it? I mean, this could be politically motivated. An attempted assassination."

"She says everyone loves her," Lacey offered cheerfully.

"She has powerful enemies," Markham continued without
listening to her. "This could be very personal. And it's really a
hate crime against all progressive thought."

"An attack on Cassie is an attack on all of us at Garrison of
Gaia, Alex," Wendy Townsend put in. "The personal is political, the political is personal. You know that."

"She says she doesn't remember anything at all from Friday." Lacey eyed the nearest elevator. She was at least ten yards
away and these two were directly in her path. *Maybe if I make
a run for it?*

"Nothing?" Wendy slid back into her line of sight. "Are you
sure?"

The toxic jungle gardenia scent was too close for comfort.
Lacey could feel her sinuses clogging. *Is perfume environmen-
tally correct?* Lacey wondered. *Must be organic. Really organic.* "Why not go and ask her?"

The elevator doors opened. A man rushed out and ran to
Wendy and spun her around. He was about six-two, wearing a
tailored gray suit, an expensive haircut over a bland face. Fit
looking, Lacey thought, but soft, like a college athlete out of
training. Moneyed. She pegged him in a similar genus, *liberal*,
but of the species *limousine*.

"How is she? Is she off critical? What did she tell you about
the attack?" The man looked from Wendy to Alex, but it was
Wendy who answered him.

"She doesn't remember anything about it." Wendy pointed
to Lacey. "That's what *she* says."

"Dude, what are you doing here?" Markham put his hand on
the taller man's chest.

"Cassandra! I'm concerned about Cassandra, of course." He
took Markham's hand away easily and looked hard at Lacey,
who noticed this big guy didn't call the patient "Cassie."

"Really, Henderson?" Markham narrowed his eyes. "I
thought you two broke up. You dumped her, for some woman?
We had to mop up the mess, remember?"

"A misunderstanding," the man he called Henderson replied.
"We're getting back together."

"Oh really! When did that happen?" Markham bristled. "Before or after you cheated on her?"

"That's between us and none of your business!"

Lacey tried to process all this surprising information. A Cassandra with actual friends? A "Cassie"? A Cassandra with an actual boyfriend? A jealous and concerned boyfriend wearing a suit? A boyfriend who wasn't the geeky Peter Johnson? *To quote Cassandra, "What kind of crazy world is this?"*

"Check the threads, Wendy." Markham seemed to be spoiling for a fight. He fingered Henderson's suit jacket. "Just feel the money. The man's gone all K Street on us." Henderson removed Markham's hand a second time. His face was hard.

"You abandoned us, Henderson," Wendy said. "How could you? Gaia needs you!"

"Not everyone wants to live in a crowded commune, Wendy," he said. "Some of us have to be the grown-ups."

"It's a group house for concerned environmental activists," Wendy snapped. "Not a commune."

Henderson snorted. He looked at Lacey. "And who on earth is she?"

"She's a reporter," Wendy said. "Lacey Smithsonian. From Cassie's paper."

"Smithsonian. Am I supposed to know who you are?" The newcomer looked only vaguely interested.

"I don't know," Lacey said. "Are you?"

"Cassie asked to see her first when she woke up," Markham said, as if Lacey weren't there. "We don't know why yet. As far as I know, they're not even friends. Are you friends?"

All eyes turned to Lacey. The new man introduced himself. "I'm Henderson Wilcox."

The name sounded familiar, but Lacey couldn't quite place him. He had a square jaw going soft and pale coloring. His expensive three-piece suit was a bit snug. Lacey introduced herself. "I'm just leaving," she added.

"You work with Cassandra?" he asked.

"At the same paper. I'm a fashion reporter." Lacey assumed that was enough of an explanation.

"Oh." The three said in unison, achieving a ragged three-part harmony.

"You weren't friends then." The gardenia cloud threatened

again as Wendy leaned in. "Why would Cassie ask for you first and not her friends?"

Markham adjusted his glasses and peered at her as if she were an exotic bug. "Don't you remember, guys, this is Smithsonian! The woman with all the lucky breaks in those murder investigations. Cassie's told us all about her."

"And a talent for praising the brain-dead conspicuous consumption of a fashion industry that ravages the planet and gives nothing in return," Wendy Townsend said.

"Tell us how you really feel, Wendy," Lacey said. "Don't hold back."

"Wendy, stop," Markham said. "She may be just a fashion reporter, but she's broken some crime stories. That must be why Cassie called her in."

"So that's what you're doing here with Cassie?" Wendy was in Lacey's face, forcing her to back up. "Finding the slime ball who tried to kill her?"

"Not exactly," Lacey began.

"The important thing is to use this politically," Wendy jumped ahead. "An attack on Cassie Wentworth is an attack on what she stood for, an attack on Gaia."

"How is Cassandra?" Henderson Wilcox interjected. "What did she say?"

"She doesn't remember what happened," Wendy said. "According to *her*."

"Cassie's conscious," Markham said, "and she didn't ask for you, Henderson. How did you even find out about this?"

"I read the paper too, like everybody else. I called as soon as I heard, but they said no visitors. I took a chance on coming over today to see how she is." He paused and seemed lost in thought. "I still care for her. You know that."

"Do we?" Wendy and her cloud of jungle gardenia turned to Wilcox.

The tough nurse strutted past and shushed them sternly. "We have patients who need their rest! And Ms. Wentworth doesn't want to see anyone else right now. You got that?" She stared them down. They all nodded.

"Where did you all meet Cassandra?" Lacey asked, edging toward the elevator.

"GOG," Wendy said. "Garrison of Gaia. We're the new proenvironmental lobbying group in Washington. I'm sure you've heard of us. Earth: Love It or Leave It." Hence the logo on her canvas bag. "I'm a lawyer and coordinator, and Alex is our lobbyist and chief counsel."

"Yes, I've heard of it." Garrison of Gaia was relatively new on the Washington scene and trying to flex its muscles. Like Greenpeace on steroids, Lacey recalled, or PETA, only not so subtle. She couldn't remember much more about it.

"Cassandra used to volunteer there," Wendy offered, "and we all lived for a summer in the Gaia Project, in the hills of West Virginia, a zero-energy-sucking self-sufficient eco-community designed to prove a sustainable human society can be carbon neutral."

"Cassie's writing a book about it," Markham said. "We would have stayed on, it was idyllic, but we have a mission here in D.C. Our lobbying mission."

"And someone is trying to stop the mission," Wendy said. "Look at what happened to Cassie. It's clearly a political vendetta. It could happen to any of us."

Lacey turned to Henderson Wilcox. "And you, how do you know Cassandra?"

"Oh, I missed the halcyon days in the mud at the Gaia Project." His tone was dry, speaking not to her but to Markham and Townsend. "The summer of love and muck. I'm just the legal mind who kept it all going behind the scenes. Someone had to."

Three angry eco-lawyers, Lacey thought. *How fun. Can I leave now?*

"He worked in D.C. at the GOG offices." Wendy loved to speak for others.

"Until the bastards from K Street came calling with briefcases full of cash," Markham continued. "You know the kind? The lying lawyer-lobbyists? The kind who would sell his reputation, and his soul, for a window office on K Street? Well, meet the newest sellout."

Lacey wasn't one to sell a window office short. Her own desk was near a window. But windows were obviously a sticking point for these people. Sounded like simple jealousy to her. "You have something against windows?"

"Only when it means you stop supporting environmental issues! Only when you switch sides to defend the Earth rapers for a fat paycheck and a few lousy perks," Markham said. "How many pipelines are going to rot out in Alaska on your watch,

Henderson? How many millions of barrels of crude oil soaking into Gaia, Mother Earth, will you be apologizing for?" He was face to face with Henderson Wilcox, his voice loud enough to raise the comatose.

"Knock it off, Alex." Wilcox turned back to Lacey and narrowed his eyes. "What my *friend* here is trying so clumsily to say is that I used to be Garrison of Gaia's chief legal counsel. I recently moved to a law firm that will actually allow me to eat food and pay my mortgage, for a change. I'm still on the same side. You tell me, Smithsonian, am I raping Mother Earth if I want to live under a roof, not freeze, and not starve to death?"

Lacey wasn't up for trick questions. This lively conversation was interrupted when the elevator doors opened and *Eye Street* reporter Peter Johnson emerged, trench coat flapping. He gazed around the hall to get his bearings and spotted Lacey. "You! What the hell are you doing here, Smithsonian?"

It was the Cassandra trio's turn to observe the moment. The mop-haired nurse strode by again with a tray of meds in her hands, death rays in her eyes.

Johnson looked scruffier than usual. His collar was rumpled around a loose and crooked tie. His trench coat was shabby and threadbare and seemed to have acquired permanent brown stains. Lacey wondered if he were really that careless, or if his fellow commuters simply felt compelled to pour their morning java all over him. It was an amusing thought.

"Hello, Johnson," Lacey said. "Imagine meeting you here. We could have a staff meeting."

"You're from *The Eye* too?" Wendy Townsend and the amazing toxic gardenia smog closed in on the new arrival.

"Peter Johnson," he said in clipped tones without looking at her. "Capitol Hill reporter, *Eye Street Observer*."

Lacey wasn't sure, but she sensed a throb of female attraction toward Johnson from Wendy. Of course, this woman also seemed interested in both Alex and Henderson. *What was with these people?* Lacey thought. *What kind of jungle pheromone does Garrison of Gaia put in their coffee?* But still, this was Washington, D.C., she reflected, and the standards of attraction were different here.

"Well, Smithsonian?" Johnson jarred her back to the moment and stood there expecting an answer. "You're not here out of friendship."

"A command from the queen herself, delivered to me via Mac Jones."

"I don't believe it! You?!" Cassandra's friends stood by absorbing the scene, blocking the hall. "Cassandra asked to see you?"

"Ask her yourself," Lacey muttered, watching for the nurse to reappear. "I'm sure you'll have this wrapped up in no time."

"Wrap what up?" Wendy asked.

"Nothing." Lacey and Johnson both said it at the same time.

"All I want to do is see Cassandra," Johnson said.

"Take a number and get in line!" Markham squared his shoulders. "We were here first!" The decibels were rising.

"You can take my place." Lacey hit the elevator button. "Time flies when you're having fun." The nurse with the evil eye was storming down the hall toward them on silent clogs, her stethoscope swinging.

"Wait a minute." Peter put his hand on Lacey's shoulder. She brushed it off. "Hey, I'm talking to you, Smithsonian."

"And I'm talking to you!" Nurse Grumpy poked Johnson in the shoulder. "There are patients here, sick patients, patients who need their rest. All of you, out of here. Now! You will not enjoy being under my intensive care. Out!" She herded them all onto the elevator together and waited until the doors shut.

The five of them rode down in an uncomfortable silence. And a cloud of gardenia perfume.

chapter 17

Freedom was a heady feeling, Lacey reflected on her walk back to the office. The air on the street was considerably less stuffy without the gardenia cloud and the bombast. She'd left the Wentworth Four in the dust while Johnson was attempting some manly strutting before Alex Markham and Henderson Wilcox, each apparently in fear that the alluring Cassandra Wentworth had every eco-lawyer in Washington pining for her.

Wendy Townsend had stood at the edge of this little tableau, perhaps waiting to claim the victor. As Lacey had breezed out through the George Washington University Hospital door, she heard the woman plead for them all to stop squabbling and get coffee at Starbucks. But Lacey didn't stick around to find out.

Lacey crossed Washington Circle and was walking briskly down K Street when her cell phone rang. She retrieved it from her purse, noticing that Cassandra's cell phone number appeared in the display. "Hello?"

"You said I was a boy! I'm not a boy! I'm a girl! My name is Jasmine. Does that sound like a boy's name to you?"

A girl? Lacey recognized the little shepherd's voice. *That tough little shepherd boy was a girl?* "Excuse me?" *A girl running alone down an alley in Shaw last night?*

"You heard me. A girl."

"You're the little shepherd?" Lacey shook her head to clear it and realized she must look like every other nut walking down the streets babbling into a cell phone. "You were wearing the shepherd's robe, I mean. I was hoping you'd call back. You're all right?" Lacey stopped and stood on the sidewalk in front of a popular Thai restaurant. She didn't want to lose the kid's attention. "Where did you get the robe?"

"Around." The girl was obviously upset, and Lacey wanted to keep her on the phone. "And I'm not Hispanic. I'm a mutt, my mom says, and that's a good thing. Chinese, black, and white. Are you blind or something?"

"I never said you were Hispanic. The police thought you were."

"That's stupid. I'm not Hispanic! I am what I am!"

"Jasmine, do you read *The Eye*? Is that where you read this?" Lacey hoped the kid was not yet another fan of DeadFed dot com.

"Yeah, I read. I can read, you know. I'm a great reader." She sighed, a grown-ups-can-be-so-tiresome kind of sigh. "I called 'cause you got it wrong about me being a boy. And I wanted to see if that lady is okay yet. Your friend Cassandra."

"I didn't write the story," Lacey protested. "And Cassandra is going to be all right."

"But you said you were a reporter."

"I am, but one of the police reporters wrote the story. I write about fashion. Clothes."

"Why did they think I'm a boy?" The voice was deeply offended and suspicious. Lacey wondered what this tough little girl would think about Damon's little man and evil alien dwarf theories.

"It was dark. You were wearing a shepherd's robe."

"Shepherds can totally be girls! I'm a girl!"

"Yes, of course, shepherds can be girls." Lacey was happy to know that feminism was not dead, but not so happy that a twelve-year-old girl could make her feel like a fool. "I'm sorry. What's your last name, Jasmine?"

"It's Lee. Jasmine Lee."

"Jasmine Lee is a beautiful name. You know, with that hood halfway down your face, I couldn't see you very well. It was hard to tell what you looked like in the dark."

"Maybe you couldn't," she conceded. "I do that on purpose sometimes. I don't need anyone gettin' in my business."

"And you didn't exactly introduce yourself."

"I had things on my mind." Jasmine seemed calmer now.

Lacey hoped Jasmine wouldn't ask for a retraction in the paper. It was much safer if the Santa Dude still thought she was a boy. "I see you kept the cell phone."

"What cell phone?"

"I don't know, maybe the phone you're talking on." Laccy heard a giggle on the other end. "Never mind. But you should know that the battery will run down and the phone will die. Maybe very soon."

"So? I can use a pay phone."

"So maybe I'd like to talk to you again. Do you have another number where I can reach you?"

"I'll call you." Lacey sighed. *Cagey kid!*

"Jasmine, about that shepherd's robe—"

"Maybe I like it. Maybe it's pretty. And I like the hood."

"It was stolen from a church. Right?" Lacey assumed there wasn't a vast number of blue-and-white shepherd's robes flooding the streets of the District.

"It's borrowed! I am borrowing it! Besides, statues don't get cold. Everybody knows that."

"That's not what I mean, Jasmine. You saw the Santa Dude. That means the Santa Dude saw you. Wearing that robe. I don't want to scare you, but—"

"You don't scare me," the girl protested, although there was a tremor in her voice. "Like you could scare me. I've seen way scarier stuff than the Santa Dude."

"But you still don't want him to find you. You saw what he did and he might remember that robe. He might come after you with another giant candy cane." Lacey paused for a minute. "I saw you last night."

"No way!" There was surprise in the voice.

"In the alley near the church." Lacey took a chance she hadn't imagined it. "I tried to talk to you."

"I didn't see you."

"I was in a car."

"A car? A really big pink car?"

"That was me," Lacey said. "So it was you in the alley." There was no response on the other end. "Do you live near the church?"

Several ladies who left the Thai restaurant stalked off on their stilettos. Spicy Thai aromas filled the air, reminding Lacey it was time for lunch. A blue-and-white Metropolitan police cruiser glided by. Jasmine was silent.

"The Santa Dude is a dangerous man," Lacey said.

"He's bad," the girl agreed. "And crazy."

"The police would like to know what he looks like. So would I."

"I don't talk to police." She said it as if Lacey were a complete idiot.

"Why not?"

"It's my policy. My personal policy," Jasmine said, as if she'd given it a great deal of thought. "Police don't care about you. You talk to police and then you need a lawyer and everybody knows they're bad news."

"They're not all bad. My best friend is a lawyer," Lacey said. *A little crazy, but a good lawyer.*

"Whatever." Now there was a bored note to the voice. "The police just take you away and lock you up."

"Why would they take you away?"

"Because they just do." The girl was getting impatient. "I have to go now."

"Wait, Jasmine, where do you go to school?"

"I don't have to tell you." The attitude was back. The girl was a tough cookie.

"Where do you live?"

"I think you're nosy."

"I'm a reporter. I told you, that's what I do."

"That sounds dumb." The girl's sigh was extravagant. "Maybe you should go to school and be something else."

Lacey ignored that advice. "You said statues don't get cold, Jasmine. Do you get cold?" There was no answer. "I could buy you a new coat," she offered, "a really warm coat. Warmer than that shepherd's robe. We could make a trade." Jasmine said nothing, but Lacey could tell she was thinking about it. "You give me the robe and I'll get you a brand-new coat."

"Really totally new? Not from some dirty old thrift store?" she inquired, interested. "Any kind I want?"

Lacey hoped Jasmine didn't have a taste for mink. She wondered if this bribe would really work, and then she wondered if it was ethical. *For heaven's sake, this is a child, not a story.* "Any kind you want. Would your mother be okay with that?"

"She would," the girl said. "She totally would."

"I'd like to meet your mom too. She could come along with us. Can you give me your home phone number or have her call me?"

Silence. Then: "I'll think about it. Maybe. I'll call you. Bye." Jasmine clicked off.

Damn! I had her and then I lost her! Lacey cursed herself for pushing Jasmine too hard. *I handled this all wrong.*

Really, Smithsonian? she thought ruefully. *What was your first clue?*

chapter 18

"How'd it go?" Mac was on his way back from the third-floor snack machine with a package of little chocolate doughnuts, a sure sign that he'd given up hope that Felicity would be feeding the troops today.

Lacey had a bag of takeout Thai food in her hands that she planned to open at her desk, but Mac waved her into his office. She clutched the bag and the plastic chopsticks, determined to have *some* sustenance this day.

"So?" He waited for her report.

"It went swell, Mac. Cassandra was rude. She insulted me. I in turn insulted her, met and was insulted by her friends, was terrorized by a cranky nurse, and finished off my mission of mercy with a fight with Sir Shabby Lancelot, who arrived to save the day, a little late and unarmed for a battle of wits. Peter Johnson, I mean." She gestured with her chopsticks. *I left out the part about Cassandra being irresistible Washington man-bait, with three drippy guys all fighting over her.* "Oh, and then the crabby nurse threw us all out."

Mac wearily raised one eyebrow, swallowed a bit of doughnut. "What the hell was Johnson doing there? He was supposed to be in the Dirksen Building at a Senate hearing."

"Hearings are boring. And hearings have recesses," Lacey said. "Maybe he packed it in and just picked up the boring written testimony."

"We don't just pick up the boring written testimony to write our stories here at *The Eye*," he scolded. "We do it the hard way. We sit through the boring oral testimony just in case something not boring happens, like the idiot witness contradicting his own boring written testimony."

"Why don't you have another doughnut?" She thought that might calm him down. He rattled the package and took one out. "Cassandra couldn't remember anything useful, Mac. Not a thing. And she named as a suspect everybody who's ever read her stuff in the newspaper. Also Felicity, she really has it in for her." Lacey opened the white paper box that held her lunch and inhaled the aroma for a moment, ignoring the storm clouds gathering in Mac's expression. "Look, Mac, Cassandra summons me and then she has absolutely nothing to tell me. I can't write one whole newsworthy sentence from what she said. Johnson is convinced he's the man for this story? It's personal for him? Then why not just give it to him?"

"This is not good." He contemplated another doughnut. "Not good at all."

Lacey took a bite of her *tom yum gai sub.* "By the way, I got a call from the little shepherd."

"Who? Oh, the kid at the scene? He called you?"

"I'm very popular in certain circles. Dante's circles of Hades, that is. Turns out she's a girl. Not a boy. Her name is Jasmine."

"Ha! How'd our fashion genius miss the fact that it's a girl?" He chomped on a doughnut. "This isn't one of those transgender things, is it?"

"No, all I can say is that it was a little murky in the alley and a somewhat stressful environment. Kid was wearing a hood pulled down low, I couldn't see any hair. She makes a very convincing little shepherd boy. Grubby, dirty face, all that. You are what you wear, Mac."

"You're slipping, Smithsonian," he said. "Boy or girl? Pretty basic stuff."

Lacey delicately lifted a lovely piece of chicken with her chopsticks. "You're right, Mac. I'm losing it." She had a hopeful gleam in her eye. "Slipping. Can't tell boys from girls. Have to leave the fashion beat, I'd say. Might have to go back to hard news. Tragic. It's a shame, isn't it?"

"In your dreams, Smithsonian. Nice try though." He ate half the doughnut, then went after the other half. "You say the kid called you?"

"Jasmine. Jasmine Lee, she calls herself. On Cassandra's phone. Apparently it went missing in all the confusion Friday night. She wanted to make sure I knew she was a girl. And she's not Hispanic either."

"She want a retraction?"

"She didn't ask for one. I told her that as a witness she might be in danger. I'm worried about her."

"Why in particular?" His fingers worshipfully hefted the second to last doughnut.

"I think she might be homeless. Or close to it."

"Homeless?" Now Mac was paying attention. "How you figure that?"

"We ran a police report about a Nativity scene at a church up in the Shaw neighborhood. Nativity figures, statues, robbed of their clothes, a shepherd among them. Jasmine more or less admitted the shepherd's robe came from there."

"She stole it?"

"She *borrowed* it, she said, and she told me very logically that statues don't get cold."

"So she knows about being cold at night." His eyebrows furrowed and he stared at Lacey. "Homeless?"

"Maybe. Or maybe she's not quite homeless, but she's running around town, taking clothes, wandering through alleys. Doesn't sound like a good stable home. She's not a boy, playing around in alleys for kicks. See, I *can* tell boys from girls."

"How old you think she is?"

"Totally almost thirteen. That's a quote."

"She's black?"

"And white and Asian, Chinese. She admitted that some people might think she's Hispanic, but she's not. She's a 'mutt,' she told me. Small but tough. And smart, evaded most of my questions."

"See what you can find out about her." Mac was a tough mutt too, but he was showing Lacey his softer side. "I'm interested in this one."

"This story?"

"This kid." He put his hands together and flexed his fingers. "Almost thirteen? A vulnerable age, an age that calls out to the vultures. She's running round town alone? She's a target for more than this nut job who attacked Cassandra. The pimps, the pushers, they'll be calling, interested in the corruption of her soul. We can't let that happen."

"Sounds like a pretty big task." Lacey had never heard Mac

use a phrase like *the corruption of her soul.* Mac looked away and seemed to make up his mind about something.

"Reel her in, Lacey," he said. "Soon as possible. A kid like that's very vulnerable. She could slide right off the radar in this town. And the cops aren't helping at all, they're looking for the wrong kid. If they're looking at all. Did you find out about her family?"

"No, she ducks it every time I ask to speak to her mother. No mention of a father. No address. Nada. I'm betting she lives in or near Shaw, near the little church."

"Does sound like the mother's not on top of things. Maybe she's got problems, drugs or whatever, or maybe she wouldn't approve."

"What can I do, Mac, except wait for the phone to ring? The battery on that phone will run out of juice soon."

"You didn't tell the police about the cell phone?"

"I must have forgot. Busy night that night."

He nodded. "Probably not important to them anyway, what with this kid being their big 'suspect' and all. Somebody steals a cell phone in the District, they can sell it inside of fifteen minutes, so why would the cops waste their time looking for it? It's gone for good. And they're looking for an Hispanic teenager in a blue jacket? They're for sure never going to find this kid."

Lacey poked around with her chopsticks, searching for more chicken. "You seem to know a lot about this stuff."

"Too much, Smithsonian."

"Do you want me to call the detective?" She didn't want to, she didn't think that Charleston would understand. The last thing Jasmine needed was to be hauled into the system without support. "Jasmine says it's her policy not to talk to the cops."

"She's got a policy, huh?" Mac chuckled. "She's heard a lot about the police then. Or seen them in action. Probably all bad, in her mind." He picked up the last doughnut and contemplated it. "They could trace the phone's location. If they have a subpoena for the cell carrier." Mac munched down the doughnut. He sat back and rocked in his chair, then leaned forward. "But like you said, the battery will go dead before they even clear the paperwork. *The Eye* has to find this child."

"Her name is Jasmine."

"Jasmine. Twelve and already swiping clothes and copping

attitude about the police. I'd say she's about ten years too old for her age."

"I don't know how to get in touch with her. When I call Cassandra's cell, no one ever answers. What about finding her through the school district? Who's on our school beat, Mac? Maybe they'll know who to call."

"Forget about the schools. They won't tell you squat without a subpoena. Besides, you'd get this kid sucked into the system. Worst thing we could do to her. You got a full name on her?"

"Jasmine Lee. I offered to swap her a new coat for the shepherd's robe."

"Good plan!" Mac smiled, much to her surprise. "If she's like any female I ever met, she'll want that new coat. See, this fashion beat is really paying off for you, Smithsonian. Now go find that child. Reel her in, Lacey, reel her in."

Apparently, it wasn't some sort of breach of journalistic ethics to lure this kid with gifts. *Mac ought to know. I'm just a fashion reporter, remember.*

Lacey gathered up the last of her lunch and returned to her desk to collect her messages. Over the weekend she had called the number Jeffrey Bentley Holmes had left on her machine Friday. He hadn't answered, so she'd left a message telling him she wasn't date material at the moment, but she would be happy to meet him for lunch on Tuesday.

She found she'd missed Jeffrey's return call, but his voice mail message said lunch the next day was fine. He left the address of a restaurant on Fourteenth Street not far from Constitution Avenue. It would be a nice break, she thought, and maybe by then, the little shepherd girl would call back. She dialed Cassandra's number again. No answer.

The next message on her voice mail was from Pastor Wilbur Dean at the church of the plundered Nativity. He confirmed what Lacey already knew: The blue-and-white striped robe had been worn by one of his plaster shepherds, now a little less splendidly dressed. There was a soup kitchen down the street, and Pastor Wilbur Dean assumed that was probably where the thieves had come from. He told her he harbored no animosity, especially if the person or persons who stole the clothes were homeless. He only hoped the robes would help them get through the cold of winter, with the assistance of the Almighty.

But if it was just a group of wild and malicious boys, he said, well, that thought really galled him.

Lacey called the soup kitchen. The woman who answered said she couldn't remember everyone who came through the line. Sure there were kids, but they had to be accompanied by an adult. The kids were just a blur, she said. She didn't pay any special attention to them. "Why you asking me, lady?" Lacey had no answers, only questions.

She headed outside to Farragut Square, where a black man named Quentin often held court with the regulars who put money in his cup. He was erudite, intelligent, and homeless. A fastidious man, his clothes were clean, his manner often playful but respectful. Quentin battled with bipolar disease, he told Lacey, and sometimes it had the upper hand. She wondered which Quentin she would meet today.

As she approached, Quentin was reading *The Eye*. He prided himself on keeping up with current events, the better to proclaim his opinions to one and all. He seemed fond of the reporters. Lacey wondered what he had done before hitting bottom; perhaps he'd been a teacher? He looked up and saw Lacey dropping a dollar in his cup.

"Hey, Smithsonian, how you doin'? You still telling those idiot politicians how to dress?"

"I do, but they never listen. Quentin, I want to ask you something important."

"Ask away!" He gestured grandly. "My knowledge is your knowledge. A little knowledge is a dangerous thing. Don't tell Woodward and Bernstein I'm your Deep Throat."

"Don't worry." Lacey smiled. "You're a confidential source. I'm interested in a homeless child who might have been here in Farragut Square on Friday night."

He rubbed his face and squinted up at her. He affected his best English accent. "Ah, yes, Friday night, Milady. Oi remember it well! All the swells! Dressed fit to kill, they was, in furs and tuxedos. Moine's at the bloody cleaners, with me top hat."

"That's right, lots of people dressed up that night, lots of parties. But there might have been a child, about twelve, wearing a shepherd's robe. Blue-and-white stripes? Maybe homeless, maybe not? Did you see anyone like that among the swells?"

Quentin laced his fingers together and dropped the accent.

"We're a long way from Bethlehem for a little shepherd boy,
Smithsonian." Lacey sighed in disappointment. "And yet . . . I
may have seen one. Would a shepherd girl do as well? A little
lamb in shepherd's clothing?"

"Quentin! You *are* my Deep Throat!" Lacey could have
hugged him, but she never hugged her sources. "Where and
when? Have you seen her before? What was she doing? Was
she alone?"

Quentin had indeed seen Jasmine Lee that night, although he
didn't know her name. He had seen her around in the past couple of weeks, recently wearing that blue-and-white shepherd's
robe. He didn't know if she was homeless or not, but several
restaurants near the square left food in their alleys in take-out
cartons for the homeless; he'd seen her getting food there. But
she never stayed in the square and ate, she took the food away,
perhaps to feed her family.

"She doesn't converse with me. Or anyone. Little lamb
keeps to herself. Smart kid. Seems on Friday night I caught a
glimpse of her blue-and-white robe, running across Eye Street."
That was all he saw.

"But Quentin," Lacey protested. "Your bench is right here
facing Eye Street! You must have seen more than that!"

"Smithsonian, I am a working man!" Quentin drew himself
up with dignity. "This is the Christmas season! Friday night,
party time, lots of people on the street, jingle in their pockets,
goodwill to men in their wallets? My best business hours, pal.
Besides, this is not my only office, you know." He seemed af-
fronted that Lacey might think he was some slacker lounging
on a park bench. "I was heading for my branch office over in
McPherson Square, two blocks east of here. I got a prime bench
on K Street! You want to make the real money in the District,
you got to be on K Street, where the legal beagles bark. None
of this two-bit Eye Street action, K Street is where it's at. Am I
right, Smithsonian, or am I right?"

Lacey allowed that K Street was where it was at. "So you
saw her run across the square and that was that?"

"That was that," Quentin said. "But I tell you something I
learned on the street, Smithsonian. That little lamb in shepherd's clothing mean something to you? Then you be on the
lookout for her. Little lambs, they always draw the big, bad
wolves."

* * *

Jasmine failed to call back. The name Lee was a dead end, and Quentin's information was tantalizing, but it led her nowhere. No schools, Mac had said. She was stumped. Lacey gave up at five o'clock and tried to make her escape from the office. She was thwarted by Peter Johnson. It was that kind of day.

"I need to talk to you, Smithsonian," he commanded.

"Not now, Johnson." She stood and grabbed her bag.

"Yes, now."

He sat down imperiously on her desk, prompting Lacey to shove him right off her desk. "Have the courtesy to at least park your butt in a chair," she said. "And not my chair."

She sat back in her broken-down ergonomic chair. Johnson picked himself up and sat in the rolling Death Chair, which for some reason usually came to rest near Lacey's desk. It had earned its moniker when a fashion writer, Lacey's late unlamented predecessor Mariah, had died in it one day, many hours before her not-so-untimely demise was discovered. The Death Chair wasn't an ergonomic model, but an old-fashioned oak armchair with a grooved bottom. Someone had painted a skull and crossbones on it. The staff cartoonist had long been suspected, despite his denials.

Sadly the Death Chair did not deter Johnson, who pulled out a notebook and pen with his ink-stained fingers. "What do you have for me?"

She could feel her eyebrows lift in surprise. "Excuse me?"

"What have you found out about Cassandra's attack? Suspects? Theories?"

Lacey shook her head. Did Johnson really think she'd spent the rest of the day coming up with suspects for him?

"My day was not so productive. What did Cassandra tell you?"

"You're the only one who's seen her in person." His pale eyes were accusatory.

"You never got to speak to her? Oh, I am so honored to be her one and only. But she told me nothing at all of any importance."

"I was only able to get her on the phone for a few minutes," Johnson said. "Felicity Pickles was the only name she came up with." He gave her his attempt at an imperious reporter's stare.

"They had a fight. Cassandra was found wearing one of those ridiculous sweaters. Felicity Pickles's sweater."

"Yes, they had a fight. And I saw her in the alley wearing Felicity's sweater, remember? But I don't think Felicity did it."

"You don't think so." He peered at her skeptically over his glasses.

Lacey leaned back and stretched. She might as well show him she was bored. "What about those friends of 'Cassie's' at the hospital?"

"They don't know anything." Johnson put his notebook down. "I asked."

"You asked them what they knew and they said, 'Nothing'? And you believe them *why* exactly?"

"If they knew something, they would have told me."

"And why is that, Peter? Because you're a reporter and they trust you?" Lacey always assumed the overwhelming probability that people who spoke to her were lying. Even if they weren't, their stories were always calculated to put them in the best light.

"My. Gut. Instincts." Johnson tapped his pen on each syllable like a conductor's baton to emphasize his words. His glasses slid down his nose and nearly off the tip.

"Oh. Right. Well, you do have a gut. So what do you think of her friends?" She thought it was too bizarre to be actually speaking with Peter Johnson for more than a moment or two in passing. And a hostile moment at that. Johnson considered himself to be at the top of the journalistic food chain and Smithsonian at the bottom. Lacey would trust a politician in front of a TV camera before she'd trust his opinion of anyone.

"Them? Both men are crazy about her, of course." He seemed to find this both obvious and irritating. "You may not have picked up on that, but I did. Wendy is her best friend. She and Alex are her housemates. They have all this complicated history with each other you wouldn't know anything about, but I—"

Yada, yada, yada. Lacey had already gotten all that. "No hidden animosities then?"

"What are you insinuating?" He shoved his oversized glasses back up his nose.

"Cassandra provokes, um, strong reactions in people." Lacey sat up and started shuffling papers on her desk. "I just wondered if you thought there was anything else motivating their hospital vigil. Impressions, theories, your infallible gut instincts?"

"No. There wasn't." He tapped his pen again. "What about your gut instincts?"

"I am not getting any more involved with this thing than I have to be, Peter." She willed her phone to ring. It didn't.

"Really? You don't want to work together on this, Smithsonian? I'm not crazy about working with you either, but Mac suggested we share information. Suggested it strongly. Now, what do you do when you get involved in one of these stories, like those murders with all the fashion stuff? Do you have a logical process, or is it just dumb luck?"

"Like my dumb luck to be having this conversation with you?" Her hands were itching to throw something at him. "I just ask questions. That's all. Ever try that?"

Lacey wasn't about to discuss her instincts, or "all the fashion stuff," or the way that clothes and looks and other little style clues suggested meanings and connections to her and sometimes told her an entire story that most people couldn't read. He was a man, what did he know about those subtle things? He wouldn't believe her if she told him, so why even start?

So far her so-called fashion clues consisted of the infamous Christmas sweater, the ubiquitous Santa cap, and the alleged giant candy cane. It was all too precious and obvious, and yet baffling. An enraged overreaction to Sweatergate? Or a clumsy attempt to look like it was, to cover some other motive? Personal or political? Calculated or improvised? Discuss all that with Peter Johnson, who just wanted to scoop her and pick her brain and copy her "process" without even respecting her? Absurd.

He referred to his notebook. "According to your supposed witness, the assailant wore a red and white Santa cap. At least a dozen guys at *The Eye*'s Christmas party were wearing those stupid things. Fashion clue?"

"Twelve new suspects? Honestly, Peter, you think it was someone from *The Eye*? No one here cares about Cassandra's little fiasco of Sweatergate, except to laugh at her over it."

"Don't call it Sweatergate! Cassandra was the victim here!"

"The victim of her own hatefulness. And what should I call it, Slap Down at the Cookie Corral?" She stopped shuffling pa-

pers in case she needed to knock Johnson off his chair. He
leaned in with an ugly expression. Lacey noticed the scalp
under his thinning hair was glistening with sweat. He was too
close to her. She stood up, glared down at him on the Death
Chair, and picked up her purse.

"It must be someone at *The Eye*. The assailant is always
close to home, Smithsonian," he said. "Every police reporter
knows that."

"That lets you out, doesn't it?" Lacey laughed. "You were
never a police reporter! You just watch the detectives on TV."

"What about our office jinx?"

"Harlan Wiedemeyer? You can't be serious."

"He's bad news," Johnson insisted. "Everyone knows that."

"There's no such thing as a jinx. Ask Mac." The thought of
poor lovestruck Harlan whaling on Cassandra with a candy
cane was preposterous. Wiedemeyer was as meek as a mouse.
Besides, Cassandra was in top shape and mounted on her bicycle, versus a tubby little guy whose only daily exercise was
hefting boxes of Krispy Kreme doughnuts from the Metro station to the office.

"And," Johnson continued, "Wiedemeyer is Pickles's
boyfriend. He could have been doing her dirty work for her."

"Harlan was wearing antlers, not a Santa cap."

"Big deal. He ditched the hat and put on the antlers to throw
people off the track."

"Yeah, good idea, so he'd stick out in a crowd where *everyone* was wearing Santa hats." Lacey wiggled her fingers over
her head, antlers-style. "And the antlers lit up, just so you
couldn't forget him."

Johnson closed his mouth tightly. Lacey folded her arms and
stared him down.

"Maybe Wiedemeyer didn't do it. But does he have an alibi?
Does Pickles?" He got to his feet and stomped off. "Find out.
That's all for now."

Ha! As if they were some sort of team, Lacey thought. Or
worse, as if Johnson were her boss on this story. Mac thought
they should work together? *What on earth was he thinking?*

chapter 19

Lacey sat back down at her desk and called Wendy Townsend at the Garrison of Gaia offices. She was just leaving, but she said Lacey could stop by the house shortly; she'd be there in twenty minutes. Because Lacey had suggested to the boorish Johnson that Cassandra's roommates might have some interesting information, maybe she should observe them in their native habitat, the "crowded commune," as Henderson Wilcox had called it. Not for Peter Johnson, but for herself. This story seemed to keep demanding that Lacey get involved with it, but she was determined to work her own angles, not his. And maybe Jasmine would call, and Lacey could try to "reel her in."

Lacey didn't care how Cassandra lived, but perhaps she could get some sort of feeling for the dynamics between the housemates. She took a moment to freshen her makeup and call Vic. Even though they didn't see each other every day, she was getting awfully used to him being around. He was working tonight, but he told her to stay safe and to call him if she needed him. She caught a cab to the Mount Pleasant neighborhood, where Cassandra and the others lived.

Wendy Townsend met Lacey at the door of the small town house and ushered her into the front room. Wendy was wearing a green and white Garrison of Gaia sweatshirt and gray leggings that bagged on her thin frame. Thankfully, her perfume had faded a little during the day. The toxic cloud was gone, but the powerful memory of the jungle gardenia lingered on. Lacey tried not to wrinkle her nose.

The house was long and narrow, with a tiny living/dining area and kitchen on the first floor and bedrooms and bath upstairs. It could have been fabulous with some tender loving care, Lacey thought. There was a fireplace with a beautiful wooden mantel and a crown molding and chair rail around the room, but someone had slapped a coat of flat dingy apartment white paint on everything long ago and now it was chipped and dirty. It looked cheap and forlorn.

Decorated in early castoffs and late Salvation Army, the room was also full of cardboard boxes. This was not the kind of place in which company would be afraid to spill something on the carpet; it was so stained Lacey couldn't even put a name to its color. *Maybe "grunge."* Two sturdy-looking bikes hung on the wall near the front door. A variety of helmets dangled from a wooden rack meant for hats and coats. Lacey wondered where Cassandra's crumpled bike had ended up.

She focused her attention on the lone framed object on the wall. It was a newspaper clipping of Wendy with her fist in the air, being hauled out of a tree by police. The headline read, TREE-DWELLING ECO-ACTIVIST DEFIANT AS POLICE SHUT DOWN PROTEST. The article detailed her efforts to save the tree from a logging company by living in it for as long as it took. Wendy lost her struggle, and her tree, but gained notoriety. Lacey didn't read the entire thing, but she got the gist. *You might fault their methods,* she thought, *but not their commitment.*

"My finest hour," Wendy said. "That poor tree. Come sit down." The woman had a hungry quality that had nothing to do with her being too thin. She stood too close to people and watched them too closely when they spoke. There was a desperately needy undertone to her kinetic behavior, almost devouring. Her smile seemed like the prelude to a shark attack.

A large yellow dog lay sprawled on a bedspread-covered sofa. The spread was covered in a second spread of dog hair. When the dog growled and moved into attack position, Lacey didn't know whether to run or stand her ground.

"Bruno! Good boy! Bruno likes you," Wendy said as she wrangled the animal off the sofa, down the hall, and through a door to the basement, which she slammed. The dog barked loudly. He sounded angry. "Don't worry about Bruno. He'll calm down soon. Have a seat."

Lacey looked at the sofa and considered how her heather tweed skirt would look covered in yellow fur. It was tweed, but *still.* "Allergies," she said, indicating the sofa. Lacey liked dogs, but she preferred dogs whose owners were acquainted with vacuum cleaners. The angry barking continued.

"Ah. Too bad. One of those people, are you?" Wendy returned with a chrome chair from the kitchen, on which Lacey gratefully sat, after giving it a wipe with her hand. "Allergies. You probably grew up in a sterile environment. You really need more contact with animals, not less. Desensitization."

"Perhaps some other time." The imprisoned Bruno body slammed the basement door, shaking the whole house. He followed up with furious barking, which matched the pounding of Lacey's heart.

"Pay no attention to the little doggie," Wendy said. "He just wants to play."

"Sounds more like he wants to have me for dinner." Lacey clenched the chair with her hands and tried to calm her racing pulse.

"You're not worried about Bruno?" Wendy's high-pitched giggle sounded as if it could slide right into a sob. "He's just a big wuvvable doggie woggie." She sprawled on the sofa arms akimbo, heedless of the dog hair. Wendy's sweatshirt had a nice even coat of Bruno's fur.

"How long have you lived here?" Maybe Lacey was being unfair about the place. Maybe they just moved in. Maybe the carpet had been stained by the previous occupants.

"Oh, four or five years, why?"

"Just wondering." Lacey tried not to stare at the decor. Stacks of books leaned against the wall in the hallway. The cardboard boxes spilled their contents on the unmentionable carpet.

"Tell me something." Wendy leaned forward, elbows on knees. "Why should Cassie want *you* to find out what happened to her? That's what the police are for, unless of course they're paid to look the other way. She doesn't even like you. And you don't like her. So why you?"

"You don't sugarcoat anything, do you, Wendy?"

"Why should I? I'm just being honest. You're just a parasite, you and the whole monolithic reactionary media. Nothing personal."

Being honest was so overrated, Lacey thought. "Does that mean you don't like me too?" she asked.

"I just met you." She gave an offhanded shrug. "If Cassie

wants you to find out what happened, then so do I. And," she added logically, "it's not like I have to like you."

"No, you don't," Lacey agreed. *Neither do I.* "Well, that's out of the way. So why don't we start." She was thirsty. A glass of water would have been nice, or even better a cup of hot tea, anything to cut the thick atmosphere of dog hair that was beginning to fill her throat and lungs, but she wasn't about to ask. Townsend apparently wasn't about to offer. "Does Cassandra have any enemies?"

"Everyone has enemies."

"Anyone specifically?"

"Besides you?"

"I am not her enemy. I am her coworker, as we have already established. But I am not her enemy." Lacey stood up. She was finding it hard to breathe in the small close room. "I'm involved because Cassandra asked me to be."

"Wow, Smithsonian. No need to be touchy. There is that chubby woman who wears all the offensive sweaters."

"They are not offensive," Lacey said, resuming the edge of her seat. "They are festive."

Wendy shrugged. "Whatever. She's dangerous, did you know that?"

"Leaving aside Felicity Pickles."

"Fine. There is also the global capitalist cabal, which is destroying the planet." Wendy changed positions and crossed her legs, raising a fog of dog fur.

"And leaving aside the dogma. Specifics, Wendy. I'm talking about threats anyone might have made to Cassandra, or conflicts, disagreements, arguments, strange e-mails, anything new or unusual or out of place."

"Not that I know of." Wendy sighed. It seemed to be really hard for her to focus on things in her immediate world, rather than the important questions facing the planet.

Think globally, slack locally, Lacey thought. "Odd visitors, stalkers, weird phone calls?"

"I don't know. We all have our own cell phones. No one even calls on the wall phone. We only use it to order takeout."

"Was Cassandra upset about anything lately?"

Wendy rolled her eyes. "Yes! That crazy sweater-wearing cookie-baking monster that you don't want me to talk about. Why are you protecting her?"

"I'm not. It's just too obvious to blame her, too easy. It feels like a cheap set-up."

"It doesn't mean she didn't attack Cassie! Because it's obvious it can't be true?"

Lacey sighed and shifted in her seat. She realized that it was getting cold in the house. The temperature outside must be falling. "How close are you to Cassandra?"

"We're best friends. You don't think I did it, do you?" Suddenly Wendy was standing up and pressing forward into Lacey's space, alarm crossing her features.

"Did you ever fight with Cassandra?"

"We're pacifists! We don't believe in violence!"

"Really? Garrison of Gaia has a reputation for violence. Arson at construction sites, sabotage against developers and logging companies. Harassment of employees. Confrontations at demonstrations. Like your stint in the tree."

"But that's for the planet!" She punched the air with her fist. "That's only to protect the environment from the Earth rapers. We don't endorse violence against humans. We *tolerate* humans!"

Lacey leaned back away from her. The dog banged against the door again and she jumped. "How about someone close to her?" she asked. Wendy hesitated. "What about Alex Markham? Did they have a good relationship?"

"Alex adores Cassandra," Wendy said reluctantly. "They've always been close. Very close. I'm not sure he's ever gotten over her."

"They dated?"

"Oh yes. Friends with benefits, you know, only more so. His feelings got in the way. I think it hurt him a lot when Cassie started seeing Henderson. Things got complicated. Listen, I have things to do." Wendy moved toward the door, a signal that it was time for Lacey to leave.

"What about Henderson Wilcox then?" Lacey would be grateful to leave. Bruno could have his sofa back. She reflected that it was funny that people say they want to talk, but then they take their own sweet time to get to the real stuff. And by the time they do, they're tired of talking to a reporter. "Wilcox said they were getting back together. So they broke up? And now he's dating Cassandra again? When did all this happen? When did he move out of this house?"

Wendy winced visibly. "I don't know, he moved out about

six months ago, he's been seeing her off and on, but he's been fair game too, if you know what I mean."

"Afraid not." Lacey was glad for her jacket, which she wrapped around her. She hunted for her gloves in her pockets. "Fair game for whom?" Wendy sighed one of those big you-may-as-well-know-the-truth sighs.

"I've been sleeping with Henderson too, all right? Friends with benefits, right? He didn't tell me anything about getting back together with Cassie. News to me."

Lacey didn't know what to say about this furry little hotbed of strange bedfellows. She tried to visualize the odd, prickly Cassandra in this shabby, dog-fur-lined passion pit. She tried to keep her expression neutral. "So are they or are they not getting back together?"

"When he heard she was in the hospital, he went running back to her. Just for the moment, a natural reaction, I think, but who knows."

"How does that make you feel, about the two of them, I mean?"

"I don't know! I mean, we're all just friends, really. The Gaia Movement is bigger than our petty little affairs. We should be able to be adults about this. . . ." She looked as if she were about to cry. Instead, Wendy opened the door. A gust of wintry air blew past them into the dirty little house. It was cold out, but Lacey felt better with the door open. She heard Bruno make one more thundering crash against the basement door.

"Wendy, I need to talk to Alex too. I thought he would be here."

"He works late a lot. But you can talk to him at Garrison of Gaia. Fourteenth, near T Street. Hope you find the jerk who almost killed Cassandra."

She slammed the door. Lacey had been dismissed. Again.

chapter 20

The Garrison of Gaia, or GOG, with its mission to honor, protect, and die for Mother Earth, was headquartered in the District in a converted garage on upper Fourteenth Street near T Street Northwest. The taxi dropped Lacey in front of the building. It had been painted green and emblazoned with the fire-red Garrison of Gaia logo. She was really racking up cab fare for *The Eye*, she thought, running around the city without a car.

Lacey took stock of her surroundings. The Shaw neighborhood was only a few blocks away, she realized, with the tiny Shiloh Mount Zion Church and its looted Nativity scene. The upper Fourteenth Street neighborhood had once been a funky haven for small independent theatres, down-at-the-heels bars, quirky shops, and long-vacant warehouses, but now it was on the same aggressive fast track to gentrification as the rest of the city.

Stepping through the front door, Lacey noticed everything looked recycled, the furniture, the carpets, the battered cubicle dividers. If Garrison of Gaia was renting this property cheap and didn't own the building, she wondered when they would face eviction. *Soon,* she thought. A tangle of plants fought for sun in windows that once had been service bays. The stomach-turning aroma of burnt coffee filled the air. A young man and a younger woman sat on the floor in the reception area next to a battered coffee table overflowing with flyers. They were stuffing envelopes. Plastic bins of stuffed envelopes were piled around them on the floor. Both wore jeans, Garrison of Gaia T-shirts over turtlenecks, and fingerless gloves. They gazed up at her with mild curiosity.

"I'm looking for Alex Markham," Lacey said. The office

was as cold as the house she'd just left. *These people don't believe in heat,* she realized. *Earth: Love It or Leave It.*

"Alex!" The woman yelled over her shoulder. "Someone to see you." She returned to her task of stuffing envelopes with flyers. The phone rang and the man reached one arm up to the reception desk behind him to answer it with a practiced formula.

"Garrison of Gaia. Mother Earth: Love it or leave it! How can *you* help?"

Lacey was distracted from the rest of this conversation as Alex Markham emerged from a dim hallway. He wore casual slacks and a blue work shirt with the sleeves rolled up. Another in his collection of Jerry Garcia ties hung loosely at his throat. Apparently he was used to working in this chilly building, or the cold didn't bother him. He combed his hair back with his fingers and looked as if he were trying to remember who she was.

"Lacey Smithsonian," she said. "You remember. From *The Eye Street Observer.* We met at the hospital."

"Of course, Lacey. Wendy rang me and said you were on your way. I was just thinking I had seen you somewhere else recently. Besides at the hospital today. Were you at the Folger Consort the other night?"

"Yes, I was." She didn't remember him, but then Vic and his parents had consumed most of her attention. Markham did look like the type who helped fill the theatre that night, with his neatly trimmed beard and tweedy look. The other two had stopped stuffing envelopes and were listening in.

"I'm a big fan of early music." Markham indicated that he and Lacey should move out of the reception area. "We have a huge mailing going out soon. Come on back to my office where we can talk."

They passed a large conference room and a small kitchen aromatic with the ruined brew. Markham's small windowless office was the last one, next to the restroom. Hardly the luxury she associated with being a D.C. legal mouthpiece, even at a nonprofit.

"Is this about Cassie?" He moved a chair from the hallway into his crowded office. In addition to his desk and ergonomic chair, there were a couple of other chairs full of red law books, open to specific pages. Briefs were stacked on the desk and piled high on a small marble coffee table and battered filing cabinets. None of the furniture matched.

"Just a few questions." This was worse than Mac Jones's office, Lacey thought. Minus the doughnuts.

"Excuse the mess." He smiled as if he could read her mind. "I really do know where everything is, I promise." Markham seemed to have a slight sense of humor, the first one she had sensed in Cassandra's crowd. She smiled.

"I'm sure you do."

He picked up something from the desk and flashed it at her: a CD by the Folger Consort. He put it in an ancient boom box and turned it on softly. "It's not really the season without the Consort, I think." Markham had a charming smile when he chose to use it, boyish and friendly.

"You like Christmas? But I thought . . ." The notes of a madrigal filled the small overcrowded office. "After all, Cassandra—"

"Well, Cassandra hates the commercialism, of course, but she tolerates Christmas."

"Could have fooled me."

"Cassie doesn't approve of cutting down a living tree and sticking it in your living room to die, who does? But she celebrates the spirit of peace and goodwill in her own way. She's not religious though, I wouldn't want you to get the wrong idea." Was it possible they were speaking of two different women? "May I take your coat?"

Manners too. So unlike Wendy Townsend. "No, thank you." Lacey didn't want to point out the obvious, that it was freezing in his office. "I can't stay long."

She sat down in the chair he had moved for her. After rearranging some piles of books and papers, he perched on the coffee table in front of her, expectantly. Lacey would have preferred him to sit a little farther off. He picked up a cup from his desk and was about to sip, then remembered more of his manners.

"Can I offer you some coffee?"

Today's blend: Burning landfill! "No, thanks. I'm just here about Cassandra."

"The doctor said Cassie's getting stronger. She'll be fine. We're all terribly relieved. But they still won't let us see her."

Lacey still had trouble thinking of her as "Cassie," and

following the tangled relationships among the housemates. "She doesn't remember anything about the attack. She may never remember."

"Is that really so terrible?" Markham mused. "Should she be forced to remember such an ugly event? Might be better this way, don't you think?" He took off his glasses, pulled a handkerchief from his pocket and wiped them clear. "Our minds protect us from the aftereffects of trauma, you know. Sometimes forgetting is best."

"But what about the guy who did it? Shouldn't he be found, shouldn't he pay?"

"Absolutely. Of course, we'd all likc to see him caught." He gazed into Lacey's eyes. "But you can't definitely say it was a him, can you?"

"Maybe not." Lacy realized she'd been wrong about the little shepherd "boy." Maybe Jasmine was wrong about the Santa "Dude." Her hands were cold. She wondered if she should have accepted a cup of coffee; not to drink the nasty stuff, but just to warm her fingers.

"You see, Lacey, I think anyone who cares about Cassie would want to spare her the trauma of remembering."

"Especially someone who knew exactly the kind of trauma she might remember."

"What are you saying?" Markham stiffened his back. "You mean the assailant?"

"Could it have been someone close to her? Usually is, you know."

"Are you inferring that it was someone here? One of us at GOG?"

Lacey gazed at him. "Maybe. What do you think?"

"I don't think so. No. Preposterous. Much more likely to be a politically motivated attack." He suddenly sounded very professorial. He stared around the little office at random. She wondered if he might grab a pad of paper and draw a diagram to show her exactly where she had gone wrong. Or write a brief.

"Assaults are not usually committed by strangers."

"I see what you're saying, but it couldn't have been anyone as close as her friends, as close as, say, Wendy and I are. It's always been strong between Cassie and me. I suppose I'm feeling guilty that I wasn't there."

"She has a habit of taking on fights with people."

"Her job, you mean? Is that how you see it? Cassie feels she has a mission. Lucky for us. We find her editorials quite valuable."

"What about Sweatergate?"

He shook his head. "I don't really know why she went off on that. It's not like her. I had no idea she was going to write such a trivial thing. We hadn't discussed it."

Discussed it? Was Garrison of Gaia pulling the strings behind Wentworth's editorials? And did that simply reflect Cassandra's own beliefs, or had she crossed some ethical line? Unbylined editorials were supposed to reflect the "official" view of the newspaper, not that of an individual, or of some lobbying or political pressure group. It was, after all, the "editorial we."

"Do you have any idea who waylaid her in the alley?" Lacey said.

"Of course not." He started to rearrange papers on his desk, a sure sign he wanted to cut this meeting short. Lacey often did the same thing, she realized, usually without effect.

"Know of anyone who was capable of attacking her?"

"Sure. That Pickles woman. Cassie was obsessing over the whole sweater thing, the way people indulge in the holiday and waste money and resources. It seems like a small thing, but it's emblematic of so much in our consumer-driven culture."

"Just for the record," Lacey said. "I don't believe Felicity attacked Cassandra."

"She's your friend, then?"

"No. I don't particularly like her. But it doesn't make sense. She'd be happy to kill someone slowly with cholesterol, but I doubt she's capable of attacking someone in an alley. And leaving her own sweater, as if to claim the credit?" Lacey took a breath and changed direction. "But I understand you and Cassandra had a relationship."

"I still have a relationship with Cassie and we're the best of friends. It was even romantic once." He paused and removed his glasses, putting them in his pocket. "A while ago. We realized we made better friends than we did—You know."

But Wendy said Markham was still carrying a torch for "Cassie." And what was the secret of Cassandra's magnetic attraction for all these quintessentially Washington men? *Aha,* Lacey thought. *That's the secret. "Quintessentially Washington men."* She couldn't imagine Cassandra's elusive allure would play anywhere but in the Nation's Capital.

The woman who had been stuffing envelopes stuck her head through the office door. "We're finished for the night, Alex."

Markham looked up. "That's fine, Sylvie. Just lock up. I'll let Ms. Smithsonian out when she's ready. Be sure to lock up both front and rear on the way out."

"Will do." Sylvie gave a short wave and was gone, leaving his office door open. Lacey heard a switch. All the lights in the office, except for a lamp in Markham's office went out. It startled her. He smiled.

"We try not to waste energy here at Garrison of Gaia."

No, they just waste coffee, and the heat required to burn it. Lacey hoped the woman remembered to unplug the coffeepot. "Who do you know who might have wanted to attack Cassandra? Any recent threats, conflicts, disagreements?"

"Cassie," he corrected her. "If it wasn't that loony Pickles woman, it must have been because of her beliefs. Cassandra was always on the attack against the polluters and defilers of the planet. Must have been one of those reactionary loonies who write letters to your paper."

Same song, different deejay. "Did she get any letters like that at home?"

"Not that I'm aware of."

"How did she and Wendy get along?" Lacey rubbed her hands together and reached in her pockets for her gloves, glad she wasn't trying to write notes with her numb fingers.

"They're friends. Old friends. We're all friends."

"Old friends with a really big dog."

"Ah, you met Bruno! Bruno's a sweetheart."

"Bruno's a trained killer. Why do you even need a dog?" Lacey slipped her gloves on and wiggled her fingers to get the blood flowing. Even her nose was cold.

"The women wanted him, originally. They didn't think the neighborhood was safe. We got him from an abused dog rescue group. Now he's sort of the house mascot. He's just an overgrown puppy, really."

Right. And King Kong was just a monkey. "Worried about anyone in particular?"

"No, Mount Pleasant just used to be that kind of neighborhood. I was mugged once, when we first moved in. Seems a lot safer now."

"So where were you Friday night?"

"Friday. You mean when Cassie was attacked in the alley." Markham shifted uneasily. "Ruling me out as a suspect? Or in? I suppose you must ask these trite questions, mustn't you? Nowhere near that alley. I was working on some papers. Here. And for the record, I'd never hurt her. I love Cassie, as a friend."

"Where was Wendy?"

"I suppose she was in her office, down the hall. When I get involved in something, I barely come up for air."

Markham stood up, stretched, and glanced at a large clock on the wall. It was only about six-thirty, but it was dark and cold and it felt much later. "It's getting late. I don't want to keep you, I'm sure you have things to do. And I have to get to the hospital and check on Cassie." He opened his office door. "By the way, there was someone else at the hospital, a man from your newspaper. Who is he?"

"Peter Johnson. He covers the Hill." She ordered herself not to make a face.

"I see." Markham pursed his lips. "His interest in Cassie seemed more than professional."

"Anything is possible." Lacey shrugged. So Markham didn't like Johnson. But she didn't like Johnson either. Markham might be wary of any man paying attention to Cassandra. Lacey stood up. "What about Henderson Wilcox?"

"Ah, yes. Henderson." He flipped on a light switch so she could see her way to the front door. "Let me show you out."

"Yes. Henderson. Well?" She wasn't going to let him squirm out of the question.

"Henderson and I used to be friends. We had a falling out."

"Over Cassandra?" She stepped over a pile of envelopes.

"Oh God no." He fumbled with the lock on the front door. "Work. Here at Garrison of Gaia." He gave her one of those looks like he was going to share something big, which usually meant it was useless information. "Between you and me, Henderson's really kind of a screwup. I always had to clean up his messes. He totally fouled up a lawsuit for us. A miracle the judge didn't throw it out."

"But you seemed so unhappy that he left Garrison of Gaia for a new job."

"I felt betrayed. Just because he's a screwup doesn't mean I want to see him change sides, especially when we're so backed up and short-staffed." Markham gestured with both hands spread wide. "Although handing the bad guys a major screwup might be a good strategy. Human nature is funny, isn't it?"

Through the glass she could see someone stringing old-fashioned Christmas lights in a multitude of colors over a store-front across the street. The sight cheered her up, but it seemed to have no effect on Alex Markham. She wanted to flee this cold little office. He opened the door for her.

"I'm not really sorry to see Henderson go," he said, "but he left us in the lurch when we could have used him, used his connections."

"So now he's got a window office on K Street." Lacey took a mental snapshot of the place. The lobby looked just as shabby as her first impression. Could Markham resent Henderson Wilcox not just for leaving them in the lurch, but for landing in the lap of luxury, while they were still toiling in the fields? *Yes, human nature is funny,* she silently agreed. "If you think of anything relevant, Markham, please call me." She handed him her card. "Listen, I don't presume to think I'm going to find out who did this. I'm just keeping a promise. To Cassandra."

"Of course. I understand. Maybe next time we can discuss more pleasant things." As they fell silent, the sounds of lutes and flutes from his Folger Consort CD could be heard. The music was beautiful and it almost elevated the moment. "Music perhaps."

Lacey stepped outside. The door shut behind her. She heard the lock turn with a sharp click.

Chapter 21

In Washington, D.C., you have to read the fine print.

Ensconced in a large green velvet chair at Starbucks, Lacey watched the D.C. cops busily engaged in one of their favorite activities: Towing an entire row of cars lined up down the block. A muscular black cop directed the towing of a silver Lexus, and a white cop was dealing with the next one in line, a black Lincoln limousine.

Poor suckers, Lacey thought. Not the cops, the drivers. No doubt they'd either not seen or ignored the hand-scrawled temporary NO PARKING signs taped below the parking meters, with their barely legible blur of prohibited dates and times. These signs were usually impossible to read until drivers were already out of their cars, and by that time, having wedged themselves into a too-good-to-be-true parking space in the District, many were tempted to take their chances. Just more fine print, and Washington was full of it. In due course of events, D.C. Parking Enforcement would tow them away to that Great Impound Lot in the sky—or in Anacostia in far Southeast, which was nearly as distant. Just another day on the job for the only District government department universally acknowledged to function with chilling efficiency. Until you asked them to find where they'd towed *your* car, that is.

Lacey arranged to meet Brooke Barton after she left Garrison of Gaia. If anyone could decipher the fine print on Cassandra's lawyer friends, it would be Brooke, Lacey's favorite attorney and slightly loony best friend. They chose the coffee shop near the Capitol on Pennsylvania Avenue because Brooke had been attending a hearing on some important matter of national security.

Happily, Lacey's observation of the towing crews was interrupted by Brooke, who dashed in the door, waved hello, and rushed to the counter for a double espresso. She was looking very professional in her gray flannel suit and red scarf, but frazzled as well. She added cream and sugar. Lots of cream and sugar.

"Have some coffee with your sugar," Lacey said. "For an alleged health nut, you really know how to fall off the wagon."

"Why fall halfway?" Brooke smirked. "If you're gonna fall, why not take a flying leap?"

"How was the hearing?"

Brooke moaned. "Deadly. Lucky me, I had to play messenger service for my idiot colleague who forgot his papers. He's got a sieve for a brain. Too much espresso, probably." Brooke added more cream to her espresso.

"And how is your brother, the idiot colleague?" Lacey liked Brooke's allegedly brilliant but terribly absentminded sibling.

"Benny's the same, the twit. He owes me big-time. Anyway it was a complete waste of time, except for seeing the Capitol itself. Always a kick. So we wound up in a confab in the President's Room off the Senate chamber. The hearing was so riveting I was able to concentrate fully on the ornate excess. Red leather sofas." Brooke sighed. "Mirrors and murals everywhere. If only the level of discourse within it could live up to that beautiful building."

"And everyone wearing a gray suit, I'll bet," Lacey said.

"Of course, but none so chic as mine, and that reminds me, I have to go shopping tonight. Must buy useless expensive presents for fellow overpaid attorneys. The holidays, you know." Brooke savored the aroma steaming out of the cup. "I need something to slap me awake after that boring hearing."

"We don't do that awkward gift exchange thing at *The Eye*. We'd be exchanging paper clips. Or staples. Or Post-its." Lacey was grateful that after coffee with Brooke she could finally go home. "So what do you buy lawyers who already have everything, Miss Lawyer Who Has Everything?"

"Something crystal, something silver, something distilled and bottled in Scotland. If you have it monogrammed, they can't re-gift it, they're stuck with it, so you won't get it back next year. I always have it monogrammed."

"Fascinating, Brooke. I knew you were the right person to

ask about the subtle nuances of interpersonal dynamics among lawyers."

"You're so right!" Brooke laughed. "I'm listening."

"And it's not for publication by DeadFed." Lacey paused. "Attorney-client privilege." Brooke rolled her eyes in silent assent. "Cassandra Wentworth woke up today. Mac made me go see her. She asked for me. Of all people."

"Wow. *Quel* scoop. And? Can she nail the bastard who attacked her? Did she know who it was, can she name him, or was it just some random madman? An evil dwarf?"

"She doesn't remember a thing," Lacey said. "Or at least so she said this afternoon."

"Damn! Did you get anything at all?"

"Yeah, I got plenty. I got insulted by Cassandra, so the knock on the head hasn't improved her personality. I got volunteered by Mac to—"

"Investigate, of course, to collar the creep who cracked Cassandra's cranium."

"Her friends call her Cassie." Lacey opened her eyes. "Rhymes with Lassie. Like she's a friendly freckle-faced kid with a big dog. Well, there is a big dog. But she doesn't seem anything like a Cassie to me. She doesn't even look like a Cassie."

"She has actual friends? I thought perhaps she had only comrades. Coconspirators. Fellow travelers."

"Oh, they are all that too. They ambushed me coming out of Cassandra's hospital room. Three of them, all lawyers, and they all work for this environmental thing, Garrison of Gaia, or did. One of them has apparently left the fold. I thought you might have heard of them."

"Garrison of Gaia." Brooke nodded. "GOG, although some call it GAG, as in gag me. They're like those people who break into laboratories to free the puppies. Only these people are not about the puppies, to hell with the damned puppies, they're all about the Earth, dude, love it or like, you know, bleeping leave it."

"I got that they're fairly extreme." Lacey noticed the tow trucks were moving the last of the limousines. "And humorless, which is worse."

"Much worse. I'm not saying they're always wrong necessarily, but humorless? A fatal flaw. Now, names!" Brooke commanded. "I need names."

"Alex Markham."

"Hmmm." Brooke fiddled with her long blond braid, which was coming loose, and then tossed it over her shoulder. "I know an Alexander Markham, must be the same. Reasonably cute, but politically in the deep woods. Not the brightest bulb on the Christmas tree. Sort of an alternative lawyer, the kind who doesn't even own a suit, even a bad one, it would be selling out to the System. Tree hugger. Rumored to be a cokehead. Does some pro bono cases, usually badly. Never seen him in a suit. Suits don't work well for hugging trees. Except lawsuits." Her eyes lit up. "You could write a 'Crimes of Fashion' column: Lawyers without suits! Stuffed shirts without the shirts! Briefcases without the briefs!"

"Stop, stop, I have unattractive pictures in my head." Nevertheless, Lacey pulled out her notebook and started making notes. "Markham's a cokehead, really? And why does the name Henderson Wilcox sound familiar to me? Expensive suit? A little too tight? Like his briefs?"

"Ah, Wilcox. Sure you've heard the name. He's the ne'er-do-well little brother of Senator Pendleton Wilcox, whom I think of affectionately as Senator Snidely Whiplash. Actually not so affectionately." Brooke mimed twirling a sinister mustache. "Square head, evil eyes, big teeth like a wolf?"

"Okay, now I know him. I've seen the political cartoons in the paper. You don't like Senator Whiplash?"

"I do like him, for comic relief. He's a major reactionary, and not in a good way. His bills never get out of committee. Although I have to make a point to remember his name is Wilcox. I've actually almost called him Senator Whiplash a couple of times."

Some of Cassandra's editorials against Senator Wilcox were coming back to Lacey, along with the words "fatuous" and "deluded." "Alex Markham apparently hates this Henderson Wilcox character because he left the nonprofit to go to a big K Street firm," Lacey said. "Went over to the Dark Side is the way I heard it."

"Wow, so Baby Whiplash made it out of the nonprofit salt mine. Interesting." Brooke mulled this over. "And here you are talking to the Dark Side over espresso! My take on why Henderson Wilcox had a job with Garrison of Gaia in the first place? Must have been a pity placement. Probably no one else would take him on right out of law school. They might not even have paid him, or not much. Another pro bono baby. Works for free, and worth every penny. Also maybe he wanted to throw a slap at his big brother by laboring for the loony left. Couldn't have been a matter of principle. Between you and me, from what I've seen of him he's not that bright and he has no real moral convictions. Runs in the family."

"If that's so, then why would a big law firm take him on now?"

"This new job? Well, big brother *is* a Senator. Probably big brother had enough embarrassment, got sick of little brother working for eco wackos. Had a word in someone's ear. Do a Senator a favor, get a favor back. Henderson is the embarrassing brother, you know the type. Politics is full of awkward siblings. Somebody has to take them in."

Lacey stretched. She ran her hands through her hair. "So what's your take on these two guys? Are they capable of assault?"

"Personally, Lacey, I think Markham has the political smarts of the tree toad that he loves so well. But his charm is razor thin. He's a snake. And in the case of poor Wilcox, the gene pool is just too shallow. I wouldn't believe a word either of them said, even under oath. But as for attacking someone in an alley with a blunt instrument? Neither one strikes me as particularly physical and aggressive. But who knows what evil lurks? Now, didn't you say there was another one?"

"A woman. She and Alex Markham and Cassandra are all housemates. And apparently Wilcox is an old boyfriend of Cassandra's who seems to be guilt-stricken that he wasn't there to protect her. Have you heard of Wendy Townsend?"

"Oh yes. The woman voted most likely to spend a year in a tree without a clue." Brooke snickered. "What was your impression?"

"She stunned me with a toxic cloud of perfume. What do you think of her?"

"The perfume!" Brooke made a face. "Gardenia, right? She's just like the rest of them, always proselytizing, always in your face, never gives it a rest for a second, can't see the forest for having a tree jammed up their— Well, you know. When you're in a meeting with her, you stay by the door so you can make a quick escape. And get a breath of fresh air. It's sad really. Wendy's always struck me as desperate, driving people away when she thinks she's doing just the opposite."

"Where do you know all these people from?"

"Oh, I thought I told you. Garrison of Gaia sued a client of ours. We won. They lost. End of story. Wasted a lot of money, theirs and the client's. Not that I consider paying massive attorneys' fees wasting money, actually, not when I'm the attorney."

"Is she capable of attacking someone physically?" Wendy Townsend had enjoyed making Lacey uncomfortable, particularly with her dog Bruno the killer beast, but that didn't make her an armed assailant.

"Wendy is pretty passionate. I think she has the temper for it, if not the strength. And she's, ah, what's the word? Unforgiving. She'll take a grudge to her grave."

"When I was at the hospital, both Markham and Wilcox demonstrated some manly snorting and pawing the ground over Cassandra." Lacey sighed. "Like a couple of bull moose bellowing over their prize doe."

"Over this shrill, mousy little woman you've told me about? Baffling. There must be something to her, or else the meek shall inherit the pheromones." Brooke and Lacey had often discussed the strange animosity between Washington men and Washington women, the problem of the apparently jammed pheromones in the Nation's Capital. Lacey was very grateful she had finally connected with Vic Donovan, and Brooke was gaga over her fellow conspiracy nut, Damon Newhouse. But it had taken time, way too much time, for romance to fall into place in their lives.

"Apparently after the attack everyone flew to the hospital to declare their undying love." Lacey shook her head. "They said they'd been there off and on since Friday night. A vigil. And then I get in to see her first. Made me Miss Popularity, I can tell you."

"Something funny is going on in this town," Brooke said. "Maybe this Cassandra Wentworth is a raving beauty and we just can't see it. Or maybe these guys have been affected by some sort of pheromone fog. Some secret chemical weapon. Weaponized female pheromones. I'll have to check with Damon."

"Very funny." Lacey laughed, one eyebrow arched skeptically.

"Okay, I'm reaching. But it's a theory." She swirled the last of the espresso in her cup. "What else are you hearing from this cult of Cassandra worshippers?"

"Cassandra volunteered at Garrison of Gaia for a while, Wendy told me. That's how they met, and they all seem to have slept with each other. Not sure about the two women, but after finding out Cassandra has actual friends, anything is possible. Cassandra has dated Markham and Henderson Wilcox, Wendy said she's been with Henderson, and she and Markham seem pretty tight. Friends with benefits. I haven't even mentioned the big killer dog that wanted to take a bite out of me for dinner."

"You're kidding." Brooke drained the rest of her sugared espresso and gazed morosely into the cup. "Maybe the pheromone jammers have been taken off the White House roof. Maybe now the CIA is pumping wild pheromones into jet plane chem trails over the District and it's all a mad CIA sex stimulant experiment run amuck."

"It's a theory, Brooke. That reminds me, I saw your mother last night." Lacey drank the last of her coffee.

"That's right, at the Nativity at that little church with the big name." Brooke grinned at Lacey. "I'm so sorry I wasn't there. This damn lawyering business really cuts into my personal time."

"I had no idea your mom and Vic's mom were such good friends."

"Yeah, apparently they just clicked. I think it's so cute. It didn't hit me that Nadine Donovan was *your* Vic's mom until Mom called me last night. Wow, small world! So did you find anything out? I thought maybe you went back to the neighborhood to search more alleys after you ditched the moms. You saw a child in a shepherd's robe. A shepherd's robe was stolen from the church. Two plus two, right?"

"So you do believe it's a child? Not an evil alien dwarf?" Lacey refrained from telling Brooke that the child was actually a girl. Let Damon Newhouse go off the deep end, Jasmine would be safer the less anyone knew about her. Maybe Damon would decide the child was a shape-shifter and could appear in any form to baffle observers.

"Of course I believe you, Lacey. Damon was just having a little fun with you. But I always listen to what Damon says, especially if he has an alternative theory. He has a lot of alternative information."

"Alternative to what? The truth?"

"Damon is my soul mate. He is a voice of wild possibility in the wilderness of mundane Washington rationality. I'm hurt."

"No, you're not." Lacey pulled on her jacket.

"Okay, not too hurt." Brooke stood up and gathered her things. "I'd love to stay, Lacey, but duty calls."

Lacey followed suit. Since Brooke was going back to work and couldn't give her a lift home, she wondered whether she could afford another cab ride back across the Potomac to Old Town or she'd have to take the Metro. Again.

"Damon didn't mention renegade circus midgets, did he? What's DeadFed going to say tomorrow? Brooke, are you listening to me?"

Back in her apartment half an hour later, Lacey changed her clothes and opened her Great-aunt Mimi's trunk. She took out some light blue wool fabric that had been stashed in the trunk decades before by her aunt. A *Life* magazine from the 1940s was open nearby, featuring schoolgirls in Washington with braided hair, wearing chesterfield coats with velvet collars. The girls looked smart and the coats looked warm. The faces were all well-scrubbed white faces. It didn't look at all like the Washington, D.C., that Lacey knew. It didn't look like the Washington of Jasmine Lee. Lacey wondered if the girl would call again. And if the offer of a new coat was enough. "Reel her in," Mac had ordered. *Fine, Mac, but how?*

Vic liked to tease Lacey about living a secret life inside Aunt Mimi's trunk, but he knew that rummaging through the trunk was something that took her out of the moment to a timeless place. It was part of her thinking process, allowing her troubles to simmer on the back burner until a solution bubbled up. Or not.

Her Aunt Mimi had stuffed the trunk with old clothes and memories, letters, clippings, photographs, surprises, mementos, the memorabilia of an unusual and adventurous life. And it was filled with patterns and unfinished suits and dresses from the late 1930s and 1940s. The dress patterns were classic styles with a touch of whimsy, fashions that flattered a woman's figure without torturing it. Lacey loved them, and she had several of the most striking patterns made into brand-new vintage clothes that fit her beautifully. How very clever, she thought, of

Aunt Mimi to leave them to her, the only woman in her family who would appreciate this gift. The wardrobe Lacey was creating from the inspirations she found in the trunk suited all of her moods, from romantic heroine to femme fatale.

The wonderful thing about clothes, Lacey often thought, was they always offered clues to a person's real character. A chance to display your own character—and a chance to peer into others', both what they want you to see and what they try to hide. And sometimes to find a clue to their state of mind, or their bank account, or occupation, or mood, or dreams. Aunt Mimi's trunk was a catalyst for Lacey's imagination, and happily it had supplied a good deal of her wardrobe too.

By this logic, there had to be something about the little shepherd girl's robe that could tell her something, she told herself. There were other clothes in the Nativity scene the girl could have taken, the more sumptuous robes of the wise men, the homespun blue of Mary. Or perhaps it was simpler than that. Maybe Jasmine took the little shepherd's robe because it was the only garment small enough to fit her, the only one left after others had plundered the stable. Was it just a leap of Lacey's romantic imagination that the shepherd's robe seemed unconsciously ironic, that a little lost lamb of a girl should choose to disguise herself as a shepherd?

Lacey picked up her cell phone and called Cassandra's number, hoping that Jasmine would recognize Lacey's phone number and answer. No one picked up.

chapter 22

Lacey had just settled in at her desk on Tuesday morning with a steaming mug of what passed for coffee at *The Eye* when her friend and hairstylist Stella Lake materialized in the newsroom.

Stella flung a copy of *The Eye Street Observer* down on Lacey's desk and pointed a bloodred, daggerlike fingernail at the article on the attack of Cassandra. "There you go again!" Stella wailed. "Involved in another crime of fashion and you don't call me? Your best friend in the whole world? Who has saved every last hair on your head over and over and over?" Stella looked closely at Lacey's hair. "Lace, aren't you conditioning?"

Lacey wondered why it was so easy for crazy people to get past the security desk, but she didn't say anything. Stella was one of her favorite crazy people, and Stella probably had the guard eating out of her hand. Or feasting his eyes on her cleavage. But this visit wasn't a good sign. It meant Stella was feeling neglected. It had been only a week or two since Lacey had her highlights refreshed and trimmed, but both she and Stella had been way too busy. They hadn't talked.

Stella stood before Lacey's desk, looking out of place. Too exotic for the newsroom. Her lacquered black hair shone sleek against her head. Her dark eyes were enhanced with false lashes and kohl. She was still channeling her silent film star look. Brass earrings that looked like clapping hands dangled from her ears. She wore a quilted red leather jacket and a black silk scarf around her neck. While the newsroom seemed to be washed in shades of watery sepia, Stella stood out in Technicolor.

"Good morning to you too, Stella."

Stella slipped off her coat, revealing a low-cut, V-neck silver sweater that fit like wallpaper. It showed off her "Girls" and provided a moment (or two) of fun for one of the sportswriters walking past. Stella smiled and gave him a big wink and a little wiggle before she refocused on Lacey.

"So just what do you have to say for yourself?"

"I didn't write the story," Lacey said.

"Yeah, but you're in it, right here. '*Eye Street* reporter Lacey Smithsonian alerted the police,'" Stella read. "This is a fashion crime. Your territory. Our territory! And I see your coworker, that Miss Smartypants I-hate-Christmas-sweaters-and-bah-humbug-let's-kill-Rudolph-the-Red-Nosed-Reindeer, gets cracked in the noggin with a handy weapon, possibly a candy cane? And she's found wearing a Christmas sweater? Which I admit sounds pretty tacky, although I personally adore Christmas. And someone tells me the sweater belongs to your Miss Cucumbers, or whatever her name is. And you don't call me to *tell* me about all this? Just what do you have to say for yourself, Lacey? Are we still BFFs or what?"

"It's Pickles, Stel, not Cucumbers," Lacey said. "Felicity Pickles. And of course we're still BFFs."

"Pickles, Cucumbers, Zucchinis, whatever. What I mean is, Lacey, how can you expect me to go to the salon and put a little zing in everyone's day and not know what is going on with you? I am your stylist, your friend, your confidante." Stella leaned over Lacey's desk and drummed her nails. "I shoulda known these things."

Lacey looked at the woman who dared call Miss Cucumbers's Christmas sweaters tacky. "This isn't a case I can do anything with, Stella. The police are investigating. All I'm doing is—"

"All you're doing is asking questions. Broken record. Ho hum." Stella mock-yawned. "I have a reputation to uphold, Lacey. You are an important news source for me. And I haven't heard from you in like *days!*"

"Well, you haven't called me either," Lacey said defensively.

"Details! You are hung up on details, missy, and let me tell you something, you are not going to get me offtrack on why I came to see you. Which is: You been ignoring your friends."

"What about you?" Lacey said. "New man in your life? No time for your friends?"

"Stick to the subject and anyway, what's the matter with

you?" Stella pointed to the mug of coffee sitting on Lacey's desk. "You lose your manners or something?"

"Sorry, Stel, come with me to the kitchen. But I have to warn you, it's bad for you. Newsroom coffee? Poisonous. Brewed from newsprint and printer's ink. And bile."

"Oh please, Lace, we got you beat at Stylettos. Who knows how many chemicals get mixed in with our brew? Half and half: Half java, half perm solution."

Lacey escorted her friend to the newsroom's kitchen. She was sleepy, and she was glad she'd worn a suit today. It was quick and easy, one of her Brenda Starr/Lois Lane looks, and it would pass muster for her lunch with Jeffrey today. In forest green wool gabardine from the 1940s with a black velvet collar, it was shapely and fit well. It didn't require a fussy blouse or too much thought. No nerve-wracking episode of *What Will I Wear Tomorrow?!* She'd found just the right dark green pumps to go with the suit. But she caught herself thinking that maybe she should switch to more of a Wonder Woman look. The magical gold bracelets and lasso were definitely accessories Lacey Smithsonian could get behind.

Stella followed Lacey, the heels of her tall black boots clicking on the old linoleum floor of the newsroom's tiny kitchen. Lacey rummaged around for a clean cup that wasn't chipped. She found one in the back of the cupboard, rinsed it out, and poured the now crisp-smelling coffee in the cup.

"Cream and sugar, please, Lace. Lots. You know how I like it. So as I was saying, Lacey." Stella added even more sugar and stirred it with a plastic spoon. "You ain't off the hook yet. You have all but ignored me, and yet I have been defending you."

Lacey rolled her eyes. "Defending me from what?"

"That editorial on Christmas sweaters? That it turns out your Little Miss Crabby-Negative-Person wrote? I knew you didn't write that snotty thing. You can do snarky, but it's always snarky with style and soul, you know? This sweater thing was just plain mean, not like you at all, except when you're neglecting your friends, like recently. Do I have to find out everything that is going on in this town from DeadFed dot com?"

"That's not news, Stella, it's science fiction." Lacey sniffed her coffee and put it down. "And it's gotten worse. It used to be just—"

"Like I said to my three o'clock perm yesterday, Lacey

Smithsonian can be snarky and smart-alecky, but she's not *that* lowdown mean."

"You think I'm mean?"

"We're all a little mean. Gives us character." Stella grinned and sipped her coffee. "Hey, this isn't bad. Anyway, as I was saying, if we weren't a little mean sometimes, we wouldn't even be breathing. But you know what I'm talking about. Like really mean, like this Cassandra person. What is her deal?"

Lacey led the way back to her desk. Stella grabbed the Death Chair and wheeled it up close, tracing her scarlet fingernails on the face of the skull and crossbones. She plopped down on it. No mere Death Chair could spook Stella Lake.

"What do you want to know?" Lacey settled back down.

"Tell me about this weird little man in the alley who got away. DeadFed says it's some kind of conspiracy against the freedom of the press or something. Or else aliens."

"Stella. Please tell me you know nearly every word on DeadFed is complete fiction, don't you? Even 'and' and 'the.' " Stella laughed. "I'm surprised you'd even read it, knowing that it's run by Brooke's lunatic boyfriend."

"That's why I'm here. For the truth. And I wouldn't have to resort to coming over if you kept in touch better. I want you to come to the salon."

"I don't need anything done right now." Lacey ruffled her hair. "See? I'm using your conditioner. My hair is drowning in your conditioner."

It was Stella's turn to yank on Lacey's hair with her practiced eye. She was a maniac about conditioner. "I'm not talking about your hair. Your hair looks great, thanks to you know who. But you gotta come see the salon! The salon is decorated. The tree is up, the light-up menorah is so cute, and we even have a Kwanzaa thingy, whatever it is. We are totally socially and politically and holidazically correct."

" 'Holidazically'? And the menorah is a nice touch, Stel."

"I'm half and half, you know. Half Jewish and half Christian and all fabulous, so I get to celebrate everything. I always get lots of great presents, me and the Girls." Stella was as excited as a kid. "Have you bought me a present yet, Lacey? I posted my wish list on my blog, in case you need ideas. I told you about my blog, didn't I?"

Lacey covered her eyes with her hands. "Wait a minute, a blog? You have a blog?"

"Duh! My daily observations and innermost thoughts! It's Stellariffic. I'll e-mail you the link. You're so last century, Lace. But about my present? No prob. We'll go shopping together. It'll be awesome."

"Stella, every time I go shopping with you, I spend money. Lots and lots of money. Too much money. And that's just on me, much less on you."

The stylist gave her a wide-eyed look. "And this is a problem *why* exactly?" Before Lacey could explain that yes, it was a problem, Stella's cell phone rang. She dug it out of her purse. "Oh, jeez, Lace! Look at the time." She pushed a button and tossed the phone back into her enormous black bag. She took a final gulp of the nasty coffee. "I gotta run, but I want to see you soon, at the salon. We'll talk. And then we'll shop."

"I'll call, I promise," Lacey said.

"You'll tell me *everything.*" It was a command, not a request.

Lacey would have escorted her to the elevator, but her own phone rang.

"Get the phone, Lacey, I know my way out, past the cute guy with the messy desk. He's totally in love with the Girls."

"Go torture him then."

Stella waved and grabbed her coat on the run. "Call me!"

The phone call turned out to be a hang-up from a number she didn't recognize. Funny how often that happened, Lacey thought. No one really wanted to talk with the fashion reporter, they just wanted to leave her messages.

"Lacey, can we talk?" This voice wasn't on the phone, it belonged to Felicity, who rarely spoke to her except to tempt her with something fattening. She was wearing a new dark green Christmas sweater that featured round sequined ornaments with a pair of black slacks. Lacey was glad to see that the Cassandra incident hadn't diminished her innate spirit. She had crossed the aisle to Lacey's desk and was offering her a piece of hot chocolate pudding cake topped with peppermint pieces. "Here, take a fork too."

This couldn't be good, Lacey thought. *Beware of Felicity bearing gifts. And she's baking again!* But the rich aroma filled the air and her stomach was rumbling. She reached for the pudding cake and hesitantly took the offered plastic fork.

"This smells good."

"It's for the Sunday food section. 'A peppermint twist on holiday fare.'" Felicity was evidently trying out phrases for her food column. "Or maybe: 'Hot, chocolate, and comforting. More than pudding. More than cake. Bake yourself a pudding cake.'"

"Thanks, Felicity." Lacey took a bite. "Delicious."

Felicity looked as if she needed more than food to comfort her. "I know we're not exactly friends," she began, but then her nerve failed her, and she dashed back to her desk for her own piece of today's featured dessert. She pulled her chair over to Lacey's desk, avoiding the Death Chair, and nibbled at the delicacy.

Lacey took another bite. The peppermint twist melted in her mouth. It was amazingly good. But would it be good enough for Vic's mother at Christmas? Tough call. This dessert had to be presented still hot from the oven, not made the day before. Lacey realized she'd lost track of what Felicity was saying. *More than pudding, more than cake, bake yourself a—*

"I know we're not exactly friends, Lacey, but, well, the police called me in again." Felicity started over. "They accused me of all sorts of terrible things. They aren't nice to me like that nice Detective Lamont who comes to see you." Her lip quivered. "How could they think I would attack someone, even Cassandra? I'm not a violent person."

"This is very tasty, Felicity. Did they come right out and accuse you?"

"No, they just browbeat me. Where was the sweater, where was it the last time I saw it, did I hate Cassandra, what was this thing about Sweatergate, can I prove I was where I said I was? It was horrible. Where did I get the candy cane? What candy cane? They didn't even offer me a cup of coffee."

Worse if they had, Lacey thought. *I've had their coffee— Police brutality.* "I'm sure everything will work out." Lacey didn't necessarily believe it. "But it would be better if you had someone to verify where you were on Friday afternoon."

"Mac said you'd help me."

"Excuse me?" Lacey put her plate down. So Mac had promised both Cassandra and Felicity that she would help? Without her permission? Behind her back? *Of course he did.*

"I'm scared, Lacey. If you need to know anything, I'm here to help," Felicity said. "Harlan too, anything you need. Let me know what you come up with, okay?" She sighed and retreated to her own desk, the very picture of woe. "And if you could be quick about it, that would be great."

Lacey stormed into Mac's office. "Were you planning on telling me you'd committed my time and efforts to help *both* of them? Do you just like the surprise element of it all? Or did you do it just to get Felicity baking again?"

He lifted his own plate of hot chocolate pudding cake and saluted her with his fork. He had the nerve to chuckle. "I had to tell them something, didn't I? You're the one ruining Christmas. I was just trying to save it. And it's your fault anyway, Smithsonian."

She slapped her hands on his desk. "My fault! How in the name of heaven is this my fault?"

"I don't mean the attack on Wentworth. I mean in general, sticking your nose into murder cases." He paused for breath and an expansive gesture. "And then somehow you just stumble over the killer, don't ask me how. It's a gift."

"I do not stumble!" She stood ramrod straight and folded her arms. "And there is no killer here!"

"You know what I mean."

"Do I?"

He concentrated on the pudding cake. "Besides, if it turns out to be one of Cassandra's hate mailers, we've already got the police on it. That's not what I want you to do."

"Hate mailers." She took a seat. "You mean one in particular? You have a suspect?"

"We're working on it, Smithsonian." He polished off the cake with a satisfied lip smack. "Anytime we get some whack job writing a crazy letter or an e-mail or posting something threatening on the newspaper's blog, we put it in the file. Cassandra called these the 'puffy letters.' Hand delivered, big envelopes. Nutcases, it seems, are rarely concise. They tend to ramble."

"Yeah." She had gotten her share of weird letters. She usually handed them to Mac.

"Your file is not as fat as Cassandra's, but it'll do."

"Huh. I thought you just tossed them in the shredder. Any clues?"

Mac downed his coffee. "They don't generally attach their real names or business cards. She does have one particularly nasty nonadmirer, so we gave the cops her file. Just today. Might get them off Felicity's case. And if he shows up again, building security will detain him. Chances are he's the assailant. Johnson thinks so."

"So that's it?" It was an odd feeling, but oddly freeing. The cops might take care of it after all. "We just wait for the cops to collar this guy? End of story?"

"No, we don't just wait! I'm interested in this kid of yours in the alley. The cops are not going to be any help with this kid. That's the story I want you on. That's great human interest stuff, especially in the holiday season. If we can find the shepherd girl it'll be good for the paper. And the best thing for the kid, the very best thing. That's the main thing."

"She hasn't called me back since yesterday. I've tried calling the number. She doesn't pick up."

"Let's hope she does, and soon, Lacey. The cops get hold of her and put her in the system, she's got no one to look out for her. Except the system." He snorted.

"Last I heard they were still looking for an Hispanic boy. What if I can find Jasmine's school and try to spot her when school lets out?"

"If she's homeless or close to it, she probably isn't even going to school! It's like this, Smithsonian: She's not a criminal. Maybe she takes something small, a robe off a statue in the stable. She's just hungry, or she's cold. But if she gets caught by that long arm of the law, she still goes to detention, some juvenile facility, some ugly, scary, soul-killing place. You're a kid, you got no voice. Maybe she'll go to a foster home. Some are okay, some are like a game of musical chairs. Too late, got no chair for you, kid! You get bumped. It's a hell of a life for a kid."

"Sounds like you know a lot about this sort of thing, like personal experience."

"Yup, I got some personal experience." Mac didn't elaborate. "We have to find Jasmine Lee. Find a place for her."

Lacey stood up. Talking about Jasmine just made her feel helpless. "I have no idea where to start. Except to wait for my cell phone to ring."

"Funny thing about my wife. You know Kim," Mac said. "She can't stand the thought of kids out on the street with no home. Put Christmas into the mix and she broods about it. I don't like my wife to brood. Bring that girl in. Make it happen. Too many kids fall through the cracks. Find this one, before she does too."

"Make it happen?" She wasn't sure she could do anything at all. "I'll see what I can do, Mac."

"Do better than that, Smithsonian."

LaToya Crawford was waiting for her outside Mac's office, with a tale of outrage over Peter Johnson's behavior. Apparently he was trying to interrogate everyone in the office who had worn a Santa cap at the National Press Club the night of the party.

"I think he's losing it," LaToya said. "He's *this* close." She squeezed two fingers together. "I mean Johnson starts babbling, insulting reporters, yours truly included, accusing editors of assault, and then he launches into something about Dostoyevsky's *Crime and Punishment*. Nobody knows what he's talking about. He doesn't either. He just thinks it's smart or something to throw in Dostoyevsky! Then he drops Herodotus on us, like an H-bomb, like we're all supposed to understand he's some brilliant-ass reporter who knows who Herodotus is, and I mean, Smithsonian, what the hell does Herodotus have to do with the fact that someone got pissed off enough to take down Cassandra Wentworth in the alley the other night? Not a damn thing, that's what."

Lacey would have said something, but at that moment she looked up and saw Peter Johnson strutting in her direction. Lacey looked to LaToya with a silent plea for help.

"Oh no, girl! It's your turn. I been on the grill already. He says another word to me I'm gonna hurt him. You are on your own with Mr. Herodotus Dostoyevsky, and watch out he don't pull Plato and Aristotle on you too. I got work to do."

LaToya had nailed Johnson. He was one of those Washingtonians who believed he was always the smartest person in the room. It never dawned on them that everyone else in the room thought they were the smartest ones too. It could be so exhausting, Lacey thought, to be caught in the same room with so many smarty-pantses.

Johnson ignored Felicity, and she ignored Johnson. But she made a show of offering LaToya a big piece of pudding cake. Lacey could see Johnson was irritated. Felicity's return to the land of pudding cake was not something to be missed. Johnson hissed at Lacey under his breath.

"So Smithsonian, come up with anything brilliant yet?"

"How could I, Peter, I'm not a genius Hill reporter like some people."

Mac passed by, heading for a coffee refill. Johnson shut his mouth and sidled on past. Mac detoured to Lacey's desk, eyeing Johnson's retreating back.

"Did you tell Johnson to interrogate the whole damned staff?"

"Ha. You think Peter Johnson would do anything I suggested? Really, Mac. No, he's working on his own theory. The assailant is close to home. He's one of us in the office. He's the monster among us. Or it's the man in the moon, and he wore a Santa cap on Friday night. Could even be you, Mac."

Mac made guttural sounds in his throat. The eyebrows were threatening. "And what's your theory, Smithsonian?"

"I know less than anyone and you want my theory?" She stared at her computer screen. It was unhappily empty. "How about, it's deadline and I don't have a column?"

Mac sighed. "You got a topic?"

"I'm thinking about it." She turned her attention to her work as he marched back to his office. The holiday season was looming over Lacey like an ominous thundercloud. There was too much to do; she didn't even have time to do her laundry or go Christmas shopping or shop for new clothes, much less make the perfect dessert for Vic's mom while saving Christmas for Cassandra and Felicity and a little girl in a shepherd's robe. And a partridge in a pear tree. Besides, what on earth would she wear to go shopping? Everything she owned was at the cleaners. Oh yeah, and she had a job to do.

Merry Christmas.

FASHION BITES

It's an Organization Town, Right?
So Get Organized for the Holidays!

The holidays! Too much to do, too little time? Do you feel like the last broken toy in the bottom of the stocking? Paint chipped, smile lopsided, stockings sagging, wardrobe that makes Raggedy Ann look well dressed? *Oh, not even that good?*

Has your closet come to resemble a tossed salad? Does "grab bag" define your fashion statement? Maxed out your to-do list in November and never caught up? You're not alone. Feel like it's the forty-fifth of December and you still haven't started your Christmas shopping? Wish a genie would pop out of a lamp every morning and hand you a giant Ziploc bag with your outfit of the day? Me too.

How do they do it, those elegantly garbed and groomed women you see on Wisconsin Avenue? They have help, obviously. They have chauffeurs and cooks and housekeepers and wardrobe consultants. Or else they don't have jobs or kids. Or their kids have chauffeurs and cooks and housekeepers and wardrobe consultants. So how do we, ordinary Washington women that we are, get to be as put together as *they* are?

Simple. We resort to the ordinary Washington woman's bag of tricks. This is an organization town. Whether Washington ever gets anything done may be a debate for the historians, but at least we are *organized*. Apply those organizational skills to your wardrobe. After all, you're a Washington woman! You can shine at the breakfast meeting, power through that ten a.m. presentation, wipe out six errands at lunch, smile through the board meeting, and still glow tonight at the cocktail party. Right?

So what's so difficult about penciling in your basic black suit and red silk blouse for Monday, and the chocolate slacks and twin set and pearls for Tuesday? You're already planning ahead for meetings, appointments, events, entertainment. Why not plan ahead for the outfits that best suit them all? Your tools are already at hand, whether fountain pen and paper or digital, Day-Timer or BlackBerry. Some women plan a weekly dinner menu for twenty. You just have to plan the weekly wardrobe menu for one: *you*.

Some examples to kick off your plan for the week:

- Monday, the board meeting. You'll look professional: Choose the black power suit, the one with the gold buttons. The gold blouse. The black heels. And that funky gold pin you inherited, just for dash.
- Tuesday, holiday shopping after dinner. Comfortable clothes you can move in, but that still get you in the door at Gucci. Your navy pants and sweater, a paisley scarf to tie it all together, low-heeled shoes to sprint down the aisles at the mall.
- Wednesday, the festive event after work. Your reliable coat dress with fancy buttons. Perk it up with gold button earrings and bracelet. Bring a change of shoes in patent leather. Wear the same heels all day and all night? *Not you*.

Plan ahead! You're already planning the events, so strategize your looks to suit. Create comfortable and stylish outfits for those meetings and parties and shopping trips, so you won't have to reach into that last-minute grab bag called your closet.

Finally, if all else fails, take a tip from Wonder Woman and switch to Plan B: Be strong, be brave, and don't forget your bulletproof bracelets. They'll never let you down.

chapter 23

It was a drizzly December day in the Capital City, cold enough to make people want to burrow inside, dreaming of a white Christmas, hoping for a snowstorm to shut the city down and give them an unplanned day off. However, snowstorms didn't count at *The Eye Street Observer*. News never takes a day off, and newspapers do not close for the weather. Every winter, management would send a memo reminding staff of the "We never close" policy.

As Lacey headed out the door into the cold she thought of Stella. She wondered how her girliest friend managed to stay warm with all the cleavage-baring outfits she wore. Stella could find a way to show off "the Girls" muffled in a down parka from nose to toes at the South Pole. Not Lacey. Forging out into the weather to catch a cab to meet Jeffrey Bentley Holmes for lunch, Lacey chose a cheerful peacock-blue raincoat to combat the wet gray weather. Very few of the drab drizzly December denizens of the District were following her colorful lead.

The cab dropped her off at Weatherfields, the new restaurant on Fourteenth Street. She breezed through the front doors behind three beige trench coats—that is, three men in beige trench coats, who looked like they had just come from a Senate hearing and couldn't wait to bore someone.

The restaurant was all blond wood and creamy interiors, and a clear four-sided gas fireplace was blazing away in the center of the room. It was very clubby and cozy, but it couldn't calm her apprehension. The host was efficient and courteous. He took her raincoat and led her to the booth where Jeffrey sat. It had a nice view of the front windows and all the beige trench coats walking through the door.

Jeffrey stood up as she approached the table, reaching over and offering his hand. Lacey hadn't forgotten how much she liked Jeffrey, she had simply filed it on a top shelf somewhere in the back of her brain. She had never really expected to see him again, but his smile told her he had very much hoped to see her.

"Lacey, it's wonderful to see you," he said without a trace of irony, which put her at ease. His smile was warm. He helped her out of her jacket and waited until she sat in the chair the host held for her. She had once been the messenger of very bad news for him and for the entire Bentley clan, but if he had been angry with her then, there was no sign of it now. Jeffrey looked wonderful as always, his perfectly cut sleek blond hair, his casually elegant and expensive-looking gray slacks and navy blazer. By the House of Bentley, no doubt.

"I understand you're not available for dates, Lacey. Except for lunch. Therefore, I take it your status has changed?"

"There is this guy." Lacey fiddled with her napkin and laid it in her nap.

"There always is, isn't there, and this particular guy would be named Donovan, wouldn't he?"

"Yes, it's Vic Donovan."

"Right. I met him at the Bentley ball in September. You disappeared and he was looking for you. About that time— about the time everything was happening." Jeffrey leaned forward, resting his forearms on the table. "He was ready to tear the place apart looking for you. I had a feeling he might be the guy."

She smiled at him. "You're very perceptive."

"That's me." He smiled back and casually picked up the menu. "You'll let me know if that status changes, won't you?"

"You'd be the first, I'm sure. Probably the only one on the list." She laughed at the thought of men standing in line for her. So unlikely in Washington, D.C., she reflected, a place where so many men were truly, madly, deeply in love only with themselves. And maybe their security clearances.

"I'd be in front of a long line, I'm sure," Jeffrey said gallantly. "You might be surprised. But I wouldn't be."

"Really? How'd you get to be so insightful?"

His lips played with a smile. "In my family, you have to read the subtext beneath all those calm collected Waspy exteriors. Or they eat you alive like piranhas."

The Bentleys had made their name in classic haute couture fashion with a liberal use of luxurious fabrics. Jeffrey's uncle was the famous Hugh Bentley, a legendary designer. But there were skeletons in their closets, and in their ancient steamer trunks, which had been disinterred vividly in articles bylined "Lacey Smithsonian" for *The Eye Street Observer*.

"Ah, family subtext. We all have some of that."

He put the menu down. "You look good, Lacey."

"So do you, Jeffrey. It's nice to see you. Last I heard you were in retreat. Thinking deep thoughts, no doubt."

"Not so much. At the monastery, it was a luxury not to think. Just to be."

"Tell me about it?"

"It's an uncluttered place, stark and beautiful. No place to hide from yourself. A chance to decompress after all that trauma in the family. I did some carpentry for the monks. That was fun and relaxing, centering. Built some shelves, lots of bookshelves. They get a lot of reading done there."

Jeffrey Bentley Holmes didn't look like someone who made a living swinging a hammer. He looked like a beautiful male model in a Bentley's sportswear ad, a role he'd also played for his family. But Lacey had seen his carpentry and design skills at the Bentley Museum of Fashion, in the District near the National Building Museum. He designed the wing of the museum that featured the Bentley family's permanent collection of designer clothing from the 1940s to the present, and he had also been the store designer and head builder for the Bentley retail stores. Jeffrey told her once he far preferred working with wood over celebrity photographers and temperamental models.

"And now you're back in Washington," Lacey said. "The city that fashion forgot?"

"Not just forgot. The city that ran screaming from." He tilted his head slightly to indicate a fashion disaster at a table across the aisle. Lacey looked up.

Ouch. Who let the Congresswoman from California wear loud plaid tights with a mustard yellow suit? Lacey wondered. *Don't Congresswomen have people to keep them from doing these things?*

"The reason I'm here? Seems there's this little public relations mess. Uncle Hugh stealing some designs long ago," Jeffrey said. He smiled. "You may have read about it."

"I seem to recall something about that." Lacey had in fact written those stories, a series of scoops that did not endear her to the rest of the Bentley family. Had they joined them for lunch, they would now be ordering Lacey's head on a plate. She thought it was a miracle that Jeffrey held no grudge.

"You didn't create the situation, Lacey. You simply shone a light on it, one that should have been turned on brightly years ago. Now, however, the family wants me to wallow in their misery with them, to try to mitigate the damage." He settled back in the cushioned booth. "I helped drag them through the muck, so I get to try to wash some mud off the family name."

"You've been called back into action for the Bentley empire?"

"I thought resigning from the board would get me off the hook. But now the family seems to think I'm the only one presentable enough to meet the public."

"Because of me." She met his eyes. "I'm so sorry, Jeffrey."

"Don't be. Because of you, Lacey, I learned some hard truths that I needed to know."

"You're not angry with me?"

"Did I come here to poison you?" He laughed. "I hope not. They tell me this is a great restaurant, I'd hate to ruin their reputation."

"But your family—"

"Sadly, you are not their favorite person. But you are one of mine."

Thankfully the waiter chose that moment to appear. He took their orders and departed quietly. Lacey and Jeffrey were silent for a moment. Jazz was playing softly somewhere.

"But why are you in Washington and not in New York? And what's this fund-raiser you mentioned?"

"According to our PR firm, the Bentleys must perform a public mea culpa."

"And that is?"

"Good works. The specific project hasn't been decided upon yet. The Bentley Foundation has not hitherto been known for its actual charity work. Lots of tax breaks, but not much real charity. And please don't use that quote. So the Bentleys are now going to be giving some healthy charitable grants to some worthy nonprofit organizations. Or I will kick some butt."

"You're not really a Bentley, are you? Were you secretly adopted?"

He grinned. "That's the nicest thing anyone's said to me all day. Maybe ever."

Charity work sounded like a good fit for Jeffrey, Lacey thought. He wasn't like the rest of the Bentleys. He wasn't consumed by greed or fear. *A changeling.*

Lacey gazed out the front windows. Rain was falling steadily, but she suddenly felt so at peace sitting there with Jeffrey. Buildings glimpsed through the drizzle looked stately and austere. Multicolored taxi cabs and black Lincoln limousines picked up and dropped off passengers. The restaurant's front doors opened at regular intervals, letting in waves of chill wind.

Brooke's own favorite Snidely Whiplash, also known as Senator Pendleton Wilcox, and his younger brother, Henderson Wilcox, suddenly blew through the door and handed their trench coats to the host. They shook off the rain, wiped their feet on the mats, and deposited their wet umbrellas in a large brass cylinder. Here were two of Brooke's least favorite political characters, come to life before Lacey's very eyes. Lacey was sorry Brooke wasn't around to give her a play-by-play commentary.

Wendy Townsend of Garrison of Gaia trailed along behind them, wearing a dark green slicker and shedding water on the carpet. She glumly refused an offer from the host to hang it up for her, a grown-up grumpy Wednesday Addams carrying her storm cloud with her. The Wilcox brothers ignored her. Were they just inconsiderate snobs, Lacey wondered, or had they really forgotten she was there? Perhaps she'd invited herself along and they were ignoring her as punishment? Wendy seemed about as welcome in this clubby atmosphere as a third-party candidate. Lacey wondered if she were blind to the hostile undercurrents that were so apparent to her. How did this fit in with Wendy's "friends with benefits" story about her relationship with Henderson? Jeffrey followed Lacey's gaze.

"Sorry, Jeffrey. Just people watching. A dedicated follower of fashion, you know."

"Understood. The Senator is always a good show. If you like train wrecks. He'll be there tomorrow night, if you're interested."

"Really? I guess you need some heavyweights." Few Washington politicians could really be classified as true celebrities on their own merits, but a Senator was always welcome at a fund-raiser.

"Exactly. The event is to announce the program and meet with representatives of various organizations who will be vying for the money. Leaving out politicians who pander for cash, of course. We already take care of them."

"You contribute to Senator Wilcox?"

"Not I, no way, but he and Uncle Hugh go way back. They have a lot in common, and the Senator is tireless when it comes to fund-raising. He'll get to rub more Bentley elbows. And maybe Bentley wallets. It's all about access. There'll be a full house."

"How much money is at stake in the grants?"

"Twenty million is in the pot right now. Broken into up to ten grants."

As if blessed with exceedingly keen hearing when sums of money were mentioned, Senator Pendleton Wilcox spied Jeffrey and stepped smartly over to them, leaving his brother and Wendy sitting at their table across the restaurant and scowling at each other. The elder Wilcox put his hand out and a good imitation of a smile on his face.

"Bentley, good to see you," the Senator said.

"Senator." Jeffrey stood and shook hands.

"Don't stand on my account, my boy." Old Snidely acknowledged Lacey's presence with a very slight nod, but he spoke only to Jeffrey. After all, Jeffrey was the potential contributor. Lacey was politically a nobody. "Looking forward to your big event tomorrow night. The Willard, isn't it?"

The Willard. Of course the Bentleys' event would be held somewhere fabulous, Lacey thought, and the stately Willard Hotel, just down the street, where the term "lobbyist" supposedly was first coined, certainly fit the bill.

The Senator seemed quite willing to stand there and jabber at Jeffrey all day. In Washington everyone knows that one's own time is valuable and the other person's time is not. The trick is to monopolize the conversation while eyeing the door for the arrival of someone more important to jabber at. But Jeffrey cut the Senator short with charm.

"So nice talking with you, Senator, I won't keep you from

your lunch. See you tomorrow." Senator Snidely shook hands again and lumbered ponderously back to his table, seeming confident of his next campaign contribution.

"Jeffrey, what kind of projects are you looking to fund?" Lacey asked.

"Nonprofits. The foundation board will battle it out," Jeffrey said. "Anything from arts groups, theatres, art galleries, to Boys and Girls Clubs, to entertainment. Has to burnish the Bentley name too, of course."

"You're the white sheep of the family," Lacey said.

"Not my doing, but I'm glad you think so. Who knew a spoiled rich kid could be saved by a small town cop on the beat?"

Jeffrey had told her the story of a mixed-up teenage brat who had totaled his mother's Mercedes, and a cop named Mike O'Leary who had taken him in hand and become a mentor and friend. The contrast between the Irish cop and the Bentleys, who were so proud of being WASPs of a certain social class, was vast. But Lacey thought the friendly O'Learys sounded like a much happier family.

"From what I heard, O'Leary wasn't just any cop. But what do you want the money to accomplish?"

"I don't know yet. O'Leary will have some ideas. I put him on the project. He's on the Foundation board now."

"O'Leary on the Bentley Foundation board? You *are* the white sheep of the family! Do you get a vote too, along with the black sheep? And the wolves?"

"Of course I do, or I wouldn't be here." Jeffrey's smile was engaging. "Lacey, even if you won't come as my date, why not come anyway and give me your opinion on the flora and fauna?"

She glanced across the room. Wendy Townsend was desperately trying to make conversation and gesturing wildly, while the Wilcox brothers ignored her and studied their menus. Lacey was puzzled. Why did they even drag her along? Just to ignore her?

"Like the Wilcox brothers? And is Garrison of Gaia going to be there?"

"With both hands out. GOG is on the list, as well as a host of public interest and environmental groups, Congressmen, Senators like our friend Wilcox, an ambassador or two. The usual suspects. But a Smithsonian would really class up the joint."

She laughed, delighted, but then was struck by a less pleasant thought. "What about your family? Your Uncle Hugh or your cousin Aaron? They're not coming, are they?"

"Don't worry." He put his hand over hers. "Meeting the public bores them senseless, giving money away makes their stomachs turn, Washington gives them hives after that fiasco the last time they were here, and Hugh has sworn never to leave Manhattan again. And they're smart enough not to mention you to me."

"Good to know." She withdrew her hand as gently as she could.

"Bring Vic Donovan if you want. I'd just like to see some friendly faces there, or the whole event will be interminable." Jeffrey pulled a creamy envelope from his inside jacket pocket. "You're already on the list. Your official invitation."

"Wow. Thank you." A fancy event at the Willard was very tempting. And it was business cocktail, not black tie, so maybe she could convince Vic to come. He wouldn't have to wear his tux, even though Lacey thought he looked so yummy in it. A Bentley event would certainly be good for a column or two.

They were interrupted by the arrival of their lunch. Spinach and chicken crepes for her, salmon for the relentlessly healthy Jeffrey. But before Lacey could pick up her fork, her cell phone rang.

"I'm sorry," she said, digging it out of her purse. "I may have to take this. Please start without me." She didn't recognize the number on the screen. "Hello?"

"Lacey?" The voice belonged to the little shepherd. "Lacey, I need *two* coats."

"Jasmine? You're not using Cassandra's cell phone?"

"Her phone stopped working. Cell phones don't work good around here anyway. But I know your number. I'm good with numbers, you know."

Lacey gestured to Jeffrey that maybe she should leave the table to finish the conversation. "Don't be silly," he whispered. "Sit." He took a forkful of salmon.

"Where are you, Jasmine?"

"I need two coats," the girl insisted.

"Okay. Two coats. Why two?" What was the girl up to now? Building a winter wardrobe?

"I need one for Lily Rose. I have to take care of Lily Rose!" Her voice expressed all the martyrdom a twelve-year-old could manage. "And I have to do *everything*."

"Who is Lily Rose?"

"My sister! You know that."

"No. I didn't know that," Lacey said. "You didn't mention her before." There was a huffy pause. "Really, you didn't."

"Well, Lily Rose is my sister!" Jasmine sighed loudly. "A blue coat and a pink coat. Lily Rose likes *pink*." From the way she sighed, Lacey assumed Lily Rose had to be a younger sister. "But the blue one has to be bigger."

"And you'll give me the shepherd's robe, right? In exchange?" Jeffrey was looking at Lacey quizzically. She covered the phone with her hand. "I'm negotiating a fashion deal," she whispered.

"Are you winning?" he asked.

"I'm getting hammered. Twelve-year-olds are murder." She shifted the phone back.

"I'll give you the robe," Jasmine said reluctantly, "but I need two coats. Okay?"

"Okay, Jasmine, it's a deal. What size?"

"I don't know, you saw me. And I've been growing. I'm almost thirteen, you know."

I don't know anything about little girl sizes! "What about your sister?"

"She's lots smaller. She's a baby. She's only ten."

"Jasmine, why don't you have a warm coat?"

"Because!" Lacey was obviously an idiot. "Because they kicked us out and threw everything we had on the street. We only got to keep a few things. Miss Charday, she took the TV. She said she'll keep it for us. It's a good TV."

"But where is your mother? Was she there when this happened?" Jasmine was on her own wavelength and didn't answer. "They threw out your clothes? Who threw them out?"

"Yeah, everything. And the people outside were stealing our stuff. Rotten people."

"You were evicted?" Her heart sank. Lacey occasionally came upon the remains of an apartment eviction while walking in D.C. Once she had seen a woman frantically trying to keep passersby from taking her clothes and her furniture, yelling it was hers, leave it alone, she would get it all moved. It wasn't stopping a crowd of people from taking their pick of her belongings.

"That's what they call it. Evicted. We had to put our clothes in garbage bags, but I didn't get them all. It happened before we got home from school."

"Can you tell me where your mother is?"

"She's coming back! She's just gone right now."

"She's gone? Where are you staying? Do you have any family to stay with? You have to get to someplace safe."

"But we only have our mom, and then she won't know that we got thrown out and she won't know where we are! So I have to stay close." The words tumbled out of Jasmine, and her panic was contagious. Lacey tried to catch her breath.

"Where did she go?"

"I don't know! She's done it before so I know she's coming back. She is! She has this little problem, this problem with drugs, and she drinks too much, but she's a good person and she's my mom and she's a good mom and she's going to come back for us!"

"All right, just be calm, Jasmine, everything will be okay. Where are you staying?" Lacey's stomach fluttered at the frantic note in the girl's voice.

"We're okay. I'm taking care of Lily Rose. That's my job because I'm the big sister. So there." There was a big sigh from the girl. The burden of the big sister. "We're all right. Really. But we need some coats!"

Lacey tried not to sigh as well. It wouldn't help to turn this phone call into a symphony of sighs. Jeffrey had stopped eating and was listening closely, watching Lacey's face. "I'll get them for you. What about your father?"

"We don't have a father. We used to but he walked out on us and we don't care about him anyway 'cause he's not a good person. He's not in a good place."

"But Jasmine, where are you staying exactly?" She tried to keep panic or judgment out of her voice. "I need to know. So I can bring you the coats."

"Sometimes Miss Charday lets us stay on her couch. Most of the time, if she isn't drinking too much. 'Cause if she is, she can't hear us at the door. I like it there, she lets me cook rice and stuff. I can cook rice really good." The girl sounded so mature, so responsible. So lost.

"Can I talk to Miss Charday?"

"Not right now! I'm not there. Sometimes if she's too drunk we stay in the laundry room. But it's really safe because there's a storage room that nobody knows about. It's warm and the lock is broken and we can get in. So you don't have to worry." She sounded like quite the little adult, but living in a crazy world.

So I don't have to worry? An overwhelming feeling of desperation came over Lacey. "You can't do that," she said. "Really, it's not that safe. How long has your mother been gone? A couple of days?"

"She went away with a man a couple of weeks ago maybe."

A couple of weeks! Lacey sat bolt upright. "Really, Jasmine, you can't stay in the laundry room. Where exactly is this laundry room, anyway?" *Yeah, like the kid is going to tell me.* Lacey's head was beginning to hurt. Jeffrey was listening intently. "Jasmine, I'll get those coats for you today, okay? Where can we meet? What time?"

"I dunno. I'll think of a good place. I'll call you."

"Where does Miss Charday live? What's her full name? What's the address?"

Jasmine yelped. "I gotta go! I'll call you. Just get the coats, okay? Bye!"

"Don't hang up, Jasmine!" Too late. Lacey hit redial on the phone. No answer.

"Trouble in the town?" Jeffrey's expression was full of concern.

"A little. I'm sorry, I have to make one more call."

"Of course." He flagged down their waiter for fresh coffee.

Lacey pulled out her notebook. She called Tony Trujillo and gave him Jasmine's new phone number to see if he could get an address. And she wanted to find a list of recent evictions in the city, going back two weeks. Tony thought it might be possible to pry the information out of the U.S. Marshal's office in D.C., which handled evictions. It was public information, after all. And, Tony said, he "knew a guy."

If Tony found the eviction record and the address, she could go there. Jasmine wouldn't be in that apartment, Lacey knew, but she might be close by. Maybe the woman that the girl mentioned, this Miss Charday, would be in the same apartment building, or nearby. After all, how far could you drag a TV? But was Charday the first name or last name? And how exactly was it spelled, Charday or Sharday? Or even "Sade," like the singer? She'd have to find her. Maybe guardian angels were watching over them. And maybe she would have a little chat with Mac. *Let's see if he really is the big expert on kids at risk.*

Trujillo said he'd try to have something for her when she got back to the office, if miracles really happened and pigs had wings. She clicked off. Jeffrey was watching her.

"Thank you for being patient, Jeffrey." Her lunch looked delicious, but she'd lost her appetite. "There's this kid—" she began. He took her hand again.

"So this is the little shepherd I've been reading about? Tell me all about it."

chapter 24

Lacey was always happy to stay away from the office, particularly when the denizens of the newsroom were irritated and on deadline. But her kids' coat-buying mission was an unexpected fashion challenge. *Two* coats, Jasmine had demanded. Pink and blue. The best plan was just to charge ahead—and hopefully not charge too much. The familiar awnings of the Macy's downtown store were comforting. Lacey decided to place her innocent faith in the children's department. Her plan was simple. She would throw herself on the mercy of Macy's.

Lacey found a sympathetic sales clerk who led her to the crowded children's winter coat racks. "But what do little girls wear?" Lacey asked.

"What's she like?"

"Smart, independent. Almost thirteen, going on twenty-one. And she has a sister about ten. I think the coats should be about the same style, so no one thinks they got the bad one, but pink and blue. Pink for the little one."

"Microfiber," the saleswoman said. "Easy care. Soft. Warm." She took Lacey to a rack of children's winter coats and jackets in every possible color and indicated two size ranges. "This is a tough season to buy for though. Changeable weather. I'll let you look around. Call if you need help."

The traditional red wool coats with black chesterfield collars called out to Lacey, looking as proper as that photo in the old issue of *Life* magazine, but they didn't feel that warm. The fluffy microfiber won. If she were a kid, she decided, that's what she would prefer. Besides, she thought a kid might think this stuff was cool. It had "micro" in it.

Following the saleswoman's size advice, Lacey picked out

two soft, puffy parkas, one a rosy pink and the other a pretty baby blue, both with hoods trimmed in white faux fur. Lacey hoped Jasmine wasn't that particular about her blues. They were three-quarter length, a style compromise to go with anything. At least they'll keep their bottoms warm, Lacey thought. A little girl of about ten ran past Lacey, dragging her mother right to the puffiest microfiber parkas. She grabbed one in lime green. "This one!" the girl squealed. Lacey smiled. Her fashion choice was vindicated.

Luckily they depleted her Christmas fund less than she'd anticipated. Normally by this time of year, she'd have all her presents already bought and wrapped. Granted she had been busy this year, with big stories and world travel and a brand-new boyfriend and the occasional murder to solve, but was that any excuse? Her mother wouldn't think so. And what on earth could she get Vic? Lacey hopped on the escalator to the next level, stepping off in men's coats. Leather jackets caught her eye. He had a couple, but they were both pretty beat up. "Distressed," Lacey called them. "Experienced," according to Vic.

She spied a warm chocolate brown jacket in a buttery soft leather. Vic would look sensational in it. She turned the tag over and saw a familiar designer label. Oh no, it was a Bentley! *That Bentley. Step away from the House of Bentley Collection, ma'am. Right now.* She put the jacket back. A Bentley leather jacket would *so* not go over well with Vic. And after having lunch with an attractive male Bentley by the name of Jeffrey Bentley Holmes, Vic might assume she was getting a personal discount. That would never do, and she couldn't afford one without it. Sadly, the Bentley jackets were the best-looking ones there, with the finest tailoring and the butteriest leather. *I give up. Maybe Vic would dig something in pink and blue microfiber. With the squealing ten-year-old's seal of approval.*

Lacey circled the floor to the down escalator. She checked her cell phone. No messages.

"Say 'Thank you Tony,' " Trujillo said. He was leaning against Lacey's desk, his long legs stretched out to show off his new chocolate brown cowboy boots decorated with howling red coyotes. He dangled a manila envelope in one hand.

"Tony! Is that for me? Early Christmas present?"

"Maybe." He lifted the envelope high above her head. "Who wants to know?"

"The woman who's going to stomp all over your pretty new boots if you don't hand that over, whatever it is." He laughed and tossed her the envelope. "So what is this?"

"I don't know, take a look."

"Does it have something to do with Cassandra?"

"Maybe indirectly. And with a certain witness in a certain alley."

"Tony, are you telling me that pigs have flown?" Lacey stepped over his legs to get to her chair, her Macy's sack full of puffy parkas in one hand, her purse and coat and Tony's envelope in the other. She dumped it all on her desk and opened the envelope. "Recent evictions! From the federal marshals' office! Oh, Tony, thank you!"

"*De nada.* That phone number seems to be a pay phone in Shaw. But evictions we got. So how do evictions figure into the style beat, Smithsonian?"

"Three guesses, Tony." She smiled brightly and opened the envelope.

"It's that little shepherd kid, isn't it? An evicted family equals homeless kids equals little crime scene witnesses in alleys behind newspapers. Did I do the math right?" She laughed and flipped through the pages. "Rumor has it that you're working with Johnson now. There's a dream team: Lois Lane and Elmer Fudd! You throwing me over for Fuddsy, Lacey?"

"Bite your tongue, Trujillo. Elmer is out huntin' wabbits. Meanwhile, you've brought home the prize carrot. At least I hope so."

Tony flashed his dazzling white smile. "I thought so. You're leaving Fuddsy out of the loop."

"Peter Johnson is loopy enough without my help," Lacey said. "Speaking of loopy, why aren't you riding herd on Kavanaugh?"

"More like house-training a new puppy than riding herd. I heard you're pissed about the story she wrote."

"About the 'Hispanic teenage boy suspect'? What makes you think that?"

Tony playfully socked Lacey on the shoulder. "Kelly's bound to get better, it's the way it works in this biz. You get better or you flunk out."

"Which way are you betting?"

"Hey, I can't do her job for her, okay? I got vacation coming up, I leave tomorrow for my sister's quinceañera and I don't want anything to screw up the deal. Least of all trouble with the junior cop reporter who thinks she's Dick Tracy."

"You're going to Santa Fe?"

"Yep, home to Ma's enchiladas and chili rellenos." He smacked his lips.

"Yum." Lacey had a definite taste for crispy chili rellenos, the way they made them in Denver. You couldn't find them anywhere back East. "So are you taking Linda Sue from the Christmas party to meet the family?"

He shrugged and stood up. "We're just friends, we're barely dating."

"I see," Lacey smirked. "Too many ladies back home?"

"And so little time," he agreed. "If I can do anything else for you let me know."

"How about taking Kavanaugh with you?"

"Bite *your* tongue, Smithsonian." Tony's boots hit the road.

Lacey sat down and pored over the marshals' eviction list until she found what she wanted. The District of Columbia had certain rules about evictions. They couldn't be carried out if the weather forecast included a fifty percent chance of snow, for example, or temperatures below freezing. But there was no snow in the forecast and the temperature hadn't fallen to that magic number yet. The list Tony had somehow sweet-talked out of a friend at the U.S. Marshals Service contained several dozen evictions. One in particular caught Lacey's eye.

One Mrs. Anna Mai Lee had been evicted just after Thanksgiving. Or at least her children were, although the list didn't contain their names. Jasmine said she'd been missing a couple of weeks. The family had lived in the Shaw neighborhood, not far from the Shiloh Mount Zion Church. Lacey grabbed her coat, notebook, purse, and her big Macy's bag of parkas, and headed for the elevators.

She had a vague recollection that she still had a fashion beat and a deadline and a "Crimes of Fashion" column to turn in. Wasn't this week's deadline coming up soon? What day was this again? She ignored that tingling impending-deadline feeling. Surely her editor would understand, her crusty editor with a soft spot for kids in trouble.

Reel her in, Mac had said. That was an order.

chapter 25

Lacey hit the ATM on the corner for cash, flagged a taxi in front of Farragut Square, and gave the driver an address off Rhode Island Avenue Northwest. She'd struck out on finding a "Miss Charday," even with multiple alternative spellings, but she hoped to find more information at her destination. On the way to the apartment house where Anna Mai Lee and her two daughters once lived, Lacey saw an elaborate mural decorating a boarded-up building. It looked like it had been a nightclub, but now it bore the inscription, BIENVENUE À SHAW, SLUM HISTORIQUE.

"Welcome to Shaw, Historic Slum"? She wasn't sure if that was supposed to be ironic or bitter. Both, she decided, and the French added yet another level of irony. Shaw was once the home of Langston Hughes and Duke Ellington, but now it had a reputation for poverty and high crime. It wasn't a part of the District Lacey knew well. Around the corner, another painted inscription in French: TOUJOURS FERMÉ. "Always Closed."

The entire Shaw neighborhood seemed to be in transition, like so much of Washington, D.C. Boarded-up townhouses with front yards full of trash and dead grass stood next to others that had been lovingly restored with fresh paint, neat little gardens, leaded glass windows, and every hallmark of urban yuppic nesting impulses. There were blocks of plain-faced public housing with iron fences and NO TRESPASSING signs. Lacey noticed a few vacant lots, corner markets tucked into the ends of row houses, a brand-new Giant grocery store with a big parking lot, and on almost every second or third block, little churches with long names, like the tiny Shiloh Mount Zion United Church and House of Prayer for All People.

Lacey had read in her own newspaper that there were more than six thousand homeless people in the city. Community activists protested the ongoing trend of forcing lower-income tenants out of their homes to make way for high-end condo conversions. More and more families in the District found themselves living on the street. The slightly luckier ones crowded into already too-small apartments with relatives or friends. They were the "roving homeless," whose numbers apparently now included two small girls with more courage than sense.

The cab stopped in front of a compact four-story apartment building where the Lees had lived. It had a plain institutional look, squatting among more ornate neighbors. The brick had been painted brown once. Now it was chipping off.

Lacey stepped into the small entryway between the front door and the interior door and buzzed the bell for the manager. She heard a slow shuffle of flip-flops as a woman took her time walking to the locked interior door. A kerchief covered her hair and a cigarette dangled from her mouth. She wore denim capris and a red sweatshirt that read, WHAT ARE YOU LOOKING AT? Lacey guessed her age at a hard-earned forty.

The woman cracked open the door to the foyer and parked herself in the doorway. "Yeah?" A light-skinned African American woman, she took a squinty-eyed look at Lacey and drew on the cigarette. "You lookin' to rent, I got nothing for you. This ain't yuppieville. Not yet, it ain't."

"I'm a reporter. I'm not looking to rent."

"A reporter?" A little interest flared in the woman's eyes. She stepped into the small foyer, opened the front door, and scanned the street for the camera crew. "What kind of reporter?"

"I'm a newspaper reporter," Lacey said. "I write for *The Eye Street Observer*."

The woman blew smoke from her mouth and nose, not quite in Lacey's face, but close. "Not *The Post*?"

"Sorry."

"Me too. Name's Thelma DelRio. D-e-l, capital R-i-o. Spell it right if you use it. Now, whatta you want to know?"

"A family was evicted here recently. The Lee family. Right after Thanksgiving."

"Yeah. I hate it when there's kids. Breaks my damn heart, it does," Thelma said. "Two little girls. Nice. Quiet. But whatcha gonna do? I ain't the landlord. Lady don't pay the rent, landlord don't like that. 'Fore you know it your butt's out in the street."

"What were the kids' names?"

"Um, Jasmine's the older one. Little firecracker, she is. Little one's quieter, her name's, uh—Lily something. Lily Rose."

Bingo. "Can I see their old apartment?" It wasn't likely it would tell Lacey anything, but maybe it would give her an idea of what kind of life they led.

"Nah," Thelma shook her head. "Occupied. Folks who actually paid first and last month's rent and a security deposit."

"What kind of apartment is it?"

"What kind of dumb-ass question is that?" Thelma took another drag on the cigarette, then blew it out with her next words. "What do you expect? An apartment. Bathroom, kitchen, living room, bedroom. Not bad as they go."

"How long did the Lee family live here?"

"'Bout three years," Thelma said. "Miz Lee, she had a job. Some restaurant somewhere. Then an office job. She tried hard for those kids. Then she stopped trying so hard. Drugs, liquor, lost her job. Arrested. They was on food stamps. Stopped paying rent. I cut 'em some slack, but only so much I can do. Takes awhile to kick 'em out, you know. She stopped coming home. Left the kids alone a lot. She'd come back, go away, come back. She was sorry. Anna Mai told me she was sorry a hundred times. Well, ma'am, 'sorry' don't pay the rent."

"Oh, Lord, those poor kids."

"And that Jasmine, what a little grown-up she is! Taking care of her sister, making sure they get fed. More sense in her little finger than her damn mother has in her whole body. She's the parent in that family. And that Lily Rose, sweet little girl."

"Do you know if they had any friends in the building? Or in the neighborhood? Someone they might stay with? Perhaps a Miss Charday? Is there a Charday in your building?"

Thelma gave her a sharp look. "I mind my own damn business. Don't know no Chardays."

Lacey was pretty sure she knew Miss Charday. "Do you know where the girls might be now? Where I can find them?"

"How am I supposed to know that? Do I look like some kind of babysitter?" Thelma was back on her guard. She took a final drag and flicked the butt into a dead bush by the door. "I don't know nothing," Thelma said. "I didn't know nothing yesterday when that man come sniffing around asking about the Lees. And I ain't gonna know nothing if someone else come round my door tomorrow. Reporters or no reporters."

"There was a man?" Lacey tried not to show her alarm. "Was it a cop?"

Thelma thought about it, then shook her head. "He wasn't no cop. Didn't look like no cop. Dressed better. You know cops." She stepped back into the doorway and lit another cigarette, taking a long slow drag, blowing out impressive, foul-smelling rings.

The Santa Dude? Or someone from DeadFed dot com snooping for a story? "Have you seen him around here before?"

"Don't know." Her eyes narrowed. "White guy. All look alike to me. Sorry."

"Look, Thelma, this is important. Those kids, Jasmine and her sister, they could be in danger. I just want to help them. If that guy comes back, would you call me?" She pulled out her business card and offered it to the woman. "And don't tell him anything. He's up to no good."

"Hell, I coulda told you that." Thelma squinted and read the card. "Lacey Smithsonian. *Eye Street Observer.* That you?"

"That's me. I have some new coats for them."

Thelma looked at the bag. "Maybe I should hold on to them for the girls, if I see them."

"No thanks. I need to see the girls myself, make sure they're okay. Don't worry, Thelma, I'll tell the world how good you were to them when they lived here, how you tried to help them."

"Well, don't tell 'em that," the woman finally said, smiling for the first time and showing her gold tooth. "I got a reputation to uphold. Don't want every damn fool in the city thinking I'll give 'em a handout. But long as you ain't no damn social worker. It's Thelma DelRio, in case you put my name in the paper." She stepped back into the hall and shut the interior door hard.

"Yeah," Lacey said to the closed door. She turned and surveyed the neighborhood. "You're a peach, Thelma. And if the Santa Dude comes back around, I hope you're even less help to him."

She walked the couple of blocks to the little stone-and-brick church, and the Nativity where Jasmine had "borrowed" the shepherd's robe. It looked very different in the daylight without the Christmas lights and the crowd milling around Vic's mother's wild pink Cadillac. The crèche looked forlorn and bare.

Lacey knocked on the church's locked door. No answer. Perhaps there was never anyone there except at services. She walked around the church. The vacant lot with the stable looked scruffier. The Holy Family, the Wise Men, and the plaster shepherds were still waiting for the Christ Child. The missing robes had still not been replaced.

Jasmine, where are you? She gave up and headed back to Rhode Island Avenue to hail a cab back to the office.

"That bastard. That flaming bastard," were the first words she heard as she stepped off the elevator at *The Eye* after her visit to Shaw.

Her eyes followed the sound of Harlan Wiedemeyer sputtering in anger. The chubby little Wiedemeyer was a small thundercloud of righteous indignation storming down the hall toward Lacey and Felicity's corner of the newsroom. Felicity sprang up and offered him a piece of her famous chocolate pudding cake.

"Harlan, honeybunch, are you all right? What happened? Have some cake!"

"Me! Harlan Wiedemeyer, questioned by the Metropolitan police!" he managed to get out before flopping down in the Death Chair. Wiedemeyer's face was flushed, his coat flapped open, and his tie was askew. His thinning hair stood straight up, apparently from rubbing his head in frustration. "That twisted bastard."

"Harlan, what's wrong?" Lacey's plans for polishing her next "Crimes of Fashion" column went straight out of her head. How can a reporter pass up a good "twisted bastard" story?

"Johnson! That pea-brained bastard Peter Johnson dropped a dime on me," he said. "As if any phone call cost a dime these days! But you know what I mean. He turned me in to the police like I was a common criminal. As a suspect, a suspect, in the Wentworth assault. As if it weren't ridiculous enough to suspect Felicity."

Felicity's blue eyes never left Wiedemeyer's face. They were wide with horror and full of tears. She wrung her hands and helped herself to a piece of her own pudding cake.

"Questioned like a common criminal," Wiedemeyer complained bitterly. "That bastard Johnson told that Detective What's-His-Name that I might have had something to do with the attack. Something about the antlers I was wearing. Antlers! I always wear antlers at Christmas! How does that make me a suspect?"

"Oh, Harlan, no!" Felicity's plate of cake went back on her desk. "Johnson turned you in because he thinks I did it and you covered it up? Or he thinks you smacked her in the head for me? How could he think that?"

"As if I'd waste my time on Cassandra Wentworth," Wiedemeyer continued. "As if I'd waste a perfectly good ten-pound candy cane on her! Stupid bastard. It was a setup. Can't he see that?"

Typical of Johnson, Lacey thought. He'd always struck her as a vindictive guy and a lazy reporter. Always going after the small story, the easy quote. And now he was after the easy suspects in Cassandra's attack. Maybe Johnson would catch a bad case of the Wiedemeyer Jinx. No one deserved it more.

Wiedemeyer straightened his rumpled brown jacket and patted down his hair. He picked up the plate of pudding cake that Felicity had offered him. "As if I would attack Cassandra in the alley. As if I would attack anyone, except in print." He took a bite of dessert and moaned softly. "It's perfectly clear she's got enough enemies without me."

"Was it awful, Harlan?" Felicity asked.

He patted her shoulder. "It wasn't pretty. Cops are worse than reporters, you know. At least reporters try to get the story straight. What I want to know is"— Wiedemeyer took a big bite of cake—"is this: Why keep asking me the same stupid questions? 'Were you in the alley?' No, why would I be in the alley? 'Did you wear a Santa hat in the alley?' No, I wasn't in the alley! I told you I was in the party wearing antlers, and there are pictures to prove it. 'Where did you get the Santa hat when you went to the alley?' I give up!"

Lacey was enjoying this story. "Go on, Harlan."

"Then the cop asks me, 'Did you have a grudge against Wentworth?' " Wiedemeyer sighed and shook his round head. "Well, you know, that's a little hard to answer, considering that she's such a pinch-faced bitch and everybody hates her and she's tormented and hurt my dear Felicity. But a grudge? No, not a grudge exactly."

"Oh, Harlan," Felicity sighed, lovestruck.

"So I said, 'Well, no more than anyone else who's ever met her.' "

"What happened then?" Lacey asked.

" 'Does Wentworth have any enemies,' this big cop asks me. I say, 'Have you read the editorial page? She's got nothing but enemies! They've got social clubs! Open a phone book, there they are. Of course she's got enemies.' "

"Did he actually read her editorials?" Lacey asked.

"No, of course not. He's a cop. I said, 'Cassandra Wentworth has antagonized half the population of Washington, D.C.' Now I'm not sure that's really true. Our own readership surveys show that only two percent of our readers ever get to the editorial page. But I'm sure she's infuriated at least half of *them*." He took another big bite of pudding cake for the strength to continue. "The detective seemed to be getting a headache. Finally he told me to not leave town." Wiedemeyer finished the cake and smacked his lips. He dropped the paper plate in the trash can. "You gotta do something, Lacey. This whole Cassandra mess is just ruining Christmas. You gotta get to the bottom of this. I mean, isn't this sort of thing right up your alley?"

From the street outside came the sound of screeching brakes and the impact of metal on metal. Lacey ran to the window, Wiedemeyer and Felicity hard on her heels. More reporters crowded to every window overlooking Eye Street and Farragut Square. Below them on the sidewalk, Peter Johnson stood frozen, his car keys dangling from one hand. He looked stunned, but unharmed. A Washington Metro bus had crashed into his car, which he had apparently just stepped out of only a moment before, after parking it at the curb. In the Metro bus loading zone, which was clearly marked NO PARKING. It was totaled. A wheel was spinning lazily in the middle of Eye Street.

Lacey had only one thought. *Jinx, one. Johnson, nothing.*

chapter 26

Lacey cradled the phone between her ear and shoulder.

"How was your day?" Vic's deep voice was as comforting as a warm blanket. "Are you knee-deep in Mimi's trunk yet?"

"Ha. You think you know so much." Lacey held up a coat-and-dress pattern she had just selected from the extensive collection of vintage patterns preserved and protected in Aunt Mimi's trunk. She sat on the floor, the better to poke lovingly through the treasures in her treasure chest, Mimi's vintage fabrics, patterns, photos, letters, and magazines from days gone by. "I am not knee-deep in Mimi's trunk. I'm in it up to my neck."

The broad shoulders of the woman in the cover illustration were no doubt helped by pads sewn into her no-nonsense trench coat. The pattern was from the early World War II era: Strong capable women were all the rage. This woman looked like she could knock down a Nazi or two with a well-placed punch, or perhaps pull a pistol from a cleverly tailored interior pocket and stop the Nazi war machine. That woman, Lacey thought, would have no problem finding two lost little girls.

"So you're communing with Aunt Mimi's spirit. Does she have any answers from beyond?" His voice was gently teasing.

"Maybe. It helps me think, you know."

"Thinking is good. Can I help?"

Lacey set the pattern down and leaned back against her dark blue velvet sofa. "I don't know what to do, Vic." She sighed deeply and closed her eyes. "Jasmine's just a kid, this is probably all just a big game to her, and she won't call me till she's good and ready."

"Or when it gets good and cold. You might not have to wait much longer, darling. The weather is changing. You still have those parkas ready?"

"Parkas won't be enough to save them if they end up on the street. There are so many predators out there. What can I do, Vic, recruit your mother and her pink Caddy and drive up and down every alley in the District?" She couldn't banish an image of two cold little girls huddling in doorways, with the pimps and pushers just biding their time.

"Lacey." She liked the way it sounded when he said her name. "This might help. I'm putting a little surveillance team in her last known neighborhood, the area where they lived and the church where she borrowed the robe."

"You're doing what?" She opened her eyes and sat up straight. "A surveillance team?"

"They'll be watching for them. Kids are hard to find, but you never know, they may get lucky."

"Oh my God, Vic, that's so great!" It had never crossed her mind that he would do something like that for her, or that he even could, as if he had some vast network of secret resources to spread around. She knew his dad's security company was stretched pretty thin these days, but Lacey had underestimated him. And this must really be costing him, she thought. "Who are they?"

"Just a couple of my guys who need some extra hours. For Christmas shopping. They're good."

"How are they surveilling?"

"Urban standard. Beat-up van, just this side of legal, so it looks like it belongs in Shaw. They'll take turns walking the neighborhood, check out the local flora and fauna, watching for a little shepherd. They'll check Eye Street too, they'll do a loop."

Lacey was almost, but not quite, speechless with gratitude. "That's so wonderful, Vic."

"I'd like to see you tonight, Lacey. I need your opinion on something. The guys will call me if anything breaks."

Every bone in her body seemed to ache with exhaustion, and not to mention her flagging spirit. She'd returned home after work only when she decided she could do nothing productive in the office. She knew it wouldn't be safe for her to roam around the streets of Shaw alone on foot, and probably she would find nothing anyway. Without a car, she was stuck. Stella was working at the salon. Brooke was up to her ears in a case. She had almost called on Nadine and the Pink Flamingo. At moments like this she really missed her old Nissan 280ZX.

"You'll pick me up?"

"In fifteen minutes, if that works for you. If we get the call, we'll head straight to the kids. I promise," he said. "What do you say?" His voice was honey on her nerves. "I'm close by, I'll be there soon."

By the time Vic pulled into the circle drive of her apartment building Lacey had washed her face, redone her makeup, put on a rousing red sweater over her jeans for a little color therapy, and grabbed her red leather jacket. She climbed up into the Jeep.

"Do I smell coffee?" she asked.

"I picked up a café mocha for you. In the cup holder."

She fastened her seat belt and reached for the steaming cup. "Thank you. It's a little spooky how you know this stuff, Vic." He swung out of the circle drive.

"Professional boy scout, ma'am. Gotta be prepared."

"Where are we going?"

"Reporters just have to know everything, don't they?" He kept his eyes on the road.

"That's right."

"It's a surprise."

Lacey raised her eyebrow at him. She wasn't really a surprise kind of person. "Then just drive, darling. I'll commune with the coffee." She hoped it was decaf, but she'd probably be awake all night anyway, she thought, worrying about Jasmine and Lily Rose.

Vic turned right onto South Washington Street, which turned into the scenic George Washington Parkway north of Old Town. Lacey loved the Parkway paralleling the Potomac River. The rain had stopped and the night had turned crystal clear. The monuments across the river were striking. She could see the Jefferson Memorial at the Tidal Basin, the Capitol on the National Mall, the Washington Monument, and the Lincoln Memorial. The Parkway took them beneath the Memorial Bridge, which featured huge matching statues of warriors on horses facing into Washington, with their backs to the traffic from the Virginia side.

"That's the perfect metaphor for entering the Nation's Capital," Vic said, as he often did. "Being greeted by a pair of giant gilded horses' asses."

"Majestic horses' asses, though. As horses' asses go."

They drove on in cozy silence until Vic spoke again. "How was your lunch with Bentley?"

"It's actually Jeffrey Bentley *Holmes*," Lacey said. "He says he'd happily drop the Bentley, except he's been called back into the family biz. They think he'd be wasted in a monastery."

"And what do you think?" Vic glanced her way.

"He's not cut out to be a monk."

"Too bad. How was lunch?"

"Lovely, until Jasmine called. I really couldn't eat after that. Too bad, the chicken crepes were delicious." She realized she was being coy. She didn't mean to be.

"Not exactly what I was after." He gave her a look. "Where did he want to take you as his date tomorrow night?"

"Some big fund-raising cocktail event. Now we're both invited, Vic. It's at the Willard." Not that the Willard would tempt Vic the way it tempted Lacey. "I love the Willard. You want to go?"

"Maybe. You told him about us then?"

"Well, I was tempted to just run off with him at lunch, Vic. You know, the clothes, the furs, the jewels, the limousines, the lifestyle, none of which he has actually offered me. Oh, yes, the glamorous life of a Bentley woman! The fantasy dimmed ever so slightly when I pictured his cousin Aaron and his Uncle Hugh trying to murder me. Again. Not to mention what his mother might do to me. So when all was said and done, I decided to dump the Bentleys and come back to you, Sean Victor Donovan."

"Oh were you gone? I hadn't noticed."

She punched him playfully in the shoulder. "Of course I told him about us, you handsome jealous thing, you."

Lacey thought she detected a hint of relief in Vic's smile, but she didn't press it. She left out the part about telling Jeffrey she'd call him first if things fell through with Vic. That was the sort of emergency backup plan a girl should keep to herself. Lacey smiled at him and he put his right hand on her left knee and squeezed gently.

"He's a mighty rich boy," Vic said.

"I hear you're a rich boy too."

"Comfortable, Lacey. Comfortable."

She laughed. "Like Bill Gates is comfortable?"

"Nobody is that comfortable. And the Bentleys aren't comfortable, they're just uncomfortably rich. I'm nowhere near Bentley rich." Vic gave her a sidelong look and pulled off the Parkway onto Chain Bridge Road.

"Have you forgotten that I fell for you when I thought you were just a small town cop turned P.I. and I figured your net worth might be a full tank of gas in this Jeep?"

It was Vic's turn to laugh. "Pretty good cover, huh."

"All this stuff about being 'comfortable' you pulled on me *later*, cowboy. Bait and switch, I call it."

They turned off Chain Bridge into the town of McLean, the tony suburb where Vic's parents lived, and then onto his folks' street. Their house was quite spacious, but it was not one of the obnoxiously large McMansions that were multiplying like mushrooms. An oh-so-comfortable neighborhood, Lacey decided. Vic was renting a townhouse not far away. Lacey assumed he was just driving her past the Donovans' place so she could see the neighborhood's Christmas decorations. Two soaring pine trees decorated with old-fashioned colored lights anchored the drive that led to the senior Donovans' home, and the roof was outlined with Christmas lights as well. In the front room, an enormous decorated tree blazed away through the front window.

"Your mother's already decorated everything!"

"She's like that. If everything's not done by the first weekend in December, she feels she's failed in her duty as a McLean matron."

"Oh, no." Lacey could feel herself pale. "I haven't even figured out what to make for dessert yet."

Vic parked the Jeep and touched her face. "She won't care what it is, Lacey."

"Men are so silly." She kissed him lightly. "Of course she'll care."

"We're here." He turned off the engine.

"Is this some kind of setup?"

"Don't worry, they're not home."

"The lights are on," she pointed out. "Your mother wouldn't leave the house with lights on a live tree."

"Oh, they're at the neighbors. I just want to show you something." He hopped out of the Jeep and opened the passenger door for her. "Please."

The front door opened and Nadine bustled out with a huge smile on her face. "What a nice surprise!"

Vic looked chagrined. "Didn't think you were gonna be home, Mom." Lacey pasted a smile on her face and squeezed his arm meaningfully.

"Is that a nice thing to say?" Nadine said to Lacey. "Sean Victor, you thought you'd sneak your girlfriend into the house while we were gone?"

"Um, not exactly." He looked guilty.

Nadine wrapped Lacey up in a warm hug. "Lacey, it's so nice to see you. Come on in and I'll get you both something to drink," she said.

"I just came to show Lacey something, Mom. We won't be long."

"Is this about that old BMW of yours out in the garage?"

Vic groaned. "Mother—"

Lacey turned to Vic. "You have a BMW? But you always drive the Jeep."

He took Lacey's hand and told Nadine they'd be back inside later for that drink. He led her around the house and opened the door to the garage. Next to the shocking pink Caddy sat a perfect BMW 2002tii, freshly painted in forest green.

"Vintage 1974," Vic said. "The last year for the tii model. Completely rebuilt. Runs really great. I know you like vintage cars. Me too."

"It's beautiful, Vic," she said, walking around the car and admiring its details. It was a proud-looking little car, with its squarish but jaunty shape and big round headlights. The fresh green paint gleamed under the garage lights. Lacey thought the whole car looked brand-new. And it was definitely Vic's color, but it didn't seem quite like a car for Vic somehow. Too cute, perhaps.

"Engine's rebuilt. Low mileage." He gave her the little Bimmer's highlights. "Fuel injection actually works. Fast, reliable. I replaced all the rusted panels with galvanized steel. And this model's got the bigger, safer bumper. It's the last year they imported the 2002tii. This car is from when BMWs were still cool, before they became shameless overpriced yuppie bait."

"You worked on this car?" Lacey said. "I missed the part about you being a car mechanic too."

"Um, I'm handy." Vic flashed his killer smile, white teeth against his olive skin. It was devastating when he looked at her like that. "These things are notorious rust buckets, but I've taken care of all that. I work on it over here because my dad is the tool king of Northern Virginia." He waved at the garage wall, covered with cabinets and tools hanging on hooks, a large and intimidatingly well-organized display. Everything from hammers and saws and drills to nails and screws and washers in jars, chainsaws, power sanders, power augurs, timing lights, things Lacey didn't even recognize.

"It's a great car, Vic. Wow. I've always liked these. It's so cool." She caught herself just short of saying it was adorable, it seemed like such a girly thing to say. She opened the door. "Sheepskins on the seats?" It was a nice touch, a Colorado touch. She rubbed her hands over them in appreciation.

"To keep your cute bottom comfy."

"You mean we get to drive this tonight instead of the Jeep? All right!" She caught herself. "Not that I don't love the Jeep and all that."

Actually, Lacey resented Vic's green Jeep ever so slightly. It always ran. It never seemed to break down, unlike her late lamented 280ZX, which had spent more time with Lacey's mechanic than with her. It never got itself stolen, unlike her poor abused Z, which had been stolen and turned to a life of crime. All the while, Vic's darn Jeep Wrangler just kept running and remained rock solid and unmolested.

"I wasn't thinking about me," he said. "I was thinking about it for you."

"Is it for sale? You're really gonna sell your project car, your baby?" She needed a car and she loved this one. The forest-green color was almost identical to Vic's Jeep. "How much?"

"It's not for sale, Lacey. I'm not gonna sell it. It's for you. It's a Christmas present."

"A car! You want to give me a car?" A wave of astonishment mingled with panic washed over her. "A car?! I can't accept a car!"

"Why not?"

"Because! It's a car! It's too much. I mean, nice girls don't accept cars, for heaven sakes. What would people say?" Lacey meant people other than Stella, who would think it was totally cool and that Lacey must have done something right for a change. Or people like Brooke, who would want to take a fast test drive and tell her about all the spies she knew who had once owned or driven or stolen a 1974 BMW 2002. Lacey meant nice normal people.

"What do you care what people would say? What anyone would say?" He stood there, looking impossibly handsome with his dark curls falling over his forehead and his eyes looking at her full of amusement. That was a good question. She'd have to think about it.

"Well, I don't know exactly."

"You're my girl, aren't you? You think I want you walking the streets unprotected?"

"But it's a *car*, Vic! I can't just take—"

He put his arm around her and steered her to the driver's side door and opened it. "Why don't you check it out? It has a few extras. Let me show you. Try out the sheepskins."

In a mild state of shock, Lacey eased herself onto the sheepskin-covered seat. Her hands slid over the steering wheel and adjusted the rearview mirror. She moved the seat and noticed that it fit her very well. That Vic Donovan was a clever guy. But a *car*?

"I installed a GPS navigation system," Vic said. "That little screen on the dash."

"To keep track of me?" she said.

"I was thinking so you won't get lost, but keeping track of you is a better idea."

"A stereo?" Her fingers ran over the shiny buttons. "Does it work?"

"It better, I just installed it. This thing came with an eight-track. They didn't have CD players back then, but now it does. Brand-new air-conditioning too."

She gazed up at him, her eyes very wide. "How can I possibly accept this?" Her moral sense was deeply conflicted. This was like a car guy's equivalent of a marriage proposal and a diamond ring, but she wasn't about to say that. And the car *without* the marriage proposal was like—a proposition? *Or is that just my mother talking?*

"Honey, it's just an old car," he said with a grin.

"An adorable old perfect vintage BMW! With a brand-new stereo! And air! And sheepskins! Lord, these feel good, are these made from real sheep?"

"Merry Christmas." He leaned against the car and smiled, peering into the window at her. "So you like it."

"'Merry Christmas'?" She was horrified.

He held back his laughter. "What did you think I was getting you for Christmas?"

"I don't know, a sweater, or a CD, or something. You know."

"Oh, Lacey." Now he was laughing. "Come on. And I did get you a CD, by the way. It's in the glove box. Ella Fitzgerald singing Christmas carols. Gotta have something to try out the new stereo."

"Well, what am I supposed to get *you* now? A yacht?!" She was dumbfounded. What indeed? A leather jacket, even one by Bentley, seemed so insignificant now. And a nice jacket would be pushing her budget, even before she'd bought two unanticipated little puffy parkas.

"How about the image of you behind the wheel?" Vic pulled her out of the car and kissed her. "And you are making our Christmas dessert. I'll take a slice of that legendary pecan pie cake."

"Are you making fun of me?"

"No. You're all I want for Christmas. I have you, Lacey, and that's enough. Unless I scared you off with this." He held her tightly. "After all, you've been known to bolt when men get serious about you."

"That's not true!" It was sort of true, but she didn't want to admit it. She couldn't look at him.

"It was all over Sagebrush when that cowboy asked you to marry him. You bolted like a spooked deer."

"He told the whole town he proposed! Everyone in town knew I said no. I couldn't stay after that." The man she'd been seeing then, a rancher, *not* just a cowboy, had wanted to keep her with him forever in Sagebrush, Colorado. She couldn't imagine being embalmed in a barren, claustrophobic little boom town where the temperature often touched forty below in the winter. And he wasn't the right guy for her to be embalmed with anyway. Lacey told the cowboy no, and then she hot-footed it out of town. It would have been too awful to stay, she thought. For both of them. Vic was off-limits at the time, being just barely separated from his wife and in the process of getting a divorce. So she left Sagebrush behind and headed east.

"You're not going to bolt on me, are you?"

She certainly felt like bolting. "It's a car, Vic!"

"Yup, it sure is. Are we back to that?" He sighed and folded his arms around her.

"You're so casual about this. Have you given cars to other women?" Did he make a habit of this? And if he did, what kind of car did he give the last one?!

"You're the first." He kissed her again. "But if this works, hey, who knows." The Bimmer was growing on her. "Knowing that you have a car that works is important to me, Lacey. A reliable car, but with something special, a car that fits you, a car that suits you. A car as cute and classy as you. Well, nearly as cute, anyway."

"A BMW." It told Lacey that Vic was pretty serious about this relationship. A guy doesn't give away a vintage BMW to get a date. She felt warm and cared for and scared to death at the same time.

Nadine chose that moment to pop through the door from the kitchen to the garage. "Haven't you given her that old car yet?" she said. Vic sighed.

Lacey gaped at his mother. "Were you in on this, Nadine?"

"I didn't turn any wrenches, Lacey, but let's just say not much gets past me here, especially in my own garage," Nadine said. "It's cold out here, why don't we go inside and have some eggnog while you give her the keys?"

Lacey was certain she looked like a deer caught in the headlights. Vic suggested a test drive before their eggnog. She looked at the car. It really was adorable. It must have been a lot of work. It would be incredibly rude to turn it down. Maybe if she drove the car her feelings would sort themselves out. Christmas was still weeks away. Surely she still had time to decide? She realized she'd taken the keys from Vic's hand. It wouldn't hurt her to take a test drive. Maybe up to Shaw to look for Jasmine again.

"Let's hit the road, cowboy," she said. "You said there's a CD in that glove box?"

FASHION BITES

Don't Be SAD:
Get Help for Seasonal Apparel Disorder!

Tweed on the beach? Flip-flops in the snow? You've got Seasonal Apparel Disorder! Consult a mirror. Call your stylist. Get help *now.*

Seasonal Apparel Disorder, also known as SAD, is caused by a clash of seasons, the real one outside and the imaginary one you're dressed for, the season inside your head. Perhaps it's already spring in your heart or summer in your sandals, but when the Beltway is coated in black ice and the forecast is freezing drizzle followed by more freezing drizzle with a good chance of freezing drizzle and you're frozen to your flip-flops, my diagnosis is SAD.

SAD victims fill the streets of Washington, D.C. Recognize them by their shivering state of denial, their touching belief that it's still half past summer, that fall will last forever, and winter will never come. Winter comes late to Our Nation's Capital, but come it does. SAD sufferers cling to their summer dresses and sandals. They eschew stockings. Their winter coats are in storage and they've lost the key. They are dazed and confused and wondering what to wear, and who can blame them! What are the rules? There used to be rules, sensible, easy to understand and easy-to-follow rules such as: No white shoes after Labor Day. Believe me, frostbite is not fashionable, nor is heatstroke stylish, but both threaten the cluelessly clothed when the weather starts to change.

Yes, it is difficult to deal with unpredictable transitional weather, but remember, it doesn't just taunt you personally, it torments all of us indiscriminately. When the seasons shift, it's cold in the morning and hot in the afternoon. It freezes when they predict balmy; it monsoons when they say dry. It did this last year, too, remember? Why? *It's Washington, people!*

What's the solution? Clothes. The right clothes. And a few simple rules and some basic advice. Take responsibility for your own wardrobe decisions. Catch a weather report. Sure, it's often wrong here. But if torrential downpours are predicted, grab the umbrella, ditch the sundress. Don't just assume the Washington weatherman is always wrong, simply because Congress is. (Congress is paid to be wrong. Meteorologists are wrong because it's a *science.*) Weathercasters give us secret clues, subtle hints like wind chill factors and humidity indexes. These clues can tip you off to wrap yourself up in wool and microfiber up to your eyebrows, or reach for the bikini and sunblock. Get a clue. Here are a few more.

- When the weather is changeable, it's time to layer. Think jackets, vests, wraps, shawls, and a pair of gloves in your purse. Think versatile layers of easy-on, easy-off midweight clothing, not the single overstuffed Everest-rated parka over the bare halter dress. Layer, layer, layer!
- Breathe! Humidity is our middle name here. Humidity makes everything worse, cold colder, heat hotter, and both can happen in the same twenty-four-hour period. If your clothes don't breathe, you won't either.
- When it's cold, tights and hose are your friends, unless you really like the look of dry, flaky legs and the feel of goose bumps. Under your tights you may still have the goose bumps, but *no one will see them.*
- Oh yeah, remember this: Never wear flip-flops to the White House, Congress, or the Supreme Court, summer, winter, spring, or fall. Not ever. That's not just SAD, that's silly. But you already knew that, didn't you?

chapter 27

On Wednesday morning, with a chill in the air and winter fast
approaching, Lacey could no longer deny her inner sweater girl.
No, not thick bulky novelty sweaters, not the dreaded Christmas sweaters that had inspired the fiasco that was Sweatergate,
but the soft warm sweaters of winter. There would be no Seasonal Apparel Disorder for her.

For workdays Lacey liked silk, cotton, merino wool, and
cashmere sweaters. Turtlenecks, V-necks, pull-ons, all went
with suits for an easy, carefree style. Lacey selected a violet
cashmere sweater to wear with a flared black wool crepe skirt
and high heeled—though not excessively high—black leather
boots. A black wool crepe coat with velvet collar completed the
outfit. But the Bentley reception after work, where nonprofit
types would hobnob with members of the Bentley Foundation
and vie for the inside track to foundation money, posed a trick-
ier problem. It was after all, sponsored by the famous fashion
design firm. She couldn't go looking like just any reporter.
Lacey did what working women everywhere do: She packed a
change of clothes to take to the office.

From the famous Aunt Mimi collection, she selected a vintage fitted blouse in heavy, almost crocheted, creamy white
lace. The top featured a soft ruffle down the décolletage that
showed off her neck, a nipped-in waist accented by a burgundy
sash, and a graceful peplum that dipped lower in the back. A
cultured pearl necklace and earrings, also from Aunt Mimi's famous trunk, would complement both looks. Although she
would be weighed down with the extras on her daily commute,
Lacey thanked her late great-aunt.

The outfits would be fine, but the shadows under her eyes

were not. Lacey had tossed and turned half the night, worrying
by turns about two little girls lost in the District and Vic's lovely
but preposterous Christmas present. After one glorious test
drive across the Potomac to Shaw and back, she left the beautiful green BMW parked in his folks' garage in McLean for temporary safekeeping. She was tempted but conflicted, and after
all, she told Vic, it wasn't Christmas morning yet. He just
smiled and told her to take her time, the BMW wasn't going
anywhere without her.

Vic's surveillance team reported no sightings of the girls in
Shaw or Farragut Square. They came up empty on their first
night on the job, and they asked for more information, which
Lacey couldn't supply. They were stalled. Lacey was stalled.
Christmas was stalled. Everything seemed to be stuck, waiting
for the Santa Dude.

When Lacey strode through the lobby of *The Eye* that morning a commotion was under way. She couldn't even see the
tastefully decorated Christmas tree for the uniformed D.C. cops
tussling with a tall man in a navy blue dress coat. Mac was in
the corner talking with Detective Charleston, the cop on Cassandra's case. A smug-looking Peter Johnson stood by them,
eavesdropping.

Lacey elbowed her way through the crowd to listen. Pushing to the front of any room was a skill she'd honed as a journalist. The detective glanced her way, but he made no move to
stop her. Mac said nothing. He kept his eyes on the man in the
middle.

The subject of everyone's attention was a tall wiry man, his
mouse-brown hair shot through with gray. Lacey placed his age
somewhere in his fifties. His eyes were large and pale behind
wire-framed glasses, and he seemed an unlikely object of police
attention. His voice, however, was strong and betrayed a large
measure of outrage. Lacey inched forward to stand at Mac's
elbow.

"False arrest, that's what this is!" the man was shouting.

"We're not arresting you yet, Mr. Graybill," the detective
broke in. "We just want to ask you a few questions." He
smacked a puffy business-sized envelope in his hands.

"I have every right!" the man he called Graybill spluttered.
"My First Amendment right to express my opinions."

"You don't have a right to make threats of violence," Charleston didn't seem particularly upset by the man or the envelope, and he barely seemed interested in the exchange. *Just going through the motions,* Lacey thought.

"The Second Amendment of the Constitution of the United States of America guarantees me the right to—" Graybill began.

"Let's move this along," the detective said. "We want to ask you a few questions about these threats you've been sending."

"I don't have to say a word. That's my Fifth Amendment right under the Constitution." The man's voice rose higher. "Or don't you dumb-ass bozos know that?"

"Bad move," Lacey muttered.

"Never pays to insult the police," Mac said under his breath.

"You ain't getting squat from me," Graybill declared.

"Mister, that's all I've been getting from you." Charleston was moving from bored to weary. "Let's go." The uniforms took Graybill's arms.

"What's the charge?" Graybill shouted. "I demand to know the damned charge."

"Disturbing the peace."

"Bull!" The man struggled to remove the strong arms of the lawmen.

"How about stalking. Resisting arrest."

"You just said I wasn't under arrest. False arrest! I have witnesses, all of you here saw this." Graybill swiveled his head at the bystanders.

"Keep going," Charleston said. "I got a whole book to throw at you, including assault with a deadly weapon. Attempted murder."

"You're out of your mind," Graybill said. "I don't know what you're talking about."

"Sure you do. A Miss Cassandra Wentworth, object of your attentions, was attacked on Friday. She's still in the hospital."

"I didn't do that! You think I'd do that? You're crazy!"

"Get him out of here," Detective Charleston told the uniformed officers. Two policemen escorted the man from the lobby. The detective nodded to Lacey and Mac.

"Detective," she said, "Does this mean your Hispanic teenager is no longer a suspect?"

"Ms. Smithsonian, to me everybody is a suspect, all day,

every day." He favored her with a weary smile. "We'll be in touch." He ambled out the door.

Lacey looked to Mac for an explanation of the scene in the lobby. Peter Johnson answered her. "Cassandra has a stalker, a letter writer. Mac and I set up this entire trap." Mac looked at him, his eyebrows clenching their fists.

"That guy? He's the nasty letter writer Mac told me about?"

"And we collared him entirely without your assistance. You've been no use on this story at all, have you?"

She took a step toward him. He backed up. "Oh, wasn't this *your* pet story, Johnson? And this guy doesn't look much like Pickles and Wiedemeyer, does he? What became of your prime suspects, the deadly duo?"

"You've just been lucky, Smithsonian, skating on that easy beat of yours."

"The fashion beat is murder, Johnson, or haven't you heard?" It really was too early in the morning for this nonsense, Lacey thought. "I suppose you're saving the world on the red tape and hot air beat."

"I am an experienced Capitol Hill reporter! I know how this town works—"

"How's your car working, Peter? Still parking at bus stops?"

"Upstairs, both of you," Mac ordered. "You just saw what happens when you disturb the peace at *The Eye Street Observer*." He marched them to the elevators.

"Hold that elevator!" LaToya leaped in just as the door closed, holding a large sack in her hands. It smelled like hot cinnamon rolls and filled the elevator with a heavenly aroma. "What did they get that guy for?"

"Writing threatening letters," Johnson said. "Stalking. Assault. Attempted murder."

"What? No way!" LaToya's eyes were wide. "This is all about Cassandra Wentworth, isn't it?"

"Perception is one of your skills, LaToya," Johnson replied.

"Ooh, attempted sarcasm, Johnson! You got a learner's permit for that?"

"Silence!" It was an order from Mac.

LaToya threw a meaningful look at Lacey as the doors opened. "I expect the whole story from you later, girl, with all the dirt." She shook her bag of hot rolls under Mac's nose and flounced away to her desk.

Lacey followed Johnson to Mac's office. But she slipped in faster and grabbed the only open chair. Johnson leaned against the wall, arms folded over his soft belly like a Buddha. His glasses slid down his nose.

"Okay, the stalker," Lacey said. "Who, what, where, and when? I already got the how, but I would be curious about the why." She crossed her legs and leaned forward.

"Cassandra makes a difference," Peter snapped. "She has an impact. That earns her enemies. Saving the planet is more important than saving a buck on a pair of shoes."

"Focus here, people," Mac ordered. "Those letters I told you about, Smithsonian, the ones from the same very nasty source?"

"Big, fat, hateful letters," Johnson put in.

"They've progressed from 'You can't write your way out of a paper bag' to 'Why aren't you dead yet?' " Mac said. "They were hand delivered, in response to her editorials. The letters were getting increasingly unhinged. Cassandra's editorials were also getting a little unhinged, you may recall," Mac sighed. "There has been some discussion about reining her in. But no one expected this attack."

"How do you know this guy in the lobby is the letter writer?" Lacey asked.

"It's him, all right," Johnson said. "Didn't you hear him?"

Mac sighed. "The letters have common elements, style markers, physical characteristics. Very few crank letter writers cross the line to assault, of course. But we were making a case. Quietly. Johnson here helped."

"I returned to the hospital yesterday," Johnson obviously meant this as a slap at Lacey, who had not returned to visit her. "Cassandra told me she was being stalked. I only wish she had confided in me earlier." Johnson rubbed his eyes. "The letters frightened her, but Cassandra put a brave face on it. She just said it was her job. She got lots of letters, but these were the worst."

"We put building security on watch for the guy who delivered the worst letters. Signed by 'Joe Citizen,' " Mac continued. "We tightened our procedures. Joe Citizen was required to sign the log when he delivered his letters. That's how we finally got the name Stephen Graybill. He could have just signed it 'Joe Citizen.' Idiot." Mac opened a drawer in his desk and pulled out a pile of papers. "Copies of his letters. Cops have the originals."

"So when he showed up today," Johnson added, "we were ready."

Lacey tried to feel some relief. But there was something about the man's face when he heard himself charged with Cassandra's attack. It looked to Lacey like shock, disbelief; not guilt. But perhaps Graybill simply felt self-righteous, not guilty.

"I have to hand it to you, Peter," she said. "You managed to get a lot of information from Cassandra. All of which Mac could have told me himself."

"There were threats on her voice mail too," Johnson went on, ignoring her. "She told me she had the feeling lately she was being followed."

"Did she tell you, Mac? Or anyone else at the paper?"

"That she was being followed? Not that I know of," Mac said. "Maybe she didn't have time to dwell on it until she was in the hospital."

Lacey needed some air and some coffee. "What about this Graybill guy? What's his story? Did Cassandra ever see him following her?"

"At a distance, so she didn't have a detailed description. This Stephen Graybill character fits the profile, though. His life seems to have fallen apart." Mac spread the letters out on his desk. "All we got are these, but the cops will get more out of him soon, I hope. He owned some kind of small business that got shut down a few months ago, some environmental impact problem, polluting a water supply. His wife left him, he filed for bankruptcy. Apparently he had nothing to do but sit at home and surf the Web and read the papers. And then Cassandra wrote something about how polluters should be put out of business with regulation and confiscatory taxation and allowed to starve to death like the parasites they are." Mac shook his head ruefully. "You remember that one? That started the letters."

That sounded like Cassandra, Lacey thought. So this down-and-out small business owner took the politically correct Cassandra as his personal demon. To the level of stalking and assault? "So he fixated on her? What kind of small business was it?"

"Something that poisons the atmosphere and pollutes the earth," Peter quoted Cassandra without irony.

"I don't remember. It's in here somewhere. Then there was the chat room incident." Mac sounded tired and rubbed his face. Among *The Eye*'s new outreach efforts to attract readers were the accursed online chats in which reporters were "requested" to participate. There was no extra pay for this extra duty, but it was considered insubordinate to refuse this particular pain in the neck.

Personally, Lacey hated the chats. The few she had participated in consisted of a nerve-wracking hour answering questions on style trends and sometimes personal self-defense tips. Before she could finish one answer, five more questions would pop up. If she paused for a moment to frame a thoughtful answer the chatters would start chatting with each other and leave Lacey out of it entirely. Other days there would be no one online to talk to her at all, just the sound of crickets. A real ego boost either way. It was nice to hear Cassandra had to suffer through it too. But then, Cassandra never missed a chance to insult someone. Why pass up insulting strangers online?

"Smithsonian, you still with us?" Mac was staring at her.

"Sure, Mac, it's just that my brain starts to flatline when I hear the words 'chat room.' "

"How typical of you," Johnson said snottily. "I adore the chat room. My readers are politically sophisticated and unusually well informed, thanks to me."

"There it went, I flatlined again," she said. "Back to Chatty Cassie. What happened?"

"Tech ops had to block this guy from the chat room because of his tone and his threats," Mac said. "Several times. He started logging in with different names."

"How did you catch him?"

"Same threats, same catch phrases, same clichés. Worse than a brand-new sportswriter," Mac said. "So he was ejected."

"More rejection," Lacey said. "Poor guy could get a complex."

"He was angry and abusive!" Johnson's voice rose. "Or didn't you get that, Smithsonian?"

"Children, knock it off, for pity's sake." Mac picked up

Graybill's letters and stacked them. "It escalated, apparently, to the point where he was following her."

"What did he write about Sweatergate?"

"He didn't. And that term was only going around inside the paper," Johnson seethed. "Why don't you pay attention?"

"Why don't you kiss my—"

"Hey," Mac said. "If you two want to fight, take it outside. He didn't write about the Christmas clothing editorial. Who knows why?"

"But if he didn't write about the sweaters, then why—" Lacey said.

"Writing wasn't enough anymore!" Johnson was in her face. "He attacked her."

"I'm glad you're the smartest man in the room, Peter. Where would the world be without geniuses like you? But where did he get the damned sweater, genius?"

Mac stood up. Johnson retreated from Lacey, breathing hard, his lips a tight line. But Lacey wasn't thinking about Johnson, she was thinking about the man in the lobby. He was dressed for a day in a Washington office, maybe a little shabbily, but no worse than a typical reporter. Better, in fact. He was mouthy, but not very physical.

"That guy looked to me like a letter writer, not an attacker," she said.

"Which doesn't mean it couldn't have been him. He could have snapped," Mac pointed out. "The police think he's probably the assailant in the alley." Lacey picked up some of the threatening letters from Mac's desk and looked at them.

"'Joe Citizen'? He's just a blowhard. Why on earth would he wrap her up in a Christmas sweater? He didn't even complain about the Christmas sweater thing. It's not one of his hot-button issues, is it? And if he did do it, how was he able to grab Felicity's sweater, which he somehow stole without anyone at *The Eye* noticing? Did he sneak upstairs, past the guards, and grab it right off the chair in her cubicle? How would he even know where to find it?"

"Sometimes these guys escalate," Mac said. "Nuts can be very clever. As for the rest, Smithsonian, let the cops figure it out." Lacey was shocked that Mac was taking the easy way out on this, just like Johnson, jumping to the simple conclusion. She threw the letters down on Mac's desk.

"The cops!" she said. "Oh, I feel much safer now! And if this guy whacked Cassandra, what the heck is he even doing here today? Has anyone even peeked in today's envelope? Is he gloating over putting her in the hospital? Might be good to find out. Maybe he's got a complaint about Peter Johnson now, maybe he thinks people shouldn't park at bus stops! I think you bagged the wrong guy, Mac. He may be a letter-writing nutcase, but he's not the guy in the alley with the Santa cap."

Mac and Johnson were dead silent. Lacey opened the office door and then stopped.

"Good work, Peter," she said. "Now that you've nailed the nonassailant, at least Pickles and Wiedemeyer are off your list of suspects." She let the door slam behind her.

Word traveled fast in the newsroom. Word that a suspect in Cassandra's attack was in custody and that he wasn't from *The Eye* elicited sighs of relief. Even if Cassandra wasn't well loved, she was a fellow journalist. Assaulting her was like attacking their newspaper.

Lacey didn't feel the same relief. It bothered her that the assailant, whoever it was, had apparently also threatened her little shepherd. It bothered her that someone had been nosing around the girl's neighborhood asking questions. It bothered her that the cops and even Mac were stuck in what looked to her like a dead end. It even bothered her that Johnson was an arrogant idiot, though she told herself she should be used to that by now. But if the attacker wasn't Stephen Graybill, who was the Santa Dude?

She was way behind on everything she could actually call work. Today was her deadline for her weekly "Crimes of Fashion" column. Felicity and Wiedemeyer weren't around. It was quiet in her corner, but there was a persistent buzz in the newsroom about the man in the lobby. Lacey worked the morning away.

Finally at noon she gave up trying to make sense of her end-of-the-year fashion piece. She picked up her coat and purse and headed out to take a walk and pick up some lunch. She needed to walk, to think, to pray the phone would ring. She didn't even care who was on the other end of the line, she thought, she was in no mood to talk to anyone. And then she corrected herself.

Except Jasmine.

chapter 28

Lacey saw the man's reflection in the window of Filene's Basement and tried not to react. She could tell he was watching her and waiting for a moment to catch her eye. She wasn't going to let him until she was ready. This close, she saw his sharp nose and his ears sticking out through the thin hair, his breath coming out in short puffs.

Either Stephen Graybill hadn't been arrested, or he'd escaped. She doubted this thin, weedy man would have the strength to break the hold of two burly cops. Graybill hadn't been charged, she concluded. But she had just enough doubt about him to make her feel a sharp pang of fear.

She wondered if he'd done this with Cassandra, lurking in the background while she was window-shopping. No way, she decided, Cassandra would never window-shop. And could Graybill surreptitiously pull some hidden holiday weapon on Lacey, say a giant candy cane? Not here on busy Connecticut Avenue in broad daylight, with his reflection very clear in the glass.

There was no sense letting her tension build any longer. She turned around quickly and looked right at him. Graybill backed away and met her eyes pleadingly. He had that eager confessional look she recognized so well as a reporter. This was a man who wanted to tell her his story. She relaxed. The only danger, she thought, was that he might try to talk her to death.

"You're Lacey Smithsonian?" His voice was more controlled now.

"You're Stephen Graybill."

"I gotta talk to you." He extended his hand, but she didn't

take it. "I'm not dangerous. I wouldn't hurt you, or anyone. Really. Swear to God."

"Not the way I hear it. So they didn't arrest you?"

"No. They didn't arrest me because they got no case. They got no case because I didn't hit her. How crazy is this whole thing? I've never attacked anyone in my life. Physically, anyhow. I know my rights. They said they want to question me some more, but I got an alibi. And I got a good lawyer."

"What's your alibi?"

"Friday night services. I take my mother. She's the only person left who talks to me. Call my lawyer. Hell, call my mother."

Graybill wrapped his oatmeal-colored muffler around his neck. Standing outside in the cold was probably a stalker's occupational hazard. He looked chilled and his cheeks were chapped.

"Listen, Smithsonian, can I buy you coffee? I'd like to talk to you. Quietly. You have a reputation for listening to people, for finding the truth even if you write about that stupid fashion stuff."

"Such a compliment. Ten minutes, and I'll buy my own coffee." It was her flaw, she knew: She always wanted to know the whole story. Her plans to escape the office for fresh air and freedom evaporated.

"A woman after my own heart," he cracked. They picked a Starbucks at the end of the block. They bought their beverages and found a small round table in the triangular shop. The midday December sun streamed through the windows.

"I'm not gonna waste your time, Ms. Smithsonian," Graybill began. "I just want you to know I'm not the one that beat up your friend Wentworth." He took a gulp of hot coffee. "I'm not saying I didn't want to sometimes. That woman sure can piss people off. She pissed me off. But I didn't do it."

"Why do you care what I think?"

"You're the one who caught those killers, right? They say you're like a crime solver or something."

"Please don't tell me you have been reading DeadFed dot com." She breathed in the aroma of her café mocha.

"I don't know what your beef is with them. They worship you. You're like their superhero or something."

She cursed Damon Newhouse's creeping influence. "You

know of course that everybody at *The Eye Street Observer* was
pretty relieved to see the cops drag you away this morning.
They think Cassandra's attacker is off the streets now. They
think it's you."

"Bunch of pelican heads." He gulped his coffee. "Got their
beaks in everybody's business. You ever watch pelicans at the
beach? Damn big nosy birds. So what do you think, Smithsonian?"

"I think you should give up writing letters to the editor. Find
a nicer hobby. How did you get Cassandra's name in the first
place? Our editorials aren't bylined."

"Oh, that was easy. I called up your office mad as hell one
day and they told me to send an e-mail through the paper's Web
site. So I check the Web site and there's her name and e-mail
address: Cassandra Wentworth, Editorial Page Editor. Pretty
simple."

"What was today's letter about?"

"It was stupid, I guess. I wrote this stupid letter complaining
about all the stupid typos and mistakes and factual errors your
paper makes. I wrote your ombudsman, not Wentworth. Newspapers should have higher standards, you know."

"Did you complain about her Christmas sweater editorial?"

"Christmas sweaters!" He rolled his eyes. "Gimme a break.
Who freakin' cares?"

"It didn't make you so angry that you stole a Christmas
sweater from our office, waited in the alley for Cassandra Wentworth to retrieve her bike from the garage to ride home,
knocked her over the head with a giant candy cane, and then put
the sweater on her to warn her never to mess with the sacred tradition of the holiday sweater ever again?"

"What are you, nuts?"

"No, but that's what some people at my paper think."

"They're nuts. What do I care what some shiksa thinks
about Christmas? I'm Jewish, for God's sakes! I care about
her lies about American business, about capitalism and
democracy, about small business owners! The small business
owner is the guy who made America great!" He stared at
Lacey. Then his shoulders slumped. "Never mind. You don't
think I did it. Thank God. At least you get it. I can see you
get it."

"No, I don't think you attacked Cassandra in the alley, Graybill. But I could be wrong. I do think you threatened her, stalked her, scared her. I think you're a loose cannon."

"Ha!" He waved his hands like a conductor looking for an orchestra. "I wrote some crazy letters! I been goin' through a tough time! Okay, I'm an idiot, all right? I'm sorry. As for stalking, I saw her leaving work a couple of times. I wanted to talk to her, but I never even got close." He leaned in conspiratorially. "I'll tell you one thing. She's a royal bitch."

"And tell me, what am I?" Lacey realized she would listen to anyone, even this nut.

"You're okay. You got an open mind. You can see I'm not a bad guy. Look, I don't even believe in violence. I was a conscientious objector once. I'm a good guy."

"The jury's still out on that one."

He raised his hand as if swearing an oath in court. "You don't like me? No problem, I don't blame you. Lots of people don't like me. But you're listening to me. You're okay in my book."

Lacey stood up. "I have to get back to work."

"You're going to find out who clobbered the little witch, right?" He gave her a pleading, desperate look. "Right? And when you do you're going to prove it wasn't me. Get me off the hook. 'Cause this Cassandra Wentworth thing, with the cops and lawyers and all, it's really ruining my holidays, you know what I mean?"

He should form a club, she thought, along with Trujillo and Pickles and Wiedemeyer and Mac. The Lacey-will-find-the-answer-and-save-the-holidays club.

"I've got a job, Graybill. Keep your lawyer on retainer, you'll need him." She tossed her empty cup in the trash.

"Thanks. I'll be seeing you," he said. She hoped he was wrong.

If Lacey had thought she was going to slip back into the office quietly and start sorting out press releases and writing a column, she was wrong. Wiedemeyer was sitting on the edge of Felicity's desk and she was standing beside him, giggling and leafing through the pages of a new cookbook. This was a pretty good sign that Felicity was ready to start feeding her fans in the newsroom again. The pudding cake the day before was just the tip of the sugar-coated iceberg. They stopped chattering when they saw Lacey.

"Is it true? They got the man who attacked Cassandra?" Felicity's face was full of hope, and her new yellow sweater was full of dancing gingerbread boys and girls. "Did they figure out how he got ahold of my sweater?"

"I can't believe that flaming bastard Johnson was instrumental in the capture," Wiedemeyer complained. "It's preposterous, in fact, I bet he's just taking credit for it. But did you hear about his car? He'd let his insurance lapse just before the bus hit it! He is so screwed. Poor bastard. Ha! Serves him right."

"Capture?" Lacey noticed a few other reporters had edged in to listen. She hung up her jacket and sat down at her desk. "Well, I'm glad everybody's so relieved." *At least until they find out he wasn't arrested.* She wasn't going to spoil the moment. *Why ruin their Christmas?*

"Did you have any idea about this guy?" Felicity asked.

"Um, not specifically." Lacey looked away. "But Mac mentioned there was a crazy letter writer."

Wiedemeyer invaded her cubicle, cornering her, with Felicity close on his heels, cookbook still in hand. "I can't believe you didn't figure it out with your radar, your mojo, your killer magnet," he lamented.

"My mojo?" Let Johnson take the credit, maybe he could develop a magnetic attraction for the weirdos. Perhaps it came with the Wiedemeyer Effect. "You should ask Johnson what's up," Lacey said.

"Johnson! But Lacey, he told the police I did it!" Felicity crowded into the cubicle too. "Just because I went home from work to find another sweater, and I was alone. No alibi. Then he told the police that Harlan did it. He's a bastard."

"He set me up," Wiedemeyer complained. "Then the little bastard told the police we obviously did the attack together, because we're just that diabolical. Like we've got the time. Why, I can't believe that bastard Johnson's got two working brain cells!"

Lacey straightened her back. "But everyone is relieved now?" She adjusted the blinds on her window to keep the glare off her computer screen.

"Joy and jubilation!" Wiedemeyer beamed. "Of course

we're relieved this stalker's been arrested. I'm sorry you didn't collar him, Lacey, but this solves the whole thing."

She couldn't help putting up a cautioning finger. "I wouldn't jump to that conclusion just yet."

"What? Why not? What do you know, Lacey?" Wiedemeyer plopped down on the edge of her desk. "Felicity, she knows something we don't! You don't think he did it, do you, Lacey?"

"He wasn't arrested," Lacey said. "The cops questioned him. They let him go."

"You mean he's still out there?!" Felicity squealed, biting her lip. "The guy who tried to murder Cassandra in the alley? Oh my God."

"Don't just sit there like a sphinx, Smithsonian," Wiedemeyer demanded. "What do you think? Did this whack job do it or not? He must have, it must have been him, right?"

"Yes, Lacey, tell us! Please tell us!"

"Smithsonian." Mac's voice boomed from down the hall. "My office. Now."

Lacey grabbed her notebook. "Oh gee. Gotta go, guys. Sorry."

Mac probably wanted to know what her Friday column would be. She had no idea. She hoped he wasn't going to spring the dreaded and inevitable year-end, what's in, what's out, what's hot, what's not, New Year's story assignment on her yet. Or the top ten fads of the last year, or the top ten fashion predictions for the coming year. She hated these cliché stories. Mac made her write them anyway, year after year.

Her predictions would, as usual, include what she wanted to see and had no real hope of seeing: Clothes that fit and that ordinary women could afford, structured fashions that flattered the figure, and classic lines that would last for more than one season. Her fashion predictions were notoriously inaccurate, but nobody at *The Eye* seemed to mind, least of all Mac. Lacey tried to consider it a noble one-woman crusade for good taste. Perhaps she'd have to come up with the best and worst trends for the coming year. Mac liked that one too. Lacey was compiling ideas as she headed for his office, so he'd think she'd actually been planning something. White shirts, in or out? Black sweaters, hot or not? Brown is the new black? Size zero is the new two?

Mac was wordsmithing something when she stuck her head

through his doorway. His head was down, his eyebrows drawn in concentration.

"You bellowed?" she said.

He straightened up and gave her a weary stare. "Cassandra wants to talk to you."

"Will this torment never end? Where is she, is she home yet?"

"No, still in the hospital, but feeling feisty."

"What is it this time?"

"She wouldn't tell me." He returned to the papers on his desk.

"What about Johnson? She told him about the stalker. I'm sure he could squeeze the truth out of her. If not a lot more."

"Don't give me any more grief, Smithsonian."

"But it's the season for giving, Mac. Oh, all right, I'll give her a call."

"No. Go see her. In person, Lacey." It was an order, another in a long line. "People spill more information face to face. You know that."

Yes, she knew that. "Did you tell her about the drama in the lobby? Cuffing her mad stalker?" She leaned against Mac's wall, her arms crossed.

"Yes."

"Was she relieved?" Lacey persisted. "Did you tell her the cops turned him loose? Did you tell her he has an alibi? Did you tell her he wasn't the guy in the alley?"

"You are not interviewing me." Mac glared at her. "Yes, I heard he was cut loose. You were right and we were wrong. Happy now? Go talk to Cassandra." He sighed deeply, as if she were just another tragic interruption in his day. "She wants you. I have no idea why."

"She probably wants to throw things at me."

"Don't go throwing things back. She's a sick woman. Humor her, okay?"

Lacey rubbed her eyes. "When is somebody going to humor me, Mac?"

"Don't get any wise ideas." He stood up and reached for his coffee cup. "Maybe Cassandra can tell you something she can't tell Johnson. You've seen how those two are together, they can barely speak. Turns your stomach. Maybe she can be honest with you. God knows why. Maybe she's a masochist. But go see her, it might be important."

"She can talk to me because she doesn't like me? That makes a lot of sense."

"You have a gift, Smithsonian." He actually laughed. "It's the season for giving, right? So give me a break! Now get out of here."

chapter 29

Cassandra looked more alive than the last time Lacey visited, but she still wore that look of pained superiority. The big bandage was gone, replaced by a smaller, neater one. Someone had cleaned her up a little, but she still had clumps of hair that looked like they were stuck together with dried blood. It was not an attractive look. *Not her fault,* Lacey thought.

"I heard you were going home soon," Lacey said.

"Tomorrow, they tell me, if I behave," Cassandra said. She was sitting up in her hospital bed, surrounded by stacks of newspapers.

"Looks like you've been busy."

"Trying to catch up. Mac said the cops questioned my stalker."

Lacey set her purse down in the chair. She tossed her coat on the purse. It looked like she would be here awhile. "Word travels fast. Did he also tell you they let him go?"

Cassandra nodded. "I thought this was all over, but now it's not." She seemed to be holding back tears. "If it wasn't him, who was it? I'm so confused. And I don't understand the part about the candy cane. It's so weird to use that for a weapon. How bizarre is that?"

"What about the sweater?"

Cassandra looked away. "They say it was all meant to send me a message, hoisting me on my own candy cane, so to speak, because of that sweater editorial. Do you think this man they caught at the paper could still be the one who attacked me?"

"I think letter writers write letters. They pour all their anger into their diatribes," Lacey said. She remembered the confusion on Graybill's face when he was escorted out the door by the police. And their little chat at Starbucks. "I'm not sure they have a lot of energy left after that. He seems to have an alibi, anyway. I don't think it was him."

"Did you see the man? I think I've seen him, but only out of the corner of my eye."

"Tall, skinny, muddy brown hair turning gray, dull complexion, a navy dress coat. Wire-framed glasses." Lacey crossed her arms.

"That's the man." A tear trickled down her cheek and she rubbed it away. "But it's not him? That's what you're telling me?"

"Probably not. Why didn't you tell me about the letters, and being stalked?"

"I didn't think you'd understand how awful it is. Everyone knows how strong you are. Smithsonian tangles with killers. Smithsonian defends herself with hair spray! Smithsonian this, Smithsonian that. But being threatened and stalked is different, it's so insidious, so psychological. You have no idea. I am a target for hatred, I took on that burden knowingly. But you, you just stumble into these things, who knows why, you're just the lousy fashion writer."

"Thanks for clearing that up for me. I haven't been insulted in at least twenty minutes. And actually, I'm a pretty good fashion writer. So why exactly did you call me here, Cassandra?" This was getting neither of them anywhere.

"I remembered something. Something important."

"What? Something about the attack?"

"No, I wish it were. Something that happened when I was still in the office. After you and I had words. I remember that too." Cassandra took a deep breath. Was an apology about to spill out? Lacey wondered. "This isn't easy, but I have to get it out. So please, don't interrupt me."

"I haven't said a word. Go on."

"I came back. I walked down the aisle between your desks, yours and Felicity's. I wanted to say something else to you, I don't remember now what it was, but you weren't there. No one was around. And I—I'm not proud of this—" Cassandra took another breath and rubbed her hands together. "But you have to understand, I was so angry, and you were so—so flippant! So— I don't know. Flippant! Snarky!"

"Flippancy in the first degree. Aggravated snarkiness. I

blame Lacey Smithsonian for all the *snarkasm* in the world. Everyone does." Lacey sat down and made herself comfortable. "Lacey's ruining Christmas too, did you know? My secret plan. Today, Washington. Tomorrow I will ruin Christmas all over the world."

"Yes, flippant! Just like that! Right now!" Cassandra flared her nostrils.

"Sorry." Lacey put up her hands in peace.

"There was this idiotic Christmas sweater hanging on the back of Felicity's chair when I went past it," Cassandra recalled. "I'd never seen anything like it. It was worse than all the others. Garish, tacky, expensive. Hideous. I couldn't take my eyes off it."

"You should have heard what it did to 'Jingle Bells.' "

"It was right there, staring at me! Like an insult. A slap in my face. It was the Queen Mother of all tacky Christmas sweaters. I couldn't stop myself. And I—I—"

"You took it? You took Felicity's sweater *yourself*?" Cassandra nodded, her eyes welling up with tears. The sweater may have been an affront to good taste, but it was someone else's property. Lacey refrained from stating the obvious: Felicity would certainly kill Cassandra when this came out. With her bare hands. "But why?"

"I don't know! It was the strangest impulse. It was hanging there like a rude gesture. It was made of petrochemicals, there wasn't a single natural fiber in it, it served no useful purpose to the planet, it was an affront to everything I believe in. I wanted to destroy it." Cassandra looked at her hands. "I've never stolen anything before in my life. I'm so ashamed."

"You stole the sweater that Felicity ordered specially for the Christmas party so she could amuse everyone. Wow, Cassandra, talk about ruining Christmas. Way to go."

"I told you I'm not proud of it," the woman snapped. "But I realized that someone should know because—"

"Because it changes everything," Lacey completed her thought. Things looked even worse for Felicity now, she thought. The food writer finds her prize sweater missing, the ultimate example of what Cassandra was railing against, assumes Cassandra stole it or destroyed it, runs after her, finds her with it, goes berserk, and has a giant candy cane in her hands for heaven knows what reason, but there were such weapons available at the newspaper Christmas party. She beats Cassandra over the head with it and leaves her lying in the alley in the prize sweater, because it had been defiled by Cassandra's touch. And because it would serve Cassandra right to be caught dead wearing the gaudy Christmas sweater she hated so much. It all fit so neatly. Cops would like that theory, it was big and neat and obvious. But then who on earth was the Santa Dude that Jasmine saw in the alley? *Graybill? Now my head hurts too!*

"Did you put the sweater on?" Lacey needed to clarify that point.

"Are you insane? It was all scratchy and unnatural."

"What about the candy cane?"

"I didn't see a candy cane. I don't even remember what happened in the alley. Or who did it." She closed her eyes. "Oh, this is so awful, why can't I remember?!"

"Have you told the police all this yet?"

"No." Cassandra looked horrified at the thought. "Only you."

Lacey realized that if Cassandra took the sweater it turned some of the other theories on their heads. Where did that leave Stephen Graybill? If Cassandra had it with her, it simply presented anyone the opportunity to imply the attack was all tied up in Sweatergate. And Lacey had assumed nothing in the world would make Felicity part with that precious sweater. But what if Cassandra had polluted it? Would she leave it on Cassandra's body to make a point?

And how did I get into this mess, caught between the two people I like least in the entire newsroom?

She picked up her coat and noticed the flower arrangement next to the bed. Two dozen roses with holly and berries and tiny candy canes, wrapped with a large red ribbon. It was very pretty, if a little ironic. She looked at the card. "For all our tomorrows, Henderson." The arrangement must have cost a lot of money, but then, Lacey thought, he could afford it. *The Eye's* puny arrangement was drooping.

"No flowers from the Gangsters of Gaia?" she asked.

"Oh no. We believe cutting flowers is a violation of the plant's rights. But they brought me all the newspapers so I could catch up. They thought it might jog my memory.

Maybe it did." She waved her hand at the stack of newspapers on the bed.

"Doesn't cutting down a tree to make newsprint to print a newspaper violate the tree's rights?" Lacey asked. Cassandra rolled her eyes. "Just trying to follow along, Cassandra. So why didn't you call Peter Johnson about the sweater, once you remembered it?"

"Mac said you were working on this. He said Peter needed to cover that emergency appropriations bill on the Hill. That's more important than my little troubles."

Leave it to Cassandra, Lacey thought, to think an appropriations bill trumped life and death. Or maybe Mac was diverting Johnson off this story?

"So Peter is out of your life and Henderson is in? I'm confused, Cassandra. It's pretty obvious that you and Johnson have, um, unexpressed feelings for each other."

"It is not obvious!" The patient suddenly sat up straight, then she grabbed her head and sank back down in pain, closing her eyes. "I have . . . a history with Henderson, and I think I can help him keep his priorities straight, especially now that he's taken that new job. He's impressionable, and that lifestyle it offers, it will tempt him to—to go over to the other side. It would be wrong of me to let him go. I'm tired now. Please go."

My pleasure, Cassandra. "Take care. Call me if you have another memory breakthrough." Lacey picked up her bag, checked her cell phone for messages that weren't there, and left.

She started walking down the hall, head down, lost in thought, and nearly bumped right into Henderson Wilcox. As if Cassandra had summoned him by speaking his name, the little brother of Brooke's "Senator Snidely Whiplash" appeared before her. He wore a blue suit and a big smile full of relief.

"Ms. Smithsonian? We've met briefly. Henderson Wilcox." He patted his red power tie into place with one hand and extended the other. "It's wonderful news, isn't it? A suspect being arrested? The stalker who wrote those terrible letters?" *Oh really?* Lacey let him have his moment, Cassandra could burst that bubble herself. "We were all placing bets on whether you'd be bagging yet another killer. Attempted killer, of course. Now

that it's all over, I'm surprised to run into you here. Another interview with Cassandra?"

"Oh, just girl talk," Lacey said, smiling.

"She told me someone else at the paper had a hand in the assailant's capture?"

"Can't bag 'em all." She smiled brightly. *Let him get a load
of Johnson.*

"Then the hunt is off for the other suspect you saw?"

"What suspect?"

"The kid in the alley, in the shepherd's robe? It was in the
papers. Yours and the *Post.*"

At least he hadn't mentioned DeadFed. Lacey buttoned her
coat and fished her gloves out of her pockets. "Oh, you know
how newspapers are. Full of misinformation. But isn't Cassandra looking better?"

"Better every day. When I think of what I could have lost—"
He shook his head.

"I understand you and Cassandra are an item."

"We've always meant a lot to each other. Now even more."

"Where were you when she was attacked?"

"Ah, yes, the obvious question. I was not that far away,
sadly. I was at my firm's Christmas party at the Army Navy
Club on the next block. And I understand you were just inside
The Eye's offices at the time. All the while Cassandra was lying
there on the ground."

Lacey saw the cranky nurse from the other day heading
briskly down the aisle toward them. Wilcox noticed her too and
motioned her over to the chairs in a waiting area, apparently in
no hurry to reach Cassandra. Lacey perched on the edge of a
chair overlooking the street. She gazed out the window. People
were bustling, Christmas shopping. It seemed that city dwellers
never strolled, they were always rushing about. Lacey would
rather be out there too, in the fresh cold air, rather than inside
among the mingled smells of medicine and disinfectants and
Henderson Wilcox's cologne, a sickly sweet, metallic aroma
that reminded her of high school boys drenched in their first af-
tershave. It was nearly as overpowering as Wendy Townsend's
jungle gardenia scent.

"I heard you guys were taking a break from each other,
you'd broken up."

"We did take a break," Wilcox was saying. "But this incident shocked some sense into me." He looked down at his manicured hands and a look of remorse crossed his face. "I realized what I could have lost."

"What about Wendy Townsend? I gathered you were more than friends too."

Wilcox shook his head. "Wendy has this fantasy about me. If I were you, I'd discount half of what she says. Don't get me wrong, but—"

She rubbed her nose. "I got it. Just friends with benefits."

He had the grace to flush. "It's a complicated little dynamic. Wendy and I have a history and we've grown closer since this happened, but I have to take care of Cassandra, first and last."

"Her friends seem to think you've sold your soul for a posh K Street law office."

"Alex. It was Alex, wasn't it? He likes to say I abandoned the cause of Garrison of Gaia. That's a lot of crap. He refuses to see you can accomplish a lot more if you're well connected and working from the inside. You don't have to break the law and use violence and polarize people. And Alex has always been a little jealous over me and Cassandra. And Wendy."

"He's jealous?" Did Alex Markham hate Wilcox because of the cause, or because of Cassandra? And poor Wendy's always the also-ran?

"Ancient history. Let's not talk about Alex. What have you heard about this stalker? How long was he after Cassandra?" He leaned over her, making her feel small next to his bulk. She slid away to gain some more space.

"I'm sure the cops know more than I do."

"But what have you heard?" Wilcox was way too close. She stood up to get a little more breathing room.

"Nobody tells me anything, Wilcox! You know how people clam up around reporters." *Or else they talk my ear off.* "I just wondered if someone else could be after Cassandra."

He smoothed his hair. "I suppose there could be more than one unhappy reader. We've discussed her finding a new job, with a lower profile. We can't go through this again. I'll take her away for a while when this is all over." He opened and closed one large fist. "I wish I could get my hands on that little creep."

"That doesn't sound very lawyerly."

"Maybe I'm not very lawyerly. Believe it or not, Miss

Smithsonian, ice water doesn't flow in all of our veins. Some of us have passions."

When Lacey finally managed to shed the overbearing Henderson Wilcox, escape the hospital, and return to the newsroom, Mac wasn't there. She left a message on his voice mail. Felicity wasn't there either, and she didn't answer her cell. No Wiedemeyer. No Trujillo, he'd left for Santa Fe. Vic hadn't called her back; probably on a job or in a meeting. Lacey tried to concentrate on "Crimes of Fashion," but it was impossible. The shadows over her desk grew long and then disappeared. The phone didn't ring. She shut off her computer with a sigh. Mac and Felicity hadn't reappeared. *Another productive day. Reel her in, Mac says, but Jasmine won't take the bait. Go see Cassandra, he says, and Cassandra puts me right back in the middle of this feud with Felicity.* But she wasn't about to write up Cassandra's latest revelation without talking to Felicity and Mac. *Damn, I should be out Christmas shopping!*

It was time to get ready for the Bentleys' cocktail party. She was getting used to changing in the ladies' room at work, and changing her clothes would help her shake off the frustrating day. *New outfit, new perspective. You are what you wear.* The creamy lace blouse that had been Mimi's made her skin glow and the fit was perfect. Lacey was reasonably certain no one else would be wearing anything like it. She refreshed her makeup and realized she still hadn't heard from Vic. Would he meet her at the Willard or not? She left him another message.

Lacey wished she could just go and have a good time, but she would be going with a heavy heart and a shopping bag full of puffy little girls' coats. If Jasmine called, she wanted to be ready to abandon the cocktail party and jump in the nearest taxi. Back at her desk she found Mac waiting for her. He launched into her without so much as a hello.

"People are protecting those kids, Lacey. Jasmine and her sister. Someone must know. But no one is talking, not their friends, not the pastor, not the neighbors. Not to you, not to the cops, not nobody."

"Why not, Mac? And don't you want to hear the latest bombshell from Cassandra?"

"Later. One headache at a time. Those kids come first. People are protecting them because they don't want them separated. They don't want them to end up in the system. Everyone is hoping their mother comes back and they'll have another crack at being a family. That's my theory, and I'm right. So this is the deal, Smithsonian." He leaned on her desk while she gathered her things to leave. "You get ahold of those kids. You tell them there's a place, a foster home, not one of the bad ones, but one where they can stay together till their mother comes back. They'll be safe and they won't be pulled apart."

"I'll tell them, if I can find them. If she ever calls me back. But Jasmine is pretty stubborn. We could still try the schools, couldn't we?"

"If the schools get involved, they'll be at the mercy of social workers, the foster system, the courts. They'll be split up. Their mom will end up in jail. We're trying to save this family, not destroy it." He pursed his lips. "You have a gift, Lacey. Find them. Convince them. Gently."

"And where is this magical foster home? They might want some details before they take this leap of faith. I want some details too."

"Our home. Kim's and mine. We'll take care of them. We're trying to expedite things. We want to be the foster parents for these girls. I've got the paper's lawyers working on it."

"You, Mac?" Stunned, Lacey tried to keep a straight face. She didn't know if she would laugh or cry. "You've gotta be—"

"Don't look at me like that, Smithsonian! I am as gentle as a lamb! A lamb! You got that?" He glowered at her. He didn't look like a gentle little lamb. "Now, you call me the minute you get ahold of these kids! We'll come running. I want to save them before they get thrown to the lions." He stood up and stretched. "There are lions out there. Lions and tigers and bears. Never forget that."

"Mac, I have no idea where to start looking for Jasmine and her sister! Vic even has his people working on it, but nothing's happening. Any suggestions?"

"Yeah, I suggest you get off your butt and go find those kids."

"Jasmine said she'd call and it's getting pretty cold out there." Lacey showed him the bag of puffy coats. "She really wanted these coats. So maybe—"

He picked one up and admired it. "Good job. She'll call, Lacey."

"Maybe if I light a candle to Saint Jude."

"Whatever works. Don't fail me, Lacey. My wife is planning Christmas with those little girls. So am I."

Great. One more Christmas I can ruin.

chapter 30

The Willard Hotel was decked in its best Christmas finery. The impressive columns outside the front doors of one of the District of Columbia's most storied hotels were wrapped in white lights and evergreens, punctuated with big red velvet bows.

Inside, a lavish Christmas tree awash with ornaments took center stage among a throng of well-dressed patrons. There was a hubbub of a Christmas party in the lower level below the lobby, but the Bentley event filled the ornate Crystal Room on the lobby level. One of Lacey's private goals for the evening was to have a mint julep, the Willard's special signature mint julep, with Vic upstairs at the Round Robin, the hotel's premier bar and a legendary Washington establishment. If Vic could meet her there. And unless her phone rang. Then all bets were off.

It was Wednesday, a work night, so most of the partygoers were in dressy business/cocktail attire. In Washington that meant black and gray suits and little black cocktail dresses. Lacey's off-center fashion sense was vindicated. Her antique lace blouse and black skirt and high-heeled boots didn't look a thing like the Washington standard little black cocktail dress, so correct and so boring.

Some attendees were less boring than others, she noticed. There were theatre people present, apparently planning on extracting money from the Bentley Foundation *dramatically*. They were wearing their own version of creative cocktail attire.

Lacey stood transfixed at the vision of a pale thin woman in a tight gold lame miniskirt, tiny black glasses, black turtleneck, black tights, and shocking pink high-top sneakers. She was sipping champagne with a man wearing some sort of ankle-length ceremonial military greatcoat in blazing scarlet, resplendent with gleaming medals and buttons and swinging gold epaulets, and thigh-top boots right out of a pirate movie. He looked like something from some nineteenth-century parallel universe, or perhaps from the wardrobe room of a Gilbert and Sullivan operetta. They appeared to be having a wonderful time.

The festive mood was marred by Alex Markham and Wendy Townsend arguing loudly near the Christmas tree. Their little group home, or the "crowded commune," as Henderson Wilcox had called it, seemed to be an unhappy home without Cassandra. *Who would have thought that gloomy Cassandra could be someone's Little Miss Sunshine?*

Markham was wearing an olive green corduroy jacket over a khaki shirt with an olive green tie and khaki slacks and hiking boots. *"Dressy business attire" means different things to different people,* Lacey reflected. *It might mean just wearing your clean Wellies as opposed to your muddy Wellies.*

Wendy Townsend looked like the woman most likely to fail a *Glamour* fashion quiz. She was wearing all black: lumpy sweatshirt dress, quilted microfiber vest, tights, lug-soled Doc Martens. She looked like an aging Goth teenager, still moody, dark, and depressed, and proud of it. Clasped tightly in her arms was a thick manila envelope. The two of them were shouting at each other nose to nose, faces flushed red with anger. When they saw Lacey they fell silent and stared at their shoes. She was about to say something noncommittal, like "Hello," when a more elegant distraction arrived.

"Lacey, there you are!" Jeffrey Bentley Holmes appeared at her side and saved her from having to engage with the argumentative Gaia gang. She was relieved to see him. He took her arm and ushered her into the party. Cameras flashed as they walked through the room. "Let me look at you. I'm no designer, you know, but I detect a rare and lovely vintage blouse. I'm glad Uncle Hugh isn't here to steal it."

"Brave words, Jeffrey."

"Where is that Vic Donovan of yours?"

"He's meeting me here later. If he can get away."

Jeffrey was accosted by a Congressman and his wife, and he smiled at Lacey and shook his head apologetically. He extricated himself a moment later.

"I don't want to keep leaving you in the lurch tonight, but there are some very aggressive hustlers here. My head is being stuffed full of worthy nonprofit projects. If I get dragged away, I'll catch up with you as soon as I can—" Another hustler appeared at Jeffrey's elbow, trying to angle him away for a private word.

Lacey smiled and waved Jeffrey back to his job. She filled a small plate of hot canapés from a buffet table and declined an offered glass of champagne. She needed a clear head tonight. She settled for a sparkling water at the bar.

"Smithsonian." Lacey didn't have to turn around to recognize Detective Broadway Lamont's dulcet tones. Lamont was bearing down on her right. He cut in next to her and demanded coffee from the barman, black. Then he took her elbow, not nearly as smoothly as Jeffrey had. "Let's talk."

"Don't be shy, Broadway. What are you doing here?"

He led her to a back table, far away from the hungry multitude crowding around Jeffrey Bentley Holmes. Lacey felt a little uneasy at his presence, but she wasn't about to let Lamont see that.

"Don't keep me waiting, Lamont. Read me my rights." She was in no mood to volunteer information about Cassandra or anything else to the police. Besides, Lamont was with the Violent Crimes Branch and in the District that usually meant homicide. "If they're alive, we don't touch 'em," he had once told her. "This isn't about Cassandra Wentworth, is it? Last I looked, she was very much alive."

"Little birdie told me someone at *The Eye Street Observer*"—Lamont stressed every syllable for effect—"was interested in recent evictions in the District."

"Which are handled by the U.S. Marshals' office," Lacey said. "Not the Metropolitan police. And especially not Violent Crimes. So where do you come in?"

"Oh, little birdies are everywhere."

"So are you, apparently. Out with it, detective! Please."

"We got a body. Dead woman. No, it's not the Wentworth woman."

"What woman?" Lacey took a deep breath. "Where? How long has she been dead?"

"A while. Not a pretty sight. We have some ID, but it could be stolen. We don't have a positive yet on the body." Lacey said nothing. "ID says her name is Lee. Asian, thirty-three years old. Anna Mai Lee. Mean anything to you, Smithsonian?"

Jasmine's mother. Lacey realized she'd been holding her breath. She let it out with a deep sigh. "What happened to her?"

"Why, Smithsonian, I do believe I've gone and spoiled your appetite." She scooted her plate of canapés over to him. "Thanks, don't mind if I do." He picked up an appetizer and popped it in his mouth. "Now, where were we? Oh, yeah. What happened to her? Looks like she got her head bashed in."

"Like Cassandra Wentworth?"

"A little different. This attack was fatal." He gave her one of his amused looks. "I know what you're thinking, but this is nothing as weird as a big old candy cane. Something more logical, like a tire iron, metal pipe, something round and heavy. But yeah, she was hit over the head. What can you tell me about that?" Lamont ate an egg roll. Lacey felt sick to her stomach.

"I don't know who she is."

"Okay. Let's say you don't, for the moment. Why don't you and I converse on why you're interested in evictions in the District of Columbia? Funny coincidence, this dead woman being on that eviction list your paper wanted."

He loved to talk, Lacey gave Detective Lamont that much. A sense of the dramatic, no doubt calculated to encourage suspects to confess before they had to witness the climax of his performance. Her thoughts were a jumble. She decided she'd just keep him talking as long as she could. Maybe Vic or Jeffrey would arrive before he really did read Lacey her rights.

"So what does her being evicted have to do with her being murdered?"

"Good question. See, this woman was evicted from her apartment, but technically it looks like it happened after she was already dead. She wasn't around for the big ceremony. People cry and beg for mercy and just a little more time to make the damn rent, and then they follow their worldly belongings out the door onto the street. You ever see one? Ugly damn business, eviction."

"I've never seen an eviction in progress. Sounds awful."

"Then why you were so interested in that eviction notice? You know something about that woman? About why she's dead? Because if you do, Smithsonian, you better start squawking. Little birdies want to know," he growled.

Lacey gazed around the room, willing herself not to tear up, to remember she was a tough, cynical reporter. Jeffrey was surrounded by grant-seekers hustling him for money, crowding around him like an emperor. Vic was nowhere to be seen. No one was about to rescue her from Broadway Lamont. The big tough birdie was waiting.

"I had a hunch," she said at last.

"About?"

"About the little shepherd. The kid I saw in the alley, who witnessed the attack."

"That Hispanic teenager?" Lamont didn't seem angry. He bit into a shrimp canapé.

"The kid that I said looked mixed, Asian and black and white." He nodded. "It turns out she's a girl."

"A girl. See, you do know something. How do you know that?"

"She called me on Cassandra Wentworth's cell phone."

He glowered at her. "You forgot to tell my buddy Charleston about a victim's traceable cell phone being missing from a crime scene?"

"I have such a bad memory sometimes."

"You and everybody else in this damn town." He laughed a deep rich laugh. "Why'd she call you?"

"She hit redial when she found Cassandra, looking for help. She got me, and I came out and called nine-one-one. Later, after your buddy Charleston, and my paper, got it all wrong, she called to let me know in no uncertain terms that she was a girl, not a boy."

"You didn't know she was a girl? You're some kind of fashion expert and you can't tell a boy from a girl? I worry about you, Smithsonian. That's more than just a fashion clue, that's basic equipment, you know what I mean?"

"It was dark! She had the hood pulled down over her face. She acted like a little street tough. So sue me. Jasmine also called to find out how Cassandra was doing, if she would live. She was worried about her."

"What do you know about this kid?" He took out a notebook and pen.

"Her name is Jasmine. Jasmine Lee. Her mother is Anna Mai Lee. She told me she 'borrowed' the robe. She was cold. And she was cold because some people came and threw all their things out of the apartment onto the street. Sounded like an eviction to me." Lacey put her face in her hands.

"What's the matter now, Smithsonian?"

"Jasmine told me her mother was coming home. She was sure of it."

"Not gonna happen. Not if that ID checks out. Damn shame. She got a father?"

"No," Lacey said. "Tell me about her mother, Lamont. Does she have a record?"

Lamont shrugged. "Not much. Looks like she had a good job for a while. Then one day, who knows, she fell down a rabbit hole and that hole was full of drugs. A couple of arrests, but the charges got dropped. She must have had a sharp lawyer. But Ms. Lee must have fallen off in her rent months ago. Evictions take time, but the weather's been warm enough, and landlords want folks out well before Christmas. Nobody wants to evict around Christmas," Lamont said. "Nobody wants to look like a damn Scrooge."

"What happens if you find Jasmine?"

"Kid has to be questioned, of course. Both cases. Wentworth and her mother."

"I don't know, Lamont," Lacey said. She thought of that little girl with this huge intimidating cop. Lamont threw her his exasperated look, one of his best.

"It's not like we're going to beat her with rubber hoses, Smithsonian! You maybe, but not a little kid. Children always get to have a parent or a legal guardian or a lawyer present. No matter how bad they are."

"There won't be a parent now." And what if there was no legal guardian, Lacey wondered. Jasmine would get some junior public defender for an advocate. Pro bono. They'd end up in the system, Jasmine and her sister Lily Rose. "Jasmine Lee had nothing to do with either assault, you know."

Lamont put his notebook away. "She's a material witness in an assault, which could be connected with the murder of her mother. At the very least she may know her mom's drug connections, and odds are that's probably who killed her. This kid is a person of interest." Lamont got to his feet. "You know the drill, Smithsonian. You got information on this, you call me. Your memory suddenly improves, you call me. You see that kid, you call me. You got some kind of wacky fashion clue, you call me." He lifted himself to his feet. "I got a feeling we'll be talking soon. Sooner the better."

She stared him down. "Jasmine Lee did not attack Cassandra."

"Hell, I know that, Smithsonian!"

Lacey straightened her shoulders and stood up. "What about your Detective Charleston? Where is he in all this?"

Broadway Lamont smiled his broad pearly smile. "You call me. Detective Charleston, he don't understand fashion clues like you and me. And I'm working a homicide. Homicide out-ranks assault. You call *me*, you got it?" He plucked the last canapé off Lacey's plate and lumbered off through the crowd.

Lacey knew she would have to call Lamont eventually, if and when Jasmine resurfaced. But she wouldn't be responsible for splitting up those two little girls. They would be taken into custody and put into some kind of juvenile detention hell before being parceled out to a state facility. They'd be scared to death, despite Jasmine's veneer of toughness. Jasmine and Lily Rose didn't seem to have much in the world besides each other, a tipsy lady who let them sleep on her couch and in her laundry room—and a stolen shepherd's robe.

What if Lacey or Mac could get to them first? Mac was already invested in their future, along with his wife. If Mac and Kim could get to them, they would have a home, a Christmas tree, and most of all, a safe haven. Lacey had to find Jasmine and convince the girls to trust her. But how could she tell them their mother would never be coming home? She fished her cell phone out of her purse, just in case. Lacey was lost in thought when she looked up and saw Henderson Wilcox standing there. It felt like déjà vu.

"You look like you've lost your best friend," he said.

Lacey forced a smile. "Oh, not me. Having a swell time. Nothing more fun than a Washington cocktail party."

"And it's an honor to have one of Washington's leading jour-nalistic lights with us."

Who? Where? Me? Apparently this kind of ass-kissing was his idea of idle flattery.

"Yeah. Right. I'm a little surprised to see you here, Wilcox. I thought you'd be at the hospital with Cassandra."

"She needs her rest. She's going home tomorrow. We're thinking of taking a few days out of town. But I'm here because my family knows the Bentleys. I couldn't very well beg off." He nudged her. "And you seem to be a special friend of our host too."

So that's why he's sucking up to me, to get to Jeffrey, she thought. *I should have known it wasn't my charms. Any guy who's sweet on Princess Cassandra of the Planet Catastrophe won't see much in me.* She decided to change the subject completely.

"The police didn't charge that alleged stalker, you know," Lacey said.

Wilcox's expression hardened. "So she told me. But it's only a matter of time."

"Do you think she'll ever remember what happened? Who attacked her?"

He shook his head. "The doctors don't think so. But the important thing is that's she's getting better. She'll be our Cassandra again, the same as ever."

Yeah, that would be wonderful, Lacey thought grimly. "Unsettling that the guy is still out there, don't you think? Maybe he'll try to get to her again."

Wilcox downed his champagne. He set the glass on a passing waiter's tray and took a fresh glass. "Then we'll just have to make sure she's safe until he's put away."

"How do you explain the Christmas sweater she was found wearing?"

"The sweater?" He looked blank. "I don't know. The guy obviously had some sort of twisted fixation on her. Or on Christmas. Who knows."

"Funny Christmas fixation," Lacey said. "That stalker of hers is Jewish."

"You don't say." He moved on smoothly. "The important thing is that Cassandra is going home tomorrow. She's all I care about." His eyes followed an attractive young woman in a fitted Nancy Reagan red wool suit.

"So how long have you two been together?"

He dragged his attention back to Lacey. "About three years now. We met at Gaia. We're both very passionate about the planet, both very politically engaged." He shifted the subject again. "We're a political family. You know my brother, don't you, Senator Pendleton Wilcox? Let me introduce you." He steered Lacey's elbow to where his elder brother was holding court. Suddenly she was tired of men grabbing her elbow. She shook his hand off. *Don't handle the reporter!* The younger Wilcox stepped back as the Senator turned to them.

"Miss Smithsonian, a pleasure," the Senator said, looking over her shoulder for someone more important. His mouth formed a cold toothy smile. To Lacey it looked like the devouring maw of a predator. "And what is it that you do again?"

"I'm a reporter," Lacey said.

"Really?" His ears pricked up. "For *The Post*? I haven't seen you at the Judiciary Committee hearings, I'd have noticed you, believe me. What's your beat again?"

"Not *The Post*. *The Eye Street Observer*. And my beat is fashion."

"Ah. *The Observer*. Right. And the fashion beat must be so—" The Senator shot a look at his younger brother that said clearly, *You idiot! Why are you wasting my valuable time with this insignificant peon?* "Nice to meet you, now if you'll excuse me, I—"

Lacey turned on her heel. *When you're being cut dead,* she thought, *always try to get in the first cut!* She walked away as fast as her boots could travel. Jeffrey Bentley Holmes intercepted her.

"Lacey, I'll be making a few remarks in a minute. Will you join me up front?"

Relief washed over her. "I'd be delighted, Jeffrey! You have no idea how nice it is to see a friendly face—"

Her cell phone buzzed in her hand and she jumped. She flipped it open.

"Hi, Lacey! It's me! Can we have our coats now? It's really cold out here!"

chapter 31

"You're off to meet the little shepherd girl?" Jeffrey asked.

"Yes, I have to go. I'm sorry I'll miss your—"

"You won't be missing much, trust me. You'll be safe?" He walked with her to the hotel lobby.

"Of course. I'll be fine."

"I can try and meet you later, when I can get away from this thing."

"Jeffrey! You don't have to do that. You have people to see here."

"Are you kidding? Miss a chance to meet your famous little shepherdess?"

"Well, I'll try to call you later, after I meet the girls."

She collected her bag of puffy coats and caught a cab to the meeting place Jasmine had picked out, a McDonald's just off U Street Northwest on Fourteenth, not far from Jasmine's neighborhood. The fast food joint with its harsh lighting and sullen air was a jarring change from the glorious and festive Willard Hotel. Lacey wondered if she would recognize Jasmine and her sister unless the girl was still wearing the blue-and-white robe. As people kept pointing out to her, she'd thought Jasmine was a little shepherd *boy*. But when the cab pulled over she spotted them instantly. Two little girls were waiting impatiently outside the McDonald's, stamping their feet and skipping, trying to keep warm. She paid the driver and the girls ran up to her, Jasmine in the lead.

"Lacey! Lacey! It's me! Did you bring our coats?"

Lacey would have known Jasmine's wise and wary eyes anywhere. And her shepherd's robe, which looked a little the worse for wear. Jasmine held her little sister's hand tightly. Lily

Rose wore a thin nylon windbreaker that was much too small for her. It was snug across her shoulders and the seams were splitting open. Neither one had gloves. They looked up at her eagerly and Lacey saw they both had the same almond-shaped dark eyes. Both girls had unruly masses of curly black hair that fell to the middle of their backs and kept flopping in their faces. No one had been overseeing their grooming lately. They looked like two little girls very much in need of their missing mother.

"We're cold!" Lily Rose was jumping up and down, trying to peek into the bag.

"I have coats for both of you," Lacey said. "Have you eaten today?"

"I'm starving!" The little one pulled on Lacey's coat toward the door.

"Hi, I'm Lacey." She put out her hand and the girl grabbed hold of it and shook it vigorously. "Who are you?"

"That's Lily Rose." Jasmine opened the door. "She's my baby sister. Can we get anything we want?"

Lacey thought she must be doing this all wrong. She should probably insist on feeding them something healthy instead of fast food, she needed to turn them over to Mac, and she needed to call Broadway Lamont, as soon as Mac gave her the go-ahead. But she couldn't bear to see them so hungry and neglected. They skipped in ahead of her. Lacey herded them to one of the back tables, all too aware they were still visible from the street. She kept her eye on the doors.

Lily Rose bounced while Jasmine waited, holding her breath, her hands waving up and down as if she would burst. Lacey opened the bag and pulled out the coats, hoping they would like them.

"Mine is pink! Oh wow! It's pink!" Lily Rose grabbed her coat, rubbing her face against the soft microfiber. She plunged her little hands into the faux fur trim around the hood. She looked up at Lacey to make sure it was okay, it was really hers.

"Yes, it's all yours." Lacey turned to Jasmine and pulled out the larger baby blue parka. For the first time, Jasmine's face opened in a wide beautiful grin as she held the coat, stroking the fabric.

"Oh Lacey. It looks really warm. Thank you." She nudged her little sister. "What do you say to Miss Lacey, Lily Rose?"

"Thank you, Miss Lacey." Lily Rose had already taken off

her too-small jacket and was unzipping her gift. Jasmine helped her sister put on the pink coat, then she handed her shepherd's robe to Lacey and snatched up the blue coat. Lacey folded up the tattered robe and tucked it into the bag with a sigh of relief. The girls were jumping up and down and hugging each other, twirling in circles.

"Mine's prettier!"

"No, mine's prettier! It's pink!"

"They're both equally pretty," Lacey broke in. "But they really look a little too big. We could take them back and get smaller sizes."

The girls cried "No!" in shocked unison. Jasmine zipped hers up. "We'll grow into them," she said decisively. And a coat in hand was worth two in the store.

"If you say so. But I think you need something else too." From the bottom of the bag Lacey pulled out two pairs of gloves to match the coats.

"No way!" Jasmine took the blue pair from Lacey's hand. "Cool!"

"Mine are pink too! And they're only a little big. See?" Lily Rose already had the pink pair on her little hands. "I love them."

"Thank you, Lacey." Jasmine prompted her sister again and Lily Rose said a fervent thank-you. Lacey thought they must have had a very good mother. Once.

The restaurant was nearly empty. Two women chatted in Spanish behind the counter. A few people nursed their coffee at tables, trying to shake the cold. Lacey knew she needed to tell the girls their mother wasn't coming back for them, she needed to convince them to trust her about a foster home. And she needed to talk to Jasmine again about what happened in the alley. She had no idea where to begin, the words were not coming to her. Maybe feeding the girls would be a good place to start.

"I'm glad you like your coats. Now let's eat! Order anything you want."

The girls raced to the counter to order burgers, fries, and sodas. Lacey ordered a coffee and paid the bill. Jasmine and Lily Rose wanted to keep their new coats on, but she persuaded them to take them off, just while they ate.

"How long has it been since you two have eaten?"

"We had lunch at school," Lily Rose said.

"So you've been going to school?" Lacey said.

"We have to be really good until our mom comes home," Jasmine said. "And they feed us lunch."

Just follow the rules and life is supposed to work out, Lacey thought. Why didn't life always work out that way? Jasmine pushed her hair out of her face and Lily Rose mimicked her big sister. Just as Thelma DelRio had said, Jasmine was quite the little grown-up, making sure they went to school to get their lunches. They must have had some help from a few adults, adults who wouldn't turn them in to the authorities, hoping their mom would come home and everything would be all right again. Mac knew what he was talking about.

"I have some things I want to ask you about, Jasmine." Lacey's throat constricted. Two sets of dark eyes looked up at Lacey. "You remember the woman in the alley?"

"Cassandra," Jasmine said. "Oh no! Did she die?"

"No, she's going to be okay, thanks to you, but she doesn't remember what happened. You finish eating and I'll talk, okay?" They nodded.

"She can't remember a thing?" Jasmine swallowed.

"Nothing from the alley. But she remembered something else. The crazy sweater that you saw in the alley, the one the Santa Dude put on her? The sweater that played 'Jingle Bells'?" Jasmine stared at Lacey and kept eating. "Cassandra had it along with her, she took it from someone, as sort of a prank. For a long time, I thought the Santa Dude was after Cassandra, for a lot of reasons. But you know, the more I talked to people, the more I began to think that maybe Cassandra wasn't the one he was looking for. Somehow she got in the way and so he attacked her instead. Maybe he was after someone else, and Cassandra just tried to stop him."

The sweater was the misleading thing. When Cassandra confessed to taking it, all the little theories, neat and otherwise, fell apart. Cassandra had the sweater with her in the alley before the attack; she probably didn't even know what she was going to do with it, maybe just throw it in the Dumpster. The Santa Dude, according to the little shepherd, put it on the woman after he hit her repeatedly. And then he laughed. So the sweater meant something to him, but he hadn't brought it with him. Lily Rose took a long slurp of her drink and looked from Lacey to Jasmine and back again.

"But they knew each other," Jasmine said. "I heard them."

"I know you did, I believe you. But I also think you have something more to tell me, Jasmine. Maybe you have the key."

"I don't have a key. I don't even have a place to live anymore," Jasmine said, sadness creeping into her voice.

"Jasmine, did you know the man in the alley? You know, the Santa Dude?"

The girl looked down, her hamburger clutched in her hand. "I told you, I don't know who he is. I don't know his *name*."

Lacey could have kicked herself for not being more aware of what she was asking the first time she talked to Jasmine, when she thought the girl was a little shepherd boy. *What kind of reporter am I?* she thought ruefully. *Journalism 101!*

"It's not your fault, Jasmine, I didn't ask you the right question. Now I know you don't know his name, but you did recognize him. The Santa Dude. Who is he?"

Jasmine shrugged. Lily Rose said nothing. She looked at her big sister for reassurance.

"It's important, because I think maybe he was chasing you, not Cassandra," Lacey said. "And I don't want him to find you."

"He knows my mother." Jasmine put her half-eaten hamburger down and sighed deeply. Lily Rose did a perfect imitation of her sister.

"He knew your mother?" Lacey had to stop herself from joining in the chorus of sighs. The dots were starting to connect. The Santa Dude knew Anna Mai Lee. She had been killed, and Cassandra might have been killed. "I have something to tell you about your mother." The girls waited. Lacey took a deep breath. "It's not good news. It's very bad. I'm sorry." Lacey thought this might be the hardest thing she had ever had to do.

"I know," Jasmine said quietly. "Something bad happened to her. He did something bad to her, or she would have come back for us by now. He killed her, didn't he?"

"I think so. I talked to the police." Lacey took the girls' hands. "It doesn't look like your mother is coming home again. They found a woman's body. They think it's her." Lily Rose started crying and clutched Lacey's hand. Jasmine tried to be strong, but tears were coursing down her cheeks. She leaned against Lacey and cried. "I'm so sorry."

Lacey hugged both girls and her eyes filled with tears. The girls cried quietly. She didn't push them to stop. Life at McDonald's went on around them. The other customers ignored them. Soon their tears eased up and Lacey had napkins ready to wipe their eyes.

"We really thought maybe she wasn't coming back this time," Jasmine said, still trying to be the brave little grown-up. "It's just that we didn't ever hear it for actual really sure until now." Tears still streaked her face. "You know what I'm saying?"

"I know. But let's try to figure this out. Jasmine, what were you doing in that alley? And what was he doing there?"

"He was with my mother the last time we saw her. She left with him." Jasmine played with her fries while she talked, rolling them around, stacking them up. She had lost her appetite. "She said they were going to a party. She wore her red dress and she looked really pretty. But she didn't come back that night and she didn't come back the next day and she didn't ever come back, not ever. She didn't even know we got kicked out of our place." Jasmine wiped her eyes with the back of her hand. She pushed the long locks out of her eyes again. "I saw him hit her one time, he hit her really hard and he called her stupid. But he didn't know I saw him." She scowled at the memory.

"What were you doing on Eye Street?"

"I know where you can get free food, from the restaurants there. It's a long way, but we were hungry, so I go there. I was crossing the park, you know, across from where you go to work."

"Farragut Square. Is that where you mean?"

"The man was there, with the dumb Santa hat. Like a Santa Dude. He was walking. He was dressed up like he was going to a big party, wearing a tuxedo. But my mother wasn't with him."

Lacey recalled the people in black tie she had seen walking to the Army and Navy Club across the Square. There were Christmas parties all over the city that night, including *The Eye*'s party at the National Press Club. Lots of men in tuxedos and Santa caps.

"He's got this big candy cane in his hand. Probably full of drugs. They did drugs together a lot." Jasmine looked into Lacey's eyes. "I think that was why she liked him, he always had drugs. I only wanted to know where my mother was! I asked him where she was. He didn't pay any attention to me, because I'm just a kid, you know. Anna Mai's little girl, you know, but I'm not so little, am I? He just walked right past me like he didn't know me. So I picked up some rocks off the ground." She slipped out of her chair and mimed picking up imaginary rocks. "Like this! And I threw them at him, just to make him pay attention to me. Like this! I said, 'Where's my mother?' " Jasmine's voice carried, but no one bothered to look over at her. " 'Where's my mother?' I kept asking him. He wouldn't talk to me. He kept just ignoring me."

"You were throwing rocks at him?" Lacey could picture Jasmine doing it.

"Yeah. A lot." Jasmine looked away. "And then I hit him and he looks at me and he just comes after me fast like he's going to grab me and hit me, like he hit my mother. But I'm not going to sit around and wait for it, like she did. So I took off running. And that's when it happened."

"You ran into the alley?"

She nodded. "I threw another rock at him and I had a head start so he couldn't catch me. I hid behind the Dumpster. He was too big to get in there. And too clean. He wouldn't like it back there, all dressed up."

"How did he end up hitting Cassandra?"

Jasmine raised her eyes to Lacey's and shook her head. "I didn't see all of it. She came out of the garage with her bike and she saw him running after me and she yelled something at him and I hid. She knew him, I think, but I couldn't hear what she yelled. She seemed really surprised and mad. He tried to ignore her like he did to me. He was pounding on the Dumpster to try to make me come out. She ran up to him and grabbed his arm. He tried to get away from her, but she started yelling and hitting him with her bike helmet. Then he took his big candy cane and hit her. He covered her mouth and kept doing it. That's how I know what happened to my mother. But I didn't really know till you told me she was—" Jasmine stopped and gulped back fresh tears. "That's why I didn't want your friend Cassandra to die too, I guess. But I couldn't help her 'cause he was too big. I had to hide from him." Her eyes were filling up. "He wanted to kill me too." Lily Rose burst into tears and buried her face in Lacey's arm again.

"Jasmine, listen to me. You really did help Cassandra. You

saved her life when you called me." Lacey waited while Jasmine drank some of her soda and Lily Rose blew her nose. "How did he know your mother? Can you tell me?"

"They partied and stuff. They did drugs together. Drugs make you stupid. That's what she told us, but it didn't stop her. I hate drugs and I hate him."

"Did he sell your mother drugs?"

"We don't have any money. He just knew these guys who had drugs and he gave her drugs for free. He *rep-re-sen-ted* these drug guys, she said. He was my mom's lawyer too."

"Her lawyer was giving her free drugs?"

"I think it was for sex. You know. We know all about sex, Lily Rose and me. We learned it in school. Mom said this lawyer dude was too smart to get caught so it was okay, and not to worry about her. But she got caught and he helped her. She never told us his name, so I don't know his name. He's creepy. She just called him the Lawyer Dude. Or Mr. Lawyer Man. Like she would say, 'Jasmine, take care of your sister, I gotta go see Mr. Lawyer Man.'"

She said it blithely, but Lacey blanched. Anna Mai Lee couldn't pay a lawyer; she must have had Legal Aid or a pro bono defender. Was this the "sharp lawyer" Broadway Lamont mentioned, the one who got her charges dropped? And how many lawyers did Cassandra know? Probably a lot, but two very intimately, that Lacey was aware of. Alex Markham and Henderson Wilcox. Whoever it was, the name would be on the court documents.

Tomorrow I'll know who the Santa Dude is.

chapter 32

"Can we have an apple pie now, Lacey?" Jasmine asked in a tiny voice. All this talking seemed to have used up her energy and she needed replenishment.

"Of course." Lacey got them all hot apple pies and another cup of coffee for herself. She checked her cell phone while she waited at the counter. No messages. She needed to call Mac. And Vic. And Jeffrey now too? After dessert, she thought, then the girls might be ready to trust her to take them to a safe place.

Jasmine blew on her pie to cool it down. Lily Rose followed suit. They ate their pies silently, and Lacey let Jasmine take her time.

"There's something else we need to figure out. Where you guys are going to live," Lacey said. "You can't sleep in the laundry room forever. It's not safe. You have to have more than that. You need a real home."

"We can stay with Miss Charday," Jasmine said. "She doesn't even notice us 'cause she sleeps a lot of the time. We're quiet. We're being really good."

"I know you are, Jasmine, but you aren't even getting all your meals."

"She lets us eat potato chips," Lily Rose said. "And leftovers sometimes."

"It's really not safe for you there." Lacey could feel their fear of leaving familiar surroundings, but she needed to lay out her case for Mac and Kim. She needed to be sure they trusted her. Handing them over to Mac and Kim, or to anyone, without their trust would just feel too awful. She wasn't about to deceive them.

"We'll be fine," Jasmine said. "We take care of each other."

"The Santa Dude could still be after you. He's a dangerous guy."

"He won't find us. We don't live at our place anymore 'cause they made us leave."

"But he's tried to find you. I know. He was asking Thelma DelRio where you were. She told me." Jasmine's eyes got very big. Thelma must be one of the adults keeping them off the street. Lacey surveyed the restaurant again; she'd been watching the doors ever since they entered. It was important to stay calm and not let them see she was frightened. Lacey tried to reconstruct what she had told all the Gaia gang, Cassandra, Wendy, Markham, and Wilcox. Had she let anything important slip?

"We have to find you a safe place to stay," she started again.

"Can we stay with you?" Lily Rose asked.

You bet, guys. We'll have McDonald's every night. "That's really not a good idea." Lacey took a deep breath. "I know some great foster parents who really want you."

"No! Fosters are terrible!" Jasmine said hotly. "They'd split us up." She stood up and grabbed her new coat as if to make a run for it. Lacey put a hand on her arm, gently but firmly. Jasmine waited, watching her face.

"And I need my sister!" Lily Rose's eyes filled up with tears again. "I want to be with my sister."

"All they want is the money," Jasmine said bitterly. "We know all about foster parents. They kick you out. They make you go somewhere different every year."

"And they beat you," Lily Rose said. "And they starve you!"

"Have you ever been in foster care?" Lacey asked.

Jasmine thrust out her chin. "No! Because we have a mother and we're being good!" The tears threatened again.

"Sit down for a minute," Lacey said. "Please. I have a plan. There are these people I know. They're really good people."

The older girl glared at her. "Right, where'd you hear that fairy tale?"

"Really," Lacey continued. "A couple. They have a big house with lots of room for two girls. They're friends of mine. Very good friends."

"What color are they?" Lily Rose asked.

That question caught Lacey off guard, but she realized it was natural. The girls were an ethnic mix, they'd be sensitive to that.

So were Mac and Kim. "Well, the dad is mixed, black and white. And the mom is Asian-American. They look a little bit like you." The girls looked at each other, their mouths open in amazement. "I'm not making it up, honest. They like kids. And they aren't doing it for the money. They have enough money."

"What are their names?" the little one chirped.

"His name is Douglas MacArthur Jones. We call him Mac. He's my boss, I see him every day, and his wife is Kim. They're looking forward to meeting you."

"Mac and Kim?" Lily Rose looked at her sister for direction.

"We can stay with Miss Charday." Jasmine stood up again. "She's got our television. We need our own TV."

"Sleeping on a sofa in an apartment with someone who's passed out all the time? Or in a laundry room and never getting fed? I don't think so. I'm sure that Mac and Kim have a television. And you'll be together. And I'll come see you to make sure you're okay."

"Do you promise we'll be together?" Jasmine's face was fierce. "And you'll come see us?"

"Cross my heart." Lacey crossed her heart solemnly.

"And hope to die?" Lily Rose waited for the rest.

"And hope to die," Lacey said. "I don't say those words lightly. Is it a deal?"

"Maybe. If it doesn't work out, can we come and stay with you?" Jasmine said, no doubt thinking Lacey was the world's biggest pushover.

It's my own fault, she thought, *I bought them coats and apple pies.* "You wouldn't like it. I've been told I'm really mean."

Jasmine smirked. "How mean could you be? You brought us coats."

"Are you really mean?" Lily Rose rubbed the fur on the collar of her coat. "You don't look mean."

"Pretty mean. I'd make you sleep in a real bed instead of a laundry room and wash your faces and comb your hair."

"My hair!" Jasmine wailed and grabbed her hair, embarrassed. "It's really bad, isn't it? I lost my hair band. I need another one."

"Me too," Lily Rose said sadly. "I need clips and I don't have a comb. I lost it somewhere." She shrugged extravagantly and grabbed her hair with two hands and pulled. It was full of snarls. Lacey helped the girls with their new coats and slipped on her own. Jasmine helped Lily Rose with her zipper.

"We'll take care of your hair. It'll be really pretty when it's clean and combed."

"But no cops, Lacey," Jasmine said. "We don't talk to the police. It's our policy."

"Yeah, I know it's your policy. Well, let me tell you something. The cops have a policy too. It's called 'We don't care what kids think,' and sooner or later, they're going to find you. But this way you'll be together and you won't be all alone. You'll be okay."

"No cops!" Jasmine squealed. A few people turned around to stare at them.

"Inside voices, Jasmine," Lily Rose stage-whispered.

"No cops," Jasmine said again, softly.

Lacey grabbed her bags and ushered them out the door to find a cab, holding their hands. She thought she had them, if she could just keep the forward momentum.

"Now. You can trust me, and I'll make sure you have a home with great foster parents who will take care of you. Or you'll be in the system with just the cops and no one to take care of you." The girls were thinking about it. They didn't make a run for it. "If you choose me and Mac and Kim Jones, then you'll have a home with your sister, and the Santa Dude will never find you."

"What's going to happen to him?" Jasmine asked.

"He's going to go to prison." *I hope,* she added silently.

"What if we don't like these foster parents of yours?" Jasmine's tough guy look was back.

"You will, trust me. And if the cops find you and you don't have a guardian, you both get swept up in the system, you go to juvenile facilities, and you might get split up."

"No, Miss Lacey." Lily Rose pulled on Lacey's hand. "You can't do that to us."

"I don't want that to happen either, Lily Rose. I'm on your side. So what's it going to be, Jasmine? You're the big sister. You're in charge. You have to decide. It's time." Lacey waved her hand at the traffic and a purple cab pulled over for them. She opened the back door and ushered the girls in. She sat next to Jasmine and shut the door. The driver waited for instructions. Jasmine was silent.

"Come on, Jasmine." Lily Rose bit her lower lip. "Please? I

don't want the Santa Dude to get us. We have to stay together. We're a family."

"Okay," Jasmine finally said to her sister. "We're gonna trust Lacey. 'Cause she came and helped me and the lady in the alley, right? And 'cause she came and bought us coats and apple pies. And 'cause if it doesn't work out we can go and stay with her. Okay, Lily Rose?" Lily Rose nodded. Jasmine turned to Lacey and shook hands. "It's a deal, Lacey. We're trusting you. But we have to get our things at Miss Charday's, please? We have to tell her good-bye. And we have to tell her thank you."

"I left my things there too," Lily Rose said. "All I have in the world, the whole world. And then can we go?"

They had a deal. Lacey breathed a sigh of relief. "Where does Miss Charday live?"

"Right across the street from where we used to live. Can we go right now?"

Of course. The kids had stayed in their own neighborhood, close to home. Lacey hugged Jasmine and Lily Rose together and they giggled. They suddenly seemed so small, just two armfuls, even wrapped up in their puffy new coats. "We'll go see Miss Charday together. But first, I know a place where we can get some bands for your hair and a couple of combs, okay? We'll make you pretty."

Lacey told the cabdriver to take them to Dupont Circle. Now that the decision was finally made, both girls seemed enormously excited by this big adventure. Jasmine took Lacey's hand and squeezed it tight.

"I never been in a taxicab before!" Lily Rose said.

Lacey reached for her cell phone. She'd reeled them in.

chapter 33

The cab dropped them in front of Stylettos, the salon just off Dupont Circle where Lacey's friend Stella Lake was the manager. Stella's blue menorah with multicolored lights was lit, even though Hanukkah was at least a week away. Next to the menorah in a blaze of pink lights sat a four-foot-tall pink feather tree decorated with pink flamingos, purple balls, and a riot of colorful hair accessories, clips, elastic bands, and pretty painted porcelain barrettes. The girls stopped on the sidewalk to gawk at the holiday decorations, bouncing up and down outside the salon's front windows. Lily Rose announced that she wanted the pink tree. Jasmine wanted one in blue. And she wanted all the pretty menorah candles too.

It was just before eight, but to Lacey it felt like two in the morning. There were a few customers left in the salon, their heads covered with foil wrapping. Stella was stocking shampoo bottles in the displays and applying pink bows everywhere. She pounced happily on Lacey the instant she and her wards walked through the door. The girls hid behind Lacey's legs and peeked out at Stella.

Stella had shed her usual Stylettos smock, and she was wearing a long-sleeved, skintight black sweater with an eye-popping neckline. No winter cold would stop her from showing off the Girls. Her black Lycra stretch pants were also skintight over shiny gold stilettos. Her black hair was slicked back à la Rudolph Valentino and her makeup was just as dramatic.

"Lacey! It is about time! I have been expecting you!" Stella inspected her friend's outfit. "Uh-oh, all dressed up for a party? So let me see, let me see!" Lacey unbuttoned her coat to show off her outfit. "Aha, got to be from the Aunt Mimi collection.

Nice, classy, elegant. Nothing I'd ever wear, but nice. But you know, Lace, I really could have done something better with your hair. Something sophisticated? A French twist or something, to show off your neckline? You know, something sort of 'Our Miss Brooks' meets Naughty Miss Lacey."

Lacey smiled. "There was no time, Stella, I'll explain later. We can't stay long."

"Stop! Who is this 'we'?" Stella eyed the two little girls peeking around Lacey. Lily Rose stared at the exotic Stella. "So what have you brought me here? A couple of little Christmas presents? For me? You shouldn't have! Are they adorable or what?" Lacey made introductions. Stella examined the girls' hair with a professional scowl. The girls giggled. Lacey's friend seemed to be amusing them so far.

"They are adorable," Lacey said. "But we need some rubber bands for their hair and some combs and maybe a quick brush-out and then we have to meet—"

"Ha! That's not all they need." Stella hefted a handful of Jasmine's tangled curls. "These girls need the works. Shampoo, cut, blow dry, conditioner. Both of them."

The girls' eyes went very wide. "Uh, I'm not sure about all that, Stella," Lacey cautioned. "We're on a timetable here."

"Lacey, look at this hair, it hasn't been washed in weeks!"

Jasmine's sullen look returned. Stella's assistant manager Michelle took over soothingly. "Ah, good hair," she declared. "Strong and healthy. It will be so pretty when it's washed."

"Can we really?" Jasmine looked to Lacey.

"Of course you can," Stella said, ignoring Lacey's look of alarm. "I'll put it all on Lacey's tab. No probs. So what do you say, girls? Something different? Short and spiky? Buzz cuts?"

"No cutting!" Lily Rose grabbed her hair so Stella couldn't cut it. "Maybe braids?"

"Stella! No teasing the girls! And no buzz cuts," Lacey warned. "They have beautiful hair." Their long hair was probably their mother's pride, she thought. They probably looked a lot like her.

"I'm just funning you, Lace." Stella laughed. "You should have seen the look on your face." She addressed the girls. "Did you see that look? She totally cracks me up. So maybe we just trim a couple of inches, shampoo, condition, blow dry?"

"It's been a super long day, Stella. We have to be out of here by—" She looked at her watch. "By nine o'clock. Latest."

At nine they would go see Miss Charday. Lacey had called Mac and Vic; neither answered, but she left messages. By nine she was sure they would get back to her, and they could meet them in Shaw to help explain the situation to the woman who had been helping the girls. And if their hair was clean and braided and the girls looked happy, Lacey thought, Miss Charday would be easy to win over.

"Oh ye of little faith." Stella snapped her fingers and things started happening.

Lacey gazed at the girls' expectant faces. They looked dirty and neglected, but at least their stomachs were full of burgers now. Who knows how long they had been running from street to laundry room to couch, without a mother to take care of them?

"And in the spirit of the season, Lace, I'll give you a discount," Stella said.

"A real discount?" Lacey inquired. Stylettos' basic rates weren't expensive, but Stella loved to pile on the à la carte services and then alarm her customers with the terrible fate their hair would face without her tender loving care. And lots of expensive "product."

"Totally. Two for the price of one." She ushered the girls back to the dressing room to hang up their new coats. "So what are you two doing here with Lacey?"

"We're getting away from the Santa Dude," the younger one said.

"Lily Rose!" Jasmine gave her sister a look.

"It's a secret," Lily Rose told Stella earnestly. Lacey rolled her eyes.

The stylist's eyes lit up like the jackpot on a pinball machine. "Well, you've come to the right place. I love secrets."

"Stella," Lacey warned.

"Lacey tells me all her secrets. Now, you tell your Auntie Stella all about it." She gave Lacey an evil grin and whisked the girls away to the shampoo bowls, where no secrets could withstand Stella's magical massaging fingers. Lacey grabbed an empty salon chair. There was a message on her phone from Vic. She called him back: No answer. She left another message. She finally reached Mac, who picked up on the first ring.

"Mac, I've got the girls," she said. "We'll be at an address in Shaw later, in about an hour. Write this address down, are you ready?"

"You've got the girls? Both of them? That's terrific! Why not meet now?"

"We made a little stop first. It's a little hard to explain."

"You are right there with them, aren't you?" Mac growled.

"Of course I am. And it'll take you a while to get to Shaw, so—"

"So what's the holdup?"

"No holdup. They loved their coats, they were hungry, we had to eat, we had to talk, and now we're with Stella, getting all cleaned up and pretty."

"Your crazy hair stylist? Smithsonian—"

"Listen, Mac, they're willing to try the foster-parent thing as long as they're not split up, but it was a tough sell. They'll be much happier when they're clean and pretty. It's a girl thing, Mac. Ask Kim about it. Now, we just have to pick up their things and talk to this woman they've been crashing with. It's important."

"Nine o'clock sharp, Smithsonian." He repeated the address.

"Bring Kim." Kim would soften his grumpiness. "Maybe ten after."

"We're both coming, Kim wouldn't miss this for anything."

"Good, I don't want you to scare them, you big grouch. They're just little girls."

"Smith—" he started to say, but she hung up on him.

Lacey gazed in the mirror and caught the reflection of Jasmine and Lily Rose being herded back to their respective stations from the shampoo bowls, wearing towels on their heads and Stylettos' smocks that on them fell almost to the floor. Michelle took Jasmine. A stylist named Jamie, in a festive shag with red and green highlights, took Lily Rose.

"Where did you put their clothes?" Lacey asked Stella.

"In the wash," her stylist said blithely. The salon had a washer and dryer in the break room to handle the endless wet towels. "Those spiffy new coats are in the closet, they are very proud of them. You're the aces, Lace, getting those girls new winter coats. But the rest of their things were filthy, and I run a clean salon." Lacey couldn't argue with that. The mirrors and chrome shone and the floors were spotless, every snipped hair neatly swept away. "So where's their mother anyway?" Stella asked. "I kept trying to get the rest of the story. The little one's a doll, she wants to talk and talk, but the older one keeps shushing her up."

Lacey shook her head. "Their mother's not coming home anymore."

"Gotcha. Poor babies. So where you takin' 'em?"

"Mac wants to foster-parent them, Mac and Kim. You know, Mac, my boss?"

"Jeez. Poor babies. So what's this whole 'Santa Dude' thing all about? Spill, Lacey. You got another killer after you? What's it got to do with that thing that happened in your alley? It's not a different killer, is it, 'cause that would be like two different killers at the same time, and that would be weird even for you."

Lacey told Stella an edited version of events, emphasizing it was not to be broadcast in the salon. She demanded Stella's vow of silence.

"Are you kidding? Like a tomb I am, silent as the grave. You know that, Lacey. Who's always got your back? Me! Who's your best friend in the whole world?"

Vic called back. Lacey filled him in and he agreed to meet them at Miss Charday's apartment building. He was still tied up on something classified, and she and the girls would have to take another cab to the Shaw neighborhood. Lacey found herself wishing she'd accepted the little green BMW waiting for her in Vic's parents' garage. *Why am I being such a fool about taking the car,* she wondered. *I need Vic, and I need a car! Are we a couple or not?*

"Are you all right, sweetheart? Here you've bagged your little shepherd girl, you really did it, but you still sound blue. Can I help?"

She didn't know where to begin. "Um, I'm fine. It's been a busy night, Vic, and I just feel so bad for these girls."

"Me too. Stay safe, and I'll see you soon."

Lacey promised to stay safe. She clicked off just as Stella and her crew presented Jasmine and Lily Rose for her approval, in their now-clean clothes, still warm from the dryer. The girls ran to Lacey to show off their haircuts. Their hair shone and fell in soft curls around their shoulders. They still needed baths, but at least now their hair and hands and faces were clean and bright. "My hair feels so good," Lily Rose said. Jasmine smiled at her little sister. They looked like little angels. Mac and Kim wouldn't be able to resist them, Lacey thought. Nobody could.

The girls admired their reflections in awe and slipped on their new coats. Laccy was a little surprised at their resilience, how they could shift from grieving for their mother to reveling in their clean clothes and hair. But they had known somehow that their mother was not coming back, they had told her, and in the weeks since she had left them, they'd switched into survival mode. Pleasures had been hard to come by, and Lacey wasn't about to deny them this moment.

"You come back and see me again, okay, girls?" Stella said to them.

"We will, Auntie Stella," Lily Rose promised. "It was fun. I love my hair."

Stella laughed, walked them to the door and held her hand out. Lacey pulled out her credit card, hearing the *ka-ching* of the register in her head.

"You need some good shampoo for the girls. I got just the thing."

"Of course you do." Lacey looked at the price tag. "Stella, this is twenty dollars!"

"But don't they look pretty? It's got conditioner. And it's cheap, because you don't have to use so much. Just mix it with water."

Two sets of dark almond eyes pleaded with Lacey for the shampoo. *Sucker!* She was pleased to think Mac Jones wouldn't be such a pushover with them. "Oh, all right." *The Eye* was definitely paying her back for this. Or Mac personally.

"Thank you, Stella," Jasmine said. Lily Rose followed suit after a polite tap from her sister.

"Thank Lacey, girls," Stella said, "she's the one paying. I just supplied the creative artistry."

"Thank you, Lacey," Jasmine said.

"Thank you, Lacey!" Lily Rose launched herself at Lacey and embraced her tightly. "I love my hair and my pink coat."

"You're very welcome." Lacey gently disentangled herself from the girl to retrieve her credit card and the bottle of shampoo, which she slipped into her coat pocket to have one less bag to carry around. It was nearly nine o'clock. "We have to go now."

"Lacey, lunch. Tomorrow."

"Sure, Stel, I'll call you." Lacey put a hand on each girl's shoulder.

"I'm not on till two tomorrow, so I'll be at your office at twelve-thirty for a complete report," Stella promised. "Lunch is on me."

"It's never on you. And I'll be too tired to talk."

"Whatever. I'll pump you full of coffee." Stella handed each girl a barrette from Stylettos' pink feather tree. "Merry Christmas and Happy Hanukkah, and don't forget to rinse thoroughly. And condition!"

Lacey spied a taxi and dashed out the door to flag it down. She asked Jasmine to give the driver the address while she checked her wallet to make sure she could cover the fare. Just barely.

"Where are we going?" Lily Rose said.

"To see Miss Charday," Jasmine answered.

"Oh, yeah. I forgot." Lily Rose yawned and leaned against Lacey.

"What's Miss Charday like?" Lacey asked.

"She's okay. She doesn't care what we do as long as we're quiet," Jasmine said in a whisper. "And we don't wake her up."

"You won't have to worry about that anymore," Lacey said.

"Stella said you stabbed a bad man," Jasmine said. "With a pair of scissors?"

"Stella says you're really brave and you'll keep us safe from the Santa Dude," Lily Rose added.

"Did you really stab somebody?" Jasmine persisted. "How big were your scissors?"

Thank you, Stella. Lacey noticed the cab driver looking at her in the mirror, not scared, just wary. "You can't believe everything Stella says."

"She said it was self-defense!" Lily Rose added, and the cab driver relaxed.

"Do you have a pair of scissors now?" Jasmine said. "'Cause maybe you might need them sometime, you know?"

"Stella gave us little bottles of hair spray." Lily Rose showed Lacey her sample bottle. "She said if the Santa Dude gets too close, we should spray it in his eyes. Like Mace. What's Mace, Lacey?"

"Auntie Stella is very helpful, isn't she? Why don't we put those away now, girls."

The girls' neighborhood wasn't far from Stylettos, perhaps a mile. The taxi drove through blocks of Victorian townhouses, some renovated, some rundown, others in between. It looked prettier at night, with small Christmas trees in windows, lit with white lights or colored bulbs.

The driver turned down the block past the little stone church with the stable. No crowd of Conspiracy Clearinghouse fans tonight, the cold had driven them inside. They passed the apartment building where the girls had lived and stopped at a plain redbrick building. They wouldn't have to call up to get inside, the girls said. The lock on the front door was broken. If Miss Charday wasn't asleep, Jasmine told her, she would be watching their television. Or drinking.

Lacey paid the cabbie and scanned the street. There was nothing on this block but apartment buildings with few lit windows. It seemed empty and deserted. A cold wind swept down the street. She hoped Mac and Kim would be here, or Vic. She saw no one.

"That's Miss Charday's window." Jasmine pointed to the third floor on the corner. A reflected blue glow from the TV flickered through the window and Lacey saw the shadow of someone moving in the apartment. "Look, she's awake."

"Let me do the talking, okay?" Lacey said.

They followed Lacey into the small vestibule. The mailboxes had old names scratched out and new ones inked in. As promised, the inner door was shut but not locked. She didn't quite know why, but Lacey put her finger to her lips and quietly opened the door for them, closing it gently behind them. They took the small musty elevator to the third floor. When the doors opened, Jasmine pointed down the hall.

The door was ajar and the television was blaring. Lacey motioned for the girls to stop while she went on ahead. She peered through the gap, pushed the door open a little wider, and took one step inside. She saw a woman inside the apartment, sitting in a chair in front of the TV. This must be Miss Charday. But something made Lacey stop. Something was very wrong.

Miss Charday wasn't asleep.

chapter 34

The woman inside the apartment was dead. The smell of death was unmistakable, death mingled with alcohol. One glance told Lacey she had died violently. In the light of the TV glow the woman's head leaned far back against a shabby gold recliner. Slick blood matted the woman's hair and the back of the chair, and her face was covered with blood.

Lacey took a deep breath and willed herself not to react. She had children to think about. The girls stood silently in the hall in their puffy new coats. She closed the apartment door as quietly as she could, glad she was still wearing her leather gloves. She thought about calling the cops immediately, but the killer could still be in the apartment, waiting for them, listening. Mac and Kim and Vic were all heading for this address, but she had to make sure she and the girls were safe first. They had to get out of there.

"Aren't we going in? Isn't she home?" Jasmine asked.

Lacey shook her head and put her fingers to her lips.

"But I want—" Lily Rose began.

Jasmine took one look at Lacey and knew. She put her hand over her sister's mouth. "Shhh. The Santa Dude got her."

Somewhere in the apartment, there was a crash. He was still in there. He was looking for something, perhaps for two little girls hiding from the Santa Dude.

Lacey hit the elevator button and heard the creaky machinery start to move. Slowly. She pointed the girls to the back stairs and hurried them along. In the stairwell, she whispered, "Is there a back door?" Her throat felt dry and tight, her heart was pounding and her stomach was in knots. Miss Charday's apartment faced the street. The killer could see them if they went back out the front door.

Jasmine nodded. "The basement."

They scurried down three flights of gray concrete steps under a single dim lightbulb. Lacey opened the basement door.

"I left my teddy bear behind the washers." Lily Rose was about to duck into the laundry room where she and Jasmine had been sleeping when Miss Charday wasn't home to take them in.

"No time." Lacey tried to keep the panic out of her voice. "Which way, Jasmine?"

They heard the sound of a door slamming high above them on the stairwell and heavy footsteps pounding down the stairs. They pushed through the rusty metal basement door to the back yard, the girls leading the way. Lacey shoved a garbage can in front of the door.

"Come on!" She grabbed Lily Rose by one hand and Jasmine took her sister's other hand to form a chain and they ran for the alley.

"Miss Charday is dead, isn't she?" Jasmine said. "He killed her too?"

"Yes. We have to run." Lacey led them down the alley and past the dark backs of blocks of townhouses being renovated to attract people with much more money than Anna Mai Lee and Miss Charday. When they reached the street, they ducked around the corner and behind a tree. Lacey pulled out her cell phone, but there was no signal. SEARCHING, it said. *Searching for signal?!* she thought. *In the middle of Washington, D.C.?!*

"I'm scared," Lily Rose said in a small voice.

"I knew she was dead." Jasmine's lips were a tight line. "I knew he did it."

"We have to keep going," Lacey said. "We'll find a cab."

There were no cabs on this street. Most of the buildings were dark, under construction. They heard quick footsteps behind them. Lacey looked around the tree and saw what looked like Henderson Wilcox pounding down the alley toward them. In his hand he was swinging a long six-cell Maglite, the kind of metal flashlight cops carry as a baton, heavy enough to use as a weapon. Heavy enough to beat a woman to death.

Wilcox swung the Maglite wildly in the dark, looking for them. He must have left the fund-raiser right after she did, Lacey thought. What had he asked, what had she told him, what had he answered? Questions tumbled through her head as she grabbed the girls' hands and ran.

A large round tin garbage can sat on the corner. Lacey pushed it over on its side and sent it rolling behind them. She dragged the girls on a run down the block and across the street toward the nearest lighted building, the little church with the Nativity. There was a light on inside. Someone might be there. Lacey thought if only they could reach it, they might be safe. She heard their pursuer stumble and fall over the can with a crash, swearing heartily as he fell. Jasmine turned and looked.

"It's him, it's the Santa Dude!"

Lacey caught a glimpse of Wilcox on the ground in his own flashlight beam, his hair wild, his face contorted. Swearing as he picked himself up off the concrete, he dusted off his expensive suit, a festive red scarf around his neck. Lacey silently cursed him for forever turning a Santa cap for her into a bogeyman's accessory, and a candy cane into a weapon. And for being a murderer of children's mothers. He was back on his feet now, and he looked strong and very angry. Lacey remembered he had struck her as an ex-athlete. They turned the corner. Wilcox was out of sight, but Lacey saw the flashlight beam swing into the dark recesses behind bushes.

"My side hurts," Jasmine said. Lily Rose's face was wet with tears.

"Keep running." Lacey raced with them across the street to the side yard of the little church where Jasmine had taken the shepherd's robe. Surely a church meant sanctuary, even this tiny church. But even though the lights were on, the doors were locked. The three of them pounded on the doors. No one answered. The only place to hide was in the Nativity stable next to the church. The Christmas lights outlining the wooden structure were off and it was dark inside.

The small wooden building was three-sided, the front open to the street. The side walls looked solid, but toward the back of the right wall there was an opening concealed by two panels for actors to make their entrances and exits, before the living Nativity had been replaced by plaster statues. She pushed the girls in ahead of her. To Lacey's surprise, the stable was empty except for the manger. The Holy Family, the shepherds, the angels, the three kings: all gone. After losing their robes, Pastor

Wilbur Dean apparently decided not to risk his statues after dark.

Henderson Wilcox was still across the street and down the block, searching the dark corners around empty townhouses. Peeking past the wall of the stable, Lacey saw him shake his head and pound the big flashlight in his palm in rage. Jasmine peeked too, then they ducked as the light swung across the front of their hiding place. Lacey pulled out her cell phone. It was finally getting a signal. Vic didn't answer. She left him a brief message: They were at the stable by the church. They were in trouble. Hurry.

She called 911. It was ringing and ringing. Lacey hugged the little girls. It was getting colder and snow had started to fall, fat chunky flakes like the inside of a snow globe. Their breath made white clouds. Lacey heard her name on the cold air.

"Smithsonian!"

She pulled the girls close and they huddled at the back of the stable, behind the manger. She looked at her phone: The connection had been dropped. SEARCHING FOR SIGNAL. She cursed silently. *Are we in the middle of nowhere up here in Shaw?!*

There were bales of hay stacked high at the back on either side of the manger, taller than Jasmine, with a thin aisle behind where actors could wait for their cues. A hiding place. Jasmine and Lily Rose tucked themselves behind the hay on the right side near the hidden exit. They peeked out to watch Lacey as she pulled the shampoo bottle from her pocket. She opened the cap.

"What are you doing?" Jasmine crept out from behind her hay bale.

"Not sure. Maybe something to slow him down. If he gets any closer."

"The Santa Dude?" Her eyes were grave. Lily Rose was right behind her.

"Yes. At my signal, I want you two to run out the back way, okay? Don't wait for me. If I'm not with you, just run and don't stop. Run to the big grocery store way down the street and get help. Got that?"

"Got it," Jasmine said. The girls nodded and watched with big eyes as Lacey poured twenty dollars' worth of Styletto's shampoo over the straw in the front of the stable.

"Now," Lacey whispered. "Hide and stay put until I signal, or he goes away. Not a word, and we'll be safe."

"Not a word," Jasmine put her finger to her lips.

"Not a word," Lily Rose repeated.

All three of them crouched down behind the hay bales. Lacey's hands were shaking, but the girls seemed to have complete confidence in her. She wished that made three of them. They heard Wilcox making his way toward them, his shoes scuffling on gravel and trash, first on the sidewalk and then on the church property and the vacant lot next to it.

"You think you can hide from me, Smithsonian?" His voice was a low growl. "From me? You're not going to mess this up for me! Not now! Not like this!"

Lacey's mouth went dry. His voice grew slightly louder, then softer; he must be walking around the little church, searching for a way in. The girls were looking at her, holding their breath, straw sticking out of their clean hair. Lacey shook her head: *Wait!* He was walking away, still growling threats and curses. Lacey took a long slow breath and tried to visualize where his voice was coming from. He was heading away. They were almost safe. Then something terrible happened.

Lily Rose sneezed.

Lacey felt her heart stop. Maybe he hadn't heard. Maybe the wind had smothered the sound, or the hay bales. Maybe it only seemed like the world's loudest sneeze to her, echoing off the walls of the little stable. Then she heard Wilcox laugh softly. He turned around.

"So there you are. Hiding like dogs in the manger." Footsteps on the gravel moved closer to the back of the little stable. Lacey wondered if she could lift one of the hay bales to throw at him. One of them budged when she pushed it, but it wasn't much of a weapon. Her foot bumped into something. Peeking out from under loose hay was a shepherd's staff, roughly made, just a long stick rounded at the top. It might have gone with Jasmine's robe. Lacey picked it up and thanked some helpful angel, or Pastor Wilbur Dean, for leaving it behind.

"Want some candy, little girls?" He laughed again, just outside. Lacey was getting sick of the sound of his laughter. *Why is this so funny to him?* she wondered. *What kind of psychopath is this guy?* "A candy cane? They're making them bigger this year, biggest candy canes you ever saw, the better to bash your heads in, little girls. Big girls too. Sorry, I don't have a candy cane for you. But I've got something better." He banged on the back wall of the stable with something long and heavy, his Maglite.

Lily Rose looked like she might sneeze again. They crouched down in their hiding place, ready to run. Lacey waited, clutching her staff.

"Answer me when I talk to you," Wilcox demanded with a kick to the wall, one wall, then the other. "I'm not someone you ignore!" He waited for an answer; he made no move to the front of the stable. Apparently he wanted to flush them out the front like a flock of pheasants. "Come out of there."

Lacey waited. She wanted him right in front before she sent the girls out the back. Wilcox's footsteps stopped and he banged on the wall behind them again and again, making the girls jump. Jasmine put her hand over her mouth to keep from screaming, and Lily Rose imitated her. Lacey was afraid he might come in through the actor's entrance, which was on the dark side of the stable. But he changed direction and stomped to the front of the stable, pounding on the wall with each step. He reminded her of a soldier of Herod, ordered to kill all the infants in Bethlehem in hopes of murdering the Child in the manger.

Lily Rose sneezed again.

"That's right," came the answer from the front of the stable. "Sneeze all you want. I know where you are."

Lacey peeked over the straw. Wilcox stood before the stable peering in. His shirt was open and his tie was missing. The lethal Maglite was in his hands, illuminating the falling snow. He seemed indifferent to the snow settling on his shoulders like a white shawl, lying thick on his hair and eyebrows. His face was contorted in a grimace and his eyes were slits: the "squintchy" eyes of Jasmine's Santa Dude. This was not the well-connected Henderson Wilcox who tried to impress Lacey with his K Street office and his brother the Senator. This was a killer. He stared at her, dead-eyed, more chilling than the snow.

"What do you want, Wilcox?" Lacey stood up behind the hay bales, holding the staff out of sight with both hands. Only her face was showing. She nudged Jasmine with her foot and the girls crept quietly out the back to safety, and to get help. She hoped.

"Where are the little brats? I want all of you."

"They're right here with me," she lied. "But you can't have them."

"You can't stop me, Smithsonian. With what, a bale of hay? You gonna sneeze me to death? You're no detective, you're nothing but a two-bit reporter."

"Be fair, Wilcox. The paper's thirty-five cents a copy. So that's maybe two-and-a-half bits." The snow was falling harder. Vic must be coming soon, she thought, or the police, or even Mac. *And Christmas.*

Wilcox stopped to catch his breath. He thought he had them all bottled up. *He's a damned lawyer,* Lacey thought, *and lawyers love to talk, don't they? So let's keep him talking.*

"Why do you want them?" Lacey said. "They're just little girls."

"No way. I'm not telling you anything. You're trying to ruin me, just like she tried to do, but you can't do it, I won't let you. Come on out."

"Who, Cassandra? She'll remember what you did to her, you know. Someday."

"Cassandra will never remember what happened. Trust me. She will never remember. I'll make sure of that."

"Why did you have to attack her?"

"What the hell was she doing there in that alley?! And then she wouldn't let go of me! She never could let go, never stop preaching at me. You know how infuriating she could be. She grabbed hold of me, all I wanted was to make her let go." He was just standing there, swinging his Maglite. *What's he waiting for,* Lacey wondered?

"You were chasing Jasmine," Lacey said. "You knew who she was."

"Anna Mai's little brat. Throwing rocks at me in the street? Trying to embarrass me right there in Farragut Square? In front of the Army Navy Club? What if people saw that? What if people wondered how this filthy street kid knew me? What if people started asking about her mother?"

"They found Anna Mai's body."

"Yeah, yeah, I saw you with that big cop. I knew I had to take care of the brats before you got to them. Thought I could do it without you even being here. Never a good idea to screw with a reporter. You figured out a few things, Smithsonian, I give you that. Cassandra said you would."

"But not the sweater, Wilcox. Why did you put the sweater on her?"

He laughed. "I knew she hated the whole Christmas thing. She even managed to start in on the big candy cane I was carrying, right there in the alley. It was just a prop for a skit at the Christmas party for God's sake, but she goes berserk on me."

"What happened with Anna Mai?"

"A druggie! Clingy needy bitch. I defended her pro bono, they assigned her to me, but she wanted more, she wanted to be with me. A common drug addict? With me, a Wilcox? She would have ruined me. But she wouldn't go away. She wouldn't let go."

A theme, Lacey thought. "So you had to kill her?"

"All I'm trying to do," he said with a dramatic sigh, "is to change my life for the better. Stop being a screwup. Live up to being a Wilcox. That's a good thing, isn't it?" She thought he was almost crying. His shoulders were shaking; with rage or remorse? *Is he having a breakdown?* Lacey wondered. His voice became quiet, almost reasonable. "I just want to get out of the sewer, out of the backwater, out of the stinking nonprofits with those screwy tree huggers. A lousy sixty grand a year! For a Wilcox! Who are they kidding? Damn it, a chance for K Street, is that too much to ask?"

Lacey's arms were aching from holding the shepherd's staff so tightly. *Say something,* she told herself. *Just say anything. Just keep him talking!*

"So you want to be like your brother?"

"I am like my brother! I deserve to be! I'm a Wilcox!" he roared. "But you and people like you keep getting in my way."

"What about the woman back in that apartment?"

"She wouldn't give me those brats. I had to do something, didn't I? Didn't I? I had to! And a Wilcox does what he has to do! Now give me those damn kids!"

The breakdown was over. His voice had turned from reason to rage. Wilcox lifted the Maglite and took a step forward into the stable. Lacey held her breath. She crouched down behind the hay bales. He took another step and another, and then Lacey sprang up and leaned into the hay bales with all her might, toppling them over onto him. She saw the surprise in his eyes.

Wilcox took a startled step back and slipped on the straw, slick with shampoo. He fell flat on his back underneath the hay bales.

"Damn you, you meddling bitch! Damn it, I'm going to kill you first and make the brats watch!" Wilcox scrambled furiously in the slippery straw with one hand, trying to get to his feet without dropping his heavy flashlight. He kept sliding and falling in the sodden mess, flailing around like a large and dangerous walrus. He got to his knees but then slid back down again, banging his head against the wooden manger in the center of the stable. Lacey fled out the actor's entrance with the staff in her hands. She looked around, looking for Vic or Mac, wondering which way to run, when she felt a tug on her coat.

"Are you okay?" Jasmine asked.

"Jasmine! I told you to run! To go get help! Where's your sister?"

"We stayed here to help you." Jasmine pointed to a tree whose lower bows dipped to the ground. Lacey saw a flash of Lily Rose's pink coat. "We hid behind that big tree."

"Go get your sister. Go get help. Run. Now!"

"You all die first!" Wilcox emerged from the front of the stable covered with shampoo and sticky straw. He staggered toward them. He'd lost his big flashlight somewhere in the stable. He lunged at Lacey with both hands.

She swung her shepherd's staff like a baseball bat and hit him hard right in his gut. Wilcox gasped for air and doubled over. A snowball came out of the shadows by the tree and hit him in the face. Lacey spun around and saw Lily Rose making snowballs and Jasmine ready to throw another. She ran toward him, arm cocked to throw.

"Jasmine, Lily Rose, no! Get out of here," Lacey yelled at them. "Run away!"

They paid no attention to her. The next snowball hit Wilcox in his open mouth as he screamed curses at them. He straightened up and wiped the snow from his face and made a lunge for Jasmine. She ducked. He leaned over and reached for her, and she shot Stella's hairspray directly in his eyes.

Wilcox howled and clawed at his face. Lacey smacked him again in the gut. He yelled something and blindly grabbed the end of the staff and pulled her toward him. She held on, tugging back on it. Jasmine sprayed him again and then retreated to her sister, who was still piling up snowballs. Lacey pulled her staff away from him.

"I'll kill you all! You and the brats, just like their mother! I'll kill you!"

Lacey whacked him again, as hard as she could, first across his stomach, then across his back at kidney level. He sank to one knee and howled again. Lacey yelled right back at him.

"Go to hell, Wilcox, you monster!"

"Monster! Monster!" the girls cried. They rained snowballs on him as he struggled to his feet. Wilcox grabbed Lacey's staff and gave it a vicious pull, knocking her off balance. She let go and fell in the snow. She tried to roll away, but Wilcox was right on top of her. She looked up and saw him lift the staff high over her head to strike. Another snowball pasted him in the face and he shook his head. The girls were screaming and Wilcox was growling and Lacey was scrabbling to get to her feet in the muck, and suddenly there was Vic Donovan, diving at Wilcox in a flying leap and bowling him over backward into the dirty snow.

Lacey grabbed the girls. She retrieved the staff, ready to use it if she had to, and they huddled under the tree and watched. Wilcox snarled like a rabid animal and the two men wrestled and grappled and slid around in the slick churned-up snow. She couldn't tell who had the advantage. But as soon as Vic got one arm free, he put his fist into the other man's face twice and then rolled him over onto his belly and jammed his face into the snow. Vic stood up and put one boot on Wilcox's neck and bore down. He pulled Wilcox's right arm up behind his back until something popped and the man on the ground bellowed in pain. Lacey caught her breath. Vic pulled the other arm back to meet the first and cuffed them together and then looked around for Lacey. The boot never left Wilcox's neck until the cops arrived.

"Nice timing, Vic." Lacey threw herself at Vic. "Glad you could make it." Jasmine and Lily Rose jumped up and down and hugged each other. "Very glad."

"I'm so sorry, Lacey." He hugged her hard. "I didn't get your message right away. What the hell's wrong with your phone? I got here as soon as I could. What the hell happened?"

"We hid," Jasmine said.

"And I sneezed," Lily Rose said, with an exaggerated shrug. "I couldn't stop. It just came. It's my hay fever."

"And Lacey hit him and hit him and tired him out," Jasmine said. "We helped her."

"I can see you did." Vic laughed out loud and hugged the girls as they wrapped their smaller arms around Vic and Lacey.

"He's the Santa Dude!" Jasmine told Vic. "Are you Lacey's boyfriend?"

Lacey laughed too, and the stress seemed to break suddenly and they were all laughing. Except for Wilcox, who seemed very unhappy in the snow, breathing hard, his eyes closed in agony.

"My brother is a United States Senator," Wilcox mumbled through the pain of his injured arm, spitting out snow and dirt and straw. "I'm going to sue the lot of you!"

"Bad luck for you," Vic drawled, "Senators hate having scummy little brothers in prison for murder. He may never speak to you again. I guess that's at least two murders, assault, and three or four attempted murders? You've been pretty busy, for a K Street lawyer."

"I'll press charges! False arrest, assault, all of you, assault and false imprisonment. You all assaulted me. You broke my damn arm, and I'm a Wilcox!" Vic adjusted his boot and Wilcox shut up, his face in the mud.

"Smithsonian! What the hell is going on?" She heard a familiar gruff voice, and behind it the sound of sirens coming closer. She could see other cars pulling up, some with flashing lights.

"Glad you could join us, Mac. Just where on earth have you been? Didn't we say nine o'clock?"

Mac Jones trudged toward the little church and the Nativity, bundled up in a trench coat, red earmuffs, and a red and green scarf. His wife, Kim, was holding Mac's hand and smiling. She'd seen Jasmine and Lily Rose hugging Lacey's legs where they stood over the downed Wilcox. Mac threw a sour look at the broken man handcuffed on the ground.

"What kind of mess have you gotten us all into now, Smithsonian?"

"Nice to see you too, Mac. Hi, Kim." Lacey took the little girls by their hands and presented them. "I'd like you to meet Jasmine Lee and Lily Rose Lee."

chapter 35

The Metropolitan Police and Detective Broadway Lamont arrived on the scene. Lamont announced he had another damn dead woman to deal with in an apartment down the block, and if this little circus in the snow wasn't connected to it somehow and nobody here in the Nativity stable was dead, he had "bigger and deader fish to fry." Lacey led Lamont to the stable, where they found Wilcox's lethal Maglite under the straw, still slick with shampoo and fresh blood. Lamont decided he could spare them a little of his precious time. Soon he had Henderson Wilcox taken to the Violent Crimes Branch to be interrogated and charged with multiple murders and miscellaneous lesser offenses. Mac and the big detective had a chat out of earshot of Lacey and Vic. Lamont came back and said he would talk to all of them later, and they should "stay local." He would see the girls the next day, and he favored Lacey with a wink. Mac said he and Kim would be there with them, along with the legal staff of *The Eye*.

Jeffrey Bentley Holmes showed up in a limousine with thermoses of hot chocolate and boxes of cookies from the Willard Hotel. He hadn't been able to reach Lacey, he said; he'd been worried, and he finally reached Vic just as Vic was en route to Shaw. Jeffrey said he just wanted to offer his support, and his hot chocolate and cookies were appreciated by all. Especially Jasmine and Lily Rose.

After all the police procedure was over for the night, Lacey caught Jasmine looking up at Mac, clouds of doubt in her eyes. Lacey sat down next to her in the back of Jeffrey's warm limo. "I know he looks mean, but really he's not. He doesn't even hit reporters. Some reporters might deserve it sometimes. Not me, of course."

"He doesn't look that mean," Jasmine said. "I just don't know about all this. You know."

"They want both of you. You and Lily Rose. They won't split you up."

"But Lacey," Jasmine began, chewing on her lower lip. "But what if I just can't stand it?"

Lacey put her arm around the girl's shoulders, thin even under her puffy new parka. "Then I will come and kidnap you myself."

"Do you promise?" Her almond eyes were large and serious.

Lacey glanced over at Mac and Kim. They were holding hands and talking quietly with Lily Rose, and Lily Rose was smiling and giggling and eating a cookie. Mac was laughing too. She had a feeling this foster family would work. And if it didn't, well, they were small, and Lacey did have a second bedroom.

"I promise. Cross my heart."

Mac turned to them and addressed Jasmine. "Why don't you and I have a little talk?" He took Jasmine's hand and they went into the stable to talk. Mac sat down on a bale of hay and she stood next to him. This made them approximately the same height, and Mac and Jasmine conversed face to face and scowl to scowl.

Kim and Lily Rose and Vic and Lacey waited for the verdict. They edged a little closer. They couldn't hear what was being said, but Jasmine seemed to raise a lot of objections. There were gestures and shrugs and sighs. Finally, Mac put out his big hand for Jasmine to shake.

"Deal," he said solemnly. "Are we ready to go home now?"

Jasmine nodded, with one last piercing look at Lacey. "Remember, you promised." Then she turned to Mac and put her tiny hand in his large one.

In that moment, Lacey imagined she saw the weight of the world fall from Jasmine's shoulders. Jasmine had decided to let Mac carry that weight for a while. She let him zip up her new coat for her.

Lily Rose ran to her sister. "They have a Christmas tree, Jasmine, and a bedroom just for two little girls."

Jasmine smiled at her sister. "No one's going to keep us apart."

Vic gave Lacey a hug and she wiped a couple of tears away. "It's really late, Mac." Kim gave each girl a hug. "We've got to get them home." Mac put his arms around his wife and completed the family picture. It was weird, Lacey thought, how well they all seemed to fit together.

"What are you looking at, Smithsonian?" Mac said.

"I think I'm looking at Santa Claus."

Nothing ruined Lacey's mood the next day, not her overdue column, not her long chat with Broadway Lamont, not even the preposterous story on DeadFed dot com, which Damon Newhouse peppered with adjectives, alliteration, and angelic intercession. There wasn't a space alien or small assassin in sight.

CHRISTMAS MIRACLE IN SHAW!
CANDY CANE KILLER CAUGHT.
SMITHSONIAN AND LITTLE SHEPHERDS
FEND OFF FURIOUS FIEND.
SENATOR'S SIBLING A SLAYER!

Newhouse must be in conspiracy geek heaven today, she thought. Brooke too. Maybe she would forward Damon's resume to Mac after all. Just for laughs, and a little holiday goodwill. And if he actually hired him, Mac would either turn him into a real journalist—or have him bronzed and put on display in *The Eye*'s lobby.

On Christmas Eve, Lacey dropped by the office for half a day. There wasn't much to do. Half the newsroom was off. Cassandra was on an extended leave to cope with the troubling fact that her ex-boyfriend had tried to kill her. On the bright side, a judge had denied Henderson Wilcox bail and bound him over for trial on charges of murder, despite the anguished pleas of Senator Snidely Whiplash himself. Lacey noticed Peter Johnson had taken time off as well. Perhaps, she thought, he would persuade Cassandra to leave "the commune" and the Gangsters of Gaia.

Felicity's legendary Christmas cookie party had taken place after all, right down to the personalized gingerbread boys and girls. There was even one with Lacey's name on it. Peace was restored to the newsroom. But now it was Christmas Eve, and Felicity's desk was dark. She and Wiedemeyer were nowhere to be seen. Lacey was alone in her corner of the LifeStyle section, part of the skeleton staff required to be on hand just in case news broke out. *But if a Christmas tree falls in the forest with no one to report it,* Lacey wondered, *is it still news?*

An impromptu party gathered in an alcove near the staff kitchen. They'd turned off the overhead newsroom lights and lit candles. A motley repast of seasonal goodies was spread out on a festive green and red holiday tablecloth draped over an un-used desk. There were cheeses and bread and ham and roast beef, platters of Christmas cookies, red and green plastic cups of rum-spiked eggnog garnished with nutmeg. Lacey helped herself to some cookies and eggnog and chatted with LaToya.

"I don't mind coming in today," LaToya was saying. "No news is good news, I always say. Also free rum, pretty good eggnog, and I get New Year's week off. Cheers!"

Lacey raised her plastic cup in a toast. She was waiting for Vic to pick her up for some last-minute shopping. Then they would bake their cake for tomorrow's dessert, something from the festive fiends of *Southern Living* magazine: a chocolate macadamia pie with wildly improbable (and labor-intensive) chocolate leaves. Their dessert had better be good, it had a tough act to follow: Nadine's standing rib roast. After baking their pie together tonight, she and Vic would go to Midnight Mass.

Lacey wondered where Mac had disappeared to. He seemed quieter since the girls came to live with them, most likely worn-out from playing dad. He seemed happier too. He didn't need to come to work on Christmas Eve, but he showed up anyway. Lacey knew Mac generally appeared any time food appeared. She fixed a plate of assorted goodies and a cup of eggnog and headed for his office. It was Christmas, after all.

But Lacey stopped, mesmerized, at Mac's office door. Her gruff editor was sitting on the floor with his light-up Christmas tie thrown over one shoulder, reading an instruction manual and handing something shiny and mechanical to Vic Donovan. Vic, wrench in hand, was deep in concentration, apparently engaged in putting together a little girl's blue bicycle. Already completed and leaning by the door was a slightly smaller version of the same bike in pink.

The sleeves of Vic's sweater were pushed up, revealing his muscular forearms. The curl he always tried to brush back fell down over his forehead. Looking up, he smiled at the sight of her in the door. Lacey felt a rush of pleasure.

Mac followed Vic's glance. "Smithsonian, come on in." He noticed the cup and the plate in her hands. "Is that for me?" She nodded and handed them over.

"I didn't know you were in here," she said to Vic. "I've been waiting for you, cowboy. I didn't realize I'd stumbled into Santa's workshop."

"You learn something new every day, Smithsonian," Mac commented.

She had, in fact, learned a lot about Mac. Like what an old softie he was.

"And I'm Santa's little helper," Vic said, indicating the bicycles and instructions and tools and parts spread around him on the floor.

"You're giving the girls bikes for Christmas?" Lacey felt her eyes misting up.

"No, Santa's giving them bikes," Mac said with a straight face. "If they're good."

"Are they good?" She already knew the answer. She'd had several visits with Kim and the girls. Jasmine proudly showed her the Christmas cookies they helped Kim bake, and Lily Rose told her all about their trip to see *The Nutcracker*, her eyes very wide. They both wanted to see Stella again and they made Lacey promise to take them.

"They better be good after we finally get these things together," Vic said. "You ever build a bike, Lacey? Not as many parts as a BMW, but pretty darn close."

"They're good girls, better than I ever expected," Mac grunted. "Can you believe they never had bikes before?"

"Imagine that," Lacey said. "I guess they just had to be pink and blue."

"You know how hard it is to find pink and blue bikes in just the right sizes? At this late date? I had to order them on the Web! Good thing Donovan here showed up."

Lacey looked at Vic, reaching into his tool kit for another wrench. "Tool kit's always in the Jeep," he said. "Ready for anything, Santa." Obviously this guy had hidden talents. He could build two little girls pink and blue bicycles. He could even build a green BMW. Lacey's heart swelled with pride. And something else.

Mac finished his eggnog. "I had these express-shipped to the office so they wouldn't see 'em at home. Who knew bikes wouldn't come already assembled? You know that, Donovan?" Vic just chuckled.

Nearly everybody knows that, Mac, Lacey thought, but she didn't say it. Vic tightened the last bolt on the last bike and got to his feet. He spun the pedals and shifted the gears: Everything clicked and hummed. Mac admired the bikes, as taken with them as if he had never seen anything so beautiful. He couldn't seem to stop grinning. *Is this the same Mac?* Vic led Lacey out into the darkened hall and kissed her.

"Hey, I don't see any mistletoe," Lacey protested.

"Oh, honey, who needs mistletoe? Don't you want to kiss Santa's helper? I could build you a bicycle for Christmas too."

If you think fashion is just to die for,
then you'll love Ellen Byerrum's next
Crime of Fashion mystery,
on sale Summer 2009.
It will have you on the edge of your seat!

A **Crime of Fashion** Mystery
by Ellen Byerrum
Designer Knockoff

When fashion columnist Lacey Smithsonian
learns that a new fashion museum will soon grace
decidedly unfashionable D.C., it's more than a good
story—it's a chance to show off her vintage Hugh
Bentley suit. And when the designer, himself, notices her
at the opening, Lacey gets the scoop on his past—which
includes a long-unsolved mystery about a missing
employee. When a Washington intern disappears, Lacey
gets suspicious and sets out to unravel the murderous
details in a fabric of lies, greed,
and (gasp!) very bad taste.

Also in the **Crime of Fashion** series:
Killer Hair
Hostile Makeover
Raiders of the Lost Corset

**Available wherever books are sold or at
penguin.com**

ELAINE VIETS

Josie Marcus, Mystery Shopper

Dying in Style

Mystery shopper Josie Marcus's report about Danessa
Celedine's exclusive store is less than stellar, and it may
cost the fashion diva fifty million dollars. But Danessa's
financial future becomes moot when she's found
murdered, strangled with one of her own thousand-dollar
snakeskin belts...and Josie is accused of the crime.

High Heels are Murder

Every job has its pluses and minuses. Josie Marcus gets to
shoe-shop...but she also must deal with men like Mel
Poulaine, who's too interested in handling women's feet.
Soon Josie's been hired by Mel's boss to mystery-shop the
store, but one step leads to another and Josie finds herself
in St. Louis's seedy underbelly. Caught up in a web of
crime, Josie hopes against hope that she won't end up
murdered in Manolos.

**Available wherever books are sold or
at penguin.com**